THE LAST KING OF BRIGHTON

The new gripping mystery following City of Dreadful Night

A man impaled on the South Downs. Another skinned alive. A skeleton found beneath the West Pier, its feet encased in concrete. Brighton has been invaded. But this is no mere power struggle between rival mobsters; the motives for the killings stretch back through the decades, to an explosive forty-year-old secret Brighton's crime king John Hathaway would rather forget. But someone else remembers, and that someone has decided that revenge is a dish best served cold...

A Selection of Recent Titles
by Peter Guttridge

The Brighton Mystery Series

CITY OF DREADFUL NIGHT *
THE LAST KING OF BRIGHTON *

The Nick Madrid Series

NO LAUGHING MATTER
A GHOST OF A CHANCE
TWO TO TANGO
THE ONCE AND FUTURE CON
FOILED AGAIN
CAST ADRIFT

available from Severn House

THE LAST KING OF BRIGHTON

The Second Brighton Mystery

Peter Guttridge

Severn House Large Print
London & New York

This first large print edition published 2012
in Great Britain and the USA by
SEVERN HOUSE PUBLISHERS LTD of
9-15 High Street, Sutton, Surrey, SM1 1DF.
First world regular print edition published 2011 by
Severn House Publishers Ltd., London and New York.

British Library Cataloguing in Publication Data

Guttridge, Peter.
  The last king of Brighton.
  1. Police--England--Brighton--Fiction. 2. Gangsters--
  England--Brighton--Fiction. 3. Revenge--Fiction.
  4. Detective and mystery stories. 5. Large type books.
  I. Title
  823.9'2-dc23

  ISBN-13: 978-0-7278-9943-9

Severn House Publishers support The Forest Stewardship Council
[FSC], the leading international forest certification organisation. All
our titles that are printed on Greenpeace-approved FSC-certified paper
carry the FSC logo.

MIX
Paper from
responsible sources
FSC
www.fsc.org   FSC® C018575

Printed and bound in Great Britain by the
MPG Books Group, Bodmin, Cornwall.

*For all my family, in memory of
Ada and Jim Guttridge*

'If God had abandoned this unlucky town, he had surely not abandoned the whole world that was beneath the skies?'

Ivo Andric, *The Bridge Over The Drina*

PROLOGUE

Barbarians at the Gate

The thin oak stake was about nine feet long, blunt at one end, pointed at the other. The shaft was coated in something oily. Beside it on the grassy ground there were ropes, blocks and a mallet.

The paunchy naked man looked at these things, his eyes bulging. There was tape across his mouth. His hands were taped together behind his back. He was shivering uncontrollably, his flesh wobbling. The four men jerked him to the ground and lay him on his belly. He screamed through the gag.

They tied ropes to his ankles, then two of them pulled on the ropes to spread his legs.

The tallest of the two remaining men laid the stake between the naked man's legs, the sharp end pointing into his body. The other knelt and rummaged between the legs with a knife. He turned his head away when the man fouled himself but continued to poke and cut with the tip of the blade.

The naked man jerked and squealed through the gag. As he spasmed, the men holding the ropes pulled them taut so he could only buck.

His bound arms shook.

The tall man picked up the mallet and touched the blunt end of the stake. The man with the knife raised the pointed end of the stake and pushed it between the spread legs. The naked man shuddered.

The man with the mallet hit the blunt end of the stake. Three times. The naked man convulsed and started to hit his forehead against the earth. The man kneeling between his legs pressed with his fingers on his shaking back, checking the progress of the stake through the body. Satisfied, he signalled for the tall man to continue.

The naked man made strange mewling sounds as the next three blows thrust the stake deeper into him. Something frothy and bilious jetted from his nose. The man with the mallet paused but the kneeling man indicated he should continue. After a further three blows the kneeling man picked up the knife and leaned over the juddering body. The skin above the naked man's right shoulder was stretched and swollen. He cut into the swelling with his knife, lengthways and crossways. Blood gushed out.

The knife man crouched over the shoulder as the point of the stake emerged in three short jerks. When the tip was level with the naked man's right ear the knife man held up his hand. The man with the mallet laid it on the grass and came up beside the man he had skewered.

The skewered man's arms were twitching but otherwise he was unmoving. He was bleeding heavily from his shoulder and rectum. The two men holding the ropes flipped his rigid body over. They bound the legs to the stake.

The man's eyelids were fluttering, his face engorged. Green slime bubbled in his nostrils. The tall man bent over and tore the tape from his face. The skewered man's lips were drawn back from his teeth in an agonized snarl. He breathed in jagged wet puffs.

All four men lifted him. They carried him a few yards to a crude frame and lowered the blunt base of the stake into a pre-prepared hole. As he was lifted to meet the frame, his whole weight bore down on the stake. His body slowly dropped, and with a strange sucking noise the tip of the stake slid level with the top of his head. His chest rose and fell in impossibly rapid jerks.

Two men held the body steady whilst the other two busied themselves with securing the stake to the frame. When they had finished they stood back and observed their handiwork. The man's head lolled, his eyes rolled. He was whimpering when they left him there.

PART ONE

The Sixties

ONE

Johnny, Remember Me
1963

The axe shattered the window, sending shards of glass cascading to the carriage floor. The big man wielding it thrust his masked head and shoulders through the opening and clambered into the railway carriage. The five postal workers heaping mailbags in front of the door recoiled as he waved the axe in their faces. Behind them the mailbags tumbled as the door gave and six more men, wearing boiler suits and woollen balaclavas, pushed into the carriage. They carried pickaxe handles and coshes.

The masked men rained blows on the five sorters, hitting them across their shoulders and on the elbows, shouting at them to lie on the floor. The mailmen did as they were ordered. It was only five minutes earlier that they had heard someone outside the carriage yell: 'They're bolting the door – get the guns.'

'Don't fucking look at us,' a masked man bellowed, kicking one of the postal workers in the ribs. 'Keep your fucking head down.'

Even so, each of the men lying on the floor stole looks at the masked men as they went about their business. Whilst two of the masked men stood guard with pickaxe handles, two more stacked the mailbags together. Three others handed them down on to the railway line. The smell of sweat was keen in the air.

There were 128 bags in the carriage. Half an hour later, when the man with the axe looked at his watch, all but seven had been offloaded.

'That's it,' he shouted, 'let's move.' He saw one of the masked men glance at the remaining bags. 'Leave them.'

He remained in the carriage whilst the others dropped down on to the track. A few moments later the train driver and his fireman were dragged into the carriage, handcuffed together. The train driver's head was bleeding heavily. They were dropped to the floor beside the mailmen.

Another big man loomed over them.

'We're leaving someone behind,' he said, his voice a hiss. 'Don't move for thirty minutes or it'll be the worse for you.'

Then the masked men were gone, taking with them £2.6 million in unmarked bills. It was an hour before dawn, Thursday, 8 August, 1963.

On Sunday, 11 August, John Hathaway was sitting at the breakfast table reading about what the press were calling the Great Train Robbery in his father's *News of the World* when the doorbell rang.

The banks had admitted that the used £5, £1 and ten shilling notes stolen from the Glasgow to London night mailtrain were mostly untraceable. One bank had admitted that its money was not

16

insured so it would have to suffer the loss itself.

The police were claiming they had significant leads but they always said that. Although the newspaper was indignant that the train driver, Jack Mills, had been badly injured when he resisted the robbers, it was clear they admired the audaciousness of the crime.

So did Hathaway. From what he had read, the robbery had been planned and executed with military precision. The train had been stopped on a lonely stretch of track at Sears Crossing in Buckinghamshire, at a fake signal. It had been robbed within a strict time limit. And the robbers had disappeared into the night with no word of them since.

It reminded him of a film he'd seen a couple of years earlier – *The League of Gentlemen* – when Jack Hawkins and a band of ex-soldiers had committed the perfect bank robbery.

'Except they got caught,' he said to himself as he opened the front door. He flushed crimson.

'Did your father say I'd be popping round?' the woman standing on the step said.

'He said someone would, with some money, yes, Barbara,' Hathaway stammered. He stood aside so that Barbara, who worked in one of his father's offices, could come into the house. She looked back and he gestured vaguely down the hall, then watched as she walked, hips swaying, ahead of him. He could smell her perfume.

His heart was thumping. Barbara, some ten years older than Hathaway, looked like a softer version of Cathy Gale in the *Avengers* and was his main object of unattainable desire. Whenever

17

he went to his father's office he tried not to ogle her, at least when she might notice.

She stopped by the breakfast table and put a big brown envelope on it.

'Now don't spend it all at once,' she said, without turning. She was looking down at the newspaper.

'My paper is saying that the mastermind is somebody in Brighton,' she said. 'A miser who lives alone in one room and works with infinite care and patience to come up with criminal plans that he takes to a master criminal well known in the Harrow Road area of London.'

She turned and laughed.

'Such nonsense,' she said. She glanced from his burning face to the front of his trousers and then around the room. 'Have you heard from your parents yet?'

Hathaway's parents had gone on a touring holiday in the Morris Oxford down through France and into Spain. They were going for three weeks, possibly longer. 'Let's see how it goes,' his father had said. His mother was calling it a second honeymoon.

Hathaway shook his head.

'They only went yesterday.'

'Away for your birthday – that's a shame.' She took a step towards him. 'How old will you be tomorrow?'

'Seventeen,' Hathaway said, trying to focus on her face rather than her cleavage.

'Seventeen and this house all to yourself. I expect you'll be having a party. Probably more than one.' She took another step. 'I hope you're

18

going to behave.'

Hathaway shrugged, feeling his face burn even more, thrown by the look in her eyes. It was both nervous and calculating. He saw her glance down at the front of his trousers again.

'I'm not much for parties.'

'What about birthday presents?' she said, only a yard or so from him now. Her perfume enveloped him. 'You must like them.'

'Who doesn't?' he said. His throat was dry. She was so close he could smell her soft breath. She reached up and touched the corner of his mouth with a crimson fingernail.

'Would you like an early one?'

When The Avalons finished their set to desultory applause the landlord came over, a sour look on his face.

'Didn't think much of the audience,' Hathaway said as the landlord handed him a well-stuffed envelope. 'Didn't get in the spirit of it at all.'

The landlord looked at him but didn't respond. Instead he said: 'Hope your dad's having a good holiday.'

'From what I hear,' Hathaway said, slipping the envelope into his jacket pocket. He was nattily dressed in a dark suit with narrow lapels and trousers, white shirt and slim black tie. The other three in the group – Dan, Bill and Charlie – were dressed in the same way and all had their hair Brylcreemed back.

'Same time next week, then,' Hathaway said.

The landlord gave a faint smile.

'Looking forward to it,' he said.

19

Once they'd loaded the gear into the back of Charlie's van, they went across the road to another pub, ordered halves and Hathaway divided out the money between the band members.

'He's a miserable sod that landlord,' Hathaway said.

'It must be something in the beer,' Dan, the lead singer, said. 'Everybody in the place looked like they were at a wake.'

'Well, it is a Sunday and they were all ancient,' Hathaway said. 'Not one of them under thirty.'

'What did that woman think she was doing asking if we could do any Frank Ifield?' Dan said. 'Do I look like I can yodel?'

'Well,' Hathaway said. 'In those trousers...'

'Bugger off,' Dan said, taking a swipe at him. 'Now if she'd meant yodelling in the canyon...'

'Hark at him,' Charlie, the drummer, said. He was a couple of years older than the others. He had his comb out, peeling his thick lick of greased hair straight back into a high pompadour.

'Good gig, though,' he said. 'And you almost got the intro right on "Wonderful Land" tonight, Johnny.'

'I'm getting there,' Hathaway said. He watched Charlie patting his hair into place. The drummer saw him watching.

'Learn from the master,' he said.

Charlie Laker had been a Teddy boy since he was about thirteen. When not in his stage gear, he lived in a drape jacket and brothel creepers, and thought Duane Eddy was God and Gene Vincent sat at his right hand. He was a car mechanic but he rode a motorbike. The van was his father's. Charlie gave Hathaway grief about the Vespa he scooted around on.

'I'm thinking we might need to change our look,' Hathaway said. 'All these mop-tops in the charts.'

'I am not having a bloody mop-top,' Charlie said vehemently. 'Those Liverpool queers can do what they like.'

'It's catching on,' Hathaway said, and Dan and Bill, the rhythm guitarist, nodded.

'Having girl's hair or being a fairy?' Charlie said. They all laughed.

'We should be learning some of their songs, though,' Bill said. 'I've got that new Billy J. Kramer and the new Gerry and the Pacemakers. I can figure out the chords.'

Three out of four in the group could read music, but the simplest way to keep the act up-to-date was not to wait for the sheet music – which could be a long time coming – but to figure out the chords from listening to the singles again and again. That sometimes meant the lyrics weren't exactly accurate.

'Just something to think about,' Hathaway said, standing.

'Where are you off to?' Dan said. 'It's your round.'

'Got someone coming round the house,' Hathaway said.

'Oh hello,' Dan said. 'Whilst the cats are away. Want us to come back, help you with the cheese?'

'I can manage, thanks.'

'Who is she?' Charlie said. 'Do we know her?'

'Not that fat girl who lives at the end of your street?' Dan said.

'Bugger off,' Hathaway said. 'See you Friday.'

'Make sure you wear a johnny, Johnny,' Dan called after him. 'And for God's sake don't let her get on top of you or you're done for.'

Hathaway ignored the calls as he went out into the street and climbed on his scooter. Barbara's car was already in the drive when he got back to the house.

On Monday evening there were radio reports that the police had found the farmhouse where the Great Train Robbers had holed up. It was splashed all over Tuesday morning's papers. Leatherslade farmhouse, somewhere in Oxfordshire. On Friday two men called Roger Cordrey and Bill Boal were arrested. Hathaway recognized Cordrey's name. His dad knew him. He ran a flower shop in town.

That evening The Avalons were playing in a new pub on the edge of Hove. Hathaway had time to watch the new pop show, *Ready Steady Go*, and ogle its short-skirted presenter, Cathy McGowan, before he went off on his Vespa. He liked the theme tune, '5-4-3-2-1'.

The evening started well but quickly went downhill thanks to the six Teddy boys who were out for trouble. Even before they were three rounds of Newcastle Brown in, they'd been cat-calling and jeering. They were sitting to the right of the stage, pinched faces, big rings on their fingers that would cut as they punched.

They'd been OK at first but then The Avalons always started with Gene Vincent and Roy Orbison. It was when they moved on to some of the Liverpool Sound songs that the Teds got uppity.

The pub was only half full. Hathaway looked over at the landlord but he was deep in conversation with someone sitting at the bar.

The first coins were thrown at Hathaway partway through the group's second Shadows' cover, 'Apache'.

'Get yourself some guitar lessons,' the biggest of the Teds called, and the others cackled.

The first bottle of Newcastle Brown hit Dan in the chest a few moments later. When the second hit Charlie's bass drum, he was out from behind his kit and jumping off the shallow stage before any of the Teds had got to their feet.

As Charlie ploughed into them, Hathaway looked at Dan and Bill and pulled his Fender Stratocaster over his head.

'Bugger,' he said, laying the guitar carefully down.

Hathaway had been in his share of scraps. His father had taught him the rudiments of boxing but he'd taken up judo when he was fourteen and moved up the grades pretty quickly.

The Ted who'd thrown the coins was out of his seat and heading straight for Hathaway. Hathaway knew exactly what to do. He was going to grab the man by his velvet lapels, nut him, then do a backward roll, plant his feet in his stomach and use his opponent's weight to send him over his shoulders on to the floor behind him.

That was the theory. But when he grabbed the Ted's lapels he felt something slice into his fingers. He let go and saw the blood a moment before the Ted nutted him. He managed to turn his head to avoid getting a broken nose but the man's hard forehead hit him with a loud crack against his cheekbone and eye socket.

Dazed, Hathaway could do nothing as the man followed it up with a kick to the shin that indicated there was some kind of steel toecap inside his suede brothel creepers. The man grabbed Hathaway's own lapels, pulled him towards him and nutted him again. This time the nose went. Hathaway keeled over.

Charlie had gone under in a welter of flailing fists and feet. Dan and Bill, neither of them scrappers, hadn't even really got started. The smallest of the Teds had hit Dan on the side of the head with a bottle that, thankfully, didn't smash. Bill had slumped to the floor after a kick between the legs.

They could do nothing as five of the Teddy boys wrecked their gear. The sixth, the smallest, stood over Hathaway. He was unbuttoning his fly when the big one pulled him away. He leaned over Hathaway, who was trying to breath through his mouth as blood poured down his throat.

'Listen, Hank Marvin,' he said. 'If your dad ever comes home again, tell him this pub ain't his anymore.'

Then the six teddy boys sauntered out of the room.

* * *

24

'What did he mean about the pub not being your dad's any more?' Bill said, as the four of them sat in the emergency room of the hospital.

Hathaway shrugged, holding a wadded cloth to his nose. His fingers stung. In his eagerness to use his judo move he'd forgotten that Teddy boys habitually sewed razor blades behind their jacket lapels so that nobody could grab them to nut them.

'Something to do with the one-armed bandits?' he said, his voice thick.

One of his dad's various businesses was leasing one-armed bandits to pubs and clubs along the south coast. He had his own machines in his amusement arcade on the end of the West Pier.

'I borrowed the money off my dad for that drum kit,' Charlie said. 'He'll go mental.'

'I don't even want to think what the Strat cost my dad,' Hathaway said.

Two nurses came over. They looked disapproving.

'We'll see you all together,' one of them said. 'And afterwards a policeman will want a word.'

Two hours later, Hathaway was home. His hands were bandaged and his nose had been reset. He had a lump like a goose egg on his shin and he felt about a hundred. He wanted to telephone Barbara but he didn't know her number. He didn't really know her home circumstances. He thought she might be married but he hadn't liked to ask – he didn't want to spoil what was going on. He'd noticed a faint white mark on her ring finger, as if she took off her wedding ring

25

before she met him. And although she sometimes met him late in the evening, she never stayed the night.

He sat on the sofa listening to *Please Please Me* on his parent's radiogram, thinking about Barbara. He'd had girlfriends before but he'd been a virgin until that Sunday. She'd been patient with him. She'd seemed sad and, when he asked to see her again, anxious. But she'd agreed. Since then she'd taught him things. The evening she'd asked if he'd like her to French him had been a revelation.

She didn't like to come round to the house because she didn't want the neighbours talking, but there was a hotel she knew on the seafront down towards Hove that they'd gone to once. She paid for the room.

He was modest enough to wonder what this glamorous older woman saw in him, but he was arrogant enough not to worry about it. He was dying to brag to his friends but she'd pleaded with him not to. She said she'd feel embarrassed.

That was why she wouldn't go out anywhere with him, though he wanted her to come and see the group. The only time they had gone on a date was to a late-night screening of some Hammer horror film. They'd sat in the back row and, of course, he couldn't keep his hands off her. She'd unbuttoned his trousers and used her hand on him.

Although he was in pain, just thinking about her now got him excited. He had trouble sleeping that night.

* * *

On Saturday, the doorbell woke Hathaway. He tried to ignore it but it persisted. He put on his dressing gown and slippers and padded down the stairs. He hoped it might be Barbara. He picked up the newspaper lying on the doormat.

He squinted in the glare of the sun when he opened the door.

'Good grief, Johnny. You've been in the wars, I see.'

'Mr Reilly.'

'Sean, please. Do you mind if I come in for a moment?'

Sean Reilly was, as far as Hathaway could figure it, a kind of Mr Fix It for his father. Hathaway wasn't clear exactly what his father did – he wasn't interested actually – but whenever there was a problem he called on Reilly.

Reilly was middle-aged, in his mid-forties judging by the way he'd mentioned seeing action with his father in World War Two. But he was in pretty good nick. He moved gracefully and was well muscled. He reminded Hathaway of one of his judo instructors. He smiled readily enough but Hathaway had always found his eyes cold and hard.

'Have you heard from Dad?' Hathaway said when they were sitting on the sofas in the front room. He was suddenly anxious about why Reilly was there.

'Your mum and dad are fine. I believe they're buying some property in Spain. As an investment and for a holiday home.' Reilly crossed his legs. He was wearing cavalry twill trousers and polished brogues. 'No, I'm here to find out what

27

happened to you.'

'Oh, just a rumble with some Teds. It was nothing.'

'So I see,' he said, gesturing at Hathaway's face. He chuckled. 'Are you telling me I should see the other fella?'

'Not exactly, no,' Hathaway said sheepishly. 'We got leathered.'

'It happens,' Reilly said cheerfully. 'Any other broken bones aside from that swelling that used to pass for your nose?'

Hathaway realized he had no idea what he looked like. He stood and looked at his face in the mirror over the fireplace. Jesus. Huge yellow and black bruises around his eyes, his nose a swollen mess. He gulped.

'Ah, that'll all be gone in a fortnight, don't you worry,' Reilly said. 'Sit yourself down again.'

Hathaway sat and Reilly continued:

'I wondered what you made of these fellas?'

'Looking for trouble, like I told the police. Razor blades in their lapels, steel toecaps in their brothel creepers. They were ready to rumble.'

Reilly nodded.

'Your mates OK?'

'Charlie the drummer got a good kicking – couple of broken ribs – and Bill the rhythm guitarist has swollen goolies. Dan the singer had to have stitches in the side of his head but no concussion or anything. It's the equipment we're most bothered about. We had no insurance.'

Reilly nodded again.

'You say you spoke to the police?'

'At the hospital. We just told them what had

28

happened.'

'Was there anything you didn't tell them?'

Hathaway frowned.

'What kind of thing?'

Reilly shrugged.

'You tell me. Did these thugs say anything to you?'

'Said I needed guitar lessons.'

Reilly smiled.

'Aside from that.'

Hathaway told him what the Teddy boy had said about the pub not being his father's anymore. Reilly sat forward.

'And he used exactly those words?'

'Well, he also called me Hank Marvin but aside from that, yes.'

Reilly sat back in his seat.

'What about the landlord – did he wade in?'

'No, but he's only a little bloke. He did call the ambulance.'

'And the police?'

Hathaway thought for a moment.

'I don't know. The ambulance whisked us off to hospital pretty quickly – police might have come after we'd gone.'

Reilly stood.

'All right, then.'

'What did he mean about the pub not being Dad's anymore, Mr Reilly?'

'Sean,' Reilly said. 'I don't rightly know. Maybe something to do with the bandits, you know?'

'Are you going to tell my father what happened?'

'Do you want me to? No, I think he knows

you're old enough to look out for yourself.' He squeezed Hathaway's arm. 'You were unlucky this time but you've learned for next time.'

Hathaway touched his nose tentatively.

'I hope there won't be a next time.'

Reilly smiled.

'Tell your mates not to worry about the equipment. I'm sure we can find some way of making a claim through the business.'

'Great – thanks, er, Sean,' Hathaway said.

Reilly glanced over at the newspaper.

'Looks like they're on to the gang.'

Hathaway looked at the front page. There were photographs of three men the police wanted to help with their inquiries into the Great Train Robbery. Bruce Reynolds, Charlie Wilson and Jimmy White.

'They found their fingerprints at the farm. Seems a bit careless. As for Roger and Bill...'

'Those men who were caught at the start of the week? Is it the same Roger Cordrey dad knows? The florist?'

'It is. Bill Boal's his friend. The chances of Bill being involved in a robbery are about zero. Last thing he got charged with was fiddling a gas meter back in the forties.'

Hathaway pointed at the photographs.

'You know these men as well?'

Reilly shook his head slowly.

'I've heard of them. Hard men. Rumour is they were in that airport robbery last year.'

Hathaway remembered reading about the wages robbery committed by half a dozen bowler-hatted men armed with pickaxe handles and shotguns. A man called Gordon Goody had been tried but acquitted, because when, in court, he put on the hat he was supposed to have worn at the robbery, it was two sizes too big.

'The one Goody was acquitted for?'

Reilly laughed.

'That was a good gag with the hat.'

'Gag?'

'The story goes that he bribed a policeman to switch the hats.'

'How do you know these things?'

Reilly shrugged.

'You'd be surprised what you pick up at the racecourse.'

Hathaway nodded, feeling out of his depth but thrilled to be having a conversation with some-one clearly in the know.

'Will they catch them?' he said. 'The Great Train Robbers?'

Reilly smiled.

'Doubt it – they'll be out of the country by now, I would think.'

He moved towards the door.

'Better get going.'

Reilly shook Hathaway's hand and patted him on the arm before he stepped out of the house. As Hathaway was closing the door, Reilly turn-ed.

'Just remember one thing, John.' He smiled, but again the smile didn't reach his eyes. 'There is always a next time.'

'Oh, John.' Barbara's face hovered near Hatha-way as she seemed to be trying to figure out a

31

place to kiss him that wouldn't hurt him. She'd come straight from work but still seemed dolled up to Hathaway. She was wearing a tight skirt and an angora cardigan that clung to her breasts. Hathaway wrenched at the buttons of the cardigan.

Afterwards, as she lay on his chest, still straddling him, he said:

'Did Reilly tell you?'

'In passing,' she said. 'I had to wait an age before I was alone so I could phone you.'

'Thanks for coming round.'

She gave a low laugh.

'It's absolutely my pleasure.'

'Mine too,' he said as she rolled off him and on to her side.

After a minute or two:

'I've been wondering how Reilly heard,' Hathaway said.

'From the publican, I presume,' Barbara said, sliding her hand down Hathaway's stomach. 'He's an old customer of your dad's.'

'Not any more,' Hathaway said, giving a little grunt.

Barbara nuzzled her face into Hathaway's neck and murmured in his ear.

'How much do you know about what your father does?'

'Very little,' he said after a moment.

'That's what I thought. When I first came to see you, on that Sunday, I thought you knew far more.'

'What do you mean? Is there stuff I should know? Barbara?'

32

Barbara was sliding down Hathaway's side. 'Barbara?'

'Darling,' she said after a moment through the curtain of her hair. 'Don't you know a lady doesn't talk with her mouth full?'

TWO

Devil in Disguise
1963

'Listen to this,' Billy said, taking a single carefully out of its paper sleeve and threading it on to the long spindle of the radiogram.

'Who is it?' Charlie said.

'Dusty Springfield has gone solo. It's her first single.'

'Dusty, my Dusty,' Dan groaned, tilting his head back on the sofa. 'If only you knew what a constant companion you were to me in my bed.' He looked at the others. 'Well, you and Christine Keeler.'

'Hang on, Christine Keeler's with me,' Billy said. 'I'm not sharing her.'

'She's probably already with Johnny here,' Charlie said. 'His mystery bird.'

The four members of the band were sprawled around Hathaway's parent's living room, bottles of beer on the coffee table, half-pint glasses in their hands, cheese and crackers on plates. It was

33

Sunday afternoon, a few hours before the group's evening gig.

Charlie was riffling through the record collection. Dan had been scanning the latest *NME*.

'I only want to be with you too, Dusty,' Dan crooned, singing along in a strangulated voice to the single on the turntable. 'I've heard this on Radio Luxembourg. We could do this.'

'I've heard she's a lezzie,' Charlie said.

'Dusty Springfield a lezzie?' Dan said. 'Bugger off.'

He put on The Beatles.

Charlie said from the record stack: 'They'll never catch on. Hey, look at this – George Shearing, Ella Fitzgerald, Lena Horne – your dad really likes easy listening doesn't he, John?'

'You haven't got to the big band stuff yet.'

'Your dad's got quite a good singing voice,' Dan said. Hathaway looked at him.

'That party I came to a couple of years ago – he did that duet with Matt Monro.'

'Your dad knows Matt Monro?' Charlie said. 'Don't tell my mum that.'

'He came as a favour – my mum likes him too.'

'Your dad sounds interesting,' Charlie said. 'I've heard some stories.'

Hathaway saw Billy and Dan exchange glances.

'He's OK,' Hathaway said.

There was a lull, then:

'They chucked a car off Beachy Head today,' Billy said.

'Who did?' Hathaway said.

'Brighton studios. It's a film called *Smoke-screen*. They set fire to it then pushed it over the edge.'

'What were you doing out there?'

'What do you think? Gardening. That light-house up on the top? Anyway, there's this sexy French woman in it. Yvette somebody.'

Charlie walked back to the record collection.

'Hello, hello – here he is. Matt Monro. *Love Is the Same Anywhere*. True or false, Johnny?'

'That's my mum's.'

Dan broke into a mock-basso version of *From Russia with Love*. The four of them had seen the film together a couple of months earlier.

'Oh that Russian bint from the film,' Billy said. 'You can have Christine Keeler, Dan, and I'll have her.'

'Johnny's probably got her stashed away up-stairs too.'

They all looked at Hathaway.

'Come on,' Charlie said, walking back to the sofas and sitting down, automatically touching his bandaged ribs as he did so. 'Tell us about this girl you're being so secretive about. When are we going to meet her?'

Hathaway was dying to tell but Barbara was almost paranoid about anyone finding out about them.

'She's just somebody who works for Dad.'

'Did your dad set you up?' Dan said. 'That's very modern.'

'Ha ha. She's a stunner but really nice too.'

'Yeah, yeah,' Charlie said. 'Just tell us what she's like between the sheets.'

'Have you gone all the way?' Billy said.

Hathaway felt a lot for Barbara but he was seventeen. He fought to keep the smirk off his face.

'You have, you sod,' Dan said. 'You bloody have.'

Hathaway saw Charlie watching him. Of the three gathered round him, Hathaway reckoned Charlie was the only other one who'd actually had full sex with a girl – at least to hear him talk. But Hathaway had gone one better. He took a sip of his drink.

'She's ten years older than me.'

'Lucky bastard,' Billy said.

'Ten years older,' Charlie said, possibly sceptical, possibly jealous. 'Bet she's shown you a thing or two.'

Hathaway couldn't stop himself.

'She does French.'

'Does French,' Charlie said. 'Hark at him. A month ago he thought vagina was an American state and now he's the bloody Kinsey Report.'

Bill and Dan fell about. Hathaway grinned.

Charlie sat on the arm of the sofa.

'Should we try to get our own back on those Teddy boys?' he said.

Dan stopped laughing.

'Are you mad?' he said. 'They gave us a real kicking.'

'But they did smash up our gear,' Charlie said. He reached in his jacket pocket and pulled out a long bicycle chain. 'And next time, I'm ready for trouble.'

The others stared at him.

36

'Have you got Sonny Liston in the other pocket?' Billy said. 'Cos that's who we're going to need.'

Hathaway didn't say anything but instinctively touched his nose. The swelling had pretty much gone down now and the colour faded from round his eyes. Every time he thought about the beating he'd sustained he got angry about the Teddy boy who'd unbuttoned his fly. If the other Ted hadn't stopped him, Hathaway was sure the man would have pissed on him. He hadn't told anybody about that but he fantasized killing the little creep in various bloody ways.

'I think my father's company is going to sort out insurance,' he finally said.

'Can't it sort out those buggers too?' Billy said. 'Like your dad sorted out Nobby Stokes.'

Charlie looked at Hathaway with interest. Dan looked away. Hathaway bridled.

'What do you mean, Bill?'

Bill caught his tone.

'I didn't mean anything by it, Johnny.'

'Yes, but what *did* you mean?'

'C'mon, Johnny,' Charlie said. 'Even I heard the story about your dad and your headmaster, and I wasn't even at your school.'

'It gets exaggerated in the telling,' Hathaway said.

'I was only joking,' Bill said.

Hathaway nodded.

'I know.'

They sat listening to The Beatles in awkward silence, then the phone rang. Hathaway walked over to answer it.

'Get those dancing girls out of there now, Johnny!'

It was his father.

'Max Miller's dead,' his father said. 'Died back in May and I've only just heard.'

'Where are you, Dad?'

'Never mind that. Your mother sends her love. Your granddad knew him, you know, when he was starting out. He was Thomas Sargent back then. Lived in the same house on Burlington Street for fifteen years. Damn shame.'

'How old was he?'

'About seventy, so he'd lived a good life.'

'When are you coming back, Dad?'

There was a pause, then:

'Son, do me a favour and take a walk down the street.'

'Now?'

'No, son, next week. Of course, now.'

'But, Dad—'

'Humour me, son.'

Hathaway put the phone down and called to the others: 'I'll be back in five minutes.'

He walked down to the phone box on the corner. Somebody was in it. Hathaway hesitated for a moment then tapped on the window. The man looked round, irritated, saw Hathaway and pushed open the door a few inches.

'My father – sorry...'

'I'll call you back in half an hour,' the man said, putting the phone back on its cradle.

'Sorry,' Hathaway said again. The man waved Hathaway's apology away as he walked down

38

the street, shoulders hunched.

Hathaway stood in the booth waiting for the telephone to ring. His parents probably had the only telephone on the estate, but his father never made or took calls from there, preferring to use this phone box. Everybody on the street knew it was 'his' phone box and respected that fact.

Hathaway knew the respect came out of fear of his father. It wasn't something he liked to think about. The telephone rang.

'Johnny?'

'I'm here, Dad.'

'Johnny, your mum and I are staying out here a bit longer than we thought. Another month probably. We wondered if you'd like to join us?'

'Where are you exactly?'

'Spain.'

'Spain's a big country, Dad.'

'Showing off your geography lessons again? Humour me, son. You know I've got my funny ways.'

'I think it's called paranoia, Dad.'

'No – it's called caution, son. So what do you think?'

'The group's doing well, Dad. I need to be here, really.'

'As you wish. Your mum wants to know whether you're eating properly.'

'Of course. Is she there?'

'She's out by the pool but she sends her love.'

His mother was growing increasingly eccentric. Menopause, his father said, but Hathaway didn't really know what that meant.

His dad hung up.

Barbara came to see the group that evening. Unwillingly, but Hathaway had insisted. She sat right at the back, looking uneasy. Hathaway introduced her to the others during the break, but nobody could think of anything to say so the rest of the group left the two of them sitting together.

Afterwards, in her car, she wasn't in a talking mood. She gave him French instead.

'Did you enjoy the gig?' he said later.

'Look. They've seen me now – OK? You've proved you can pull an older woman. Congratulations.'

'I don't get what you're so cross about.'

'You wouldn't.'

'You're not being logical.'

She laughed and reached to wipe the steamed-up side window.

'One word of advice, John. Don't ever tell a woman that she's not logical if you want to keep everything that belongs to you.'

'But you're not.' He could feel spots of red burning on his cheeks. 'Don't take this the wrong way—' She snorted. 'Don't take this the wrong way,' he continued, 'but I did pull you.'

She gave him a savage look and turned away.

'I have to go,' she said, staring out the side window. 'Early start tomorrow.'

He glared at the side of her face. He was indignant.

'Sure,' he said, climbing out of the car and slamming the door behind him.

They got over it. And so it went. Two or three

gigs a week, cash in hand. Seeing Barbara for sex a couple of times a week. Long days messing about.

By October his parents still hadn't come home.

'When's Dad coming back?' Hathaway said to Reilly one Saturday. He'd come to the office on the pier, to see Barbara really. He liked to see her all demure behind her desk, knowing what she got up to with him in the hotel and the car. She didn't work Saturdays.

Hathaway had seen this old film, one of the two that had made Marlon Brando a star. *On The Waterfront*, made in black and white. And this corrupt union boss had an office in a wooden shack at the docks on a tiny pier. He often thought of that film when he visited his father at the end of the West Pier. His father's office wasn't in a shack but through the floorboards you could see the grey waters flopping between the iron stanchions below. Through the windows you just saw the sea. There was another room beyond that one, but Hathaway had never been in there.

'Soon, John, soon,' Reilly said. 'He needs to. In his absence, people are starting to take the piss. You OK for money?'

Hathaway nodded.

'I'm flush because of the money from the gigs as well. Though they've tailed off a bit. The landlord at our Sunday gig says he doesn't want us anymore and we've lost a couple of others.'

'Which pub is that?' Reilly said.

'The Gypsy, up on the Dyke Road. We've never got much of an audience so you can understand it.'

Reilly nodded.

'Write down the names of the others for me but I think I know which they are.'

That Reilly should know puzzled Hathaway. 'That housekeeper working out all right?' Reilly continued.

Because Hathaway wasn't exactly house-trained, Reilly had arranged for a woman off the estate to clean and cook for him. Hathaway wasn't always in at regular mealtimes so she left stuff in the fridge to be heated up. She was wary at first – she'd never seen a fridge before.

Sometimes Hathaway couldn't be bothered. Her cheese and onion pie eaten cold was fine but the steak and kidney got a bit congealed.

'How do you know the pubs that aren't booking us?'

Reilly stood and walked over to the window. He watched the turgid water.

'Some of the pubs we look after have chosen to go with our competitors in your father's absence.'

'Look after? You mean with the one-armed bandits and that?'

Reilly nodded without turning.

'And they happen to be the ones that aren't booking us any more?'

Reilly turned and nodded again.

'Probably.'

Hathaway left a few minutes later. As he made his way through the noisy amusement arcade next door – The Beatles' 'I Want To Hold Your Hand' blared out above the cacophony of pings and bells – he saw Charlie over by one of the old slot machines.

It was called The Miser's Dream. There was a little puppet of a miser with white hair and spectacles sitting at a table in the middle of a spooky old room. Charlie put a penny in the slot, and as Hathaway approached, the scene came to life. A door opened and a skeleton shot out; a picture slid back to reveal an ogre lurking behind it. A trunk opened of its own accord and a hooded creature started to climb out. All of this behind the miser's back whilst he continued, oblivious, looking at his piles of money on the table.

'You can keep your rigged one-armed bandits,' Charlie said, by way of acknowledging Hathaway. 'This is the one for me.'

'Rigged?'

Charlie glanced at Hathaway.

'No offence to your dad but every one-armed bandit in town is rigged so the odds are in the arcade's favour. Always have been.'

Hathaway nodded. He was wary of Charlie, who had quite a short fuse. He liked him but he hadn't known him as long as the other two in the group.

'So we're still on for the gig at the Snowdrop tonight?' Charlie said. The Snowdrop was a pub on the edge of Lewes, down the end of the Cliffe High Street.

'I said we'd be there for seven. Money's not bad, and if it works out, it could become a regular.'

'You know I'm from Lewes?' Charlie said, looking at a worn penny that had a faded image

43

of Queen Victoria on one side, which he'd fished out of his pocket to put into the slot.

Hathaway looked at the side of Charlie's face, at the knotted jaw.

'I remember you saying,' he said.

'Bloody hate the place. Bad memories. So excuse me in advance if I'm in a foul mood tonight.'

'Would we know the difference?' Hathaway said, stepping back quickly when Charlie mock-lunged at him.

The two had first met when Hathaway had advertised a few months earlier for a drummer for the group he wanted to start.

Charlie had turned up in Hathaway's dad's office on the end of the West Pier in full Teddy boy mode: the drape jacket with velvet lapels, the string tie, the brothel creepers.

'What kind of music you going to be playing?' he said, looking Hathaway up and down. 'I ain't doing any Cliff Richard or Pete Seeger.'

'We'll mix it up – Gene Vincent, Chuck Berry, Orbison, The Shads – whatever else is around that's good.'

'How old are you?' Charlie said.

'Nearly seventeen. You?'

'Nineteen. That's a good age for a drummer. Drummer has to hold it all together. Keep the beat. It takes maturity to do that.'

Charlie looked round.

'What is this place?'

'My dad's. He owns this end of the pier. The firing range, the amusement arcade and the dodgems.'

44

Charlie nodded slowly.

'It smells.'

Hathaway pointed down at the gaps between the floorboards to the water churning below.

'It's the sea.'

Charlie tilted his head.

'You got a van?'

Hathaway shook his head. Charlie smirked.

'I have. You're going to need a van.' He took a pack of cigarettes from his jacket pocket, patted the other one for matches. 'What do you think about the Springfields?'

'Mum and dad music.'

'Acker Bilk?'

Charlie lit up.

'The same. I hate trad jazz.'

'I hate skiffle,' Charlie said, blowing out smoke. 'You haven't got Joe Brown or Lonnie Donnegan lurking somewhere in the background, have you?'

Hathaway smiled again.

'Are you from Brighton?'

Charlie shook his head.

'Lewes originally. We've just moved down to Moulscombe.'

Hathaway waved an arm around.

'We'll rehearse here out of hours.'

'I assume I can bring the van on to the pier – don't fancy carting the drum kit from the pleasure gardens.'

'You can.'

'And is that just the two of us?'

'I've got a couple of friends from school. A bass player and a vocalist. They couldn't be

45

here today.'

'In detention?'

Hathaway grinned and after a moment so did Charlie.

'Are they any good? '

Hathaway nodded.

'Are you?'

Hathaway nodded again. Charlie pointed over at Hathaway's guitar and amp.

'Play us a tune, then.'

The Snowdrop was packed that evening, and Charlie, though quiet, seemed OK. At the first break an old friend of his came over, an un-reconstructed Teddy boy.

'This is Kevin,' Charlie said. 'We used to pal out until I moved to Brighton.'

Kevin looked awkward. He stared at his shoes as he said:

'And turned into a mop-top.'

Charlie and Kevin went off to the corner of the bar for a drink, but Hathaway could tell by the way they were standing that the conversation was awkward.

It was snowing by the time they finished the gig so progress back into Brighton was slow. Once they'd dipped down off the Downs, Hatha-way said:

'Kevin an old friend, is he?'

'More of an ex-friend, really. Not his fault. Just bad memories.'

The others glanced at each other but nobody said anything.

Charlie filled the silence:

46

'My little brother died. Kevin and me were kind of implicated.'

Again nobody said anything until Hathaway said:

'Sorry to hear that.'

'Yeah,' the other two said, almost in unison.

They drove on past Falmer on their left.

'We seem to be losing gigs,' Dan said. 'Don't the pubs like the music?'

'I think it's to do with my dad,' Hathaway said. 'And his arrangements with the pubs for the one-armed bandits'

'What do you mean?' Charlie said, as a car overtook and pulled abruptly in front of him. It slowed, forcing Charlie to crunch his brakes.

'Idiot,' he muttered.

Hathaway said:

'The pubs that aren't using us are the pubs that aren't using my dad's machines any more. When he was away, they went elsewhere.'

'Hang on,' Charlie said. 'Does that mean we're getting these gigs in the first place because your father has influence? That it has nothing to do with talent?'

'I think the link with Dad helps,' Hathaway said.

Charlie was getting agitated.

'I'm not getting this. I'm a bloody good drummer. That fucking Ringo Starr doesn't compare—' He pressed his foot hard on the brake again. 'What the hell is going on here?'

The car in front now had a flashing light on its roof and its hazard lights winking as it slowed down even more. Hathaway looked in the side

47

mirror.

'There's a cop car behind us too. Panda.'

'If it's trouble, I don't want any tonight,' Charlie said, crashing the gears.

The car in front guided them into a lay-by. The car behind followed.

'What the hell do the rozzers want?' Charlie said.

Four plain-clothes coppers spilled out of the unmarked car in front. Two bulky coppers came out of the panda. One of the plain-clothes cops wrenched open the passenger door and waved a warrant card at the occupants. He took a deep breath and breathed out.

'I'm smelling something illegal. You darkies in disguise, are you?'

The back door of the van was wrenched open.

'What do you know – it's a bloody pop group.'

This from a red-faced, sour-mouthed sergeant whose white helmet scarcely fitted his enormous head.

'What's the problem?' Dan said.

'I think you want to say "Sir".'

'He definitely wants to say "Sir".' Another copper loomed behind the first. He too sniffed loudly. 'Smells like the casbah in here – or Notting Hill. Want to get out and empty your pockets, gents?

Hathaway looked around at what was going on. He wasn't worried about drugs – though they'd heard about cannabis, none of the band had tried it yet – he was curious about the reason for the police picking on them.

'What do you want?' Charlie said to the plain-clothes man.

'We have reason to believe there are drugs in this vehicle and we therefore intend to search it.'

'We don't do drugs,' Dan said. 'But feel free to search.'

The policeman cocked an eye into the back of the van.

'Bit of a clutter back there. You'd better get your stuff out.'

'Our stuff?'

'All of it.'

The snow turned to sleet halfway through the unloading of the vehicle. The policemen in uniform and the plain-clothes coppers were standing at the side of the road under the shelter of the trees.

'Bastards,' Charlie muttered as he lugged the big amps out. When the van was empty and the sleet had become rain that was really pelting down, the policemen gave it a cursory glance.

'OK – our mistake. On your way.'

'Are you going to help us put the stuff back in – it's pissing it down.'

'Language,' the red-faced sergeant said, wagging his finger. 'That's not our job, lads. We're crime-busters.' He touched a finger to his helmet. 'Evening all. Oh and sonny –' he pointed his finger at Hathaway – 'tell your dad Sergeant Finch says hello.'

Hathaway and the others watched them go as the rain rattled on their gear.

Charlie was looking for something – or somebody – to kick.

'Fucking bastards!' He turned on Hathaway.

49

'So we've got your dad to thank for this. Again.'

Billy and Dan looked away.

'And for a gig with Duane Eddy when he comes to Brighton.'

Charlie gave a double take.

'You're bloody kidding me!'

Hathaway grinned.

'I'm serious. One of my dad's contacts.'

Charlie did a little jig. The other two looked bemused.

'Do you think we could talk about it out of the rain?' Billy said.

'Supporting Duane Eddy,' Charlie said. 'Well, this is it. The start of the big time.'

'It's only supporting,' Hathaway said. 'We're not topping the bill with him.'

'And he is past his best,' Dan said.

'Bugger off. I suppose you think the Everlys are over the hill.'

Charlie started putting stuff back into the van.

'Well, I'd like to meet your dad – he obviously moves in interesting circles. One minute he's pally with the rozzers, the next they're pulling us over.'

Hathaway was thinking the same thing.

On the Bank Holiday weekend, Hathaway went with Dan, Billy and Charlie on to the Palace Pier. The smell of hot dogs, chips, burgers and candy floss thickened the air. After the dodgems and the rifle range, they queued for the helter-skelter, mats in hand.

'Did you read about that bloke Tony Mancini?' Dan said. 'Confessed that he did it.'

50

'Did what?' Charlie said, watching a couple of girls eating candy floss walk by.

Hathaway was watching an old woman hobbling along in a headscarf with a see-through plastic rain hat over it. It was a bright, sunny day.

'He's the Brighton Trunk Murderer,' Hathaway said. 'Killed his mistress in 1934, stuck her in a trunk that he carted around for six weeks. She was a prossie, he was her pimp. Went to trial in Lewes and got off. Now he's admitted he did it.'

The others looked at him.

'What? All I did was read the paper.'

'There were two Trunk Murders, though, John,' a voice from the other side of the cordon beside the queue said.

It was Sean Reilly, in his cavalry twill and check sports jacket.

'The first was never solved. Victim never identified because her head and arms were missing, so the killer was never tracked down.'

'Mr Reilly—'

'Sean.'

'You're on the wrong pier, aren't you?'

Reilly smiled.

'Business meeting.' He looked at Hathaway's friends. 'These gents are the rest of your group, aren't they?'

'Meet The Avalons,' Charlie said, gesturing at the others. 'Supporting Duane Eddy soon.'

Reilly nodded.

'I heard. And I believe my living-room suite has the same name.'

The boys looked at him, then at Billy, who was

51

blushing furiously. Reilly caught their looks. 'It's a superior sort of suite, mind.'

He nodded to Billy, Charlie and Dan.

'Gents. I'm Sean Reilly. I work with John's father. Enjoy yourselves.'

He waved them off as the queue shuffled forward.

'I thought we were named after some King Arthur thing,' Charlie hissed at Billy. 'But we're named after a fucking settee?'

'And two armchairs,' Billy said.

The others looked at him, then Dan said:

'Well, that accounts for three of us – what's the other one?'

'As long as I'm not a pouffe,' Charlie said sourly, and they all laughed, including, last as always, Charlie.

'I suppose I'd better be that,' Billy said, 'in the circumstances.'

'Too right,' Charlie said, and they laughed again, Billy limiting himself to a tight smile.

As Hathaway climbed the steps at the back of the giant slide, he could see Reilly making his slow progress down the pier. A couple of other men joined him fifty yards along and they walked together back to the promenade. Hathaway looked to the pier offices as he stood poised at the top of the helter skelter.

A tall, thin man was standing in the doorway watching Reilly go. A look of utter hate on his face.

THREE

You Really Got Me
1964

On New Year's morning 1964, Hathaway was in bed with Barbara when his parents came home from Spain. Hathaway was dimly aware of a car pulling up outside, then the front door slamming, but he was otherwise engaged. Only when he heard his father bellowing his name did it register.

'Bugger,' he said, rolling off Barbara so abruptly she cried out. Hathaway put his hand over her mouth.

'It's my dad.'

Her eyes widened.

'Get rid of those dancing girls, Johnny boy,' his father boomed, his footsteps heavy on the stairs. He rapped on the bedroom door. 'You've got about ten seconds to chuck them out the window.'

Hathaway scrambled out of bed and scrabbled for his trousers, his erection still evident. Barbara pulled the blankets over her head.

'Just a sec, Dad. I'm not decent.'

'What's new?' his father said through the door.

Hathaway looked wildly round the room, saw Barbara's jewellery on a chair by the window. He started towards it but his father threw the door open.

'Johnny boy.'

His father strode in, a big grin on his face, looked his son up and down. He wasn't a tall man – maybe 5' 9" – but he was big across the shoulders with a barrel chest and his presence took up space. He moved towards Hathaway, scanning the room as he did so. He noticed the jewellery on the chair. He stopped and looked over at the bed.

'Dad,' Hathaway said, flushing. 'I wasn't expecting you home. Is Mum with you?'

His father ignored him. He looked back at the jewellery. Took a step and picked up Barbara's necklace. His jaw tightened.

'Dad, why didn't you phone?'

His father's look singed him, then swept to the bed. He took two strides, still holding the necklace, and grabbed the blankets with his other hand.

'Dad,' Hathaway said, now more startled than embarrassed.

There was a moment's resistance, then his father tugged the blankets off Barbara. She lay curled up tight, her head pushed into the pillow, but as the cold air hit her she uncurled and turned to look at Dennis Hathaway. Hathaway could see panic in her eyes but her voice was calm when she said:

'Hello, Dennis.'

His father's face was savage.

54

'Mr Hathaway to you,' he said. His voice was ice.

Barbara couldn't wait to get out of the house. Hathaway tried to calm her but she was having none of it. His father had gone downstairs and was with his mother in the kitchen when Barbara rushed out of the front door. Hathaway rested his head against the door for a moment then went to the kitchen.

He could hear his mother talking then laughing loudly.

'That Ena Sharples. She's a one. She bullies Minny Caldwell so.'

'Mum?' Hathaway said, coming into the kitchen and finding his mother alone.

'Hello, dear,' she said. She was standing by the sink, washing her hands under the taps. No water was running. She laughed. 'I do like the *Beverly Hillbillies*, don't you?'

'I thought you were with Dad.'

'Your father's out in the garden somewhere. It looks lovely in the snow, doesn't it?'

Hathaway was surprised at his mother talking and laughing to herself, but he was in such turmoil that for the moment he just accepted it.

'It's *Z Cars* later,' she said. 'Though I prefer *Dixon of Dock Green* myself.'

Hathaway hadn't seen his mother for nearly six months but she gave the impression they'd been together just a moment ago. She was nut-brown and wearing a yellow summer dress underneath her fur coat.

'Do you want to take your coat off, Mum?'

'No thanks, Johnny. It's a bit parky. I've been used to exotic climes.'

She said the phrase 'exotic climes' proudly, as if it were a foreign expression she'd mastered.

Hathaway stood awkwardly.

'OK, then,' he said, unable to think of any other comment that would meet the situation.

Hathaway spent the rest of the morning in his room. At lunchtime his mother called him down.

The family ate in the dining room, looking out over the snowy garden. His mother had cooked a gammon, with all the trimmings. His father sat at the end of the long table – it could seat eight – glowering and monosyllabic. His mother dithered.

At the end of the meal Hathaway's mother went in the kitchen to do the washing-up. Hathaway had offered to do it but his father said he wanted a word in the living room.

'Put some Matt Monro on,' Hathaway's mother called from the kitchen.

Hathaway's father did so, then brought over to the sofas a bottle of whisky and two glasses.

'Canadian Club. The best whisky in the world – according to the adverts.'

'Dad, about Barbara—'

'I don't want to talk about her,' his father said, the ice back in his voice. 'I want to talk about you.'

He chinked their glasses.

'I know I'm not educated,' his father said, 'but I'm guessing that the fact you're hanging around the house all day means you decided not to go on to take your A levels.'

'It's the school holidays, Dad.'

'Oh – that would be it. So you are doing your A levels?'

Hathaway's cheeks were burning from the whisky, a drink he wasn't used to.

'No.'

According to IQ tests at school Hathaway was above average intelligence. He liked learning stuff. And reading.

'More books,' his mother would say when he came home with yet another pile. 'Haven't you got enough books?'

But he couldn't settle at school. The teachers drove him potty.

'So you're financially dependent on me?' his father said.

Hathaway put his glass down. The whisky really burned.

'The group is doing pretty well.'

His father rolled his whisky round in his glass.

'As I said.'

'What do you mean?'

Hathaway's father didn't seem to hear.

'Let's change the subject,' his father said. 'I'm afraid your mum's got worse.'

'What's wrong with her?'

'She's going through the menopause – her hormones are all over the place. Big change – it can send some people mental.'

'You're saying mum's mental?'

'Not exactly – and I hope just for the time being.'

'What does the doctor say?'

'He's given her some tablets. Valium. Brand-new on the market. Tells me it's a wonder drug.'

'I heard her talking to herself in the kitchen.'

'All the brightest people do,' his father said cheerfully. 'Usually because they find they're the only people worth talking to.'

He saw Hathaway's face.

'Don't be worried. She's fine, just a bit ... irregular.'

His father topped up their glasses then gave his son a long look.

'What?' Hathaway said.

'There's real money to be made in the pop business,' his father said.

'If we can hit the top ten,' Hathaway said.

'With me, you berk.' His father saw Hathaway's look. 'Yes, a proper job. Have you any idea what I do?'

'No – but I have been wondering lately.'

The doorbell rang. Hathaway's mother answered the door. It was Sean Reilly. His father stood and shook hands with Reilly.

'You're looking fit.'

'You too.'

Hathaway stood awkwardly and also shook Reilly's hand whilst his father poured another whisky.

'Irish, I hope,' Reilly said.

'Irish-Canadian,' Hathaway's father said, handing the glass to Reilly.

They all sat.

'Son, as you may know, not everything I do is exactly above board. But then I don't know an honest man who doesn't try to fool the taxman if

58

he can. I'm no exception.'

'I don't blame you,' Hathaway said, though he really didn't know anything about tax.

Hathaway's father and Reilly exchanged a look.

'I thought you might want to join the family firm. It would be management-level entry for you, so to speak.'

'Yeah, but, Dad, I've got a job. The group.'

Dennis Hathaway looked at his son for a moment.

'We're going to go all the way.'

'I'm sure you are, son, I'm sure you are. But, in the meantime, help your old man out a bit. You'd get a proper salary. Cash in hand, of course. And frankly the way you splash out on clothes and the latest gizmos you can always use money.'

'I don't know, Dad. What exactly would you want me to do?'

'Nothing much at this stage. But I just wanted an in principle agreement with you at this stage.'

'An in principle agreement?' Hathaway said.

His father laughed.

'I heard the leader of the council say it once. I've no idea what it means.'

Hathaway's mother and father had decided on a welcome home New Year party that night. 'Invite your friends,' his mum had said, but none of the group was on the telephone and he didn't have any friends locally. He didn't think the invite included Barbara.

Caterers arrived late afternoon. Hathaway

went up to his room whilst they took over downstairs and thought about what to say to his father about Barbara. He hadn't imagined there would be a problem, even though Barbara worked for the family business.

The family business. He wondered exactly what else that business entailed.

The party was a boisterous affair. Hathaway was surprised that his parents, after a six-months absence, had got so many people there, on New Year's Day, at such short notice.

As usual, the women gathered in the kitchen whilst the men stayed together in the main rooms. There were loud voices but also lots of murmured conversations in quiet corners. The Great Train Robbers were a main feature of conversation among the men.

Hathaway observed his parents' guests as if for the first time. There were a number of hearty but tough-looking men, bursting out of their suits.

He was standing by the radiogram helping his father change the record when Reilly came over.

'The twins are here,' Reilly murmured. Dennis Hathaway looked over the heads of the people around him.

'Better treat them like royalty, I suppose. Who's that with them?'

'McVicar. Nasty piece of work from some south Peckham slum.'

'Come on, Johnny,' Dennis Hathaway turned to his son. 'Time you met some big-time villains. They think.'

Hathaway looked over at the two stocky men

in identical, boxy grey suits. He'd seen their photos in the newspapers, usually surrounded by cabaret people or minor film stars. He followed his father and Reilly over.

'Gentlemen, an unexpected pleasure.'

'As we were down here,' one of the twins said, though Hathaway didn't know which one was which.

'This is my son, John,' Dennis Hathaway said.

McVicar looked him up and down.

'Tall, ain't he? Hope you've killed your milkman.' He laughed loudly. Dennis Hathaway smiled thinly, the twins not at all. Hathaway smiled politely but had already taken a dislike to the man.

'So you're down on business,' Dennis Hathaway said. 'If there's anything I can help you with...'

The twins just looked at him.

'Right, then, let me introduce you around.'

'Before you do that, please allow me to say hello,' a voice said.

They all turned to look at the tall, slender man who had just arrived, accompanied by a much broader man of similar height. Both men were in their fifties, Hathaway judged, and both wore sports jackets and slacks.

'Chief Constable, glad you could make it,' Dennis Hathaway said to the thinner of the two. 'Gentlemen, this is the newly appointed Chief Constable Philip Simpson, who has brought law and order to the whole of Sussex after the bad behaviour of our previous chief constable, Charles Ridge. These men are—'

'They hardly need an introduction. I even know Mr McVicar there – by repute that is.' The chief constable indicated the man standing beside him. 'This is an old friend – a bobby turned bestselling writer. Donald Watts – though you might know him by his pen name, Victor Tempest.'

Hathaway looked at the man with interest. Victor Tempest. He'd read a couple of his books. Pretty good thrillers.

'So you served together?' Dennis Hathaway said. Tempest nodded.

'Back in the thirties.' He pointed at Hathaway. 'Neither of us much older than the lad here.'

The twins and McVicar were scowling at Tempest and the Chief Constable.

'Couldn't you get an honest job?' McVicar said. He had a sneering way of talking. The twins remained expressionless. 'Were you bent?'

Tempest was a few inches taller than McVicar. He reached out and placed his hand on the McVicar's right shoulder.

'Amusing bloke, aren't you?' he said.

Hathaway wasn't sure quite what happened next. He saw Tempest give McVicar's shoulder a little squeeze and the man cried out and reeled away, clutching at his upper arm. Tempest gave a nod in the general direction of the twins and Hathaway's father, and made a beeline for a group of women by the window.

McVicar, flexing his right hand and still gripping his bicep, glared at Tempest's back. Reilly took a step to block McVicar's way as the

62

London gangster started after Tempest. One of the twins put an arm out and flashed McVicar a cold look.

Hathaway saw that the chief constable had quietly separated from the group. Dennis Hathaway grinned and started to move away:

'Enjoy yourselves, gentlemen.' He glanced at Hathaway. 'Come on, son, time you helped your mother in the kitchen.'

Hathaway's father murmured to him as he led him away:

'London hoodlums. No bloody manners.'

Hathaway got trapped in the corner of the kitchen by two of his mother's friends, one of whom kept reaching up to ruffle his hair. His mum was chattering on, not really caring who was listening.

'We were having a nice lunch when we heard the President had been assassinated. Terrible. Ever such a nice restaurant overlooking the beach. That Lee Harvey Oswald – how could he do that to such a good-looking man?'

Hathaway noticed McVicar in the kitchen doorway, ogling the younger women. He was still rubbing his arm.

When Hathaway went back into the main room he drifted towards Reilly and his father. They were standing with a small group of men that included the twins. They were talking about the Great Train Robbers. Hathaway had been following the reports avidly. Over the past few months a number of men had been arrested. There were nine in custody.

A Brighton man Hathaway vaguely knew was saying:

'I saw the smudges in the paper. Didn't do Buster any favours, mind.' Hathaway remembered seeing the Wanted photo for a Ronald 'Buster' Edwards in the newspaper back in September. 'But did you hear what happened to Gordon?'

Gordon Goody had been arrested around the same time.

'He was lying low at his mum's in Putney, then went up to see that beauty queen in Leicester. His smudge isn't in the paper, his fingerprints are nowhere in the farmhouse. But the receptionist at the hotel where he's booked a room to get his leg-over thinks he's Bruce bloody Reynolds because of the glasses he's wearing. She's seen Bruce's smudge in the paper. What are the bloody chances? And, of course, once the coppers have got their hooks in him, that's it.'

'They fitted him up?' Dennis Hathaway said. The man nodded.

'They were spinning his place when just his old mam was there. That's not on. They did an illegal search in a room he was using over a pub and claimed to find paint from the farm on his shoes. They put it there, of course.'

The others in the group were all listening but nobody was commenting. Indeed, Hathaway was struck by their silence. McVicar suddenly barged in:

'Who's the nutty woman in the yellow dress in the kitchen? She's got bats in her belfry, you ask me. Doo lally bloody pip.'

64

Hathaway's father pursed his lips. After a moment's silence, Reilly produced two cigars from his pocket.

'Mr McVicar. You look like a man who enjoys a cigar. Come and smoke one with me. I want to talk to you about a bit of business. Outside, though – Dennis's wife doesn't mind cigarette smoke in the house but draws the line at cigars and pipes. Plus, it's a bit more private.'

McVicar looked surprised.

'Bit more freezing, too.'

One of the twins whispered something in his ear.

'OK, then,' he said to both Reilly and the twin. As Reilly led the way, the twins looked at Hathaway's father. Did Hathaway imagine it or did the same twin who'd whispered in McVicar's ear give the slightest of nods? Hathaway's father excused himself.

The twins looked at Hathaway but didn't say anything. Hathaway retreated to the kitchen.

The two women who had trapped Hathaway before were washing-up. There was a bag of rubbish beside them. Before they could snare him again, he picked it up.

'I'll take this out to the dustbins,' he said.

They smiled and carried on chattering.

It was cold outside and slippery in the passage beside the house. He put the bag in the dustbin then walked down the passage to the back garden. Sean Reilly stepped in front of him, an unlit cigar in his hand.

'Where's McVicar?' Hathaway said before he became aware of the grunts. He looked past

Reilly to see his father, red-faced, kicking a shape huddled in the snow. He heard his father gasp between kicks:

'You need ... to keep ... a polite ... fucking ... tongue ... in your ... fucking ... head.'

Hathaway watched in horrified fascination as his father continued to kick McVicar. McVicar wasn't moving. He wasn't making any sound. All Hathaway could hear was his father's jagged breath and the thud of his foot making contact with McVicar's prone body.

'He's going to kill him,' Hathaway said hoarsely.

'Just a lesson in manners,' Reilly said.

Dennis Hathaway only stopped when he ran out of puff. He finished by stamping on McVicar's head then bent at the waist beside the motionless form and sucked in air. Hathaway could see the blood spreading in the snow. Dennis Hathaway turned his head towards Reilly without seeing his son.

'Get this garbage off my bloody lawn.'

'Dad,' Hathaway called out. 'What have you done?'

His father straightened up.

'It's all about respect, son. If there's no respect, there's nothing.'

'But, Dad, look what you've done.'

His father looked down at the heap in the snow.

'What? This?' His father seemed puzzled. 'This is nothing.'

But to Hathaway it was everything.

* * *

66

For the next few days, Hathaway was in turmoil. He'd seen his father angry often, but never the animal fury as he was trying to kick McVicar to death. And Hathaway had no doubt that's what his father had intended. Hathaway was repelled by the violence. At the same time, he knew there was something in him that was drawn to that kind of barbarity. He knew he had his own dark places. He knew that if he allowed himself to unleash it, he had his father's temper.

Then there was Barbara. He waited to hear from her but didn't. He tried phoning her at the office on the pier but she was never there.

On the fourth day, he went to the pier. It was bright outside but the wind cut at his face like knives. He pulled the hood up on his duffel coat, even though he thought it made him look like a gnome.

The shooting gallery was boarded up for the winter but the amusement arcade was doing desultory business. Reilly was in the office with an unfamiliar woman. There were half a dozen paraffin heaters burning round the room. Two were on either side of the woman's desk.

'Your dad's not here, John,' Reilly said. 'He's in London. Gone up to see Freddie Mills at his club.'

Hathaway liked Mills. He'd never seen him box but he'd laughed at him in the couple of films he'd made. He'd met him with his father in Brighton. He'd even competed with him at the shooting gallery outside. Best of five. Hathaway had won but guessed that Mills had let him.

'That's OK,' Hathaway said, 'I was just passing.'

Reilly stretched his neck to look out of the window at the water, as if to ask, 'Passing on to where?' He smiled and indicated the woman at the other desk.

'This is Rita. She's taken over from Barbara.'

'Hello.' Hathaway forced a smile on to his face. 'Has Barbara gone, then?'

Reilly nodded.

'Got a job abroad,' he said, looking down at his desk.

'That was sudden.'

Reilly shrugged.

'Opportunity came up and she took it.' He stood. 'The trial will be over soon.'

Hathaway knew Reilly was referring to the Great Train Robbery trial. It had begun at the end of January and nineteen people were in the dock. Others were still on the run with warrants out for their arrests.

'Roger Cordrey is the only one who has pleaded guilty,' Reilly said. 'His mate Bill is going to get screwed.'

'How come?' Hathaway said, intrigued despite his upset about Barbara's abrupt departure.

'Cordrey is refusing to implicate anyone else and everyone else is pleading not guilty. Whatever Cordrey says about Bill Boal's lack of involvement needs corroboration. But since everybody else is denying they had any involvement with the robbery, there is nobody to say he had nothing to do with it. Boal is screwed.'

68

'You know him?' Hathaway said.

'From the racetrack,' Reilly said.

Hathaway glanced at Rita and lowered his voice.

'How's that bloke? McVicar?'

'He'll mend. Eventually.'

'Won't he want to get his own back?'

Reilly drew him to the window. A flock of seagulls skirled in the gusts of wind. The sea was boisterous, huge swells rising and dipping.

'People react to bad beatings in different ways, but more often than not it breaks their spirit. He was all mouth.'

'You know the type?'

'I've been around them most of my life.'

Hathaway went closer to Reilly.

'Is my dad a gangster?'

'You'd be best asking him questions like that.'

'Would he answer?'

'No idea,' Reilly said.

'Did he send Barbara away?'

Reilly smiled again.

'You'd be best asking him questions like that.'

FOUR

Rebel Rouser
1964

Sean Reilly was at the Duane Eddy gig. He stood out like a sore thumb, smartly dressed and two decades older than anybody else. He was with a group of men at the bar.

The gig was in the Hippodrome. The group's first taste of real dressing rooms. Duane Eddy didn't hang out with them. Just said hello and shook their hands and went to his dressing room. Charlie was in awe. His backing band were British session musicians. They helped The Avalons set up their gear.

The ballroom was packed but with a potentially combustible mix of mods and rockers. The mods were on one side and the rockers on the other. The group came out and got stuck into some Buddy Holly then switched to rhythm and blues. Hathaway was glad they were on a raised stage as within ten minutes the first mod and first rocker had met in the middle for a fight. More a tussle really – punches and kicks but nobody went down. When they withdrew another three or four from each side started up.

The girls were all clustered right in front of the

stage, a lot of them leaning on the stage. Hathaway saw Dan eyeing a couple up as he sang. He dance-stepped over and leaned into him.

'Watch it – we don't know who they belong to.'

When Duane Eddy came on the rockers made more fuss than the girls. Hathaway and the group clustered at one end of the bar. Reilly gave a little wave from the other end. Hathaway excused himself and went over.

'Wouldn't have thought this was your sort of show, Mr Reilly.'

'Gentlemen, you've probably seen this young pop star around on the pier. He's Dennis's lad.'

The men around him all nodded and smiled.

'Doing a bit of business with the proprietors. And a bit of behind the scenes wheeler-dealing.'

Reilly looked over as the latest groups of mods and rockers drifted into the centre of the hall and clashed.

'It's almost choreographed,' Reilly said. 'Which is the nearest anyone is going to get to dancing tonight, I think.'

'Lot of blood,' Hathaway said.

'Head wounds bleed excessively, however minor the injury. No, this is quite restrained, I think. It could have been a brawl but it isn't. Very neat.' He looked round. 'I see the bouncers have made themselves scarce. Sensible.'

He moved across to Hathaway and spoke directly into his ear. Hathaway got a whiff of whisky on the breath.

'Recognize anyone on the left-hand side of the ballroom?'

'To be honest we've been trying not to look at anybody on either side of the ballroom.'

'Good policy when you're in the middle. But take a look now, why don't you?'

Hathaway did and almost immediately saw three of the Teds who had given them the beating in Seven Dials.

'Those three guys over there – and these two heading back to them.'

Reilly nodded.

'That little squirt and those two big fellas, and these two with bloodied knuckles?'

Hathaway nodded.

'All right, then. You enjoy the rest of your evening.'

'I want to go over,' Hathaway said.

'That would be foolhardy in the circumstances. Leave it for the moment.'

Hathaway looked from Reilly to Reilly's men ranged at the bar.

'What are you going to do?'

'Negotiate.' Reilly patted Hathaway's arm. 'Get back to your friends now.'

When Hathaway went back over to Dan and the others, he looked across at the five Teds-turned-rockers. They were in a huddle, laughing. He wondered what they had thought when they saw the group up on stage before Eddy came on.

Eddy's twanging guitar was going over big. Charlie was in raptures. Hathaway leaned over to Dan.

'Those Teds are here. The ones that did us over.'

Dan spotted them immediately.

'Bloody hell. Small town – should've thought.'
He looked back at Hathaway. 'Do you think we should do something?'

'Not here – we'd get mobbed. Maybe after.'
Dan looked uneasy.

'They gave us a good hiding last time. What makes you think this time is going to be any different?'

Hathaway glanced down the bar at Reilly. He noticed that three or four of his men had disappeared.

'We need to hold on anyway. My dad's bloke down the other end of the bar has something in mind.'

Dan looked down the bar.

'That hard-looking bloke and his oppos?'

Hathaway nodded.

Eddy finished the instrumental and Charlie temporarily reconnected with the rest of the world. He looked across at Dan and Hathaway.

'A god walks the streets of Brighton,' he yelled.

'He came by minicab, I think,' Dan said, laughing.

Charlie glanced around the room. He looked straight at the Teds and his eyes widened.

He stepped closer to the others, his hand rummaging in the pocket where he kept the bike chain.

'Have you seen who's over there?'

'We have,' Hathaway said.

'Well?'

'Well, nothing. There's nothing to be done at the moment.'

73

'Bugger that,' Charlie said. 'I'll have that big bastard.'

Hathaway still had his own rage at the one who had intended to piss on him. He was imagining broken bones. Even so. He reached up and ruffled Charlie's hair.

Charlie jerked back and patted his mop-top, into place.

'Even though you're masquerading as a mop-top we know you're really a Teddy boy through and through. I'm not sure if Teds have etiquette, but I'm sure it's not on for one Ted to attack another in the middle of a conflict with a bunch of mods.'

Charlie was staring so hard at the group of Teds that Hathaway was sure they'd sense it and look over.

'After, then,' Charlie said.

'Johnny's dad's friend said to hang on.'

'Johnny's dad's friend?' Charlie said disdainfully. 'Is your dad going to walk us home after school too?'

'It's not like that,' Hathaway said.

'I fight my own battles,' Charlie said. 'Time you did too.'

'What's your problem with my dad?' Hathaway said, squaring up to Charlie. 'I notice you didn't turn down this gig he got us.'

Charlie looked at Hathaway but ignored the question.

'I say we ambush them afterwards. The element of surprise will work in our favour. What do you say, Dan?'

Dan and Billy both looked from Hathaway to

74

Charlie. Dan shrugged.

'You going to fight your own battles?' Charlie said to Hathaway.

Hathaway was stoked up.

'OK. Just let me tell my dad's bloke.' He looked down the bar but Reilly and his friends had gone.

The Avalons were backstage by the time Eddy finished his encores. He came off in a rush, gave them all a wave and a 'Thanks, guys' and went back out to sign photographs and autographs for the long queue already in place.

'Let's go,' Charlie said.

'What about our gear?' Dan said. 'We've only just got it – don't want to lose this lot too.'

'It'll be safe enough. Come on.'

This from Charlie, who'd freaked out when the original gear had been wrecked.

Dan picked up a beer bottle, and Billy found a block of wood and he hefted it in his hand. Billy looked queasy. He looked down at his elastic-sided Chelsea boots.

'Wish I was wearing winkle-pickers.'

Hathaway looked at a long pole with a hook on the end. He'd switched to aikido and had been doing kendo. He only knew a four-strike sequence so far – two defensive, two offensive – but reckoned that would be all he needed. He dismissed the idea, though, worried that if the police got involved, he would be treated more harshly for using what was obviously an offensive weapon.

He was concerned about Reilly and his instructions, but he had been provoked by Charlie's comments.

It was drizzling when they stepped out into the alley at the back of the dance hall.

Hathaway looked to see if the Teds might be among the autograph hunters, waiting to jump them.

A thin stream of people went past the end of the alley. Charlie led the way down. He kept his right hand in his jacket pocket.

Most of the audience was only now starting to spill out into the street in front of the dance hall. There were two exits and the police, who were out in force, were ensuring mods went out of one and rockers out of the other.

There was a lot of shouting between the two tribes but the police were in a solid wedge between them. There were half a dozen police vans parked on the pavement on the other side of the street. Hathaway saw Reilly and some of his friends standing beside the uniformed police. They were all watching the audience emerge and Reilly was talking quietly to a red-faced sergeant who was nodding. It was Sergeant Finch, the one who'd asked to be remembered to Hathaway senior earlier in the week.

Hathaway saw Reilly gesture to the sergeant as the Teds emerged. The next moment, the Teds were surrounded by around a dozen police. There was a moment's discussion then they were led off and put in the back of one of the vans. Hathaway and the others looked at each other.

'Well, that's that,' Billy said, looking relieved. He took the lump of wood out from inside his jacket pocket and laid it against a wall. Dan put his bottle down beside it. Hathaway looked back over to the sergeant. The sergeant nodded at him. Reilly had gone.

Hathaway's father was in the sitting room when he came downstairs the next morning.

'Come in here a minute, will you, son?'

'What's going on, Dad?'

'That's a big question, Johnny.'

'Mr Reilly was at the Duane Eddy gig.'

'Glad to hear it. He needs to get out more.'

'Some Teddy boys were there and at the end the police took them away.'

'That's a result for law and order, then.'

'Mr Reilly seemed quite pally with a sergeant.'

His father clasped his hands behind his head.

'Pays to keep in with the boys in blue, especially in our business. What is it you're asking me, son?'

'What business are you in, Dad?'

'I've got a lot of businesses, John. My fingers in a lot of pies.'

'Are they all above board?'

His father sucked his teeth.

'There are grey areas. But if I tell you I have reached an accommodation with the police, will that put your mind at rest?'

'What will happen to those Teddy boys?'

'Probably a drug bust, wouldn't you say? Might find they were suppliers, not just users. Now let's take that as a for instance. There'll be a gap in the market there. It'll need filling. If I knew people who had access to the pills that

77

young people today like to use, I might be tempted to fill that gap.'

He was watching Hathaway closely.

'You don't pop pills, do you, John?'

Hathaway shook his head. Charlie did and Dan had tried them, but he'd never been interested.

'But you're not morally opposed to it?'

'Morally opposed?' Hathaway laughed at his dad saying those words.

'Yeah – you know? You understand there's a difference between the law and what's right?'

'Of course,' Hathaway said, feeling uncomfortable at having such a conversation with his father.

'Well, I sometimes operate within that gap between the law and what's right. People want these pills. They give them a buzz. Supplying them isn't hurting anyone. Public service, you might say.'

Hathaway glanced at his father.

'Seems to me it's only reasonable that if my son's group is providing the music, his family should profit from ancillary activities.'

'So you want me to sell drugs at our gigs?'

'No, no, no. In the pubs nobody is selling without the landlord's say-so. And the landlord's are beholden to us. You just have to be sure we get our cut.'

'Rough stuff?' Hathaway said, and his father burst out laughing.

'I don't think so,' his father said. He saw the look on his son's face. 'Not that I don't think you'd be capable of it. But your role is managerial. I have wage-packet people for anything

78

else. You don't even need to get involved with the dealers. At the end of the night, when you get your fee, you get an extra envelope too. That's all.'

At the end of Friday night's gig, Hathaway took up his duties. Dan and Bill had both gone straight off, so he left Charlie at a table drinking a beer.

'Hello, Mr Franks,' he said to the landlord at the bar. 'Wondered what the take was tonight.'

'It's your usual fee,' Franks, a burly bald man, said, handing Hathaway a thick envelope.

'No, not for that – for the ancillaries.'

The publican stared at him.

'I think my father had a word with you about the new arrangements.'

The publican continued to stare. Finally, he said:

'I was expecting Mr Reilly to do the collecting.'

Hathaway smiled.

'One grasping hand is as good as another.'

The publican nodded slowly.

'True enough. The dealer's nipped off somewhere. He said he'd be back but maybe not until tomorrow. Do you want to come back then?'

It was Hathaway's turn to stare. He could understand this sour man being irked that some youngster was taking more money off him, but he couldn't let him try it on.

'Mr Reilly will be the one to collect it in that case. He'll doubtless want a word with the dealer too, if you could arrange for him to be here.'

79

The staring match continued for another minute.

'Hang on a second,' the publican said.

He was gone for over five minutes, and Hathaway was getting steamed until the landlord returned with an envelope in his hand.

'Thought I heard him in the back – he came back sooner than expected. All the calculations are in there too.'

'Thanks, Mr Franks. My dad will be pleased.'

Charlie watched him back across to his table.

'What was that all about?' Charlie said.

'Just something for Dad.'

'These machines must be quite good little earners for your dad. He'll be worth a bob or two.'

Hathaway took a sip of his beer.

'I wouldn't know.'

'You've got the biggest house on your street,' Charlie said.

'Only because it's on the corner and there was room to extend.'

'Wouldn't he want to move somewhere a bit posher?'

'What's wrong with Milldean?'

'Nothing moving out of it wouldn't fix. If I were your dad, I'd be buying something up the Dyke Road or round Seven Dials.'

'I think he'd find them a bit snooty up there. He was born in Milldean. He's rooted there. Don't you like where you live?'

'Moulscombe?' Charlie just laughed. He took a gulp of his pint. 'You going to work for your father until the group takes off?'

'I already am, in a way,' Hathaway said. 'But it's not like a proper job.'

'Couldn't find anything for me, could he?' Charlie said. 'I hate my bloody job.'

'I'll ask him. A lot of it seems to be cash under the table if you don't mind that.'

'Same at my place. I'm just sick of wearing filthy overalls and spending half an hour every night getting the grease from under my nails. Plus, at this time of year, it's fucking cold in a garage.'

'Not much different on the West Pier.'

'But you're hardly in that office, are you?'

'That's true. I'll ask.'

'That's great. I owe you one.'

'No, we're equal,' Hathaway said.

Charlie frowned.

'How do you make that out?'

Hathaway shrugged.

'Your van.'

'The group pays for me to run that.'

'Well, you're a bloody good drummer. Anyway, I'll see what I can do.'

Charlie studied him.

'OK,' he said.

Hathaway and his father rarely coincided at home. His mother was there all the time, usually baking and talking back at the radio. Hathaway was out most nights and slept most days.

The group was earning good money but not enough for the others to live on. Hathaway felt he was rolling in money because of the new salary he got from his father for picking up the pill take. It wasn't exactly arduous work. He collected an envelope after a gig and dropped it through a night-box at one of his father's town offices.

He called in at that office late one morning. It was in the Laines, on the first floor over a jeweller, sandwiched between an antiques shop and a Baptist chapel. The Bath Arms was opposite. The Avalons had played there once but the acoustics were dreadful.

A couple of men were listening to a transistor radio in an outer office. They recognized Hathaway and waved him through. His father was alone, staring out of the window, his feet up on a big safe in the corner of the room behind his desk.

'Yes?' he said, without turning.

'Dad?'

Dennis Hathaway looked over his shoulder and dropped his feet to the floor.

'John. A surprise.'

'I was in the neighbourhood.'

'I mean that you're up – it's not noon, yet.'

Dennis Hathaway smiled and waved at a low armchair in the corner of the room.

'Doze in that.'

Hathaway sat and looked over the desk at his father.

'And?' his father said.

'You sent Barbara away.'

His father started to swivel in his chair to face the window again.

'Dad – I'm allowed to ask. I cared for her.'

'John, I don't care what wagtail you bumble. I

82

just don't want you doing it in your mother's house.'

'It wasn't just that.'

'But it was a mistake,' his father said. 'You don't know anything about her.'

Not for want of trying.

'You don't know anything about me.' Barbara had said that very thing once.

'You don't want to tell me anything.'

'You don't ask,' she said.

'I don't like to intrude.'

Now, he said:

'I know more than you think.'

His father snorted.

'You know her husband is in jail?'

'That doesn't matter.'

'It will when he gets out. You think she cares for you?'

'I know she cares for me.'

'She's scared of you,' Hathaway's father said.

'Scared of me? Me? That's ridiculous.'

'OK, strictly speaking, she's scared of me. As she should be. She disobeyed orders.'

'Orders?'

Dennis Hathaway laughed.

'I know you're a good-looking boy and you think you're a little Casanova, but she didn't just fall into you arms that first time.'

Hathaway flushed.

'She was my birthday present to you.'

Hathaway sat back. His mouth dropped open. Dennis Hathaway spread his hands.

'But that was meant to be the end of it. It wasn't supposed to carry on. She went against

83

my orders.'

Hathaway's thoughts were scattered.

'Why would she do that?' he finally said.

'Because she's an idiot and didn't believe I would punish her.'

'I mean, why would she agree to sleep with me for my birthday?'

'Because I told her to. I knew you fancied her. I saw you gawking at her every time you came in the office.'

Hathaway looked at his father's hard face. He believed him.

'You mean she's a—?'

'No, I don't mean that.'

'But you have that kind of power over people?'

Dennis Hathaway nodded.

'Oh yes,' he said.

Hathaway looked down at his sun-freckled hands.

'So when she carried on seeing me, she was disobeying you because she liked me.'

'I told you. The way she explained it to me, she was afraid of what you would do, or what you would say to me, if she stopped seeing you.'

Hathaway clenched his fists.

'That doesn't make sense. Where is she now?'

'She's working abroad.'

'That's her punishment?'

Hathaway's father tilted his head.

'Oh yes,' he repeated.

Hathaway thought some more. A look sometimes on Barbara's face. The sorrow he'd noticed that first time. He was surprised at how quickly he could assimilate it. He looked at his father.

'Are you a gangster? Like the twins? Do you run Brighton?'

Dennis Hathaway shook his head.

'The council runs the town.'

'I mean illegal stuff.'

'Crime? I'll tell you who runs the crime in Brighton. The police.'

Hathaway smiled uncertainly.

'I'm serious. Charlie Ridge, the previous chief constable, was utterly corrupt. Scotland Yard came down and made all our lives a misery. They arrested him, two of his CID officers and two members of the public. Tried to throw the book at them. Living off immoral earnings, taking bribes, running backstreet abortions, protection racketeering, robberies. He'd only been chief constable for a year but he'd been around Brighton for over thirty. God knows for how many of those years he'd had his nose in the trough. The charges only went back to right before he was made detective chief inspector in 1949.'

'What happened?'

'Ridge was acquitted, though the judge pretty much said he thought he was guilty. Said that unless there was a new chief constable, no court in future would be able to believe the evidence of the Brighton police. His CID men and one of the civilians were found guilty. Ridge got fired the next day but now he's suing the police authority for unfair dismissal as he wasn't found guilty of anything. And he wants his pension.'

'Was he crooked?'

'Of course. We paid him off same as everybody else. You had to or he'd close you down. As it was, as long as you paid, the police turned a blind eye unless you were really taking the Michael.'

'And now?'

'Well, thanks to Ridge they've got rid of Brighton police as an independent entity and are setting up Southern Police with its new chief constable, Philip Simpson.'

'The man I met at New Year with Victor Tempest?'

'The very man. And it's business as usual. Now we're paying him off. No coincidence that Simpson and Ridge both worked their way through the ranks in Brighton from the thirties onward.'

'So the head of the police is also the king of crime in Brighton. What does that make you, Dad?'

'I'm a prince of the city, son, just a prince of the city. And happy to be so. Kings have a bad habit of getting their heads lopped off.'

Hathaway's mind was racing. Personally, he was thinking, I would want to be king.

The Saint was on the television but Hathaway wasn't really watching. He had a glass of beer in front of him but he wasn't really drinking. His mother had gone to bingo and his father was down on the West Pier. His mum had left one of her Jean Plaidys on the coffee table and he was idly flicking through it, thinking hard about his father and his father's businesses. How criminal were they?

He'd asked his dad if he could find work for Charlie Laker. Charlie was with his father and Reilly now, discussing it.

He was also thinking about Barbara. He missed her but mostly he was thinking that she came to him unwillingly. Every time they'd had sex, she'd been doing it under duress. It was messing him up.

He'd liked to watch her dress, though he had to do it covertly as he made her self-conscious. When she pulled on her stockings and clipped them to her garter belt he usually wanted her again, despite her protests.

Now he thought how terrible it was that she did it out of fear. That those protests were probably genuine.

'Johnny, I hope you're not up to no good.'

Hathaway glanced at Charlie and Bill who looked at the ground.

'Mum.'

'Your dad tells me you're doing a bit of work for him.'

Hathaway loved his mother but she was away with the fairies.

'Just bits and pieces,' he said.

'How was your holiday, Mrs H?' Bill asked.

'Lovely, Bill, thank you. I do like the South of France.'

'Weren't you in Spain?'

'There too.'

'You've caught a nice tan.'

Mrs Hathaway stuck her thin arms out and looked down at them.

'I'm peeling. For the second time.'

'Mum, I'm going out now.'

'All right, Johnny. Do you want the whisk?'

His mother was baking a cake. Nobody would be around to eat it and it would sit in the cake tin until it started going mouldy and she would throw it away. She held out the whisk, coated with cake mix. Hathaway ducked his head and took the whisk, running his finger along it and putting the mix in his mouth.

'Thanks, Mum,' he said through a full mouth, his face burning.

His mother turned to his friends.

'He's always liked the cake mix from when he used to help me bake cakes. Would you like some?'

'No thanks, Mrs Hathaway,' Charlie mumbled. Bill merely shook his head.

Outside Hathaway stopped them in the drive.

'Don't either of your say a bloody thing, alright?'

Bill squeezed his arm.

'Don't worry, Johnny. Mums are like that. Mine's the same.'

'Mine too,' said Charlie. Then, after a pause:

'How do your angel cakes normally turn out?'

FIVE

Get Off of My cloud
1964

Hathaway found his father in The Bath Arms with Sean Reilly. 'You'll Never Walk Alone' was playing on the jukebox and Dennis Hathaway was quietly singing along. He broke off when he saw his son.

'Johnny boy, come and wet your whistle. You're looking very smart – don't you think so, Sean?'

'Quite the man about town,' Reilly said.

Hathaway preened. He was deeply into the mod scene now. He was proud of his suit. He and Charlie had gone down to John Collier and got suits made to measure. Both had edge-stitching, a ticket pocket, four buttons and shaped waist, though Charlie had gone for side vents whilst Hathaway decided on a sixteen-inch centre vent.

'This doesn't make me a mod, you know,' Charlie said.

'Oh yes it does,' Hathaway murmured.

Hathaway watched Charlie with interest these days. Charlie was a grafter and, like Hathaway, was keen to get on in the family business. Both were losing interest in the group. Hathaway wasn't entirely sure what work Charlie was doing – both his father and Charlie were evasive – but his father indicated there didn't seem to be anything he wouldn't do.

Hathaway touched the top button of his jacket, the only button that was fastened. 'Made to measure from the Window to Watch,' he said. 'All the mods are wearing these, though sometimes they have waistcoats.'

'John Steed has a lot to answer for,' his father said. 'Thank God you drew the line at the bowler.'

He nodded down at the newspaper on the table in front of him.

'You seen the latest on the Great Train Robbers? Thirty years apiece.'

'That seems stiff,' Hathaway said.

'It's for making a fool out of the authorities,' Reilly said. 'And not letting on they'd done it.'

'Bloody traitors to our country get less,' Dennis Hathaway said. 'Justice.' He gave a contemptuous wave of his hand.

'You said Bill Boal would suffer,' Hathaway said to Reilly. 'How do you know Roger Cordrey, Dad?'

'Always get flowers for your mother from him.'

'Has he got form?'

Dennis Hathaway grinned.

'Eighteen and talking like an old lag.'

'Cordrey used to rob trains between Brighton and London,' Reilly said. 'Started around 1961. Just opportunist stuff. He and a few mates would hang around near the guard's van. One would distract the guard and the others would steal whatever registered mail they could grab. There was no guarantee of what it would contain.

'Then Roger, sitting in his florist's shop, figured out how to change the signals to red to stop a train. After that they could steal the lot, get off the train when it stopped and bugger off with the stolen goods. One of the men in the gang was mates with Buster Edwards. That's how the Brighton gang got involved with the Great Train Robbery.'

The Rolling Stones came on the jukebox.

'And you know all these people,' Hathaway said, looking from his father to Reilly.

'From the racetrack,' both men said, Dennis Hathaway a beat after Reilly.

'Right,' Hathaway said, taking a swig of his lager.

'Listen, Johnny, there's something I wanted to discuss with you.'

Hathaway swivelled his head to look round the pub.

'In here?'

Dennis Hathaway gestured at the almost empty room.

'You see anybody listening? We can go to the end of the pier if you want. I don't trust anywhere else.'

'What is it?'

'We were wondering – Sean and me – if you wanted to get more involved in the business. A bit more responsibility. Sean isn't sure you're ready but your friend Charlie has taken to it like a duck to water, so I figured you wouldn't want to lag behind.'

Hathaway hadn't really spoken to Charlie about his new duties, although he'd been curious. Now he felt left out.

'What do you want me to do?'

Dennis Hathaway leaned forward.

'Your friends the mods and Charlie's friends the Teddy boys – excuse me, I think they're now called rockers – they don't get on, do they?'

'You could say that.'

'OK, this is what I have in mind.'

During the first half of May, Charlie and Hathaway went all along the seafront between the Palace Pier and the West Pier talking to businesses. They made a good team. Hathaway was cheerful and charming, Charlie had a dangerous edge. They didn't threaten. They made promises.

On the Bank Holiday Monday, at the end of the month, Hathaway and The Avalons were up on the Aquarium Terrace drinking coffee in the sunshine. They were all in their mod gear – turtle necks and pegged trousers. They'd been taking a bit of a ragging from a bunch of rockers sitting on the terrace but it was in good spirits. The rockers knew Charlie and liked the group.

They were planning the future of The Avalons, though Hathaway and Charlie seemed disengaged.

'Look, there's money to be made on the American air force bases in Germany,' Dan said. 'There's this competition – if you win, you get a tour.'

Charlie snorted.

'Is that a comment or don't you have a hankie?' Dan said, sounding peeved.

'These competitions are cons,' Charlie said.

Dan shook his head.

'Definitely not,' Dan said. 'Johnny Dee and the Deedevils won one to tour Sweden.'

'How did it go?' Charlie said, looking out at the Palace Pier.

'Well, they didn't actually go in the end,' Dan said, abashed. 'Two of the group are apprentices and couldn't get time off work. But the principle remains the same.'

Charlie shook his head.

'Let's stick to rugby clubs and universities and colleges. And the parks.' He looked at Hathaway. 'We have a gig in Stanmer, don't we?'

Hathaway nodded absently. He was watching an army of mods come on to the seafront on their Vespas. They parked around the Palace Pier and spread out on to it and the beach.

Next a line of motorbikes roared off the Old Steine, looped up above the Terrace and, a few minutes later, came back down Madeira Drive and parked a few hundred yards from the Palace Pier.

'Have you heard the Shads are doing bloody panto this Christmas at the London Palladium?' Billy said. 'Alongside Arthur Askey as Widow Twankey. That's disgusting.'

'You don't want to go, then?' Dan said.

'Sod off. I can understand it with Cliff – he's so square mums like him. But the Shads?'

'What are they playing?'

'Cliff's Aladdin. And the Shadows are – and this is even worse – Wishee, Washee, Noshee and Toshee.' Bill shook his head. 'What next? The Rolling Stones in *Puss in Boots*?'

'Now that,' said Dan, 'I'd pay money for.'

A group of mods came up on to the Aquarium Terrace. They came straight for the rockers, punching and kicking and pushing them out of their deckchairs. The mods outnumbered the rockers by about five to one.

'Whoa!' Dan said, starting to rise. 'What the bloody hell?'

Charlie grabbed his arm.

'Probably not a good idea.'

Five minutes later, the rockers were hanging off the side of the terrace whilst the mods were hurling deckchairs down at them. Some dropped from the balustrade to Madeira Drive fifteen feet below. Other mods surrounded them there.

That's when the rockers from lower down Madeira Drive came running, swinging bike chains and yelling. And the mods came up off the beach to mix it.

Ordinary people scattered.

'Come on,' Hathaway said to the others, and they ran across the road on to the Old Steine. Over by the Royal Pavilion, Hathaway stopped them.

'OK, Charlie and I need to get over to the West Pier. You guys should probably head home.'

Dan and Billy both frowned.

'What do you mean you've got to go to the West Pier?' Billy said.

'It's work,' Hathaway said.

'This could get worse,' Charlie said. 'You should keep out of the way.'

His voice was almost drowned out by another line of motorcyclists on the Old Steine.

'This is not a place to stay,' Hathaway said. He grabbed Charlie's arm. 'Come on, we'll go up through the Laines and drop down.'

When Hathaway glanced back, Billy and Dan were standing in front of the Pavilion, watching them go.

Two days later, Hathaway and Charlie met with Dennis Hathaway and Reilly in the West Pier office.

'How did it work out?' Hathaway said.

'It was a bloody mess,' his father said. 'Neither your mods nor your rockers exactly observed the no-go areas.'

'There were a lot more than we expected,' Charlie said.

'I think you're being a bit harsh, Dennis,' Reilly said. 'As riots go it was pretty well controlled. And we were on hand to ensure that all those who requested our protection received it. We were also on hand to pillage those that had turned down our offer. We did best out of the jewellery shops in the Laines.'

'What about the Palace Pier?' Hathaway said.

'We didn't go near, but the Boroni Brothers were enraged that they were invaded,' his father said. 'They had men out pretty sharpish but they still got trashed.'

'Who are they blaming?'

Reilly shrugged.

'They suspect us of everything but they're not saying anything at the moment. I mean, it was a riot, wasn't it? What they're planning, who knows? The chief constable was seriously cheesed off. He was caught on the hop. No warning. I told him this was going to be a regular thing – no way to stop it now. He's talking about confiscating scooters and bikes and taking them to Devil's Dyke, so they're going to have a long uphill walk to collect them.'

'Will he give us a hard time?'

Dennis Hathaway shook his head.

'He just wants a bigger cut.'

When Hathaway got in, his mum was with a gaggle of women in the sitting room. The spirits and mixers were out and they were laughing over the game of Monopoly they were playing for real money.

Hathaway knew most of them but he was introduced to two he didn't know, both much younger than the others.

'John, this is Elizabeth, the wife of Donald Watts. You know – whatsisname?'

'Victor Tempest,' the woman said. She was a slender blonde with a nervous smile. She put down her Coca-Cola. 'Hello, John.'

Hathaway nodded.

'Hello.'

'And I'm Diana Simpson, the chief constable's wife.' She was a curvaceous brunette, arching her back almost grotesquely to lean forward. She touched the corner of her mouth with a red-lacquered fingernail and Hathaway had a sudden flash of Barbara. 'I hear you're a pop star.'

'Maybe one day,' he said, wondering how both Tempest and the chief constable, both middle-aged, had got off with women twenty years younger than them. 'We're playing at the SS Brighton tonight as support for Little Richard.'

'I used to swim there,' his mother said.

'Mum – it's an ice rink.'

'It wasn't always,' she said. 'It was a swimming pool first – biggest sea-water pool in Europe. I couldn't swim from one end to the other, it was so big. Then they turned it into an ice rink. And now it's all this other stuff too.'

Hathaway gave a little wave to the group of women.

'Enjoy your game.'

'I've just gone to jail, which is a bit embarrassing for a woman in my position,' Diana Simpson said, tossing her hair. Elizabeth Watts watched her, her face impassive.

Hathaway's older sister, Dawn, was at the concert. She was home for the weekend. She lived in a bedsit in London whilst she did a secretarial training course. Hathaway was pleased to see her. She was sparky and full of life. She was perched on the ratty sofa in the poky dressing room with Hathaway, Billy and Dan when Charlie barged in.

'I didn't know Little Richard was a poof,' Charlie said. 'Fuck me.'

'He'd probably like to,' Billy said.

'He just nipped my bum.'

97

'Sparkly suit, lots of eye make-up,' Dan said. 'How did we miss it?'

Charlie looked appreciatively at Dawn.

'Excuse the language. Didn't know we had visitors.'

Hathaway introduced her.

'You work for my dad, don't you?' she said.

'That I do,' Charlie said. 'He had his son working for him but decided he needed somebody reliable too.'

'Bugger off,' Hathaway said, reaching for his guitar and taking a string out of his pocket.

'Oh, here he goes again,' Charlie said. 'Bloody Banjo Bobby.'

'What do you mean?' Dawn said.

'This is a banjo string. A "G". I'm putting it at the top of the guitar, then all the other strings one lower than they should be. It sounds great – you can bend them all over the place.'

'Until it goes out of tune,' Billy said. 'Then your chords sound crap. And it sounds crap when you strum it.'

'Chords?' Charlie said. 'In the plural? When did he learn another one?'

'Boys, boys,' Dan said. 'There are so many ways a guitar can go out of tune, it's a wonder they're so popular.'

'And you can bugger off,' Hathaway said. 'Your idea of musicianship is shaking a tambourine.'

'I shake maracas too. And play the mouth organ.'

'What, your Manfred Mann mouth organ?' He turned to his sister. 'Dan bought – by mistake, he

98

claims – a mouth organ that only plays the chords for the mouth organ riff on "5-4-3-2-1", the *Ready Steady Go* theme. He used it on "Love Me Do" and the results were diabolical.'

'I saw that Tony Jackson in a club in London,' Dawn said. 'He was so out of it he threw his tambourine into the audience and it hit a girl in the face. He nearly got lynched by her boyfriend and his mates.'

'We supported him once. He was out of it then too. He peed against the dressing room wall instead of using the loo.'

'Ugh – that's disgusting.' She turned to Charlie. 'So you're getting quite famous, supporting all these big names.'

'Holding them up, do you mean?' Charlie said, and Dawn giggled.

'Famous in Brighton,' Hathaway said.

'Do you have a following?'

'Not exactly,' Hathaway said. 'We irritate a lot of people. We'll be playing Motown and the boys will want to jive—'

'With each other, mind,' Billy said, 'not with girls.'

'And we're getting used to beer bottles being thrown at us,' Dan said.

'I never feel we've connected with them,' Charlie said, 'unless they're showering us with beer and trying to crack our skulls.'

Dawn giggled again and gave him an up-from-under look. When she looked away, Charlie winked at Hathaway.

'Good-looking lass, your sister,' Charlie said the

99

next day as he and Hathaway walked down the West Pier.

'Keep your hands off,' Hathaway said, only half-joking.

His father was ranting to Reilly about Harold Wilson when they reached the office. He was furious Labour had got in.

'Bloody bunch of lefties. Dennis Healey, Jim Callaghan, that drunk Brown. And as for Harold Wilson – we should swap him for Mike Yarwood – he couldn't do worse.'

'Good morning, lads,' Reilly said. 'How was your gig last night?'

'A triumph, Sean, as always,' Charlie said. 'A triumph.'

'By that he means nobody threw any bottles at us.'

'A breakthrough event, then,' Reilly said.

'We're gonna have to kick you out of the office in a few minutes. We've got royalty coming.'

Charlie and Hathaway both frowned.

'The chief constable is paying a state visit.'

'His wife was around our house the other week playing Monopoly with mum and her coven.'

'A looker, isn't she? I don't know what she sees in exorbitantly wealthy Philip Simpson.'

'Maybe she has a thing about uniforms,' Reilly said drily.

'Is he that wealthy?' Charlie said.

'He's coining it,' Dennis Hathaway said. 'But he's still annoyed about that Bank Holiday do and he wants us to sort out our differences with the Boroni Brothers. That's what he's coming for.'

100

'How are you going to play it?' Reilly said.

'Well, a little bird told me something that has intrigued me.'

'Wasn't a Finch, was it?' Reilly said.

Dennis Hathaway grinned.

'You two lads get into the storeroom. Listen and learn.'

Philip Simpson arrived about five minutes later. He was in his standard civvies: a checkered sports jacket, khaki trousers and brown suede shoes.

'I haven't got long, Dennis. Having lunch with the leader of the council.'

'Poor you. Frank isn't exactly a stimulating conversationalist.'

'You know him well?' Simpson said.

Hathaway leaned back in his chair and clasped his hands behind his head.

'I own him, Chief Constable. Anything you want to talk to him about, you may as well talk to me.'

Simpson shook his head.

'A finger in every pie, Dennis. You'll be trying to take over the town next.'

There was asperity in his voice.

'Not a chance, Philip. I like where I am. I'm a born liege lord. But I do like to take advantage of opportunities when they come up. I thought it might be useful to have the council in my pocket. Frank was working for me when I forced him to stand for election as a councillor. Man can scarcely write his own name. He's been cursing me ever since because of the council meetings.'

'Now he's the leader of the council,' Simpson said thoughtfully.

'And he loves being the boss man; still hates the meetings. I've had to hire someone to read the committee reports and write a one-paragraph précis of each one for him, so he has a vague idea what decisions he's making.'

'Or that you're making.'

'Far be it for me to take the credit...'

Simpson leaned forward.

'Do you control planning?'

'Astute of you, Chief Constable. Let's say I have input, yes.'

'There seem to be some opportunities for investment in the town.'

'Indeed, yes.'

Simpson showed his teeth.

'Just make sure the man with the biggest private army in the county gets his.'

'Right you are, Chief Constable, right you are. By the way, I hear you're shifting shop.'

'We're moving to St John Street, yes. We've outgrown the old police station.'

'Just as well to get away from the ghost.'

'Ghost?'

'Oh aye. The ghost of the first chief constable. Have you not felt his chill hand on your collar.'

'I can't say I have, Dennis.'

'The first chief constable was a Jew called Henry Solomon. In 1844 a young man was nicked for stealing a roll of carpet from a shop. Solomon interviewed him in his office – your office, I suppose. It was a cold day and there was a fire burning in the room. The young man got

102

angry, picked up the poker and hit Solomon across the side of the head with it – so hard that he bent the poker. There were three witnesses to this but not a one intervened. The wound in Solomon's head killed him, of course. The young man was hanged at Horsham.'

Simpson frowned.

'I'm not following.'

'History, I suppose. That station has a lot of history. Though I hear you're chucking some of it out.'

'I'm not with you.'

'I hear you've been busy destroying files. Not evidence of police wrong-doing, I hope?'

Simpson clasped his hands in his lap.

'Who's been talking to you? No – don't bother answering that. Old files, Dennis. There's a thirty-year rule. A clear out, that's all. But what business is that of yours? Or is some of your family business in there? Does your father feature?'

'My dad never came to the police's attention.'

'Hardly the case, Dennis. I was a copper on the beat from 1933 – one of the first to wear Brighton's white helmet – and use the new radios. Me and Donald Watts joined at the same time. Your father was well known to us, believe me. Your father ran the seafront. And the race-course.'

'Pay you off, did he? He never mentioned you. Besides, I heard the razor gangs ran the course in the thirties. Those London mobsters trying to squeeze out the locals. *Brighton Rock* and all that.'

'They were rough days.'

'Don't see any visible scars, Chief Constable. You obviously came out of it all right. Or stayed out of the way.'

Simpson looked at him.

'Why are you trying to antagonize me?'

Dennis Hathaway bared his teeth.

'You got me wrong. It's just that sitting behind your desk in your best bib and tucker, raking in your money from your own rackets and taking your tithe from mine, I don't see you as a scrapper, more a profiteer.'

Simpson thrust out his arm and pulled up his shirt and jacket sleeve. A long scar ran up his forearm.

'I won't show you my stomach on such brief acquaintance.'

'Grateful for that.' Dennis Hathaway leaned forward. 'Anyway, I was a big fan of Max Miller. Sadly now gone.'

'You've lost me again.'

'I wondered if some of those documents you're destroying are linked to the Brighton Trunk Murder. You know – thirty years ago.'

'Murders, Dennis; there were two. And, yes, we are getting rid of a lot of the witness statements. There are thousands of them. But why would that concern you – and what's Max Miller got to do with it? You're sounding as Irish as Reilly here.'

'I met Max a few times. Max did variety bills on occasion with Tony Mancini. He's the pimp you'll recall who murdered his mistress, Violette Kay, stuffed her in a trunk and kept her under his bed for six weeks until the neighbours complained about the smell.'

'I recall the case. Bizarrely, neither his landlord nor landlady had a sense of smell so they suspected nothing. He was taken to trial in Lewes but thanks to his brief – who later became Lord Birkett – he got off.'

'Then confessed to the newspapers in 1963 that he was guilty.'

'Your point, Dennis?'

'Sorry, Philip, I do go round the houses sometimes. Well, Mancini did an act on stage in which he pretended to kill women – saw them in half, that kind of thing. Pretty bad taste if you ask me. And Max had the odd chat with him. Only when he had a free evening, Max said – Mancini had a bad stutter so conversation could take longer than normal. And Mancini told him he was suspected of the other Trunk Murder too.'

'Two dead women found stuffed in trunks within six weeks of each other – even you would think there was a connection.'

'True – though the other one, the one who was never identified, had no arms, legs or head, and no clothes for that matter. Her missing head the main reason she wasn't identified.'

'I'm still not sure what your point is.'

'He told Max some of the stuff the police were asking. Did you interrogate him by the way?'

'I wasn't high enough up the pay scale,' Simpson said.

'Well, according to Max, he was asked some rum questions about certain people in town. Do you want me to continue?'

'I'm not with you yet,' Philip Simpson said cautiously.

'Abortions were run by the rozzers then as they are now. Your area of expertise.'

Simpson spread his hands.

'Still waiting for the light to come on. Oh, wait. You think I've ordered the files destroyed because I was somehow implicated? Because of links you're imagining with abortionists?'

Dennis Hathaway just looked at him. It was Simpson's turn to lean back in his chair and put his hands behind his head.

'But if that's the case, why did I wait so long?'

'Good question. Good question. Somewhere in those hundreds of statements in the Trunk Murder files there is something incriminating – but for whom?'

Hathaway picked the newspaper up and held it out to Simpson.

'Seen the newspaper today.'

Simpson looked at the cover.

'Great Train Robbers, getting what they deserve. So?'

Hathaway tapped a column low down on the right-hand side of the front page.

'I meant this.'

Simpson unclasped his hands and took the paper.

'You would have known it years ago, you being in the police force and everything,' Dennis Hathaway said. 'But the rest of us – us civilians – only just found out that somebody actually found the head of the Trunk Murder victim back

106

in 1934.'

'A couple of youngsters found a head in a tidal pool at Black Rock. They didn't report it at the time. But it was before the dead woman's remains had been found at Brighton railway station. By the time they recognized the significance of the find, it was too late – the head was long gone. Stupidity and bad luck. So what?"

Reilly walked over to a cupboard. He withdrew a bottle of brandy and three balloon glasses. Simpson nodded to his unspoken question.

'So it focuses interest on the Trunk Murder again. Makes those files you're chucking out particularly interesting.'

Simpson took a glass from Reilly. He nodded.

'What do you want?' Simpson said as Reilly poured out two measures.

'What the bloody hell do you think I want?' Dennis Hathaway said. 'I want to renegotiate our deal.'

SIX

Time is on My Side
1965

'Ice hockey?' Hathaway said. He was sitting with his father, Reilly and Charlie in deckchairs on their private end of the pier. It was a sweltering Spring day and all were wearing shorts and open-necked shirts, except for Reilly, in sports jacket and cavalry twill, still managing to stay cool as a cucumber. All but Reilly had ice cream cones.

'These Canadian guys in the war kept going on about it so I gave it a watch,' Reilly said. 'Good, aggressive game. The Brighton Tigers are among the best in the country – just won the Cobley Cup against the Wembley Lions. They play at the SS Brighton.'

'Are you a skater, then, Mr Reilly?' Charlie said.

'Sean. Used to be. I still do it from time to time. But SS Brighton is closing down in a few weeks – end of May.'

'Snow melting?' Charlie said, grinning.

Reilly gave him a look.

'It's being pulled down to make way for a shopping centre, and next to it Top Rank are building this concrete box. A monstrosity. A dance hall with bars, opening November. The old place is closing in October with the Tory party conference – there's probably a joke in there somewhere but I can't find it.'

'If it's a monstrosity, how did they get planning permission?' Hathaway said. His father just looked at him.

'It's all progress, Sean,' Dennis Hathaway said, grimacing as melted ice cream ran down his cone and on to his wrist. 'There's going to be a lot of development in Brighton over the next few years and we're right in the middle of it.'

He waved the cone at their surroundings.

'We've got to get off this pier before it rots away. Shit.' His scoop of ice cream had toppled out of the cone on to the wooden boards. He tossed the cone over the railing into the sea and wiped his hand on his shorts.

'We've got the site clearance for Churchill Square shopping centre this year. That's going to be massive. Three years' work before any shops open. We're providing the labourers. And the machinery. We're investing in Brighton's future.' He winked. 'And our own.'

Billy, Dan and Tony, the group's new rhythm guitarist, hove into view, also in shorts.

'Rehearsal time,' Hathaway said. Charlie groaned and Hathaway kind of knew how he felt. Hathaway was enthusiastic about his music but he was also drawn more and more to the family business. If he was honest, he enjoyed the respect – OK, fear – in people's eyes when they found out who he was. He knew Charlie got off

109

on bandying Dennis Hathaway's name around.

Dan had bought a Vox Continental organ on HP, under the influence of Georgie Fame and the Dave Clark Five. He'd always played piano so had got the hang of it pretty quickly. He was singing 'Glad All Over', accompanying himself on the organ, when Dennis Hathaway came in and stood at the back of the store. His legs looked like tree trunks in his shorts.

When The Avalons came to the end of the song, Hathaway said:

'Very impressive lads, very impressive. Freddie and the Dreamers will be quaking in their boots.'

'Dad...'

'Just kidding. I wanted to suggest something else to you, about the group. Wondered if you could do with a roadie?'

'We can do it ourselves,' Charlie said.

'I know you can, but you're musicians. You shouldn't have to lug your stuff as well. I've got a reliable bloke in my office looking for a bit of extra work. A grafter. I'd be happy to lend him to you. He's got his own van so that would free you up a bit, Charlie.'

'I get paid for my van.'

'But is it worth the hassle? Anyway, I'm sure we can work something out for all of you. Shall I bring him through?'

The Avalons looked at each other and nodded.

Dennis Hathaway returned a moment later with a tall, broad-shouldered man in his late teens in a white T-shirt and jeans. He had a fag in the corner of his mouth, his hands dug deep in his trouser pockets. He slouched a little, James Dean style, as he squinted through his cigarette's smoke.

'Alan, say hello to next year's chart toppers.'

He sniffed.

'All right,' he said in a cockney accent.

The Avalons were busy three nights running that week. Alan was hard-working and efficient, though he preferred to roam the front of house during their actual sets. Hathaway would see him drifting through the audience, cigarette clamped between his teeth, having a quiet word here and there. He immediately guessed what that meant and was annoyed his father hadn't told him.

Saturday night they were at the Hippodrome supporting The Who. Hathaway, Billy, Dan and Tony were chatting up some girls when Charlie jig-a-jigged over.

'Charlie – you OK? You look a bit—'

'Right as rain, Johnny, right as rain. Me and their drummer, that Keith guy – he's mental he is – you know he's pissed in his wine?'

'Pissed in his wine – why?'

'Not his own wine – the wine of that guy with the big nose. He hasn't noticed – been swigging it back from the bottle. The others know. They're cracking up in there.'

Hathaway reached for Charlie's sunglasses. Charlie reared back.

'Sorry, Charlie, but you seem a bit—'

'Did you know our roadie is a dealer on the side?' Charlie said. 'Uppers, downers, blues, speed. He's a mobile chemist that lad.'

Hathaway waved the girls away.

'Alan is dealing drugs?' Dan said.

Hathaway turned back but said nothing.

'He's a right little wheelerdealer,' Charlie said. 'He's just told me their roadie is offering us a deal on a hundred-watt Vox amp.'

'Hundred watts?' Billy said. 'That's bloody enormous. And a Vox? We gotta have it.'

'We'd never get it in the van,' Hathaway said.

Charlie cackled, jerking his body in another weird jig.

'They use an ice cream van. They nicked the amp from the *Ready, Steady, Go* studio last week. It's got the show's name plastered all over it.'

'Receiving stolen goods?' Dan said. 'We can't do anything illegal.'

Charlie looked at Hathaway.

'Yeah, right.' He cackled again. 'That Alan. His speed is bloody ... speedy. Talk about m-m-my generation.'

The others all laughed at Charlie, though Dave, Bill and Roy probably shared Hathaway's concern that a drummer on speed wasn't going to be exactly consistent keeping the beat.

Hathaway met a girl called Ruth that night. She was up for anything. The next day he took her to the open-air swimming pool at Black Rock. He spent time there when he could, usually chatting up girls rather than swimming. It was sheltered by the cliffs, so could be really hot in the sunshine. When he was a kid he'd often played in the rock pools there. Now he made Ruth shudder telling her how the head of the Trunk Murder victim had been found in a rock pool back in 1934.

He was surprised to see his father and Reilly walking around, deep in conversation with another two men. All of them looked overdressed in dark suits.

His father saw him and Ruth in their deckchairs. Ruth was wearing a skimpy bikini and Hathaway saw her self-consciousness as his father stared down at her.

'The hard life of the working man,' Dennis Hathaway said to his son.

'I'm working tonight,' Hathaway said, getting out of his deckchair and tossing Ruth a towel. He nodded to Reilly. 'What are you both doing here?'

He drew them away.

'Considering a bit of business,' Dennis Hathaway said. 'What do you think about this whole area becoming a marina? Berths for a few thousand boats, an oceanarium, an ice rink, a sports centre, tennis courts, apartments, a hotel, pubs – the works. Even a fishmarket.'

'The fishmarket doesn't do anything for me but aside from that it sounds great,' Hathaway said. 'We're involved?'

'We could be. I've got a bit of money lying around. Couple of problems, though. Getting a road in here is tricky. And the porridge makers are being a right pain.'

'Porridge makers?' Hathaway said.

'Yeah, the Quakers.'

Hathaway laughed.

'Do they still exist?'

'You bet.' Dennis Hathaway pointed up at the cliff. 'And they have a burial plot up near the gasometers. The plan needs that space.'

'Then there's the cliff itself,' Reilly said.

'Yeah, we can't touch that. Full of fossils, apparently. Dinosaurs and all that.'

'Really?' Hathaway said.

'Don't get overexcited, John. You're such a bloody kid. They're in the way, frankly.'

Hathaway gestured around.

'Will this go?'

'Inevitably,' his father said. He took Hathaway's arm. 'Me and your mum are off to the theatre tonight.'

'The Theatre Royal?'

'Nah, the Palace Pier. Good bit of cabaret.' He looked over at Ruth. 'Want to join us?'

Hathaway shook his head.

'No, thanks, Dad. We've got plans.'

His father looked over at Ruth.

'I'll bet you have.'

'We're going to see The Beatles. They're closing the Hippodrome.'

'Don't get me started on that. Are you supporting?'

'Nah – they're bringing their own support band. Some other Scousers. We'll meet them, though.'

Hathaway's father nodded towards Ruth and leaned in to his son.

'That should get you whatever you want from yon lass.'

114

Hathaway flushed and smirked.

'I've already had that.'

Dennis Hathaway was in London a lot in June for meetings. One day he came back to the West Pier with Freddie Mills, the former world champion. Mills, mashed nose and kid's gap-toothed smile, was friendly and took Hathaway on at the shooting gallery. Hathaway won, though he thought perhaps Mills had once more let him.

On 9 July, Hathaway, sprawled on the sofa in the office after a lively night with Ruth, read in the paper that Ronnie Biggs, one of the Great Train Robbers, had been sprung from Wandsworth in an escape like something out of *Danger Man*.

'He must be important,' he said to Reilly. Charlie was tilted back in a chair, his feet up on the window sill.

Reilly shook his head.

'He was brought in at the last moment. Small time – made his living as a painter and decorator.'

'Why, then? Who would bother?'

'Money,' Charlie said. 'He'd make it worth someone's while. Or someone would make it worth their own while by stealing his money from him.' He tilted the chair forward. 'Or – he threatened to talk unless they sprang him.'

'Who is "they"?' Reilly said, amusement in his voice.

'Well, I heard there were other people involved in the robbery who were never caught, never identified. Maybe he threatened to talk unless they got him out.'

'Why didn't "they" just pay someone to shaft him in the Scrubs?'

'Painful,' Hathaway said. He giggled. 'Have you ever been shafted in the scrubs, Charlie?'

'Piss off.' Charlie pointed at Hathaway. 'You thought Muffin the Mule was a sexual practice until you discovered Smirnoff.'

Even Reilly smiled at that.

'And your dad thinks music hall died with Max Miller,' he said. 'Jimmy Tarbuck has a lot to answer for.'

'As I was saying,' Charlie said. 'Biggs is sprung, killed and buried somewhere he'll never be found. Mark my words. He'll never be heard of again.'

Reilly shifted in his seat but said nothing.

Just over two weeks later, Charlie and Hathaway were sitting in deckchairs outside the office. They were arguing, first about whether Michael Caine was better in *Zulu* or in *The Ipcress File*, then about the relative merits of the Rolling Stones and The Beatles. It was a slow day.

Dennis Hathaway stomped out of the office. He went over for a low-voiced discussion with Tommy, who ran the shooting gallery, then headed over to the lads.

'Everything all right, Dad?'

'No, it's bloody not. Freddie Mills is dead. Shot in the head in his car in a yard behind his club.'

Charlie and Hathaway both struggled out of their deckchairs.

'Who did it?' Charlie said.

'They're saying it's self-inflicted. With one of my bloody rifles. I lent him it from the shooting gallery when he was last down. According to Andy, his business partner, he'd told his staff he was going off for his regular nap in his car.'

'But our rifles are just air guns,' Hathaway said.

His father shook his head.

'Adapted to fire pellets but easy enough to convert back. We have half a dozen behind the counter...'

His voice tailed off.

'Do you think he killed himself?'

His father scowled.

'Don't be bloody daft. A rifle in a car, a man of his bulk? If he was going to shoot himself, that's what handguns were invented for.'

'Who, then?' Charlie said.

'His chinkie was on Charing Cross Road.' Reilly had stepped out of the office. 'Right on the edge of Chinatown. The Tongs were shaking him down.'

Dennis Hathaway shook his head.

'It's the bloody twins. The chinkie went bust – probably because of the stuff going out the back door – and the twins got him to turn it into a club – The Nite Spot. They used to hang out there.'

'So why kill him?' Charlie said.

'As a warning to me,' Dennis Hathaway said. 'Freddie's been doing some negotiating on my behalf.' He balled his fists. 'Look, there are two main gangs in London. In the fifties it was the Cypriots and the Italians but today it's homegrown, cockney boys. Now, what you think about them depends on where you're sitting. Some say they keep petty crime down in the areas they control better than the rozzers can. Others say they terrorize the communities they live in – and live off.

'Frankly, I don't give a toss what they do as long as they stay out of my backyard. But they want to expand out of London. It's obvious they're looking at Brighton. They've been talking to those other tossers, the Boroni Brothers down here. Encouraging them to have a go at us. Divide and rule, that's their plan. But it can't happen. I won't let it happen.'

'So what do you want to do?' Reilly said. 'Pay them off? You know you can't pay them off – they'd bleed you dry. Start a war?'

'We can't win a war.'

'What, then?' Hathaway said.

'We'll have a parlay at Freddie's funeral. I want you boys to come up with Sean and me.'

Hathaway and Charlie exchanged glances. Stood straighter. Dennis Hathaway shook his head.

'Freddie Mills dead. Bloody hell.' His son thought he saw tears in his eyes. His father was both brutal and sentimental. 'First time I saw him fight was here in Brighton. In a booth down on the beach not long before Adolf kicked off. Not what you'd call a stylist but he could hit hard – and he could take it as well as dish it out. He was a light heavyweight really but he fought heavyweight, so he had to take a lot of punches. I saw him win the world championship in 1948

118

– and lose it in 1950 at Earls Court. Knocked out in the tenth round. Freddie retired after that. He had headaches the rest of his life from the batterings he'd taken. But in his day he took any punch you could throw at him.'

Dennis Hathaway growled suddenly.

'The fucking twins trying to muscle in down here. I knew that New Year when they turned up with that prick McVicar they weren't down for the sea air. But we've got to keep them the fuck away – they're fucking mental.'

'Sean told me it was only one of them,' Hathaway said. 'That the other is OK.'

'Fucking bum-bandit boxer,' Dennis Hathaway said. 'Not enough he wants to fuck you up the arse, he wants to punch you in the face whilst he's doing it. Freddie was the same.'

Hathaway looked askance.

'Freddie Mills was queer?'

'Freddie wouldn't be the first queer scrapper, Johnny boy. You never seen those wrestlers your mother likes watching, tent poles sticking out of their trunks when they get into a grapple?'

Hathaway flushed.

'So could his death have been a queer thing?' Charlie said.

'Well, there's a story that he'd been arrested in a public toilet and charged with homosexual indecency,' Reilly said. 'Plus his singer lover-boy, Michael Holliday, killed himself.'

Hathaway was a step or two behind.

'But he's married, isn't he?'

'He married his manager's daughter and they had two kiddies – girls, I think. But he was

119

queer.' Dennis Hathaway chuckled. 'Welcome to the confusions of the adult world, son,'

'I thought Holliday belonged to the poof twin,' Reilly said.

'They were close,' Dennis said. 'But then I thought he was doing Freddie as well. Anyway, his brother insists he's a real man's man and not that way inclined.'

'Aren't all queers men's men?' Hathaway said. 'Isn't that the point?'

Charlie sniggered.

'I saw him introducing *Six-Five Special*,' he said. 'Stuck out a bit. And in the Carry On films.'

Dennis Hathaway cracked his knuckles.

'You're going to hear all kinds of wild stories going round. One is that he's about to be exposed as Jack the Stripper.'

Hathaway's eyes swivelled from his father to Reilly and back.

'Really?'

Charlie didn't read the papers much.

'Who's he?'

'Since about 1959 through to now,' Reilly said, 'some guy has been choking or strangling young women – eight to date – as he's raping them. He dumps the bodies in or near the Thames. So far he's not been identified.'

'But why would they think that was Freddie Mills?' Hathaway said. 'Especially if he's queer.'

His father clapped his hand on Hathaway's back.

'More confusion. Your mum won't feel like going to Freddie's funeral. She's never got on

120

with queers. But you and Charlie are set? It'll give you a chance to see how the other half live.'

'The queers?' Charlie said.

'No, you daft sod, East End gangsters and East End showbiz types. You know Freddy made a few films. It'll be a big turnout.'

Hathaway and Charlie looked at each other. Nodded.

'Good. I want to introduce you to a couple of people. Then we'll do our bit of business with the twins. Sean, we won't go mob-handed. We'll show them what class is.'

'Will McVicar be there?' Hathaway said. Charlie gave him a puzzled look. Dennis Hathaway looked down at his hands.

'Don't see him around any more. They say he's in the foundations of the Westway. Doing something useful for the first time in his life.'

Freddie Mills was buried at New Camberwell Cemetery. Hundreds of people turned out. Hathaway and Charlie filed past the grave behind Dennis Hathaway and Reilly. There were boxing gloves on the headstone and an urn in front of it.

'See that urn?' His father nudged Hathaway. 'It's got one of Freddy's boxing gloves in it.'

'Won't someone nick it?'

Dennis Hathaway looked around.

'Not with these villains around.'

'Honour among thieves?'

'Fear.'

A big man with a flat nose tapped Dennis Hathaway on the shoulder. Dennis looked

121

up at him.

'The brothers want a word.'

Hathaway and Charlie didn't know what that word was. Hathaway's father and Reilly stayed up in London and sent the lads back to Brighton. Hathaway was reluctant to go but his father insisted.

'Nothing is going to kick off, Johnny. It's a *mi casa, su casa* thing.'

'What do you mean?' Hathaway said.

'I mean go home. Shag the arse off Ruth.'

'I'm not seeing her anymore.'

Dennis Hathaway laughed.

'OK, go and shag the arse off Charlie – in memory of Freddie.'

'He should be so lucky,' Charlie said.

'Go on. Piss off, the pair of you. I'll fill you in tomorrow.'

Hathaway was out the next day until mid-afternoon. He came home to the sound of his father raging and a woman crying. He hurried into the front room. His older sister, Dawn, was sprawled on the sofa, her hand to a bright red cheek. Her father was standing over her.

'Dad?'

'You keep out of this, John.'

'But, Dad—'

His father turned on him, his big fists clenched. His feet were planted a yard apart. His tree trunk legs made him look immovable.

'Do you want some too?'

'Dad, she's a girl. She's Dawn.'

122

'She's a tart, is what she is.' Dennis Hathaway looked more intently at his son. 'Do you know about this?'

'About what?'

'Your sister's got a bun in the bloody oven, that's what.'

Hathaway looked at his sister, her hands now over her face. She was sobbing.

'So?' he said.

His father took a step closer, his face reddening.

'So? That my daughter has been sleeping around is bad enough, but that they haven't been using johnnies is bloody diabolical.'

'I haven't been sleeping around,' she stumbled out between sobs.

'Haven't you? Is this the miraculous conception, then?'

'I've only slept with one person. I love him.'

'You're a kid for fuck's sake. What do you know about love?'

Dawn sat up on the sofa.

'A lot more than you, the way you treat Mum.'

Dennis Hathaway loomed over her again. She shrank into the cushions.

'I've never laid a hand on your mother. Never. Even though she'd try the patience of a saint.'

Dawn kept her eyes down.

'There's more to love than that,' she said sullenly.

Hathaway slid on to the sofa beside her and put his arm round her. Their father looked down at the both of them.

'If you love him you must be proud of him,

123

and if you're proud why won't you tell me who
he is?'

'I'm not telling you who he is because you'll
do something to him.'

'I'll do something to him if you don't tell me
who he is.'

'Where's Mum?' Hathaway said.

'Bingo,' his father said. 'She's got this to look
forward to.'

The telephone rang. Dennis Hathaway looked
from one to the other of them, his fists still
clenched.

'Of all the bloody days to hear this,' he said,
walking over to the phone and snatching it up.
'What?'

He listened for a minute then put the phone
down. He hurried over to the front door.

'I'll be back,' he called over his shoulder.

In the silence following the slamming of the
door, Hathaway said:

'Why didn't you tell Mum first so she could
prepare the ground?'

'Have you seen her lately?' Dawn said. 'She's
having one of her times. She's in la-la land.'

'When's it due?'

'Not for ages – I'm only about six weeks.'

Hathaway looked at his sister.

'Are you pleased?'

She smiled. 'Well, you know.'

'What about this bloke, whoever he is?'

'What about him?'

'Does he know?'

'Yes.'

'Is he pleased?'

124

'Sort of.'

'Is he going to stand by you?'

She laughed.

'Stand by me? You sound like a Victorian parent.'

'Is he?'

'Of course.'

'You're going to have it, then?'

'Dad wants me to have an abortion. Knows this doctor in Hove. Abortionist to high society, he says, as if that matters.'

'Who is the father?'

'Will you tell Dad?'

'He'll have to find out sooner or later.'

Dawn leaned into Hathaway.

'Will you tell him?'

'No.'

She kissed his cheek. 'Thanks.'

'But you'll have to tell him.'

She stood up and looked down on Hathaway, a coy look on her blotched face. It was a disconcerting combination.

'You know him, actually.'

Hathaway raised an eyebrow.

'That's my Saint look. I've been practising.'

'You're a good-looking boy but Roger Moore you're not.'

Hathaway shrugged.

'So who is it?'

Dawn walked over to the French windows and looked out into the garden. Without turning round she said:

'It's Charlie.'

* * *

Hathaway was half-watching *The Avengers* when his father came back in. He'd been thinking about Charlie and Dawn together. Getting angry.

'Where's your sister?'

Hathaway kept his eyes on the screen.

'Gone to bed in her old bedroom.'

'Did she tell your mum?'

'She's already knitting socks.'

Dennis Hathaway smiled grudgingly.

'I suppose if they get married straightaway it can be a honeymoon conception. She said she wasn't far along.'

'Six weeks. But, Dad, I have to ask – given our line of business, why do you care so much about the proprieties?'

The smile went.

'You want to be uncle to a bastard?'

'I don't care.'

'I'm hoping she won't have it. I've suggested a doctor I know in Hove.'

'Dawn said.'

'Has she told you whose it is?'

Hathaway nodded.

'And?'

'It's for Dawn to tell you.'

His father looked at him for a long moment but not with hostility.

'OK. This has come at a bad time. There's a lot going on. You know that.'

'What happened with the twins?'

Hathaway pinched the end of his nose and sucked in air. He sighed.

'Johnny boy, it's war.'

SEVEN

Paint it Black
1966

'We're moving up in the world, Johnny boy. Bought a place on Tongdean Drive. You're welcome to move with us. Dawn is. But I thought you might like a flat of your own. Got a nice one available overlooking the West Pier. Penthouse with a balcony.'

'A penthouse?' Hathaway said.

'OK – a top-floor flat – but with a balcony to sit in the sunshine. And we can semaphore each other from pier to penthouse.'

Hathaway was excited at the thought, largely for sexual reasons. The group was getting a lot of interest from local girls but he had nowhere to take them. It felt seedy retiring to the back of the van, especially as the others were striking lucky too. Well, except Billy, who seemed to draw only earnest young men wanting to talk music.

'I can stand on my own two feet,' Hathaway said. His father looked steadily at him.

'I know that, Johnny, but do it for your mother.' He leaned forward and put his elbow on the table. 'Come on, son, I'll arm- wrestle you for it.'

Hathaway groaned and put his Coke down. His father was a good six inches shorter but he was sturdy and he had powerful arms. Hathaway's longer forearms put him at a disadvantage because he had to start with a bent arm. He'd worked out the physics of it once.

'I may as well just say "Yes" now.'

'That's always the best way with me,' his father said.

The buzzer went off from the cashiers in the amusement hall and, a moment later, from the firing range. Reilly was sitting by the window with three foot-soldiers and Charlie.

'Look lively,' his father said, immediately out of his chair. They heard a clattering of feet on the other side of the office door, then it burst open and a man with a stocking over his head rushed through, a pickaxe handle in his hand.

Reilly had somehow moved, without any appearance of haste, into a position just behind the door. As the man went past him Reilly leaned forward and, with an almost delicate flip of the wrist, sapped him behind his right ear. The man sprawled forward, his wooden stave rattling across the floor ahead of him.

Dennis Hathaway picked it up and threw it to his son.

'Stay out of it but use this if you have to defend yourself.'

A half-dozen other men came roaring through the door with stocking masks and pickaxe handles.

Reilly stepped back and Dennis Hathaway moved to one side, dragging his own lead-filled cosh out of his pocket. Two of his men also had coshes; the third picked up a chair and prodded the legs at the man who was charging him. Charlie was on his feet with a flick knife in his hand, moving forward, focused.

'Don't kill anybody, Charlie,' Reilly called.

'Don't intend to,' Charlie shouted back, his voice trembling. 'Just gonna mess 'em up a bit.'

He swung the knife at the man nearest to him with a long sweep of his arm. The man fell back against the bench, and Charlie slashed at the hand that held a pickaxe handle. The man grunted and dropped his weapon as a thick line of blood blossomed on his hand. Charlie picked up the stave with his free hand and cracked it hard against the man's head. Hathaway heard something break.

Hathaway was dithering. He wasn't afraid and he was armed, but he wasn't quite sure what to do. Whacking somebody with his lump of wood could do severe damage.

Reilly dead-armed a short, broad-shouldered man with a hard blow to his elbow. The man dropped his stave, and Reilly picked it up and decked him with it. He moved to support Dennis Hathaway, holding off two men with wild swings of his stave. But more men tumbled into the room and Reilly had to swerve to avoid one man's lunge. Three men backed him into a corner.

Two of Hathaway's men were on the ground getting a good kicking. The man with the chair, backed into a corner, was holding his own.

There were four men on Hathaway's dad now,

and he was taking some blows on his arms and body, though he was defending his head. He was roaring. Charlie had pocketed his knife and was fending off two men with wild swings of the pickaxe handle. He looked enraged.

Nobody was taking any notice of Hathaway. He was aware of screams and crashes in the amusement arcade next door. He clutched the stave like a kendo stick, his hands body-width apart, and went for the men attacking his father.

He hit one of the men from behind in the angle of shoulder and neck with a downward swing, then brought the other end of the stave up to clip him just behind the angle of the jaw.

The attacker fell against the man next to him. Then a third turned from his father, swinging a stave above his head. Hathaway slid his stave through his hands, extended it in his right and thrust hard into the man's solar plexus. The man doubled up, and Hathaway brought the stave down again between neck and shoulder.

Hathaway heard a commotion, then a gun went off – so loud his hearing immediately went. Tommy was in the doorway, a rifle pointed at the ceiling. Two amusement arcade workers, also armed, flanked him. Everyone froze except Charlie, who was beating the bejesus out of a man curled up on the floor. Reilly grabbed him from behind and Charlie swung round, snarling.

'He's had enough, Charlie,' Reilly said. 'Charlie. Enough.'

Charlie slowly nodded, his breath ragged. Reilly gave a little salute to Hathaway. Dennis Hathaway kicked the man his son had knocked to the floor.

'Right, get these guys tied to chairs in the back room.' He leaned down whilst kicking the man again. 'You've got some explaining to do or you won't get any tea.'

'Somehow,' muttered Reilly to Hathaway, 'I don't think tea is on the cards anyway.'

By the time Sergeant Finch turned up with half a dozen beat coppers, the amusement arcade had been put back together. A few machines had been smashed, a lot of glass needed sweeping up.

Finch looked around, then at Dennis Hathaway. Sniffed the air.

'Love that sea smell. Heard there was trouble up this end of the pier. Report of gunfire.'

'Few tearaways messing about. We sorted them.'

'Where are they now?' Finch said.

Dennis Hathaway shrugged.

'Gone for a swim, I think.'

The dozen or so men who'd invaded the pier had all been thrown over the side after Dennis Hathaway had done questioning them.

'Can they swim?' Finch said.

Dennis Hathaway sucked his teeth.

'Most of them.'

Finch took off his helmet and wiped the inside with a handkerchief.

'And the gunfire?'

'I run a rifle range, Finchie; even you must have noticed that.'

Finch tilted his head.

131

'You should be more careful shaving, Dennis.'

'How's that?'

Finch pointed at Dennis Hathaway's shirt. It was streaked with blood. Dennis Hathaway grunted.

'And they call them safety razors.'

Finch put his helmet back on.

'OK, then. The chief constable might want a word about this. He likes a happy town; you know that.'

'We're happy,' Dennis Hathaway said. 'We're very happy.'

Finch gave a small smile.

'Be seeing you, Dennis.'

'Grab yourself a candy floss on the way out. All of you. On the house.'

Hathaway and Charlie cracked up when that was exactly what they did. Seven plods in crumpled shirts and white helmets, and a pile of gear hanging off their belts, waddling down the pier with pink candy floss stuck to their chops.

Dennis Hathaway looked at Reilly, his son and Charlie.

'Right, we got some planning to do. Reilly, let's go to your place.'

Hathaway was driving an Austin Healey these days. Charlie still preferred his motorbike but left it on the pier and took a lift with his friend. They didn't speak at first.

Things had been strained between them ever since Dawn's pregnancy. The day after Dawn had told Hathaway about Charlie, he'd gone to confront the drummer. He'd tracked him down

132

in a coffee bar under the arches near the Palace Pier.

'What the fuck have you been playing at?' he said, standing over Charlie.

Charlie indicated the seat opposite him and blew into his coffee.

'This is the café where Tony Mancini worked as a bouncer back in the thirties. The Trunk Murderer?'

'I know who Tony Mancini was. What's that got to do with you putting my sister up the duff?'

'Sit down, Johnny, for God's sake. You're looking a right prat.'

Charlie saw Hathaway's fists clench.

'Johnny, think carefully about what you do next. If you start something, it won't stop. You know that about me. I don't stop.'

Hathaway had dragged Charlie off enough people to know that was true. He slumped down in the seat opposite Charlie.

'I'm sorry about what happened with Dawn. It was just boy and girl stuff. I didn't take advantage of her. I like her.'

'So you're going to marry her?'

'Fuck sake, Johnny, I'm not the marrying kind.'

'My dad expects you to marry her.'

'Does he know it's me?'

Hathaway shook his head.

'Not yet.'

'I think she should get rid of it,' Charlie said.

Hathaway thrust his head forward.

'You want my sister to go through an abortion? You scum.'

Charlie watched Hathaway's expression.

'I bet that's what your dad wants too.'

'What about what Dawn wants?'

'Well, she can't want me as a husband if she's got any sense.'

Hathaway leaned back.

'Well, she obviously hasn't got any sense to be with you in the first place.'

They both looked at the table. Charlie blew on his coffee.

'Did you do it just to spite me?' Hathaway said.

Charlie looked puzzled.

'Why would I want to spite you? We're mates, aren't we?'

Hathaway looked at him, then away.

'Aren't we?'

'Yeah,' Hathaway said. 'Forget I said that.'

Under pressure from her father and Charlie, Dawn had the abortion in Hove. Hathaway took her to a posh house in a Regency terrace. The doctor was Egyptian and elderly. Dawn had seen *Alfie* and was terrified the abortion was going to be a coat-hanger job like in the film, but Dr Massiah's rooms were spick and span. Despite his age, Massiah obviously knew what he was doing.

Dawn was living back at home now. She'd given up her secretarial course. She stayed at home most of the time, her mother fluttering around her. She wept a lot.

Hathaway looked across at Charlie as they drove along the seafront.

'Dawn talking to you yet?'

Charlie shook his head.

'Probably as well. Your dad would go apeshit again.'

Hathaway could never predict how his father was going to react to things. He'd given Charlie a beating – broke a couple of his ribs and two fingers – then had accepted him back as part of the gang as if nothing had happened. Charlie's thing with Dawn was never mentioned again.

Reilly lived in Portslade on the top floor of a newly built block of flats. He had a five-room apartment with a wide balcony looking out to sea. They all sat on the balcony, a bottle of Irish whiskey and bottled beer on a table in front of them. Reilly had put a record on. Jazz.

Charlie gestured at the view.

'Very nice, Mr Reilly. Very nice.'

'Sean. Thanks, Charlie.' A motorbike roared by on the road below and the sound of its engine ricocheted round the balcony. 'Acoustics could be better.'

'Who's this playing trumpet?' Hathaway said.

'I don't know but let me pay him to have some lessons,' Dennis Hathaway said, his tumbler of whiskey clamped in his massive fist. 'Jesus.'

'Miles Davis. He's playing modally, Dennis.'

'That right? You and your highfalutin tastes, Sean.'

Reilly looked at the sun hanging above the horizon.

'Whenever that sun goes down I think of King Arthur, wounded, heading off to Avalon. The Once and Future King.'

'And whenever I think of Avalon and The

135

Avalons,' Hathaway said, 'I think of your furniture.'

Reilly grinned.

'Still a good name for a group.'

Hathaway looked from his father to Reilly.

'How long have you two known each other?'

'We were at school together. Brentfoot Primary and up through junior school. Then Sean's family went back to Ireland and we went our separate ways.'

Dennis Hathaway reached over and lightly punched Reilly's arm.

'Sean here gave me a right walloping once. You wouldn't have thought it to look it him but he was hard. Always been hard. That's how he got in the commandos and I ended up as quartermaster.'

'That's cos I was stupid and you had brains,' Reilly said to Dennis Hathaway. 'That's why I work for you, not the other way round.' He saw Dennis Hathaway's look and raised his hands. 'OK, OK – I know we're partners.'

'Damn right.'

'You were a commando?' Charlie said.

Reilly nodded.

'Where?'

'Crete and other Greek islands. Normandy. Italy.'

'Did you kill people?' Charlie asked. Dennis Hathaway and Reilly both looked at him and he shifted in his seat.

'That was the general idea,' Reilly said.

Charlie looked at Dennis Hathaway.

'Did you, Mr Hathaway?'

136

Dennis took a swig of his whiskey.

'Only anybody who crossed me.'

He looked at the others.

'We've got more legit business coming up. We're investing in the future of this town. Moving the money that we've earned in the black economy into the mainstream.'

Charlie had an odd expression on his face.

'Am I boring you, Charlie?'

'No, Mr Hathaway, not at all.'

'Only?'

He grinned.

'I quite like the illegal stuff.'

'The Churchill Square thing is going well,' Reilly said. 'We're renting them the diggers and demolition stuff, and only our men are working on it.'

'How much is it worth?' Charlie said.

'By the end of it?' Reilly shrugged. 'A quarter of a million.'

'With delays?' Hathaway said. 'I presume we hold them to ransom.'

'Never get too greedy,' his father said. 'It causes complications.'

'We can probably squeeze another fifty thousand out of them,' Reilly said. 'But we're pushing them pretty hard as it is.'

'Fuck 'em,' Dennis Hathaway said. 'If they want to bugger up my Brighton, let 'em pay.' He glanced at Reilly. 'Sean, you should show the lads your World War Two memorabilia.' He looked at his son. 'He's got quite a collection. Show them, Sean.'

Reilly raised his eyes but picked up his glass

and led Hathaway and Charlie back into the apartment, and into a small room down the corridor. It had a wall of windows looking out to sea. The other walls were lined floor to ceiling with books.

'Didn't know you were such a reader, Mr Reilly,' Hathaway said.

'I was at Trinity before the war. '

'Is that Cambridge?'

'Dublin, you oik.' Reilly walked over to a cabinet and switched a light on inside it. Charlie and Hathaway looked down at a collection of guns, daggers and medals. Charlie pointed at a gun.

'That's a Luger,' Reilly said.

'How did you get it?' Charlie said.

'Its owner had no further use for it.' Reilly pointed. 'That's a Webley. My gun of choice.'

'That's an SS dagger, isn't it?' Charlie said. 'How—?'

Reilly stopped the question with a look.

'Lot of medals, Sean,' Hathaway said. 'All yours?'

Reilly nodded.

'Don't be fooled by medals. Most of them are given just for showing up.'

'What exactly did you do in the war?' Charlie said.

'I killed people, laddie,' Reilly said. 'Up close and personal.'

He pointed to a dull bladed knife.

'Usually with that.' He held up his hands. 'Sometimes with these.' He pointed again. 'Often with that Webley. And just occasionally with one of those.'

He indicated a hand grenade in the corner of the cabinet.

'Is that live?' Charlie said.

Reilly nodded.

'But it's OK as long as that pin is in.'

He led them back to Dennis Hathaway.

'Impressed?' Dennis said.

Both young men nodded.

'Nobody messed with Sean back then. For that matter, nobody messes with him now, if they've got any sense.'

'Those blokes earlier on the pier didn't have much sense, then,' Hathaway said.

Dennis Hathaway leaned forward and put his glass down.

'Let's get to that. The Borloni Brothers were behind it, as you've guessed, and that thin-faced creep, Potts, put the gang together.'

Hathaway had a flash back to a Bank Holiday Monday on the Palace Pier when he'd seen Potts seething with hate as he watched Sean Reilly depart.

'But they were encouraged by the twins,' Dennis Hathaway continued, 'Now, I don't want to take the twins on directly, despite what they did to Freddie, but I do want to end this stuff in Brighton.'

'What about the chief constable?' Charlie said. 'Isn't that what he's here for?'

Dennis Hathaway's look lingered on Charlie. Charlie looked down. Not forgiven, then.

'He's finished. Digging himself a big hole that he's going to fall into sometime soon.'

139

'But he can come down hard on us,' Hathaway said.

'Can he?' Dennis Hathaway chuckled. 'We have Philip Simpson by the short and curlies. Remember that time a couple of years ago he came to the pier office and we talked about his destroying files to do with the Brighton Trunk Murder – the unsolved one?'

Hathaway and Charlie both nodded, Charlie lighting up a fag at the same time.

'Well, a lot of them survived, thanks to a quiet word with Sergeant Finch.' Dennis Hathaway gestured at Reilly. 'Meet Mr Reilly, archivist of this parish pertaining to the Brighton Trunk Murders.'

Reilly ducked his head and gave a mock salute.

'So Philip Simpson was the Brighton Trunk Murderer?' Hathaway said.

His father grimaced.

'You daft sod. Of course not. But there are witness statements in the files that put him in a very bad light. Not directly about the murder, but about corruption in the police force. Him and his mate Victor Tempest – two corrupt cops among many.' He gave Charlie a cold look. 'Particularly statements from a certain high society abortionist based in Hove. One Dr Say Massiah.'

Hathaway recognized the name. The elderly Egyptian who took care of Dawn.

'Who has been kind enough to write down his reminiscences of those golden days,' Reilly said, 'before he retires to the West Indies.'

Charlie looked uncomfortable.

140

'And the Borloni Brothers? We kill them?'

Reilly and Dennis Hathaway exchanged glances.

'This "we" being who, exactly?' Reilly said.

Charlie exhaled cigarette smoke and glanced over at Hathaway.

'Me and John. About time we got blooded. Right, Johnny?'

Hathaway and Charlie were running at full pelt along the Palace Pier, their feet thudding heavily on the wet timber. Hathaway was grimly determined, Charlie spurred on by rage. Charlie was ahead. They zig-zagged between punters who had already been scattered by the two men they were pursuing.

What a fucking cock-up. As he ran, Hathaway was listening to the loudspeakers strung out along the length of the pier. They were transmitting the commentary on the World Cup final. He wanted to shoot somebody when he heard Helmut Haller put West Germany in the lead some twelve minutes into the game. He had the gun to do it.

A collision with a gaggle of giggling girls eating candy floss threw Hathaway out. Charlie swerved by them as West Germany took possession again. He was waving his gun around. The girls screamed.

Hathaway righted himself and saw the Boroni Brothers disappear into the covered Palace of Pleasure. Charlie, only twenty yards behind them, was running like his life depended on it. The collision with the girls had winded Hathaway and now he could only trot round the side of the Palace of Pleasure. He flattened himself against its wooden wall as he saw the Boronis come out of a side entrance.

They darted looks around, then dashed over to the Ghost Train. They scrambled on to the last carriage as it started off. The doors to the shed clanked open and the carriage jerked through.

Charlie found Hathaway.

'We've got to get in there. There's a back entrance.'

Charlie and Hathaway hurried round the back of the large shed. A metal door swung open easily. They slipped inside.

It was dark and noisy. Amplified cackles and shrieks and roars. Flashes of light as gruesome figures were illuminated.

Charlie and Hathaway waited for the train to clatter closer.

'See you on the other side,' Charlie shouted as he flitted away.

Hathaway was standing beside a Dracula who raised his cape and roared as the ghost train approached. Hathaway heard the screams from the passengers. There were two flashes, then two more. Screams again. Hathaway tightened his grip on the gun in his pocket. He stood for a moment then turned away.

Back outside, Charlie and Hathaway forced themselves to go slowly, hands clamped over the guns in their pockets. Hathaway glanced at Charlie's expressionless face. Charlie stopped and looked up at one of the loudspeakers. He grinned. Geoff Hurst had equalized.

* * *

'Bizarre killing of Pier owners. Pursued by clowns then shot to death in Ghost Train.'

Dennis Hathaway threw the newspaper down on his desk and looked at Hathaway and Charlie.

'Only clowns I know are you two. Anything you want to tell me?'

They shook their heads.

'You were at home watching Geoff Hurst score his hat-trick, I expect.'

'Charlie was round at mine. Few beers. They think it's all over ... well, it is now.'

Reilly quietly observed them from the window.

'Whoever did do it was pretty clever with the clown disguise. No way of being recognized.'

'Must have been sweating like pigs, though,' Dennis Hathaway said. 'The wigs and the greasepaint.'

'We have to hope for their sake they were careful about where they got the clown outfits from. Not to mention the guns.'

'You're right there, Sean.' Dennis Hathaway scrutinized his son and Charlie. 'If you two were doing it, for instance. Not that you would have been since I specifically told you to forget any idea of offing the Boroni Brothers. But, for the sake of argument, if you were, where would you have got the costumes?'

'And the guns,' Reilly said.

'Thanks, Sean,' Dennis Hathaway said. 'And the guns.'

Charlie cleared his throat.

'The guns you'd get up London, I expect.

143

Round Fulham way, maybe? Stand-up friends of Jimmy White?'

'Jimmy White,' Dennis Hathaway said. 'Poor sod. Gives himself up because he's been bled dry on the run and he hopes to get a deal. Bastards give him eighteen years. And another Great Train Robber bites the dust.'

'Buster and Bruce are still out there,' Reilly said.

'Do you know where?' Hathaway spoke for the first time.

'Mexico, I heard.'

'They'll be running through their money too,' Dennis Hathaway said. 'And the clown costumes?'

'Buy them outright, mix and match them.' Charlie shrugged. 'Not a problem.'

'And disposal after?' Reilly said.

'Dad always says that's why God created the sea,' Hathaway said. 'It keeps its secrets.'

Dennis Hathaway chuckled.

'Fucking dressing up as clowns. Chasing them along the pier. Wish I could have seen that. Fucking hilarious.' He turned to Reilly. 'Where are we on that thin-faced cunt, Potts?'

'I've put the word out.'

Dennis Hathaway nodded and turned back to the lads.

'OK, you pair of pistols, I've got stuff to show you.'

Dennis Hathaway pointed down at the motorboat dipping in the water in West Pier dock.

'Handy little craft that. Takes about four hours

144

to get to France. You know that Mr Wilson, in his infinite wisdom, has put a limit on how much money you can take out of the country with you? It's your money but he doesn't want you spending it abroad. That limit is fifty pounds, which, frankly, wouldn't keep Johnny's mother in Campari and sodas for a weekend, never mind a fortnight's holiday in Ibiza.'

He indicated the boat again.

'So we shift money in that. And then bring diamonds back in. There's a couple of shops in the Laines we've got an arrangement with.'

'How often do you do the crossing?' Hathaway said.

'Every week. We vary the days and the times of departure, and sometimes we meet a fishing boat from France in the middle and do the swap there. But that can be a bit hairy if the sea is rough. A couple of times we've just offloaded stuff on the beach here.'

'And the customs don't suspect?'

'The customs have their work cut out at the airports and Newhaven. They can't control hundreds of miles of coastline. Doing it on the beach here is a good wheeze, because there's so much else going on it's just like hiding in plain sight.'

Hathaway looked down at the motorboat, polished and varnished. He glanced at Charlie.

'So you want one of us to look after the operation?'

His father nodded.

'Not me,' Charlie said. 'Thanks very much, Mr H., but I get seasick.'

'I'll do it,' Hathaway said.

145

That evening The Avalons were playing in the Snowdrop in Lewes. All except Charlie crammed into Hathaway's Austin Healey. Charlie preferred his bike. Hathaway said little as he drove. He was still trying to come to terms with what he and Charlie had done. Well, Charlie really. Charlie had insisted they should just go ahead and kill the Boronis, even though his dad had rejected the idea. He had got the guns. He had got the clown costumes. He had shot them both.

Hathaway knew he had his own dark places, places he kept hidden from everyone, but he had been shocked – and a little frightened – by how eagerly Charlie had taken to killing. He now believed Charlie capable of anything.

The lads were blabbing in the car but he only half-listened. He liked playing with the group but the real juice was his day job. He was looking forward to his first trip to Dieppe.

He looked up at a footbridge that crossed the road. Cows were walking in procession across it, silhouetted against the blue sky.

'Wow, look at that,' Dan said, laughing. 'Surreal.'

'That's why I don't want a convertible,' Billy said, scrunching down in his seat. 'One of them falls on you, you're screwed.'

Dan gave him a look.

'What? You think a cow is going to fall on you?'

They all sniggered.

'Not just a cow,' Billy said.

'You mean a cow and something else? A giraffe maybe?'

'I didn't mean that—'

Hathaway laughed along but tuned out. Thinking about his dark places.

After the gig – which represented the first outing for Bill's newly bought sitar – they sat around over a drink and Hathaway realized how distant he and Charlie now were from the other group members. Bill and Dan, in particular, were getting even deeper into music. Alan, the drug-dealing roadie, sat quietly, a reminder to Hathaway of the way the group straddled his two lives.

'Folk music is really taking off,' Billy was saying.

'Folk music?' Charlie said, incredulous. He pointed at his hair. 'Bad enough I'm looking like a Liverpool pooftah. Now you want me to turn into Peter, Paul and bloody Mary?'

'Actually, it's worse than that,' Dan said, laughing. 'These folk groups don't even have drummers.'

Everybody laughed but Charlie looked thunderous.

'What – you're trying to dump me?'

'No!' Billy said. 'But we've got to look at what's going on. Dylan. Simon and Garfunkel. Their new album is beautiful. There's a couple of songs we could cover—'

'Beautiful?' Charlie snorted. 'Since when was rock music beautiful? We get people dancing; we don't do beautiful.'

'Beautiful gets the girls,' Dan said.

'I don't have any problem getting the girls,' Charlie said.

Hathaway glanced at him.

'We've got to move with the times,' he said after a beat.

'Which are a'changing,' Dan and Billy said together, then laughed.

'Sound of Silence' came up on the jukebox.

'I love this Simon and Garfunkel song,' Billy said.

Charlie scowled.

'I don't like any of that sentence.'

'No, really. This is a great, great track. We could do three or four songs from the new album. "I Am A Rock"—'

'No way am I doing Simon and Garfunkel,' Charlie said, fishing out a packet of cigarettes from his pocket.

'We need to be writing our own stuff like Paul Simon does,' Dan said. 'That's where the money is.'

'So who's our writer?' Hathaway said. 'Cos it isn't me.'

'I've been working on a couple of things,' Billy said. 'Wondered if we might give them a try.'

They all reared back in their seats to look at him.

'Dark horse,' Charlie said.

'Crazy horse,' Hathaway said.

Hathaway met Charlie by chance in a new club in the Laines a couple of days later. Charlie had

148

definitely started feeling his oats. The drugs were making him even more aggressive. Charlie was with a new girlfriend called Laura. Hathaway was in a booth with a girl from the pier. It was busy but there was one stool free at the bar. As Laura started to sit on it, her miniskirt riding high, the man at the next stool looked down at her thighs.

'Seat's taken,' he said, continuing to look at her legs.

Charlie hauled him off his stool.

'Yours is free, though, right?' he said before he left him sprawling on the ground.

The man looked up at Charlie.

'Piss off out of here,' Charlie said.

'I'll be right back,' Hathaway said. He made sure Charlie could see him approach in the mirror behind the bar.

'Happy as Larry, boys and girls?'

Laura was staring straight ahead and Charlie had both hands round his beer glass. His pupils were enormous.

'Johnny boy, what a delightful surprise.'

Hathaway caught the barman's eye. The barman hadn't intervened but he was looking sour. Hathaway could see he was wondering whether to call the police. He palmed a tenner and slid it across the bar. The barman took it, nodded and moved away.

'Dad wants us to get into pop management,' Hathaway said. 'Reckons there's big money there.'

'Whatever,' Charlie said, staring at his reflection in the mirror.

Hathaway did a drum roll on the bar.

'Great.'

Charlie took to managing groups like he'd been born for it. He signed up about two dozen local groups straight off. Brought an edge to his management work. Dangled a big London wheeler-dealer out of a fourth-floor window by his feet when he tried to steal one of his acts. He stubbed a lighted cigar into the forehead of another rival.

'Fuck, Charlie,' Hathaway said.

'People I scare are going to have to look over their shoulders for the rest of their lives,' Charlie said.

Dennis Hathaway was impressed. At the end of the pier he reminisced.

'There's this one guy I know. He was born in Manchester back in 1926. His dad made raincoats. Age fourteen, in the war, he sang in his local synagogue and tried doing a comedy turn. He was rubbish. Sat out the war – mysterious illness that kept him in hospital until the day the war ended, then miraculous recovery – and then became an impressionist – Jimmy Cagney and all that. He actually did the London Palladium. Max Miller said he stank. Maybe he realized it. Anyway, he turned to management, promotions. Worked out of his local phone box.

'We've had dealings with him. Has his Rolls Royce and his flash jewellery. Manages the Small Faces. Pays off Radio Caroline to play the music from his acts. Pays the Small Faces a salary and gives them a London house, a Jag and driver, and all the clothes they want. No real money, though.'

He looked at Charlie.

'So far as I'm aware he doesn't commit arson, though.'

Charlie looked levelly back from behind his sunglasses. Hathaway frowned.

'Arson?'

'As I understand it, when a certain record company didn't want to release one of Charlie's new groups from its existing contract, its office was burned down.'

'All I know,' Charlie drawled, 'is that the group was released from its contract two days later.'

'And the accountant?' Reilly said.

Charlie held out his hands, palms up.

'I wanted to make sure he never had a child. So I got my tools out and battered his penis. I could have battered his head but I didn't. I just wanted our fucking money.'

'What?' Hathaway said, both repelled and fascinated.

'Charlie here was using an accountant he thought had cheated us,' Reilly said. 'He grabbed him at home, took him somewhere – not sure where, Charlie – and went to work on him.'

Dennis Hathaway was watching Charlie with a mixture of fascination and respect. Hathaway's main emotion was fear.

EIGHT

Season of the Witch
1967

'Since when did you join the Grenadier fucking Guards?'

Dennis Hathaway was in his shirt sleeves on the boat. He peered at his son's red Victorian uniform, then at the medals on his son's breast.

'And it looks like you've had a busy war.'

'I got it in Carnaby Street,' Hathaway said.

'The medals? Fighting tourists?'

'The whole thing.'

Hathaway and Charlie had gone up to Carnaby Street in the summer sunshine. They smoked dope on the train. They wandered London in a daze – dazed by the cannabis, dazed by the life there. Carnaby Street was buzzing, 'Sergeant Pepper' pumping out of every shop, incense and marijuana in the air, the pavements crowded with dolly birds and hipsters.

'This is it,' Charlie said. 'The centre of the fucking universe.'

'I thought that was Worthing,' Hathaway said.

'You look a twat,' Dennis Hathaway said now. 'You know that?'

Dennis Hathaway was peering at his son,

screwing up his eyes against the sun. There was a splash of white on his forehead. Suntan lotion he hadn't rubbed in properly. The sun flickered on the water behind him.

'It's the fashion, Dad,' Hathaway said, still a little stoned from his breakfast joint.

'To look a twat? And what are those things on your feet?'

'Plimsolls.'

'Very useful on route marches.'

'Handy for boats, though.' He swung himself out on the ladder. 'Coming aboard, Cap'n Birdseye.'

Dennis Hathaway came up close to him once he was on deck.

'I'm worried about you, son. I hope you're not using our own bloody product.'

'You know I'm not.'

Hathaway sniffed.

'Well, you're smelling of something illegal.'

'That's patchouli, Dad.'

'Patchouli? What the fuck is patchouli.'

'Elaine got it for me.'

Dennis Hathaway tilted his head as if listening for something.

'Elaine? New one on me. She's your latest quim, is she?'

'She's special, Dad.'

'Is she, Sergeant Pratt? Is she? I've got some news for you. Come below.'

Reilly was sitting behind the small table in the cabin of the boat. He blinked when he saw Hathaway.

'John hasn't got long for this meeting, Sean,'

153

Dennis Hathaway said. 'He's off to fight the Zulus.'

Dennis and his son both sat down at the small table.

'We got a problem in Milldean,' Dennis Hathaway said. 'Gerald Cuthbert is trying it on. The twins pushing him, of course. Not only that, he's trying to muscle in on some of our other business further west. He knows Worthing is ours but he's had his lads down there.'

'I haven't noticed anything,' Hathaway said, frowning. 'I would have seen.'

'That's what I would have hoped,' his father said quietly. 'But when were you last in Worthing?'

'Of my own volition?'

'You don't need to say any more. Charlie looks after it, doesn't he?'

'He does.'

Hathaway saw his father and Reilly exchange a glance.

'Right, we'll have a word with him,' Dennis said.

'I can do that—'

'He's your friend.'

'I can do that.'

After a moment his father nodded.

'What about Cuthbert?' Hathaway said.

Reilly coughed.

'We'll take care of him.'

'Are we done, then?' Hathaway said.

'Not yet. The chief constable has summoned us to a meeting.'

'What kind of meeting?'

'The it-never-happened kind. On the Palace Pier. Next week. He wants peace and harmony in the town.'

'Is that what we want?' Hathaway said.

His father rubbed his cheek.

'Once we run it, sure.'

Hathaway had met Elaine at a poetry reading in The Ship. It was part of the first Brighton Arts Festival. Yehudi Menuhin was playing his violin. Flora Robson was in *A Man For All Seasons* at the Theatre Royal. Pink Floyd were performing in the West Pier ballroom. And there was poetry. Concrete Poetry, whatever that was. And The Scaffold with Paul McCartney's brother. Billy was keen to see them. Charlie opted out but the rest of The Avalons went along because of The Beatles connection.

It took place in an oak-panelled old room at the rear of The Ship. There were no chairs. Everybody sat on the floor. Even with cushions scattered around it was uncomfortable. Hathaway became aware of a girl sitting just behind him and not just because of the exotic perfume that wafted over him.

'Am I in your way?' he said, half-turning, trying not to look up her skirt. She had good legs and an impish smile.

'What is my way?'

He blushed.

'I mean, can you see?'

'You? Perfectly. What about you? Have you seen enough?'

She had seen his eyes flick down between her

155

legs.

'Not nearly enough,' he said.

She stayed with him that night but at dawn insisted on walking barefoot on the beach. On sand, Hathaway could understand. But Brighton was all pebbles and stones. He grimaced at every step.

She was doing American Studies at Sussex. She sprang unfamiliar names on him. Bellow and Updike, and people she called 'the hipsters': Kerouac, Burroughs, Tom Robbins, Thomas Pynchon. A man called Noam Chomsky featured at the heavy end of discussions. Hathaway was out of his depth but she didn't patronize and he was interested in the things she said.

They saw each other every night for a week. She had a fierce appetite. He didn't know what she saw in him, although he knew he was OK at sex, thanks to Barbara long ago. He thought it was perhaps also a class thing. She was middle class. She liked roughing it. She called him Mellors once, then laughed. He didn't get it at the time.

On the first night he'd asked her what her heady perfume was.

'Patchouli.'

'What's patchouli?'

'A musk-based perfume. Perfumes are either musk or flower-based. Musk smells of shit, essentially.'

'Lovely.'

'James Joyce was a bicycle-seat sniffer, you know.'

'I'll take your word for that,' Hathaway said,

not knowing who James Joyce was.

'Musk and ambergris are low-down dirty smells, hence the link with excrement. Then, during the eighteenth century, when aristocratic women had to pretend to be modest, perfume makers developed sweeter floral scents. Then it changed again during the French Revolution. Am I boring you?'

'No, why?' Hathaway said, his voice muffled.

'You seem more interested in my left nipple.'

'A man can do two things at once.'

Elaine laughed.

'Not in my experience.'

Hathaway lifted his head.

'Go on.'

'Under the Terror, what perfume you wore indicated your allegiance. You could get the guillotine if your handkerchief smelt of royal perfumes – lily or *eau de la reine*, water of the queen. The Directory, Consulate and Empire marked the return of strong perfumes with an animal base. Josephine liked musk, ambergris and civet.'

'How do you know all that?'

'I'm at Sussex. That's the kind of history they teach.'

When Hathaway next saw his father, he was holding court in the back room of the Bath Arms.

'And I'm telling you, Mr Reilly, that I want these scumbags found. I want them teaching a lesson.'

A schoolboy had been found sexually assaulted then strangled up Roedean way.

'And the police?' Reilly said.

'I don't think there'll be anything left for the police.'

'Since when did we start doing a copper's work for him?' Reilly said.

'Since we started getting protection money from people. They pay for protection, we provide it.'

Reilly smiled thinly.

'Didn't realize we actually fulfilled those obligations.'

'I thought that was protection from us,' Charlie said with a laugh.

Dennis Hathaway looked from one to the other.

'Well, you're both wrong. You think we're all take and no give? These people rely on us. Some nonces kill a young lad, a schoolkid with his future all ahead of him. On my patch. On *my* patch. Somebody is taking the Michael. And I won't stand for that. Not for an instant. So I want these men found and I want them bringing to the pier, and then we'll see what's what.'

'What's in it for us?' Reilly insisted.

'Reputation. I told you – nobody is going to take the Michael on our turf. If we're not in control, then it's anarchy and we don't want to go back to that. That's what we fought a war for.'

Reilly raised an eyebrow.

'Not exactly.'

'Mr Reilly you're starting to annoy me. We fought a war so that true-born Englishmen could remain free, and we even gave freedom to the frogs and a few worthy orientals along the way.

No need to thank us, lads.'

'As you say, *Mister* Hathaway,' Reilly said, leaning over to pat Dennis Hathaway's arm.

'So just bloody well get on with it, will you?'

'As you say.' Reilly got to his feet.

'Anything I can do?' Hathaway asked.

'I don't know? Is there?' His father looked at him. 'Put the word out on your rock 'n' roll circuit that we want information. We'll pay.'

Hathaway nodded.

'OK, Dad.'

'You understand, do you, son, that it's all about a code of honour?'

'Dad?'

'We look after the people who pay for all we have. Violence we save for others in the same business as us. And scum like the men who've done this to someone on our patch. We don't target civilians if we can help it.'

'I know that, Dad.'

Over the next few days, a dozen or so nonces were hauled down to the pier and given beatings of various degrees of severity in the storeroom beyond the office. None admitted to the crime, all named names. There were buckets of water constantly at hand to sluice the blood down into the sea. A half a dozen other men gave themselves in to the police and owned up to other offences.

Hathaway went off on a smuggling trip to Dieppe and Honfleur. He arrived back on a sunny day, the wind fresh. He climbed up the ladder from the bobbing boat and stopped by the firing range for a chat with Tommy and Mickey.

'Dad in the office?' he finally said.

Mickey nodded.

'He's got a lot on, mind, so be cautious.'

'The prodigal son returns,' Dennis Hathaway said when he looked up from his desk and saw his son. 'How were the Dieppe lasses? Supposed to be the prettiest in France.'

'I've got a girlfriend, Dad.'

'You're too young to be a monk.'

'I'm hardly that.'

'Aye, well.'

'Anything I should know?'

'We soldier on, John, we soldier on.'

'Any word on the men who killed that lad?'

'Let's say the moving finger writes and having writ moves on.'

'You've been at the Rubaiyat again, Dad – Mum warned you about that.'

His father laughed.

'Cheeky sod. I bet you don't know how it goes on?'

Hathaway sat down in the chair on the other side of his father's desk.

'Actually, I do. I learned it for just such an occasion.'

'Let's hear it, then.'

'...nor all your piety nor wit shall lure it back to a cancel half a line—'

'Nor all your tears wash out a word of it. Or to put it a Brighton way – no good crying over spilt milk.'

'Whose milk has been spilt exactly?'

'All you need to worry about is your piety, young Mr Monk – don't waste the best years of

160

your life on getting too serious about just one girl.'

'There's more to life than having sex with lots of girls,' Hathaway said as Reilly walked in.

'Listen, Mr Reilly. Life's young philosopher.'

'The lad's in love. Let him enjoy it.'

Hathaway flushed.

'I wouldn't go that far...'

His father looked at him intently.

'When are we going to meet this girl, then?'

'Do you want to?'

'I know your mum does – see if she approves. Not that mothers ever approve, mind.'

The chief constable's meeting on the Palace Pier was an odd experience for Hathaway. He knew his father had something on Philip Simpson because of the Brighton Trunk Murder files. Simpson knew it too, so whilst he was being all high and mighty, he had to skirt around Dennis Hathaway. Reilly and Charlie were there, Reilly in a safari jacket, Charlie looking like Big Breadwinner Hogg with his kipper tie, wide lapels and flared jacket.

Hathaway was surprised to see Gerald Cuthbert there. He and his three heavies still favoured the Krays' look – box jackets with narrow lapels over big chests.

He didn't think anyone was carrying a gun, although Sergeant Finch's double-breasted civvy suit bulged oddly. He knew Charlie had his flick knife and assumed Cuthbert and his men had knives or knuckledusters or both. There were a couple of CID men in sports jackets and jeans.

Two men arrived late. Slender, Italian-looking, in sharp suits. Luigi and Francis, cousins of the murdered Boroni brothers. When all the men were seated, giving each other hard looks, Philip Simpson began.

'We've got to get some harmony in town,' he said. 'There is stuff I can turn a blind eye to and stuff I will not tolerate. Above all, I don't want killings, like last year's incident with Tony and Raymond Boroni.'

'For which nobody was brought to justice,' Luigi Boroni said, shooting Dennis Hathaway a cold look.

'Investigations are continuing,' Simpson said. 'The case is being actively pursued.'

'Why don't you ask some of the people round this table?' Luigi said.

'Why don't you go fuck yourself?' Dennis Hathaway said.

It took a moment, then the Boronis, Reilly and Dennis Hathaway were all on their feet.

'Gentlemen! Gentlemen!'

Simpson was standing too, and his CID men had moved in to subdue anything that might kick off.

Dennis Hathaway kept his eyes fixed on Luigi but pointed at Cuthbert, who was sitting jiggling his foot.

'First off, Philip, I want to know what the fuck that scum is doing here. He's a loan shark ripping off hard-working people, a scavenger who feeds off of our leftovers. He doesn't respect the demarcation lines we've set up in the past. He needs to be firmly squashed. And if you don't do

162

it, I will.'

One of the CID men stepped in front of Cuthbert as he stood.

'And as for the Boronis,' Dennis Hathaway went on, 'I don't know who killed their cousins. All I heard was that two clowns killed two clowns. They were messing with the twins. Seems to me anyone could have killed them – their friends as easily as their enemies.' He pointed now at Luigi. 'All I want from these guys is an assurance they're going to keep Brighton for Brighton and not bring in out-of-towners.'

'Now there I agree.' Simpson raised his voice. 'There's enough business going on for all of us. We don't need out-of-towners here. We don't want them. I won't have them.'

'With respect, Chief Constable,' Cuthbert shouted as he tried to push past the CID officer to get at Dennis Hathaway. 'What you want and don't want don't stack up to much against those London boys. They've taken on the Met and won. If they want to take over down here, I don't see how you're going to stop them.'

Simpson gave him a hard look.

'Leave that to me.'

It was always difficult for Hathaway to switch gear from his day job to the group. He was feeling more and more distanced from The Avalons. But he was also trying not to think about the more brutal things he was involved in. He couldn't forget looking back as he and Charlie walked off the Palace Pier in their sweaty, scratchy clown costumes to see the Boroni Brothers emerge from the ghost train shed, slumped forward in their seats, soaked in blood. Then the screams.

He thought the meeting on the Palace Pier today was going to end up that way but, in fact, the kettle didn't really boil at all.

'Well, that was a waste of time,' Charlie said as the four West Pier men headed back along the Palace Pier.

'On the contrary,' Dennis Hathaway said, 'that was bloody great. Look at who's against us – third raters.'

'What about the twins?' Hathaway said.

His father had just grinned.

Tonight they were on the West Pier supporting Pink Floyd. Elaine would be somewhere in the audience with some of her student mates.

Tony and Charlie turned up together. Billy and Dan turned up at seven prompt, in military jackets and jeans.

The Avalons had proper dressing rooms for a change, but they all went out on the pier and leaned over the balustrade. They shared a joint.

'How are you doing, gents?' Hathaway said.

'Not great actually, John,' Dan said.

Hathaway tilted his head.

'Oh?'

'We're a bit worried about what's going on with the group,' Billy said.

'Things are going great, aren't they?' Hathaway said, passing the joint along.

'Onstage, yes, but offstage, no...' Dan tailed off.

164

'Offstage?' Hathaway said. 'What about offstage?'

'Look, what you and Charlie want to get up to is up to you,' Billy said. 'But we just want to be in a successful rock 'n' roll band.'

'And we think,' Dan said, 'that the stuff you're doing is putting that success at risk.'

Hathaway looked puzzled.

'What stuff are we doing exactly?'

Dan shook his head.

'C'mon, John. Don't treat us like fools. The two of you are selling drugs with our roadie friend, Alan. And you're both busy managing other acts. We hardly even have time to rehearse and there's a lot of new music we should be covering.'

'We want you to stop dealing at our gigs,' Billy said.

Hathaway looked from one to the other.

'Well, that's going to be a bit complicated,' he said.

They waited for him to go on.

'I mean there are other people involved. They wouldn't be too happy if we chucked it in.'

'Couldn't they find other people to do what you're doing?'

'Again, it's not that simple.'

Hathaway seemed to ponder. Pointed at the joint in Dan's hand.

'Look, I know you guys smoke dope. You don't see anything wrong with it. We all think it should be legal, but until it is Charlie and me are providing a service.'

'But it's illegal. You could end up in prison.

165

And we could easily be accused of being accomplices.'

'Not a chance of either of those things.' Hathaway said.

'Oh – really.'

'Really. The police are in on it.'

'Bugger off. The entire force?'

'People that count. Look, I'm trusting you with this. The fix is all the way in.'

Dan and Billy looked at each other. Billy spoke.

'OK, but there's something else. The direction the group is going. Bill and me, we want to go an acoustic folkie route.'

'Folkie?' Charlie said, disgust in his voice.

Hathaway put his hand on Charlie's arm. He knew that Bill and Dan rehearsed a lot together. Bill had been teaching Dan guitar.

'OK, here's a deal. Why don't you set up as a duo and run a folk club?'

The other three looked at him with varying degrees of surprise.

'You want to break the band up?' Charlie said.

'You're sacking us?' Billy said.

'How are we going to set up a folk club?' Dan said.

Hathaway latched on to Dan's remark.

'As you know, my dad's company has branched out into pop promotion. Managing bands, running tours – and running clubs. We've been thinking about a folk club.'

'Nobody told me,' Charlie said.

'Didn't think you'd be interested in a folk club, Charlie, and your hands are full managing acts,'

Hathaway said. 'Anyway, Dan, we wouldn't expect you to run it but maybe you and Bill could host it.'

Bill and Dan looked at each other. Nodded.

'We could do that.'

'So that's the end of The Avalons?' Charlie said.

'Not necessarily,' Hathaway said. 'There's no reason why you couldn't do both, is there?'

Billy shook his head.

'Of course not.'

Hathaway looked at Charlie.

'You OK with that?'

Charlie didn't say anything for a moment. Then:

'As long as I can manage these two.'

Bill and Dan laughed. Uncertainly.

Hathaway took Elaine down to Cuckmere Haven. After a walk along the shingle beach beneath Beachy Head, the chalk cliff glaring white in the sunshine, they got fish and chips in newspaper from the café and sat on a bench looking out to sea.

Although Elaine was doing American studies she wanted to be an actress. She also wanted to go to India.

'What do you want to do with your life, John?' she said. 'You can't want to spend it all in Brighton.'

'Course not.' He gestured to his left. 'I'm fond of Eastbourne too.'

She punched his arm.

'There's this film called *Blow Up*; looks like it

167

might be your cup of tea,' he said. 'Bloke called David Hemmings – I met him in Brighton last year when he made a film about a pop band here. Do you fancy seeing it?'

She smiled and sucked on the straw in her bottle of pop.

'Here endeth the discussion about John's future.'

'Well, what about you?' he said, a little heat in his voice.

'You know about me. India for six months, then acting.' She leaned into him. 'Come to India with me. We'd have a groovy time.'

Hathaway kissed her forehead.

'Except that I'm not a footloose student, I'm a working man. I can't just chuck in my job and head east.'

'Sure you can; you just have to want to.'

She reached into her voluminous handbag and pulled out an A4 book. She laid it beside her and continued to root.

'What's that?' he said.

'My diary, volume three.'

'Must be a serious diary.'

'Oh it is. Have you heard of Anaïs Nin?'

'Is it an Indian takeaway?'

'Ha ha. She's my inspiration. Ah, here we are.' She brought out a parcel wrapped in brown paper with a red ribbon around it.

'A little gift for you.'

Hathaway was touched. He'd never, ever had a gift from a girl.

'John Donne,' he read on the cover of the first book.

'Most beautiful love poetry in the world – but don't get any soppy ideas. Just wanted to bring a bit of beauty to your cynical soul.'

'Soppiness discouraged. Got it.'

He looked at the other book.

'What is it?' Hathaway asked.

The cover was red plastic and the book a bit bigger than the prayer books they used to have at school.

'It's the words of Mao Tse-tung,' Elaine said. 'Give you something to think about.'

She looked at him earnestly, which made him want to shag her even more than usual. A girl with a passionate mouth trying to look serious always did that to him.

Hathaway looked at the book.

'That chink who keeps sending death squads to kill James Bond and finance nutters like Blofeld?' Hathaway said. 'He's a Commie, isn't he?'

'Communism is more complex than that. At Sussex there are Trotskyists and Leninist-Stalinists. Mao is the world's most rigorous Leninist-Stalinist, so now a lot of people are calling themselves Maoists.'

Hathaway flicked through the pages. Elaine grinned at him.

'Where'd you get it?' Hathaway said.

'They're free to anyone who wants one.' She grinned again. 'Ninety million in print round the world.'

'But you're always telling me I'm a filthy capitalist.'

'You can change.'

169

Hathaway thought about the business he was in.

'I wonder,' he said.

When they walked back to the car park, a police car was parked beside his Austin Healey. Sergeant Finch was lolling against the bonnet, face turned up to the sun. He stepped forward when he saw Hathaway approach.

'Sorry to disturb your day, John, but the chief constable would like a word.'

Elaine looked from him to Hathaway, wide-eyed.

'Am I being arrested?'

'Arrested?' Elaine said. 'Why?'

'No, no,' Sergeant Finch said, attempting a smile. 'He'd appreciate a word. If you're too busy, I'm sure he'll understand.'

Hathaway nodded.

'OK.'

Elaine had come out of shock.

'OK? It's not bloody OK. This is police harassment.'

'Elaine.'

'Why on earth would they want to talk to you?'

'Elaine.'

'Let me phone my dad's lawyer—'

'The chief constable is a family friend.'

Elaine stepped back.

'Your family is friends with a pig? Oh man.'

'Johnny. Sorry to spoil your day. Please send my apologies to your girlfriend. A lovely girl by all accounts. But I wanted a little chat with you. Do

170

sit down.'

'Chief Constable,' Hathaway said, taking the proffered seat.

'Please, Johnny, call me Philip. There's no formality here. I've broken bread at your house. Well, your dad's house.'

Hathaway nodded then waited.

'Have you heard the news? The Brighton police are officially no more. It's now the Southern Police Force.'

'Is that why you wanted to see me?'

'No. Actually, it's about your dad. I wanted a quiet word.'

'Shouldn't you be talking to him?'

'Well, as you know, he's not the easiest man to talk to when he's got a bee in his bonnet.'

Hathaway frowned.

'Has he got a bee in his bonnet?'

'Exactly what I wanted to ask you. See, I thought we had a gentleman's agreement around town. I thought that meeting on the Palace Pier made that clear. I allow you a certain leeway and you respect the law in other areas.'

'I thought that's what we were doing.'

'Did you?' Simpson clasped his hands. 'Your dad seems determined to hog all the action. I hear he's just taken control of the baggage handlers at the airport to help facilitate his smuggling activities.'

'Chief Constable—'

'Philip—'

'I really don't know why you're talking to me about this. I'm in the music business. I manage and promote a few bands, book them into

171

venues.'

'And the ancillary stuff.'

'I never got to university. Ancillary?'

'The little extras. We know your legit business – and it ain't all that legit – the pop industry is like the bloody Wild West. Be that as it may, we know that's just a front for your drug dealing, your protection rackets.'

Hathaway thought for a moment.

'What point are you trying to make, Philip?' Hathaway was trying to sound calm but he knew he was out of his depth.

'The deal was that brothels, abortions and protection were mine.'

Hathaway flushed.

'I don't touch brothels.'

Philip Simpson adjusted his desk pad.

'Not you – your father. Jesus, I don't care about the smuggling as long as I get my tithe, but he can't do everything. Does he want to be Brighton's Mr Big? Does he?'

Simpson was red-faced with anger. Hathaway tried to remain impassive.

'Tell him that's my role.'

'Why don't you tell him yourself?' Hathaway said, standing abruptly. 'Or don't you have the guts?'

The chief constable reddened further as he too stood and leaned forward, his fists planted on the desk.

'Listen, sonny, don't mistake friendliness for softness. I'm asking nicely but we can do it a different way. Don't forget who has all the real power and a private bloody army if I choose to

172

exercise that power.'

'Didn't do your predecessor much good, did it?' Hathaway said. He smirked, though he knew he shouldn't.

The chief constable reached over and pressed an intercom button.

'Come on in.'

Hathaway looked from the chief constable to the door.

'Oh – what? The rough stuff now?'

The chief constable watched the door swing open. A constable came in.

'You know each other, of course.'

Behind the constable, Barbara came hesitantly into the room.

NINE

I'm a Believer
1967

Hathaway tracked down his father in the Hippodrome.

'We got bingo in half an hour,' his father said. 'I expect your mother will be down.'

He looked around.

'Look at this place – beautiful. Started as a circus, you know. Built by Frank Matcham. I've seen so many great shows over the years. And now it's a bloody bingo hall.' He shook his head.

'Progress.'

'Dad, I need to talk to you.'

'What's that?' Dennis Hathaway grabbed for the red plastic-covered book Hathaway had put on the table.

'The thoughts of Mousie Tung,' Hathaway's father said, chucking the book on his desk. 'Jesus Christ – you're gonna start giving all your money away to the poor?'

Hathaway pursed his lips.

'I think that was Jesus, Dad.'

Dennis Hathaway stood, shoulders forward, the small book swallowed in his big hands.

'I suppose this is more of that stupid nonsense from your privileged student mates, is it?'

'Elaine gave it to me, yes.'

Dennis Hathaway snorted.

'I like Elaine, don't get me wrong. She's a beautiful gal and I like her spirit, but Jesus, she has some barmy ideas.'

Hathaway fidgeted. Elaine wasn't why he was here, but still he said:

'She wants us to go travelling in India, visit some ashrams.'

'Are they Commies and all, these ashrams?'

Hathaway smiled and was relieved to see his father did too.

'They're places, Dad, not people. Places of spiritual retreat. The Beatles went there and Twiggy.'

'Oh well, very deep and meaningless, then, clearly.'

'Meaningful,' Hathaway murmured.

His father's smile went.

174

'I mean exactly what I say: meaningless. We're put on this planet to look out for ourselves and our families. Everyone else can watch out for themselves. Do you think Mousie is watching out for others? He's top of the tree, mate, and he wants to stay there. Funny how all these communist countries, where everyone is equal, all have a dictator at the top of them. Kruschev, Castrato, Mousie...'

Hathaway recalled a phrase Elaine had used:

'It's called the dictatorship of the proletariat, Dad.'

His father took his time.

'Is it?'

Hathaway struggled for Elaine's words.

'It's a phase any communist society must go through—'

His father snorted again.

'The proles have never dictated anything to anybody. That's why they're proles. You weren't raised to be a prole; you were raised to be a governor.'

'But governor of what? Dad, there's something I need to talk to you about.'

'What – has your girl got a bun in the oven?'

'About the family business.'

'What about it?'

'I've just seen Barbara.'

His father sat back. Looked over to the man behind the bar.

'Find us a bottle of whisky and a couple of glasses will you, Des?'

Des nodded.

'Not for me,' Hathaway said.

'Yes, for you. This is a club – well, used to be. In a club you have a proper drink.'

Hathaway shrugged then leaned forward.

'Dad, it's about—'

Hathaway's father put up his hand.

'Not before the drinks, son. Protocol, you know.'

They waited until Des had brought over the whisky and two glasses full of ice. Dennis slouched low in his chair, looking round the room.

'Canadian Club – very nice. Thanks, Des.'

'No problem, Mr H.'

Hathaway watched Des amble back over to the bar area. He looked back at his father who was pouring two stiff measures.

'Cheers, son.'

His father took a swig, Hathaway a sip. The whisky burned.

'Tell me about the brothels,' Hathaway said.

'What brothels?'

'Your brothels.'

'Our brothels, you mean. That's a long story.'

'And the teenage prostitutes.'

Dennis Hathaway put his glass down.

'What has Barbara been telling you? And what is she doing over here, by the way?'

Barbara had looked thinner, older. Much older. Worn.

'Hello, John,' she said. Her voice was the same.

Hathaway felt himself flush. As he stood awkwardly, Barbara came over and reached up to

176

kiss him on the mouth. Her lips were dry and her breath was sour. Hathaway looked down at her, then over at Simpson.

'This really is the rough stuff, Chief Constable.'

Simpson smiled.

'Not at all. It's what in America is now known as a reality check.'

'The reality being?'

'Your father is running women and young boys and girls for prostitution in Brighton.'

Hathaway looked at Barbara. He was surprised to feel his heart beating at an odd rhythm.

'That's not good,' he said. 'I didn't know about the teenagers.'

'Fuck good,' Simpson said. 'All I care about is that these are my areas that your father is impinging on. I control the teen sex. In fact, I control all the brothels.' He walked over to Barbara and cupped her chin in his hand. 'Which is where our Barbara comes in.'

'Get your hands off her.'

Simpson dropped his hand and stepped back, smiling.

'Steady, John. Barbara, tell this innocent about the brothels you run with his father's business partners in Antwerp and The Hague. And the little import-export business you have going.'

Hathaway looked at Barbara. He couldn't read her face. Her expression was cold but pained.

'Tell me.'

'I send youngsters to work for your father over here from the Continent and back to the Continent from here.'

Hathaway looked at her for a long, long moment.

'You're kidding me, right?'

Simpson coughed.

'I'm afraid not, John. Barbara here is a whoremonger – and indeed, a whore, though that's by the by.'

'You're a prostitute? Dad said—'

'You didn't know, Johnny?' Simpson said. He pretended to stifle a yawn. 'Dearie me.'

'I wasn't when—'

Hathaway stood.

'Why is she here?'

'Well, she's here because she needs treatment for cancer, but I'm afraid that isn't going to stop her going to prison for a very long time, unless your father lets me in. And I'm sure you wouldn't want that on your conscience.'

Hathaway looked from one to the other, his heart still racing.

'I'll get back to you,' he said, stepping out of the room.

'She's here for cancer treatment,' Hathaway said. 'And Philip Simpson is threatening to put her in prison unless you stop what you're up to.'

He told his father about his meeting with Simpson. When he'd finished, his father said:

'You've heard about the law of supply and demand.'

'Meaning?'

'Meaning we're in the supply business. We supply what people want. And, as it happens, men want women. Does that come as a surprise

178

to you?'

'The kids, Dad. I was talking about the teen-agers.'

'Well, that's a specialized market, in theory, but you'd be surprised how many men like them young. Girls and boys. And not just the over-twelves, so you know. Infant schoolkids.'

'That's disgusting. And how could you make such a fuss about that young lad being murdered by a perv then provide them for other pervs?'

'That's complicated – it was rape and murder for one thing. But I draw the line at the under-twelves. And correct me if I'm wrong, but don't your pop groups have groupies around that age? Do they think twice about having sex with them?' Hathaway's father took another swig of his drink. 'Do you?'

'I've never—'

'I don't care if you have or not. What I do might be distasteful to you, but I wouldn't be doing it if there wasn't a market. Supply and demand.'

Hathaway leaned back.

'OK. So this is the family business.' He looked up and away. Finished his drink in one. 'What about Barbara?'

'I'm sorry to hear about her illness. I wish she'd told me. As for prison, I'll have a word with Simpson. Are you going to see her again?'

Hathaway took a long drink of the whisky.

'Probably not.'

Simpson hadn't stopped Hathaway leaving but Barbara had come after him.

'Johnny!' she called down corridor after cor-

179

ridor as he sped away without looking back. And the last thing he heard her shout, her voice breaking: 'Like father, like son – you're just as big a bastard as your dad.'

He glanced across at his father.

'Mephistopholes,' a voice called from the bar. Reilly was leaning there, his hand held out. Des put a glass in it and Reilly sauntered over. He grabbed a chair and in one fluid movement sat down and reached for the bottle.

'Who's he?' Hathaway said.

'You didn't know Sean was a scholar, did you, Johnny? But he is. So who's this Mephy guy?'

'Mephistopholes. He tempted Dr Faustus with the promise of anything he wanted in return for his soul.'

'Oh yeah – Liz Taylor got them out on stage somewhere a couple of years ago playing Helen of Troy. Would have liked to have seen that.' He looked at his son. 'No offence to your mother.'

Hathaway ignored his father.

'So what?' he said to Reilly.

'Your father is offering you everything you want in return for your soul.'

'Not exactly,' Hathaway said. 'We're having a different conversation.'

Reilly looked at Dennis Hathaway.

'But that's the conversation we were going to have. And Sean's poetical,' Hathaway's father said. 'Has these odd ideas. A literary man.'

Hathaway looked at Reilly.

'You mean I should ignore the fact that the family business exploits children.'

'Exploits children?' Hathaway's father shook

180

his head. 'We're providing a service, I told you. Every bit of business we do – all of it – is providing a service.'

Hathaway looked from his father to Reilly. Reilly gave him a little smile and poured a glass of the Canadian Club.

'I believe this is known as the tipping point, Johnny. For you, that is. You can walk away from the family business or you can embrace it. In its entirety.'

'I'm not getting any younger,' Hathaway's father said. 'Next year I'd like to hand things over. Your mum's not well, as you know. I'd like to retire with her to Spain. You know we've got some properties there.'

Hathaway reached for the bottle. He looked at his father. He looked at Reilly. He poured himself a drink. He topped up his father. Reilly shook his head when Hathaway tried to pour him a drink.

Hathaway sat back. He looked over at Des, who was pretending not to listen at the bar. He gestured around the Victorian auditorium.

'Not exactly the top of the mountain looking down on the world.'

'So you do know Dr Faustus,' Reilly said.

Hathaway looked at him.

'I know the Bible,' he said. He gestured to his father. 'Obligatory Sunday school.'

'It can all be yours,' Dennis Hathaway said. 'You can be a Prince of the City.'

Hathaway looked down at his hands. Clenched them. Said just one word.

'King.'

* * *

'What is this – fucking Prohibition all over again?' Some days later Dennis Hathaway was looking at Charlie and Hathaway dressed like thirties gangsters in wide-lapelled, baggy-trousered striped suits. 'I can see Bonnie but which one is Clyde?'

'This is the fashion, Dad,' Hathaway said.

'Yeah, I know that. I saw the film. That's why all the gels are in berets and midi-skirts. I saw that Warren Beatty when he was over in London a little while ago. Shags anything that moves, apparently. He was with that Hove girl, Julie Christie. I was in the World's End pub down the end of the King's Road with Bindon, when Bindon did his helicopter thing, and Beatty almost choked on his orange juice.'

'Bindon?' Hathaway said.

'John Bindon. Small-time villain with a huge dick. He's an extra in a lot of films. Plays thugs, usually. Typecasting. Twirls it round like a helicopter blade. Bindon shags all the film stars. Might only be an extra but he's got a lot of extra, if you know what I mean.'

'And Julie Christie is from Hove?'

'Missed your chance there, John. She used to work in rep at the Palace Pier theatre after she got expelled from St Leonards.'

'When?'

'Back in the late fifties.'

'Dad, I was about thirteen.'

His father raised an eyebrow.

'So? When I was thirteen—'

'Dennis,' Reilly said quietly.

182

'Yeah, well. Another time.' Dennis Hathaway waved at Charlie and Hathaway.

'Sit down. I got some news. Hot off the presses. Philip Simpson is resigning next year. Scotland Yard hot on his tail.'

Hathaway nodded.

'Is that it?' his father said, sitting back in his chair. 'Is that all the excitement you can muster?'

'He's still upset about Julie Christie,' Charlie said. 'How will that affect us?'

Dennis Hathaway's smile back at Charlie was conspiratorial and Hathaway felt a twinge of jealousy.

'What do you think, Charlie?'

'Nature abhors a vacuum,' Hathaway blurted before Charlie could say anything. His father looked at him and laughed. 'I always said you read too many books. But you're right, you're right. Now, look, if you're serious about this, we need to do it together.' He pointed at Hathaway. 'And if we're doing it together, you've got to give up these ideas of travelling in India barefoot and giving all your wealth away.'

Charlie chuckled. Dennis Hathaway turned to him. 'Plus, there are other people going to have the same idea. We need to keep hold of what we've already got and move quickly for the rest.'

'We go after Gerald Cuthbert?' Charlie said.

Dennis Hathaway shook his head.

'Not overtly. He's too close to the twins. But Simpson seems to think they are on their way down. For now we out-manoeuvre Cuthbert but

183

we don't go for him head-on.'

Charlie and Hathaway both nodded.

'Am I clear?' Dennis Hathaway said.

'Sure, Dad.'

'Charlie?'

'Whatever you say, sir.'

Dennis Hathaway gave him an intense look.

'I don't want to hear about any clowns running amok in Milldean.'

Hathaway and Charlie went to the folk club towards the end of the evening for after-hours drinks. They were overdressed so left their jackets in Hathaway's car and went in wearing waistcoats over rolled-up shirt-sleeves and gangster trousers. There were still thirty-odd people sitting around drinking and listening to Bob Dylan on the jukebox. A lot of straggly hair and beards. Women with long plaited hair and dirndle skirts.

Bill and Dan were both in granddad T-shirts and second-hand waistcoats these days. They both had walrus moustaches. Bill had turned vegetarian and was living in Lewes. As Hathaway and Charlie walked across to them, they saw a swelling around Dan's eye, the beginnings of a shiner.

'What happened?' Hathaway said.

'Bit of a barney,' Billy said, tugging at his moustache. 'Dan got in the way.'

'Folkies fighting?' Charlie snorted. 'I thought they were all peaceniks. Little boxes, little boxes, all that frigging Pete Seeger stuff.'

Hathaway grinned whilst he tilted Dan's head

to look at his eye.

'Charlie is off again. You know it's changed, mister.'

Charlie ignored him.

'What did they do? Hit you with their lutes? Or their sandals?'

'It was this one big bugger,' Dan said. 'He's on stage and his manager tries to leave without paying him. He's sees his manager legging it, stops singing, shouts "Oy, he's got my fucking money", drops his guitar and chases after him down the centre aisle.

'He catches him, virtually turns him upside down to get the money out of his pockets, gives him a couple of slaps for trying it on, then turns back to the stage. I've come down to stop the fight and he whacks me in passing, goes back up and finishes singing "Spencer the Rover".'

Charlie laughed.

'What's the world coming to when even a fucking folkie can best you, Danny?'

'Fighting's not my area of expertise.'

'Well finking and fucking aren't either, so where's that leave you?'

'Easy, Charlie,' Hathaway said. 'That eye must hurt like hell.'

Charlie clamped his arm round Dan's shoulder, despite Dan trying to shrug him off.

'Sorry, mate. Only kidding you.'

Hathaway glanced over as the door opened and was surprised to see Sean Reilly walk in. He was even more surprised to see him in jeans and an open-necked shirt. Reilly gave him a little nod and walked to the far end of the bar.

'Scuse me a sec,' Hathaway said. He walked over.

'Sean?' he said.

'John. Wondered if I could have a quiet word?'

'Is Dad OK?'

'He's fine.'

'Has he got something for me?'

Reilly shook his head.

'No. This is just me. Wondered if I could pop round your place?'

'Tonight?'

Reilly shrugged.

'If it's not too late – you're a late-night person, I think. Tomorrow if not.'

Hathaway didn't show his puzzlement. Or, indeed, his suspicion.

'Sure,' he said. He looked at his watch. 'About one?'

Reilly nodded.

'Thanks, John.'

'Don't tell me you're a fucking folkie too, Mr Reilly.'

Charlie had wandered over and now slapped Reilly on the back.

'Sean. More of a blues man, I suppose. Son House, Blind Mamie Forehand, Big Mama Thornton – that kind of stuff.'

'You might as well be talking a foreign language,' Charlie said, leaning close.

Reilly smiled and raised his glass.

'Here's to music in all its forms.'

At one in the morning, Hathaway led Reilly on to his balcony. The lights had gone off on the piers and along the seafront, but the moon was full, casting its cold brilliance over the deserted scene.

'You've made me very curious, Sean,' Hathaway said. He indicated the briefcase Reilly had brought with him. 'Especially with that.'

Reilly looked down.

'Oh that.' He reached in and withdrew a pile of thin books. 'I've seen you're a bit of a reader, John,' he said.

'It's Elaine. She's studying American literature. But you wanted to see me in the middle of the night to lend me books?'

Reilly smiled.

'I've been carrying them round for days. Just thought I'd take this opportunity. American literature, eh? Not enough good books at home for her? Well, the Yanks have always been good at finishing what somebody else has started.'

'She says they've colonized our imaginations.'

'Does she now? That's a nice bit of phrasemaking.'

Reilly passed the books across to Hathaway.

'I don't think she invented it. It would be from one of her lectures.'

He looked at the cover of the top book on the pile.

'*The Great Gatsby.*'

'That is one up to the Americans, that book there. A perfect little thing. If she's studying American literature, you'll impress her casually flaunting that around the place.'

Hathaway frowned.

'I don't need to impress her, Sean.'

187

'I'm sure you don't, but nevertheless a bit of impressing never goes amiss. Stores up points for the future, when your stock may have dipped. And I'm sure some of her literary friends will be stuffed full of opinion.'

Hathaway smiled and shuffled through the other books.

'I've taken the liberty of proposing that the best of English literature is actually Irish, which I know is an Irish kind of thing to say. *Ulysses* is a mountain you need to come up on slow, when you've trained a bit, so to say. So here's by way of a foothill.'

'*Portrait of the Artist As A Young Man* by James Joyce. You know he was a bicycle-seat sniffer?'

Reilly gave him a look.

'Apparently.' Hathaway said.

'You'll see I've chosen them all for their brevity, attention spans being what they are among young people today.'

'Flann O'Brien?' Hathaway said, holding up the next.

'Sheer comic genius but he also understands the world better than any politician or priest.'

'*At Swim Two Birds* – strange title.'

'Strange book. And your last one is a gift from God. W.B. Yeats. Read his "Aedh wishes for the cloths of heaven" and she'll be putty in your hands – though I'm sure she already is.'

Hathaway grinned and nodded.

'Thanks, Sean. But I don't quite understand...'

Sean took a drink and looked up at the moon.

'I'm not sure I do. I just ... your father isn't a

188

sensitive man.'

'Agreed.'

'You're how old now?'

'Twenty-two.'

'Well, you can understand it. At your age most men of your dad's generation were killing each other. But, still, the family business...'

'What about it?'

Reilly's eyes glittered.

'It kills the soul,' he said softly. 'Before I took up soldiering I was all kinds of things. Maybe I'll get back to some of them one day.' He pushed out his lower lip. 'But probably it's too late.'

Hathaway put the books down on the floor beside him.

'I'll take a look at them, I promise.' He gave a false smile. 'If only to impress Elaine's poncy friends.'

'What I'm trying to say, John, is that I wasn't really joking about the Mephistophelean pact. Once you fully commit to the family business, there's no way back.' He looked at Hathaway sharply. 'But maybe it's too late already.'

Hathaway watched him over the rim of his glass.

'I don't hear you talk about your sister much.'

'Dawn? Dawn goes her own way, as always.'

'From what I hear, she could do with some brotherly support.'

'It was only an abortion, for God's sake,' Hathaway said. 'Women have them every day.'

Reilly looked at him for a long moment, then dropped his eyes.

'And Barbara? Do women get cancer every

189

day?'

'Probably. Is she why you're really here? Did she send you?'

Reilly shook his head.

'She has more class than that.'

'Class? Running seedy Dutch brothels?'

'They're quite classy too, actually. The clientele are usually judges and senior politicians.'

Reilly leaned over and put his hand on Hathaway's arm.

'Don't you owe her anything?'

'The price of a few fucks?' Hathaway said.

Reilly removed his arm and sat back. He looked into the sky again. A seagull swooped silently by, ghostly in the moonlight.

'Maybe it's too late for you already. Did you or Charlie shoot the Boroni brothers?'

Hathaway refilled their glasses.

'Slainte,' Reilly said, chinking his glass against Hathaway's and keeping his eyes on him.

'Charlie,' Hathaway said.

Reilly gave a small nod.

'But you both had guns?'

Hathaway's turn to nod.

'Did you get rid of them?'

'Charlie did. Mine hadn't been fired.'

'Get rid of it. Some people say a gun is just a tool. And, of course, it is. But a gun is also a seducer. A gun wants to be fired. And, sooner or later, whoever has one will fire it.'

'So what should I do if I don't go into the family business?'

'You've met this bright young girl, Elaine.

190

Think about a future with her.'

'In an ashram in India? Will that save my soul?'

Reilly gave a low laugh.

'Your dad isn't really Mephistopheles. Your soul is still safe.'

'Is yours, Sean?'

Reilly looked into his glass.

'No, there's no hope for me. I'm for the fiery pit all right.' He pointed at the books. 'Books feed my spirit. Music too. But nothing can save my long-lost, long-damned soul.' He started to rise. 'But you give those books a try some time. If only to wean yourself off those penny dreadfuls you and your father favour.'

Hathaway nodded absently, still seated. Knowing what neither Sean nor any living being knew: that his soul had been lost years before and there was nothing he could ever do to save it.

TEN

Happiness is a Warm Gun
1968

A brisk wind blew along the promenade. The full-skirted frocks of the women crowded in the entrance to the West Pier billowed and fluttered. A couple of bonnets flew into the air and off into the sea. The soldiers in their puttees and tin helmets milled around, smoking and flirting with a gang of suffragettes.

A short, rotund man with long sideburns stood beside a camera talking earnestly to the man peering through its lens. He was wearing white slip-on shoes, a flat cap and black, shiny PVC coat. The entrance to the pier had 'World War One' written in neon in an arc over it. A sign below it read: 'Songs, battles and a few jokes'.

The Avalons were clustered together in their American uniforms near a bunch of students in period costumes, who were to cheer them on as they entered the First World War by marching along the pier into the main theatre. A cricket ground scoreboard had been set up partway along the pier to provide the war's results – lives lost and yards gained.

Charlie was scratching underneath his helmet.

'This bloody thing is making my head itch.'

'Did you ever see that anti-war film John Lennon did?' Billy said.

They all shook their heads.

'It was good,' Billy said, looking down.

'So that's Big X,' Dan said, looking over at Richard Attenborough in his PVC coat.

'Brilliant in *Brighton Rock* when he was our age,' Hathaway said. 'Really chilling.'

As he spoke, he was straining to catch sight of Elaine among the other extras. His father was trying hard to get her a speaking part, but in the meantime she was playing one of dozens of Vanessa Redgrave's suffragettes.

'Oh, oh, oh, what a lovely war,' Dan sang under his breath.

A month or so earlier, Hathaway had visited Elaine on campus sporting his new look, in-spired by Steve McQueen in *The Thomas Crown Affair*. Inevitably, her room door was open and, equally inevitably, a gang of people were lounging there listening to The Beatles' *White Album*.

Hathaway in his three-piece herring-bone suit looked around for Elaine. Everyone was bare-foot, wearing T-shirts and sitting cross-legged, some sprawled on the cushions scattered over the floor. A couple of joints were being passed haphazardly around. A boy with a goatee beard and a long scarf twirled round his head offered one to Hathaway.

Hathaway shook his head. He was feeling like Thomas Crown dropped into an episode of *The*

Monkees.

'Is Elaine here?'

'Is anybody really here?' the man said drowsily. 'We're just figments of your imagination, man.'

'Yeah, right.' Hathaway raised his voice. 'Anyone know where Elaine is?'

Silence. Hathaway repeated the question. A voice from behind him, lazy, slurred:

'Who's Elaine? And who the fuck are you, Mister Three-Piece Suit?'

'Steve McQueen in that movie – he wishes.'

'Who's anybody?' the guy who'd offered Hathaway the joint said, and Hathaway thought about decking him. The whole doped-up lot of them, actually. Though that seemed mean as one of his guys had probably sold them the dope.

'This is Elaine's room,' he said, adjusting his waistcoat. 'She lives here.'

'Oh, that Elaine.'

'That Elaine.'

One man looked round the room, waved his arms slowly but expansively.

'She's not here.'

Hathaway chewed his lip.

He found Elaine sitting straight-backed on the steep grassy incline behind the hall of residence.

'Big sky,' he said, looking up and around at the blue flecked with white vapour.

'Hey, you.'

She scrabbled to her feet and grabbed his face. He put his arms round her waist and lifted her clear of the ground.

'I've got some good news for you,' Hathaway

said.

She ran her fingers down the edges of his lapels and gave him a questioning look.

'You're coming to the ashram with me?'

Her breath smelt of tangerines, her skin of patchouli.

'You've got an audition for a part in the film they're making on the pier.'

'This is no time for films. There's a lot going on.'

'What do you mean there's a lot going on?'

'Benny burned the American flag outside the senate house and Dave threw a pot of paint over the guy from the American embassy.'

'Because?'

'Because? Because those who defend US policy in Vietnam are stained with the blood of thousands. The flag of the United States was burnt because every day napalm dropped by US planes burns Vietnamese people to death or inflicts the most dreadful wounds on them.'

'OK. Thanks for explaining. What's going to happen to Benny and Dave?'

'They'll be kicked out. Rusticated.'

Hathaway composed a solemn expression.

'Serious times, indeed. But, look, this is an anti-war film. *Oh! What A Lovely War.*'

'I've seen the play! It's a musical – I saw it at the Wyndham, though Joan Littlewood did it years earlier in the East End.'

'Well, they're filming on the seafront all the way from Madeira Drive down to the West Pier. And planting sixteen thousand burial crosses on the Downs over Ovendean way.'

'So how can you get me an audition?'

Hathaway was hot in his three-piece but he liked pressing against her.

'Well, they're doing a lot of shooting on the West Pier. In fact, it's closing down from April to August to accommodate the shooting. Which will affect Dad's business. And Dad's providing security. So he can have a word. No promises, mind. But if worst comes to worst, they're looking for loads of local extras. All The Avalons are going to try to get on it.'

She looked up at him and he couldn't figure out exactly what thoughts were passing in quick succession behind her eyes.

'Your dad's got that kind of clout?'

Hathaway shrugged.

'We'll see.'

She tilted her head.

'OK,' she said.

He disentangled himself and reached into his jacket pocket.

'I know you get disgustingly long holidays, so I wondered if before that, during your Easter break, you might want to go away for a couple of weeks.'

'Of course,' she said, taking the proffered plane tickets. Her eyes widened as she read them. 'Greece!' she said, trying not to squeal.

Hathaway had been thinking a lot about the things Reilly had said that night on the balcony. He'd thought about the buzz he got from working in the family business and tried to compare it to a life imagined with Elaine. He read *The*

Great Gatsby and liked it – but then he was drawn by the fact Gatsby was a successful boot-legger. And he thought about the violence he'd been willing to do. The violence he might have to do.

He'd tried to be more caring to Dawn – and even to his mother – but his old life at home seemed to be someone else's life. By the time he got round to seeing Barbara in the hospital, her treatment had finished and she'd gone. Not back to Europe, though. According to Reilly, his father had paid her off – generously – and she'd got out of the life. But nobody knew where she'd gone.

He'd never been away with a girl – never spent so much concentrated time with anyone. Greece was an experiment, to see if he could live a normal life. Elaine's friend, Gregory, almost derailed it before it got started.

'Greece is a no-go country,' he said. He was a man who favoured the Jesus look with long brown boots. 'A military junta is in power. There's no democracy.'

Hathaway took the 'helping support the people with his drachmas' line and Elaine went along with it. The thought of two weeks in a beautiful country with bright sunshine might have had something to do with it. Barnie, Elaine's non-political poet friend, recommended Hathaway buy a copy of a book called *The Magus*.

'Essential reading for the island-hopper,' he said, nodding sagely.

Hathaway had a suitcase; she had a rucksack. They ate the first night in the Plaka in Athens.

Hathaway cautiously, Elaine with gusto. They spent the night in a hotel on Omonia Square, the noisy bustle of the streets never pausing. Piercing whistles; the grinding of gears; an ill-tempered cacophony of car and scooter horns. Fumes came up through the window then through the air conditioning.

Hathaway hadn't realized Greece was so oriental.

The next morning they'd taken the train down to Piraeus and boarded a ferry to Spetsi. For ten days they island-hopped: sunbathing, swimming, drinking ouzo and retsina and making love. On the last weekend they boarded a ferry to Hydra.

Stepping off the boat at a narrow dock, the first person they saw sitting outside a restaurant on the dock was Leonard Cohen, with a gaggle of beautiful women. Cohen clocked Elaine, braless in her tight white T-shirt and denim mini skirt, and watched her as she walked by.

Elaine pretended to be insouciant about the attention but Hathaway could tell she was excited. He didn't mind the singer/songwriter giving his girlfriend the once-over – that was part of the music business – but he quickly got cheesed off with having to give the local lads the hard eye.

They spent the next day on a scrap of beach, Elaine topless (of course). Hathaway was nearing the end of the book. He'd started it on the plane and had really got drawn in. Some old guy called Conchis was orchestrating a whole series of things affecting the central character and

Hathaway wanted to know why. He didn't much like the central character, who was pretty much a poncy git, but the story drew him along.

Elaine casually suggested they go to the restaurant on the dock that evening. She tried to hide her disappointment that Cohen wasn't there. Cat Stevens, however, was. He had his back to the room, presumably to avoid drawing attention to himself, but Hathaway went to the toilet and noticed him on his way back.

In the time it took him to have a piss, two Greek guys had started chatting up Elaine. They hung around for a bit when Hathaway came back but eventually took the hint from Hathaway's attitude. They sauntered off, casting disdainful glances back at Hathaway and making comments in Greek.

'Pricks,' Hathaway said.

'They're just guys,' Elaine said.

Hathaway scowled.

He finished *The Magus* late the next morning on their beach and threw it against a rock in disgust.

'What?' Elaine said, looking up from her battered copy of *The Lord of the Rings* trilogy.

'The bloody bastard,' Hathaway said. 'I don't bloody believe it.'

'What?' she said again, laughing.

'Aren't books supposed to explain by the end what's been happening?'

'Not always.'

'I don't mean the kind of books you study, I mean regular books. Stories. This guy John Fowles has just been stringing me along. It's like a five-hundred-page shaggy dog story with no punchline.'

'Did you enjoy the stringing along?' she said.

'Yeah – but part of it was wanting to know why it was all happening.'

She smiled.

'If only.'

'At the end the guy is sitting on a park bench waiting for someone to turn up to tell him why he's been dragged through shit through most of the book – admittedly on a beautiful Greek island by beautiful twins, but even so. And nobody turns up. And the last sentence of the bloody book—'

'Calm down, John – they'll hear you in Piraeus.'

'The last sentence of the bloody book,' he said in a loud whisper, 'is in fucking Greek!'

She laughed at that and rolled over towards him. They went for a dip and he checked out a rock for sea urchins, then he pressed Elaine against it and started to have sex with her. Suddenly she cried out as she trod on a sea urchin with the one foot that she was using to try to keep her balance.

It would have been funny if her bikini bottoms hadn't drifted away and if, as he was hoisting her out of the water, one of the Greek men from the restaurant hadn't come by.

Hathaway didn't notice him at first. He was busy examining the sole of Elaine's foot. He'd located the black dot on the fleshy pad below her big toe where the spine had broken off when he saw movement from the corner of his eye. The

Greek man was standing leering at Elaine's nakedness.

Hathaway gave him a hostile look and grabbed a towel to thrust at Elaine.

'We're not alone,' he said.

She looked over.

'Who cares? That's Yannis – we met him last night.'

'You met him last night,' Hathaway muttered, trying to pick at the black spot with his nails. Elaine yelped.

Yannis stepped off the road, calling something in Greek.

'We're fine, thank you,' Hathaway called, adding under his breath: 'so fuck off.'

'You need to make water on it,' Yannis said, dropping down on to the patch of sand, his eyes fixed on Elaine's still naked breasts.

'What?' Hathaway said.

'Pee-pee? Do pee-pee.'

'Who?'

'You.' Yannis grinned at Elaine. 'Or I will if you wish.'

He patted his crotch, leaving his hand there, the grin widening.

'You're serious?'

'Chemicals. The spine comes out.'

Hathaway looked from him to Elaine.

'Well, are you going to do something?' she said through gritted teeth.

'Not when he's standing there.'

'Jesus, this is no time to worry about the size of your cock.'

'I'm not fucking worried,' Hathaway said, 'I

just want this guy to fuck off.'

Yannis's smile disappeared.

'You say fuck off?'

'For God's sake, will somebody piss on my foot?'

'Piss on your own bloody foot, you're so clever,' Hathaway said, thrusting his chin out and taking a step towards Yannis.

Yannis was in flip-flops; Hathaway was barefooted. Hathaway knocked him down with a roundhouse kick that caught the Greek on the side of the head just above his left ear.

Yannis fell heavily. Hathaway heard the hollow clunk as his head hit rock. He stepped forward and picked up another rock, raising it to smash down into Yannis's face. Elaine screamed his name.

His father had wangled Elaine a speaking part in *Oh! What A Lovely War* but Hathaway wasn't sure whether she'd taken it as, after Greece, she wasn't speaking to him. He couldn't see her anywhere in the crowd and then he and the other Avalons joined the procession on to the pier. They did it once, twice, three times before Attenborough declared himself satisfied. It had taken five hours.

'Well, if this is film making, you can keep it,' Charlie said. 'I've had more fun watching paint dry.'

Hathaway sauntered off, still in his uniform, down to his father's office. Halfway there, he saw his father walking towards him, flanked by Victor Tempest, Tempest's wife, Elizabeth, and, in a very short skirt, the chief constable's wife.

'How's the war going?' his father shouted before they all met and shook hands.

'No action yet,' Hathaway said, giving the women his best smile and trying not to ogle the length of bare leg on show.

'John,' Tempest said. 'You should say hello to the scriptwriter on the film – I assume you're still reading spy thrillers?'

'I am, Mr Tempest – Mr Watts, I mean – I don't know what I should call you.'

'Victor Tempest is only my working name. Why not call me Donald?'

'All right, Donald. I'm not sure this is my kind of film, really.'

'Great cast, though,' Donald Watts said. 'All doing it for a nominal sum. Johnny Mills was telling me he got Attenborough involved. Dickie wanted to do a film about Gandhi but said he'd have a go at this. He phoned up Olivier – you know he lives in Royal Crescent? He's not been well but he agreed to do it for peanuts, then everyone else came on board.'

'I see,' Hathaway said. 'But what's that got to do with thrillers?'

'You've read *The Ipcress File*?'

'Of course. Len Deighton. Very good.'

'Well, he wrote the script for this film.'

Hathaway was impressed.

'I'll look out for him.'

'Do that. If I'm around I'll introduce you.'

Tempest turned to Hathaway's father.

'We'd better be getting on, Dennis. Good to see you.'

203

'I'll let you make your own way – I need a word with my son.'

'And I need the toilet,' Elizabeth Watts said. 'I'll say my goodbyes now – don't wait.'

As she disappeared into the nearby toilets and his father led him towards the office, Hathaway caught sight of Tempest and the chief constable's wife in a prop mirror leaning against the side of a stall. Presumably thinking no one was watching, Tempest had slipped his hand under the back of her mini-skirt and up between her thighs.

Hathaway was hardly listening when his father said:

'Philip Simpson has resigned and the twins have been arrested.'

Hathaway nodded absently. He was thinking about Tempest's hand slipping up between those white thighs.

'Is that it?' his father said, sitting back in his chair. 'Is that all the excitement you can muster?'

Hathaway switched focus.

'So we can let loose the dogs of war.'

Dennis Hathaway laughed and squeezed his arm.

'Soon, sonny boy, soon.'

ELEVEN

Albatross
1969

By the time Bruce Reynolds, the last Great Train Robber to be captured, was sentenced in January 1969 to twenty-five years, Hathaway was still waiting to see his father take over Brighton. Philip Simpson was no longer chief constable, though he was still visible around town and up at the racetrack. He'd become a father for the first time a year earlier but it had co-incided with him coming down with cancer. He looked like a skeleton. The twins' empire had crashed. But Cuthbert was still being a pain in the arse, and Dennis Hathaway didn't seem to be doing anything about it.

Hathaway and Charlie discussed it many times but Hathaway dissuaded Charlie from bringing out the clown costumes.

There was talk of closing the West Pier down. It was rotting at the far end – Hathaway could kick a hole in the floorboards in the office. Charlie had done so. His father tended to use his office in the Laines most of the time.

Hathaway and Elaine had limped back together. They saw each other now mainly for sex.

She had seen an ugly side of him and it repelled her, though at the same time he could tell by the way the sex had changed that she was also drawn to his brutal side.

She didn't know the half of it.

Elaine was doing her finals but she was also getting bit parts in Brighton-based film and TV programmes. Her one line in *Oh! What A Lovely War* got her an Equity card, though when the film came out her line had been cut. The camera was on her a bit – and on Charlie in another scene. Hathaway couldn't spot himself.

Elaine played the friend of a runaway in an episode of *Marker*, a TV series about a seedy ex-con who set up as an enquiry agent in Brighton. She flirted with Sid James on the Palace Pier in *Carry On At Your Convenience*. She played a go-go dancer alongside an actress called Susan George in a film called *Die Screaming, Marianne*, filmed in one of Dennis Hathaway's discos and at Brighton Station.

Hathaway was on the set for that. When Elaine wasn't around he tried it on with George – she was the sexiest girl he'd ever seen, even sexier than Judy Geeson – but she wasn't having any.

Bill Boal, the innocent Great Train Robber, died in prison just as Elaine was filming *On A Clear Day You Can See Forever* at the Royal Pavilion.

Hathaway went on the set and reported back to Charlie over a couple of joints in a pub garden out on the Downs near the Plumpton racecourse.

'That Barbara Streisand – God, the tits on her.'

'What's she doing?' Charlie said.

206

'Making a film with Irene Handl.'

Charlie laughed.

'She's made it big, then.'

'Elaine's playing one of her maidservants.'

'You know I've never actually met Elaine?'

'Yes, you have, but you were too out of it to remember. She's having a party at the end of finals – come to that.'

'What, me and a room full of students? I'll be like their granddad.'

'Nah. It'll be the usual yellow-mellow thing – music, drugs, drink, probably sex.'

'I'd say that's guaranteed for you if it's Elaine's party.'

'Nothing is guaranteed – and look, I'm warning you, Charlie, they're a weird lot.'

'What kind of weird?'

'They play mind games – makes you want to punch them – but you can't punch anybody, Charlie. That's a massive no-no.'

'Mind games?' Charlie said.

'OK, this guy Duncan, got the hots for Elaine, total wanker, he says to me with this supercilious smirk on his face, "What colour do you think love is, John?" I mean, what kind of bloody question is that? Then he says something like "What number is lust?"'

'And decking him is out of the question?'

'Totally.'

Charlie sighed.

'Thanks for the invite.'

'Charlie – what the fuck are you wearing?'

'What – the hat? It's a panama.'

207

'Not the hat, though that's bad enough. '

'My highwayman's raincoat?'

'No, mate, not the raincoat. Even though it's summer and that should be a tricorne hat to match. I'm talking about that suit. That vomit green and blue thing lurking underneath it.'

'It's paisley. It's crimplene. What more is there to say?'

'Well, for one thing, why the silver belt?'

'Came with the suit.'

Hathaway looked down at Charlie's shoes.

'Patent leather. Nice.'

Charlie looked down at Hathaway's own shoes, patent leather slip-ons.

'Yours too.'

He looked at the long kaftan Hathaway was wearing, his trousers poking out beneath it. He indicated the high roll-neck sweater.

'Bet you're hot in that.'

'The price of being trendy,' Hathaway said.

When Hathaway and Charlie arrived, Duncan and his equally pretentious friend James were both engrossed in conversation with a couple of chicks sprawled on bean bags. Elaine was effusive in her greeting – she'd clearly smoked a couple of joints already – and reached up to hug Charlie. She kissed him on the mouth.

As she led them over to her room, Charlie murmured to Hathaway, giving him a quick punch in the arm:

'She put her tongue in my mouth, you know.'

The Moody Blues were on the turntable, with a stack of other LPs above them on the spindle. Elaine plonked down on the bean bag between the bed and the old sofa. Charlie dropped on to the bed, Hathaway on to the sofa. Elaine passed Hathaway a fat joint. 'Nights in White Satin' ended and its spaciness was replaced, with a click and a clatter of vinyl dropping on vinyl, by the lugubrious tones of Leonard Cohen. Suzanne was taking him down to a place by the river as Hathaway took a long draw on the joint and remembered Hydra.

'Do you have any brothers or sisters, Charlie?' Elaine said. She was sitting up on the bean bag, leaning towards Charlie, who was lying on the bed, his head supported by one hand. Bob Dylan was singing about a joker asking a thief where the exit was.

'Not living,' Charlie said. Hathaway looked over.

'What do you mean?' Elaine said dreamily.

Charlie took another toke and passed the joint to Elaine.

'I had a younger brother. He died.'

Elaine looked at the joint, looked at Charlie. Focused a little.

'I'm sorry. Was it a long time ago?'

'What difference does that make?' Charlie bridled.

'She didn't say it made a difference,' Hathaway said, up on one elbow.

Charlie gave him a look.

'He died about ten years ago. He was nine.'

Elaine expelled smoke with a little cough.

'Jesus. I'm sorry. What was it?'

Hathaway looked at Charlie. Charlie looked

down.

'He was...'

Elaine stared at him. Hathaway could see her pupils were wildly dilated from the drug and the low lights. Here it was.

'He was burned alive,' Hathaway said. Charlie took his time looking over at him. Hathaway dipped his head. Elaine was on her knees beside Charlie, reaching out to squeeze his arm.

'I can't imagine.'

'I can,' Charlie said. 'I do. All the time.'

He looked over at Hathaway. His eyes were bleary.

'I don't recall talking to you about it.'

'It was in all the papers. Bill, Dan and me all knew it was your brother, but you never brought it up so we didn't say anything.'

Elaine's eyes welled.

'How did it happen?'

Charlie waved at Hathaway.

'You obviously know the story so well, Johnny – why don't you tell it?'

Hathaway looked from his friend to his girl-friend – her attention entirely on Charlie.

Hathaway's voice was flat.

'Charlie's brother – Roy – was with him in Lewes one day guarding a bonfire. Other kids would try to set fire to bonfires before the fifth of November for a lark, so you had to keep an eye on them. Charlie and his mate – I've forgotten his name...'

'Kevin,' Charlie said after a beat, watching Hathaway as Elaine watched him. 'You met him at the Snowdrop.'

'Kevin and Charlie were freezing their asses off. They went down the street to a café to get a cup of tea out of the wind. They left Roy behind.'

'Wasn't he cold too?' Elaine said.

'Not for long,' Charlie said.

Elaine reared up and put her arms round him.

'Oh Jesus, that was such a bloody stupid thing to say. I'm so sorry.' She kissed him on the face, and again. And again.

Hathaway watched. Charlie's eyes were fixed on him over Elaine's shoulder. Hathaway took another long toke. Elaine looked back at him.

'Bonfires all had dens inside them back then,' Hathaway said. 'Secret spaces. Roy was in the bonfire.'

Hathaway reached over with the spliff. Charlie took it, looked at it.

'Someone set the bonfire alight,' he said.

Hathaway lay back. He heard Elaine sob. He closed his eyes.

Hathaway lay on his back, lost in the drug. Christ, it was strong. He was boiling hot but he couldn't raise the energy to pull his rollneck down. He drifted in and out of the room. He rolled on to his side. Elaine and Charlie were wrapped round each other on the bed, faces plastered together, Charlie's hand up her skirt, her hip slowly rolling.

Hathaway watched, dope-befuddled. Time passed. Then:

'Hey,' he said. 'Hey, Charlie.'

Charlie, blurry, disengaged enough to look at

Hathaway.

'What are you doing?' Hathaway said.

Charlie looked puzzled for a moment. Elaine was oblivious, rubbing her leg along Charlie's body.

'What does it look like?' Charlie finally said, his voice thick.

Hathaway drifted. He looked again.

'Elaine? Elaine?'

Elaine tilted her head back. Her eyes were all dope and lust.

'It's cool, Johnny,' she said, her voice throaty.

She gasped as Charlie pulled her skirt up to her waist. Her knickers were down, stretched taut across her thighs. Charlie winked grotesquely.

'Hey, Johnny,' he said slowly. 'What number is jealousy?'

Hathaway thought he flipped Charlie the bird.

'Fuck you,' he said, or thought he did.

Charlie grinned.

'What number is love?'

Hathaway, woozy, started to get up. Got tangled in the kaftan.

'I'm warning you, Charlie—'

'What colour is despair?' Charlie said.

When Hathaway came round he was alone in the room. He was lying on the floor beside the bed on which Elaine and Charlie had been entangled. He rolled over and vomited on the carpet.

His head thumped as he got to his feet. He dragged off the kaftan and dropped it on the floor. He staggered out of the room and through a sea of tangled bodies. He clung to the banister as he walked down the four flights of stairs. What the fuck had he taken?

Charlie with Elaine. He couldn't believe it. She'd always gone on about free love and being free, and he'd always wondered whether she messed around with the dorks she hung out with and the actors on the film sets. But Charlie?

He found his car and drove carefully to his flat. He half-expected Elaine to be waiting outside. She wasn't. He didn't know whether to be relieved or disappointed. He put ice in a long glass and poured himself a Cinzano. He added lemonade. He turned on the stereo. There was a record already on the turntable. Hendrix. That would do.

He walked across to the long window and dropped into the chair, sticking his feet up on the wall. He sipped his drink as he looked out over the promenade and down to his father's premises on the end of the West Pier. There were lights on. Somebody was having a bad time.

He took a longer swig of his drink, rolling the viscous liquid around his mouth before swallowing it. He was wondering what to do about Elaine and Charlie. On the one hand he was into free love too. On the other...

He woke at dawn with a cricked neck from sleeping in the chair and a dry, dry mouth. His glass lay on its side, its contents spilled over the carpet. The needle was butting against the album label. He lifted it and put it down on the outer rim. 'The Star Spangled Banner', live and loud. The quality wasn't great – the album was a bootleg – but Hathaway liked it. The telephone rang.

He picked it up, his empty glass in his other hand. His father.

'Get over here.'

When Hathaway reached the end of the pier he could see through the office window that Charlie was standing by his father's desk. He stopped for a moment, considering this. His blood rising.

He entered the room quickly and went straight at Charlie.

'You sod,' he said as he swung.

The blow never connected as Hathaway felt himself yanked back, spun round and plonked in a chair. The chair was on rollers and he rolled back until it collided with the wall. Sean Reilly was standing over him.

His father remained seated behind his desk.

'Your point being, son?' he said.

'That dick nicked my girl.'

Charlie shrugged.

'It's the sixties, man. Swing a little.'

'At the moment,' Dennis Hathaway said, 'that's irrelevant.'

'Not to me.'

'Well, we have an emergency. By the name of Cuthbert.'

Hathaway remembered the lights on the previous night.

'You brought him here yesterday?'

He noticed for the first time how haggard his father looked from being up all night.

'Aside from being a pain in the arse, he's threatening to grass on me.'

'About what?'

214

Dennis Hathaway stood and beckoned his son to follow him into the storeroom.

'About what?'

'What do you think? About the Great Train Robbery, of course.'

Hathaway stared at his father. He'd sussed there had been some involvement in the robbery but he hadn't know what.

Cuthbert sagged against the rope that held him to a wheelchair. His feet and lower legs were encased in cement inside a tin tub balanced on the footrest. His face was bloodied, his nose splashed at a grotesque angle over his cheek. Dennis Hathaway walked towards him and kicked him in the face. Hathaway was sure he heard Cuthbert's cheekbone crack.

Dennis Hathaway started singing as he circled Cuthbert.

'There's a hole in my bucket, dear Liza, dear Liza...'

He hit Cuthbert across the side of the head with a block of wood and continued his circuit.

'There's a hole in my bucket, dear Liza.' Kick. 'An arsehole.'

Cuthbert was still breathing, as best he could, but Hathaway could see bloody gums and a swollen tongue. The light had gone from behind his eyes.

'Dad, why—?'

'Because he's scum.'

His father circled and kicked, circled and kick-ed. Tommy came into the back of the room. Whispered something to Reilly. Reilly stepped forward, touched Dennis Hathaway on the shoulder.

'And?'

'We have a problem.'

He whispered in Dennis Hathaway's ear. Hathaway saw his father glance his way.

'OK, let's dump this scumbag.'

He stepped behind Cuthbert and released the brake on the wheelchair. Reilly opened the double doors at the far end of the room and Hathaway rolled Cuthbert over there. Reilly helped him untie Cuthbert and tip the chair.

Cuthbert, still alive but a dead weight, fell forward but his feet in the tub stalled his progress. Reilly and Dennis Hathaway bent and tilted the tub. Cuthbert's weight dragged the tub to the edge of the door and he toppled over. He hit the water with a loud splash then slid beneath the surface.

Dennis Hathaway looked back at his son. Hathaway swallowed.

'That's that,' he said.

His father shook his head.

'Now we've got a bigger problem.'

'What?'

'Your girlfriend.'

Hathaway frowned until he walked back into the office and saw Elaine shivering in the corner.

She had come on the pier looking for Hathaway to apologize for the previous evening. She had heard someone singing in the wooden hut beyond the firing range. She had peered through the window. It was misted but she could make out a man tied to a chair. She noticed his feet were in an old washtub. She drew in her breath

216

when she realized the man had been badly beaten. Another man circled him with a piece of wood in his hand. Singing. She gasped when she realized it was John's father. A man with a flattened nose – Tommy – had come up behind her.

'You're trespassing, miss.'

'She saw, Johnny boy. She saw.'

They were all back in the storeroom. Charlie, Reilly, Tommy, Hathaway and his father. The double doors were still open, the sun casting a thick slab of light across the battered wooden floor. Across the tub at Elaine's feet. Hathaway watched as Tommy poured the grey gloop into the cast-iron tub around Elaine's bare feet and legs.

Hathaway looked from his father to his girl-friend. Her eyes were so wide he thought they were going to pop from her head. He moved towards her but Reilly stepped in front of him.

Hathaway looked back over his shoulder. His father shrugged.

'You can't help her, John.'

Hathaway walked over to him.

'What are you doing?'

'You know what I'm doing. Once the cement sets we throw her in the sea and we don't have to worry about her talking.'

'What has she got to talk about?'

'She saw us deal with Cuthbert, John. That's the long and the short of it.' He put his hand on Hathaway's arm. 'And now it's time for you to step up.'

'What did she really see?' Hathaway said.

His father looked impatient.

'Don't be thick, boy. She's told us. She saw how sometimes we have to do business. She now has the power to destroy me. Us. We can't be having that.'

'Dad, you can't kill her for that.'

'Can't I? Why not exactly?'

'Dad, I love her.'

His father was transformed. His face turned red and a vein stood out on his neck.

'Don't dad me, you bloody disgrace of a son. You love her. Bring out the frigging violins. Be a man for a change. It needs to be done and that's the end of it.'

'Dad—'

'What did I just fucking say? You wanted this life. You begged me for it. Or was it just the fast cars and the flash clothes? We had a deal. You signed up for this. You want to call yourself my son?' On tiptoe, he pushed his face into Hathaway's. 'The only way you're going to be my son is if you kill her.'

'Killing Cuthbert I can understand. He's like us. But she's an innocent, she has no part in this. It's not fair.'

'Fair? Who gives a fuck about fair? If you wanted to keep her innocent you should have kept your prick in your pocket. The minute you nobbed her you compromised her.' He rubbed his eyes then glared at his son. 'She saw us. End of story.'

Elaine was crying, rocking from side to side.

'I won't tell anyone, I promise—'

Dennis Hathaway whirled on her.

218

'Do you think I'm stupid, you little cunt? Of course you'll promise now. They all promise now. But do you think I believe for one moment that the minute you're off this pier you won't blab? A well-brought-up, law-abiding girl like you.' He looked down at her legs squirming in the tub of concrete. Her skirt had ridden up. She was not wearing knickers. 'Darling, I've seen a bumbo before. Show me a trick with a donkey and I might be impressed. Now keep your fucking feet still!'

'She's not law-abiding,' Hathaway said, desperation in his voice.

His father turned back to him.

'What, because she mouths off a lot? Well, by her lights. Because she goes on anti-war demonstrations and smokes marijuana? Do me a favour.' He put his hands on Hathaway's arms. He lowered his voice. 'Listen. This has to be done. There is no room for manoeuvre. So the question is: who does it? You don't want her going into the drink alive, do you? So somebody has to snuff her. Now, I think it should be you for all kinds of reasons. One, because you can't just take from this racket, you have to give as well. And, two, because I thought that your feelings for her would mean you'd do it with a certain ... a certain ... what's the word I'm looking for, Charlie?'

'Compassion?'

'Compassion. That's it. Nice word. Thanks, Charlie.'

'My pleasure.'

Hathaway laughed harshly, an edge of hysteria

in his voice. He looked across at Elaine's distraught, pleading face.

'You think killing someone you love is compassionate?'

'You always hurt the one you love, Johnny boy – the songs tell us that. Never doubt the truths in popular music. '

'She won't talk. I give you my word. Put her in my keeping. We'll go off to India together.'

'You're not going anywhere. I need you here, even if you are turning into a nancy boy. We made a deal. You're going to inherit.'

'I don't want to inherit!'

'Don't you?' Hathaway senior moved to straddle a chair over by the table. 'Don't you? Then you lied to me. That's not the impression you've been giving me over the past couple of years. *Au* bloody *contraire*, if you'll excuse my French.'

Elaine was wrenched by sobs, her whole body heaving. The concrete was harder round her legs. Dennis Hathaway caught Hathaway looking.

'She's got lovely legs, John. You've been a lucky boy getting between them. But nothing comes free.'

Hathaway looked from Elaine to his father and around the room at the impassive faces. Only Charlie looked away.

'I can't kill her and I can't let anyone else kill her,' he said flatly.

Dennis Hathaway stood.

'I don't think you want to go there, Johnny. You being a coward is one thing, but that rather limits your options so far as anyone else doing

220

what you can't do is concerned.'

'John, please...' Elaine said, clear drool running from her nose over her mouth, wet eyes fixed on him. A supplicant.

'Someone wipe her bloody nose.' Dennis Hathaway looked at Elaine and shook his head. 'Dignity, darling, is everything.'

Dennis Hathaway looked back at his son, as Reilly took a blue handkerchief from his pocket and almost tenderly wiped at Elaine's upper lip and around her mouth. He folded the handkerchief once and dabbed beneath her eyes.

Hathaway watched, then looked over at Charlie, standing rigid against the wall. Could he enlist Charlie's help to overpower the others in the room and rescue Elaine? Even as he thought it, he realized what a ridiculous idea it was. He couldn't see himself fighting his own father and couldn't see Charlie helping.

His mind was racing. He did want the life his father was offering. He did want to be a name in Brighton. He did love Elaine. He did want to have sex with every other woman in Brighton. He did want to go to India with her. But the one thing he didn't want to do was kill this girl he knew so intimately and who knew him so intimately.

'I'm not going to do it.'

His father leaned on his knees and looked intently at his son for what seemed an age. Then he stood again.

'Well, some bugger has got to do it. What about you, Charlie? You want the life even more than Johnny here. You're his mate. Help me out.

221

Help him out. Take his place.'

Charlie flicked a glance from Hathaway to his father.

'Take his place?' He looked away. 'It's not my kind of thing. Anything else – you know I'm up for anything else—'

'It's not anyone's kind of thing,' Hathaway senior hissed. 'Unless you're a fucking psycho, of course, and I don't employ them. It's just part of the business. Something that has to be done.'

Charlie looked at Elaine, slumped in the chair, quiet now. He waved a hand at Dennis Hathaway.

'I can't, Mr Hathaway. I know her and everything.'

'I know you knew her. You did her.'

'No—'

'Course you fucking did,' he jeered. 'Last night you went for a quickie behind Johnny's back. If I were your age I'd be tempted, I tell you. She's a lovely-looking girl. Get those legs wrapped round you—'

'You can fuck me however you want as much as you want.'

Elaine was sitting up, glaring at Dennis Hathaway. She jerked her head back towards Tommy.

'I'll give head to your man here. Your men can have me –' her bravado ran out and she began to sob again – 'but please, please, don't—'

Dennis Hathaway had a look of disgust on his face.

'Jesus, someone put her out of her misery.' He looked at her. 'Darling, I'd love to fuck you but I'm happily married, and whilst I'll do most

222

things, I draw the line at doing my son's girl-friend, however much of a disappointment he is to me. I'm sure there must be a rule of etiquette about that.' He peered into the tub of concrete. 'Plus, how would I get your legs wide enough apart to stuff it in you, the concrete as set as it is?'

Hathaway saw a look pass between his father and Tommy. His father shook his head and went over to a table in the corner.

When Dennis Hathaway walked over to Charlie he had a gun in one hand and a garrotte in the other. He proffered them to Charlie.

'So you're not up to it? You're not capable of it?'

'There ain't nothing I'm not capable of.'

'A double negative. Thought your generation knew better than that.'

Charlie took the left hand, walked over to Elaine, tilted her head up and fired the gun full into her face.

'Fuck,' Dennis Hathaway said, one hand up to stop the spray of brain and blood hitting his face, 'I was hoping he'd use the garrotte. Now we've got to clean this bloody place up.'

Hathaway looked down.

'I'll do it.'

TWELVE

The Man Who Sold the World
1970

A gun is a seducer. A gun wants to be fired. It exists to be fired. And, sooner or later, whoever has one will be seduced into firing it.

Hathaway's father disappeared in 1970. He left without Hathaway's mother. Hathaway should not have been surprised by how devastated she was, but he was shocked at her rapid decline once she took to the bottle. He was overwhelmed when she took her own life just a year later, in the summer of 1971.

In February 1970 Dennis Hathaway took his son and Charlie to Spain on business. Reilly went along, of course. It was the first time Hathaway had seen the family hacienda in the mountains near Granada. It was a lovely house but the grounds were like a building site. They were a building site.

Dennis Hathaway was having a swimming pool built inside a long building constructed of local stone. The roof was going to be retractable, like something out of a James Bond film.

'More like *Thunderbirds*,' his father had said, guffawing. 'Watch your feet there. That cement's still wet. Don't want to see imprints of your big clodhoppers across the floor of the pool.'

'You're having it tiled, aren't you?'

'You bet – but even so.'

Hathaway's father was in a good mood because they'd just concluded a deal in Marbella to get hashish in large quantities from Morocco, transiting to England overland through Spain and France, then shipping from a small harbour near Deauville up to the West Pier.

Charlie was, as usual, cautious around Hathaway. They had a kind of working relationship but he knew Hathaway had never forgiven him for killing Elaine.

He was half-right. Hathaway was in a place that nobody he knew would understand. What did he feel about the death of Elaine? If he were honest, on its own he could take it. But there were other things.

His father was outlining his plans. Hathaway half-listened. He had his own plans.

They'd been drinking solidly all day. On the terrace, looking at the speckled sky and the lights winking down the valley, Hathaway watched his father take another swig of brandy.

'The Great Train Robbers never squealed on each other,' he said. 'Not a one. And the witnesses knew nothing. All they saw was a bunch of blokes in balaclavas and overalls. How could they identify anyone? Bloody hell, they didn't even know how many robbers there were. Nobody did.'

'But you do, Dad,' Hathaway said.

Dennis Hathaway got a strange expression on

225

his face.

'Makes you say that, son?'

'Something you said a while back. And I heard two got clean away.'

'You know that for a fact?' his father said.

Hathaway nodded drunkenly. Dennis Hathaway sniffed.

'Remember when your mother and I went down to Spain for our second honeymoon. Left you alone for your birthday?'

Hathaway remembered.

'I remember you coming back,' he said, thinking of Barbara.

That passed his father by.

'Well, I thought it best to be out of the country at that particular time.'

Hathaway thought back.

'It was around the time of the robbery. I remember reading the papers.'

'It was two days after the bloody robbery. We were supposed to be holing up at the farm for a couple of weeks, but we thought that one of the locals had got suspicious so we had to make other plans. We split the money. There was so much of it. It was all in fivers and single notes. We didn't even bother with the ten bob notes. Well, Bruce did but he was like that.'

'So you really were one of the Great Train Robbers?'

'No big deal.'

'And you took the loot to Spain.'

'Nah, not all of it. Any idea how much space a hundred and twenty-five thousand pounds in singles and fivers takes up?'

Hathaway shook his head.

'A fuck of a lot.'

'So what did you do?'

'That lovely Oxford Morris – remember it?'

Hathaway nodded.

'Had a false petrol tank and a false bottom to the back seat. Got the tip from a Kraut smuggler. Worked well for a couple of years. The rest – well, you know about the rest – you organized taking most of it over and converting it into diamonds, buying property and so on.'

Hathaway nodded.

'But where do you hide paperwork about stuff like that?'

His father gave him a sideways look.

'Why would you want to know a thing like that?'

'Because I remember you telling me that the less paper around the better. Property leaves a long paper trail, doesn't it?'

'Not if you pay cash, son.'

Hathaway looked across at Reilly. He was standing at the edge of the terrace, his back to the others, looking up into the snow-capped mountains.

Hathaway shot his father first. He hadn't intended to but it was just the way it fell out.

Hathaway had strolled behind Charlie, but his father saw the automatic he pulled from under his shirt and lunged for him.

His father didn't say anything, but thinking about it later Hathaway assumed he was trying to save Charlie. He actually chose Charlie over his own son. It didn't really help, even at the time.

His father came out of his chair, one arm stretched out for the gun, his head down. Hathaway shot him through the bald patch on the crown of his skull. It had looked like a target.

His father simply toppled forward and knelt on the marble tiles, his head touching them as if praying to Mecca.

Charlie, half-swinging to look over his shoulder, tilted his chair and toppled, getting it tangled in his legs.

He saw the gun in Hathaway's hand and started to scrabble away on his back, kicking at the chair. Hathaway aimed the gun loosely in his direction.

'Don't,' Hathaway whispered. He looked over at Reilly, still gazing up into the mountains.

Hathaway was registering the fact that the gun had made scarcely any sound. Later he would register the fact he'd killed his own father.

Charlie was motionless.

'We've had some times, Charlie.'

'We have,' Charlie said, his voice croaky.

'But then you killed my fucking girlfriend.'

'I'm sorry about that but it had to be done.'

'Oh Charlie. Don't sweat it. I've done far worse.'

Hathaway pointed the gun at Charlie's forehead.

'Goodbye, Charlie.'

PART TWO

Today

THIRTEEN

He stood at the back of the boat, watching the propeller churning the grey water. He had four men to help him take the boat. They killed the crew straight away. The owners were tied up in their stateroom. He would torture the man and rape the woman. He didn't think about which would please him more.

Once he was bored with her, he passed the woman on to his men. By the time they threw her overboard in the turbulent waters of the Bay of Biscay she wasn't good for much. They threw her head in somewhere off Vigo.

Morning seeping into the night. John Hathaway, crime king of Brighton, woke up sweating. He rolled out of bed without disturbing the girl. A mirror streaked with white powder on her bedside table. The air still as he stood on the balcony and looked over at the skeletal remains of the West Pier.

There was a long ship moving on the horizon, red lights winking at bow and stern. The sky whitening behind it. He looked at the stretch of water between the ship and the end of the pier.

The pier looked as if it was crumbling but iron and steel don't crumble. Wood, certainly. Buffeted by salt winds and sea water, wood warped, rotted, decayed to dust. A new coat of paint every six months had been the only way to keep the end-of-pier shooting gallery and amusement arcade looking halfway decent.

Hathaway earned his pocket money until he was fifteen up a ladder painting the exteriors of his father's end-of-pier attractions. He also painted his father's office, that draughty wooden hut with gaps in the floorboards wide enough to see the water churning far below. He could still smell the fug of the paraffin heaters as the fire-hazard stoves burned all day to keep the chill at bay.

The stanchions, the scaffolding, the pier's iron frame – they hadn't rotted. They had rusted, twisted, bent. Bolts had sheared off. The pier had crumpled, not crumbled. Eventually, it would collapse into the sea. The sea that, according to Hathaway's father, kept all secrets.

Hathaway sipped a glass of water, turning away from the ruin of the pier. He was thinking of the other theory about the sea: that eventually it threw up its secrets.

Usually when least expected. He knew from his own experience that most things happened when least expected. He had learned that preparation could be both essential and pointless. Lives were changed by the unexpected. Always.

He shivered. Last night he'd had the dream again. He was drowning, out there in the chill water, sinking into its terrible depths. Tugged down, then tangled in a glade of trees. But not trees. A forest of corpses. Arms waving, bodies

232

swaying with the tide. Men in rotting suits or naked. One, little more than a skeleton, with a pork-pie hat jammed on his skull.

Some were scrawny, some were fat. Some were gagged, mouths taped. Fish nibbled at them, sea worms writhed through empty eye sockets. Rooted, each of them, in cement poured in tin tubs.

Hathaway didn't know how many men his father had taken out in his motorboat and dropped into the sea. Didn't know the ratio of still alive to already dead. But the one he never dreamed about, the one he never saw, was the one he knew for certain had been dropped off the West Pier, her face shot away by Charlie.

Hathaway's mobile rang. He looked at the number, answered.

'Early morning, Ben.'

'Sorry, Mr Hathaway. Thought you'd want to know. Stewart Nealson is dead. In a very bad way.'

And so it began again.

The scene of crime was the Ditchling Beacon on the northern edge of the South Downs. When Detective Sergeant Sarah Gilchrist arrived at the National Trust car park she could see Ronnie Dickinson, the local community policeman, sitting on a stile some fifty yards away, looking like a stiff wind would blow him away. Reg Williamson, her sometime partner and now her superior officer, bulky in an ill-fitting suit, stood beside him. Both men were smoking.

The wind gusted at her coat when she got out

of her car. A crowd had gathered in the car park, some with dogs. She looked down at Ditchling, a cluster of rooftops set among fields a few hundred feet below.

Gilchrist pushed her way through the crowd and walked up towards the two policemen. As she neared the stile she saw beyond them, further along the chalky path, scene of crime officers in white bunny suits clustered around something hanging from a wooden frame.

'What's going on?' she said. Williamson offered her a cigarette. She shook her head. 'Two years, two months, three days,' she said. 'Get ye behind me, Satan.'

Ronnie looked winded and sick. His hands were trembling.

'You found him?' she said.

'I was summoned. By a dog-walker. In his own world. He resented the walk – it's his wife's dog really.'

His voice trailed off.

'Never seen anything like it,' Williamson said, looking over his shoulder. 'Not even on the telly.'

'So what's happened to him?'

'He was impaled,' Williamson said. 'A skewer put up his arse and out the other end.'

Gilchrist clenched her jaw.

'Out of his head?'

'No, his shoulder.'

'All the way through his body?' Gilchrist said, trying to imagine it and shuddering as she did so. 'So he'd die pretty quickly once the heart was pierced.'

'The dog-walker didn't get close enough to see what had happened,' Ronnie said. 'Thought he might have been crucified because of the way he's hanging. Just as well. We need to keep this quiet.'

'Isn't crucifixion bad enough?' Gilchrist said.

'Yes, but to have someone killed like this – can't you see the headlines? "Vlad the Impaler loose on the Sussex Downs".'

Gilchrist was watching the bunny suits as they lowered the body to the ground.

'You'd be able to see that for miles around, being so high up,' she said.

'That was probably the idea,' Williamson said.

'Who's Vlad the Impaler when he's at home?'

'Ancestor of Dracula,' Williamson said. 'Some Rumanian prince back in the middle ages who fought against the Turks. Favourite punishment was to stick prisoners on the end of a spike. Let their body weight do the rest.'

Gilchrist grimaced.

'God. Do we know who the victim is?'

'Didn't get close enough to find out,' Ronnie said. 'I thought it was more important to keep people away.'

'Probably right.' Gilchrist frowned. 'How do you get from pushing a stick up somebody to drinking their blood from a bite on the neck?'

Williamson shrugged.

'I'm more of a sci-fi fan myself.'

He looked beyond Gilchrist.

'Here they come.' He saw her look at the journalists heading their way. 'The jackals.'

* * *

235

Brighton took a battering that afternoon. A storm came up, a high tide threshing the beaches, hammering at the clubs and bars on the lower promenade, slopping up on to the Kings Road, running from the Palace Pier to Portslade. By the evening the lower town was blanketed in fog. The frets clothed the seafront bars and restaurants, groping along the Old Steine and Middle Street, faltering at the steep slopes up to Seven Dials and the back end of town.

Ex-Chief Constable Bob Watts stood on the steps of the Grand Hotel watching the water sluice through the fog only to run out of energy halfway across the road.

The Kings Road was understandably quiet. However, Watts thought he could hear across the road, above the thrash and racket of the sea, the high drone of a motorboat. He listened to its engine cutting in and out in the wind. He started to turn. He was drawn back by faint flashes of light in the fog. Behind the fog. He watched them burst and die. He thought he heard the motorboat again. He went into the hotel.

He bought a gin and tonic in the ornate bar and took a table in a quiet corner. He was due to meet with Laurence Kingston, the chair of the West Pier Syndicate, the body that was raising money to refurbish the pier. Rebuild it, really. Watts had been made a committee member when he was chief constable and it was one of the few bodies that had not asked him to resign after his down-fall. The Syndicate had just been given a promise of £20 million from the Lottery Fund. Several million in private money had also been pledged.

However, Kingston had phoned Watts out of the blue asking to meet privately to discuss the fund raising. He'd implied there was a problem.

Kingston, a fussy man, was usually punctilious about time but fifteen minutes after he and Watts had arranged to meet he had still not arrived. Watts assumed the frets had something to do with it.

He was thinking about his wife, Molly, from whom he'd been separated since his one-night stand with DS Sarah Gilchrist had been made public in the aftermath of the Milldean massacre. He hoped they could find a way to get back together, but things were on hold for the moment as she'd gone to stay with her sister in Vancouver. It was part of her drink cure – she'd been drinking heavily before they broke up but had given up soon after. Watts felt guilty that he had clearly driven her to drink and was impressed by her new strength of will.

He had promised that he would keep a closer eye on their son, Tom, and daughter, Catherine, whilst she was away. Not that they cared, both off at university and critical of his behaviour. Catherine was coming down to Brighton at the weekend but he wasn't sure if he was going to see her. A fashionable DJ who lived locally was hosting his annual party on the beach. Last time the entire town had been gridlocked as thousands of people hit the party.

A man sat down on a nearby sofa. Tall, broad-shouldered, with close-cropped hair. In his early sixties, Watts judged. Watts saw that someone had done some work on his face, probably with a Stanley knife.

The man's top lip was puckered where it had been sliced open then sewn back together. His right nostril too had been sliced and sewn back, and there was a line down to his jaw that could have been mistaken for a laugh line if it weren't so prominent. From the side, Watts could see his nose had been broken. There was a tattoo covering the back of his hand and his wrist, peeking out of his shirt cuff.

The man put a mobile phone to his ear and began a murmured conversation. Watts had more of his drink and looked across the room. It was quiet, with a mix of foreign and British tourists, some of them looking stiff and awkward in the elegant surroundings.

His father, Victor Tempest, the once best-selling thriller writer, had told him that when they lived in Sussex this had been his favourite bar as he liked to watch the London villains flash their cash. Watts preferred somewhere more informal himself.

Across the room he recognized a man with a small moustache and a self-important posture. He looked at him for a beat too long. The man looked back and his eyes widened. He stood and walked over to Watts.

'Ex-Chief Constable,' the man said, standing over him. 'How nice to see you.'

'Well, well – Winston Hart, Chair of the Police Authority.'

'You must be relieved it's all done and dusted.'

'Milldean? Swept under the carpet, don't you

238

mean?'

'Still banging on, then,' Hart said.

'Still a pompous twit, I see,' Watts said.

Hart tugged at the corner of his moustache.

'What are you doing these days?' Hart said.

'I'm pretty busy,' Watts said.

'On the motivational speaker circuit?'

Watts laughed.

'Never realized you had a sense of humour, Hart. How's your son?'

Hart flushed. His illegitimate son, Gary Parker, had murdered and dismembered a flatmate and was now confined in a secure establishment.

Watts's phone rang. He picked it up from the table beside his drink.

'Excuse me,' he said. 'Good to see you.'

Hart walked back to his table. Watts was expecting his caller to be Laurence Kingston apologizing for being late. It was Jimmy Tingley, his friend and deadly comrade-in-arms.

'I've just heard that Stewart Nealson has been killed.'

'Sorry to hear that. Who's Stewart Nealson?'

'Remember the grass we met in the Cricketers with his partner, Edna the Inebriated Woman?'

'The accountant for Brighton's crime gangs?'

'That's the one.'

'And he's been murdered?'

'In a rather nasty way, apparently. I don't have the exact details but he was found up near Ditchling Beacon.'

Watts glanced back to the sofa as he was listening to Tingley. The scarred man had gone.

FOURTEEN

Anna went to the kitchen first, as usual. She was surprised that the radio was already on but she was late this morning. It was tuned to the local radio station, Southern Shores. There was a smell of gas so she checked the cooker. Everything was turned off. She opened a window to let the smell disperse.

As she filled the dishwasher she listened to the news broadcast. Since she'd arrived in Britain she'd improved her English best by listening to the radio. A lot of the colloquialisms still went over her head but she understood more each day.

'A man was found murdered in horrific circumstances by a dog-walker on Ditchling Beacon yesterday morning. Police haven't yet released the man's identity or the exact details of his death, but there is speculation that he may have been crucified.'

Crucified? Did she hear that correctly? Like Our Lord Jesus Christ? Anna shuddered and finished loading the dishwasher. She left its door open whilst she went through to the living room for the wine glasses she was sure would be there. Mr Kingston enjoyed entertaining and his friends all seemed to enjoy wine.

'The council has released details of the

arrangements for dealing with Saturday's Party on the Beach...'

The phone started to ring. Anna screamed.

Laurence Kingston lay by his gas fire, impeccably dressed in a smoking jacket and cravat. His mouth was open. His tongue hung from it, bent at an odd angle, lolling obscenely over his cheek.

Kate Simpson held her phone against her ear with her shoulder as she typed the 'News Just In' into the system. She could see through the glass that, in the studio, Steve, the morning show presenter, had clocked it. The phone rang on without Laurence Kingston, chair of the West Pier Syndicate, picking it up.

'Just in,' Steve said. 'Bad news for the West Pier. If you've been along the prom this morning you'll have seen that yesterday's storms have brought down the middle section and done damage to other sections of the already battered pier. This will be bad news for the West Pier Syndicate who have just got money in place to restore the pier to its former glory. We hope to have a comment from the Syndicate's chairman, Laurence Kingston, in the next news report.'

'Not if I can't get him, we won't,' Kate muttered.

She'd been trying Kingston for the past half-hour but she only had his landline. For all she knew, Kingston was already out at the pier surveying the latest wreckage.

'Can't raise him, Steve,' she said through the headphones. 'We don't have his mobile.'

241

'It's big news, Katie – find him.'

Find him. Kate looked up the West Pier Syndicate and found a list of its committee members. There was one familiar name. She phoned ex-Chief Constable Bob Watts.

Sarah Gilchrist was looking at the autopsy report for Stewart Nealson, the man found at Ditchling Beacon. Reg Williamson was looking out of the window, his head tilted to see further down the seafront.

'West Pier is pretty much gone after yesterday's storm,' he said.

'He lived for a few hours – can you imagine?'

'Vlad's victim?'

'Reg!'

'Once the news is out you know that's what he's going to be called.'

'The stake was angled so that it missed all vital organs. Missed the heart, the liver, the kidneys.'

'Was that by chance, do you think, Sarah?'

'The alternative is that these guys knew what they were doing. And that's alarming.'

'You think it was more than one person?'

'Don't you? That frame? Holding him down – I don't see it as a one-person job. And digging that deep hole in the flint must have been a real pain.'

'Are CSI telling us anything else?'

'They're still up there. It's pretty unforgiving ground, though, so don't hold your breath.'

Gilchrist's phone rang.

'It's Bob Watts.'

She coloured.

242

'Hello. Is this a social call?'

'Alas, not,' he said. 'Two things. Have you time?'

'Well—'

'Won't take long. Kate Simpson just phoned me for Laurence Kingston's mobile number. The radio wants a quote about the further collapse of the West Pier. Thing is, Kingston stood me up last night, which is not like him, and I've not been able to raise him since then.'

'Laurence Kingston,' Gilchrist repeated, indicating to Williamson to write the name down.

'And the second thing?'

'I was down by the West Pier before I was due to meet Kingston and I saw some flashes of light in the fog. And perhaps the sound of a motor-boat.'

Gilchrist frowned.

'What are you saying?'

'Well, thinking about it, I believe the pier was firebombed.'

'Firebombed?'

Williamson looked over as he tapped keys on his computer's keyboard. Then he looked back at the screen and scribbled something down.

'It won't be the first time,' Watts said.

The West Pier had been firebombed twice before in the past couple of years.

Williamson handed his note to Gilchrist.

'OK, I'll pass it along,' Gilchrist said to Watts. She scanned Williamson's note. 'And I'm afraid Kingston won't be answering his phone. I'm sorry, Bob. His cleaner found him this morning. A death by suicide.'

243

* * *

Kate Simpson was stymied until Kingston phoned her back. Steve was blaghing on, in his mid-morning banal flow. She glanced at the morning newspaper and her father's name jumped out at her. Government adviser William Simpson to be given new responsibilities. She pushed the newspaper away. She'd been avoiding facing the fact that her father was somehow implicated in the Milldean massacre. In the course of the investigation she had found out more about her father than any daughter should have to know.

She was finding it difficult to deal with.

Steve buzzed through.

'Are you seeing these emails about the West Pier?'

Kate looked at her screen.

'People are reporting seeing flashes of light in the fog. There are suggestions the pier might have been firebombed again.'

John Hathaway was sitting on the deck of his boat, taking in the late afternoon sun. The boat was his secret hideaway, although anyone serious about tracking him down would have no trouble finding it, as it was usually moored just a few hundred yards from his bar in Brighton marina.

He did usually take the minor precaution of never coming out on deck until he was a mile or so out at sea, as he was now. But he knew that was stupid, as anyone could see him getting on the boat in the first place.

244

He looked at the men facing him in a semi-circle. Smart lads, every one. He never just hired muscle, those bulked-up idiots from the local gyms who spent their nights standing outside pubs and nightclubs.

These men were ex-military and all had some semblance of a brain.

'Stewart Nealson is dead,' he said, 'Tortured and killed in a particularly horrible way. Not all of you know him, so for those who don't: he's our accountant and the accountant of a couple of other gentlemen in our line of work. His death jeopardizes our plan – and, indeed, may have come about because somebody suspected our plans.'

'Fuck,' Gavin said. He was a carrot-top and the sun had brought his freckles out. 'Is that why he was tortured?'

'Possibly.'

'How'd they know to get suspicious?'

Hathaway shrugged.

'Stew was discreet but he might have said something that somebody picked up on.'

'But you're not calling it off?'

'Of course not.' Hathaway had heard the early reports of the West Pier suffering further injury. 'In fact I'm more determined than ever. But we'll have to do a little more planning, just in case.'

'The basic plan remains the same?'

'Absolutely. I wanna hit them where it really hurts. Teach them a *big* bloody lesson.'

Ex-Chief Constable Bob Watts was sitting in a

meeting with the deputy chair of the West Pier Syndicate. Theresa Henderson had heavily gelled hair. She was wearing a tight-fitting red trouser suit. Watts thought she looked like a distaff Hillary Clinton. He wasn't sure how she made her money but he knew she had plenty of it. She leaned forward and parted her scarlet lips in a smile.

'Bob, we could do with some informal help here.'

Watts looked at Henderson warily. He liked her but he didn't trust her.

'Help with what?'

'The damage to the West Pier.'

Watts waited. She clasped her hands and leaned forward.

'We're going to have a nightmare with the insurance company on the pier. We need to be clear what has happened.'

Watts looked out of the window. They were sitting in The Ship sharing a pot of coffee. People hurried by outside, struggling with the gusting wind.

'I believe you have a notion the pier was firebombed,' Henderson said.

He looked at her. He'd never got the point of hair stiffened with gel or spray. He imagined for a moment trying to run his hand through her hair. His fingers would get stuck about a centimetre in.

'I'm certain of it,' he said. 'A fire in a storm hardly makes sense otherwise. We both know the Palace Pier people aren't happy about any competition from the West Pier development.

246

Everyone assumes they firebombed it twice before. Who else is it going to be?'

'The situation could be more complicated than that,' Henderson said.

'In what way?'

'You're the policeman. Don't you think it likely that it's connected to the death of our Chair? Rather an odd coincidence that he should die on the same morning.'

'Coincidences do happen but I take your point,' Watts said. 'In what way connected, though? What aren't you telling me?'

'We think there might have been something fraudulent going on.'

'Laurence? You know he asked to see me the night of the storm but he didn't show up.'

'I didn't know,' Henderson said, sitting straighter. 'But, yes, we think it was Laurence.'

'"We" being?'

'Alec Henry and me.'

Alec Henry was the West Pier Syndicate's treasurer. Watts looked at Henderson. She grimaced.

'We're talking twenty million pounds here, so I guess that's a temptation for anyone.'

'Do you know what he'd done?'

'Not exactly. We just know there's something weird going on with the grants for the development.'

'What kind of weird?'

'Possibly fraud on a massive level. The thing is, if it gets out the whole project will be in jeopardy.'

'You want me to hush it up? That's not really

247

what I do.'

Henderson looked at him for a long moment. Watts guessed she was thinking he'd somehow hushed up what happened in Milldean. He didn't say anything.

Henderson leaned forward. 'Do you know the name John Hathaway?'

Watts nodded.

'What do you know about him?'

'A major player in Brighton. Almost certainly a major criminal, though he's never seen the inside of a prison cell. He's involved?'

'His name has come up a couple of times.'

Watts looked out of the window again.

'OK. I'll look into it.'

The UK coastguard found the blood-spattered boat drifting at dawn, within sight of Brighton's piers. Gilchrist saw the report flash on to her screen. She shouted over to Reg Williamson:

'Listen to this. The UK coastguard have boarded a boat that was drifting off the coast of Brighton, swept into shore by yesterday's storm. A luxury cruiser registered in Ravenna. The boat was deserted except for the carcase of the owner, an Italian industrialist hanging from the wheel.' She read on. 'Ugh.'

'What?'

'He was naked. Worse than naked. '

'How worse?' Williamson said.

'He had been skinned.'

'Jesus. Did someone send us back to the Dark Ages and not tell me? One guy gets impaled, another gets skinned.' He thought for a moment.

'I don't like to ask, but did they find the skin?'

'Doesn't say. Blood everywhere. His wife, a former actress twenty years his junior, and the crew are missing.'

'And the perpetrators?'

'The dinghy from the vessel is missing. I assume they came ashore somewhere.'

'In Brighton, do you think?'

'Who knows? But don't you think two such barbaric crimes must be linked?'

Williamson reached for a cigarette.

'I've a horrible feeling they are.'

FIFTEEN

Jimmy Tingley, ex-SAS, current status ambiguous, telephoned Bob Watts, disgraced ex-chief constable of the Southern police force. Watts said:

'I'm on the train,' then wished he hadn't.

He was looking out of the window as the train crossed the high viaduct just beyond Haywards Heath. He loved the view across to Ardingly College and its Gothic chapel. He eased his neck in the stiff collar of his shirt. He was thinking about the West Pier but he was dressed for an interview. Funds were running low and he needed to get a proper job.

'Nealson died in a memorable way.' Tingley said.

The train went into a deep cutting. Watts frowned at his reflection in the train window.

'Hello?'

Watts waited, glancing down at the front page of the *Guardian*. The second lead announced the imminent publication of the report into the Milldean Massacre, in which four civilians had been shot and killed by armed police. He was aware of the rush of the train above the wavering phone signal. His phone rang again.

'There are tunnels coming up,' he said. 'I may lose you. You said memorable?'

'To you and me.'

Watts frowned.

'What do you mean?'

'I mean,' said Tingley and the signal was snatched away. But Watts had clearly heard: 'Vlad the Impaler.'

Watts looked down at his phone. Then at the tremor in his hand.

After his interview, Watts phoned Tingley.

'How did it go?' Tingley said.

'Pointless. Who wants a disgraced cop?'

'Sorry.'

'Did you say Vlad?'

'I did.'

'Can you meet?'

'Where?'

'Cricketers?'

'Nah – I've moved on. Let's meet in the Bath Arms.'

'Big change.'

'It's a couple of hundred yards away. And it

250

has free wi-fi.'

'Don't give me too many shocks at once, Jimmy. New pub and new technology? Next you'll be drinking a proper drink.'

Watts phoned Sarah Gilchrist next.

'I'm meeting Jimmy in the Bath Arms. Want to join us?'

'No offence intended, Bob, but some of us work for a living.'

'This *is* work. We can help you with Stewart Nealson's kebabbing.'

Tingley looked pretty banged up.

'You OK?' Watts said, sitting down beside him. Tingley had a laptop on the table in front of him. The light from the screen gave him a terrible pallor and highlighted the black around his eyes.

'Lost focus – my mistake.'

'Where?' Watts said. Tingley was a gun for hire and the government sent him to all the world's hotspots.

Tingley took his drink.

'Rum and pep. Loverly.'

Tingley, discreet as ever.

'What's with the high-tech?' Watts said.

'It's all about intel. You know that, Bobby.'

'And what intel are you looking at?'

'Vlad the Impaler. I've been thinking about this. Those two in the bed?'

Watts nodded. The police operation that had gone disastrously wrong in the Milldean suburb of Brighton and had wrecked Watts's career. It had been the armed entry into a house to arrest an armed robber. In the course of the operation four unarmed civilians had been shot dead. One had been identified as a local male prostitute but the others had never been identified. DNA indicated that two of them – a man and a woman who had been in bed together – were from somewhere in the Balkans.

'So now the Serbian mafia have come for payback.'

'Do you think Vlad could really be here?' Watts said.

Tingley stared straight ahead.

'God, I hope so.'

The Bath Arms was on the junction of two of the laines. A jewellers faced one side of it, a church converted into a pub the other. Watts and Tingley saw Gilchrist walk past the church in her civvies through a jumble of people. Jeans, white T-shirt and leather jacket were her off-duty uniform. She came into the pub, saw them, then about-turned and went out again.

'Excuse me a sec,' she called over her shoulder. She approached two people. One of them scowled, one of them grinned, then both moved away.

'Pickpockets,' she said when she rejoined the men. 'All this jostling makes easy pickings.'

'That's very proactive of you,' Watts said.

She smiled.

'Just didn't want to disturb our meeting by having to nick 'em. They'll be back when we've gone, and in the meantime they'll just shift shop to the North Laines.'

Watts looked at her hands. Her right fist was

tightly clenched.

'My dad used to come here in the thirties,' he said. 'Selling information to the papers about the Brighton Trunk Murder.'

His father, Donald, successful thriller writer under the name Victor Tempest, had been a bobby on the beat in Brighton in the early 1930s. Watts tried to picture him now as a young man propping up the bar.

'This Stewart Nealson thing,' Gilchrist said. 'He was alive when he was found. They'd taken great care to miss the vital organs – the stake didn't touch any of them.'

'How long had he been impaled?' Watts said.

'All night.'

'Poor sod.'

'You know the worst thing?'

'Worse than that?'

She nodded.

'What?'

'To have done it like that means they had obviously done it before.'

Tingley and Watts looked at each other.

'Takes you back,' Watts said.

'Doesn't it just.'

Gilchrist looked from one to the other.

'What do you know about this?'

'You know you said there was a theory those two in the bed in Milldean massacre were Albanian,' Watts said.

She nodded.

'Any chance they could be Serbian?'

She shrugged.

'You two going to tell me what you know and

253

I don't?'

Watts gestured to Tingley.

'The historical, fifteenth-century Vlad the Impaler was Rumanian. Transylvanian actually. He ruled Wallachia. He's supposed to have been the source for the Dracula myth.'

'So I've heard. He was a vampire. How have you picked up on this guy's nickname so quickly?'

Tingley ignored her question.

'Actually, the historical Vlad was best known for resisting the expansion of the Ottoman Empire. And for his cruel punishments. Pretty cruel age, though. His elder brother was blinded with hot iron stakes and buried alive. When Vlad came to power he burned people alive, decapitated many – but most of all he impaled hundreds.'

'I don't get the Dracula link.'

'The family name was Dracul.'

'OK. But now you think he's loose on the South Downs. You're sure you haven't been spending too much time in Lewes?'

'Jimmy and I served in the Balkans in the nineties,' Watts said. 'I was with the UN peacekeeping forces; Jimmy was doing – well, what Jimmy does. That's when we first encountered another Vlad, real name Miladin Radislav.'

Watts had been stationed in Travnik, a hilltop village just north of Visegrad in Bosnia. He had been staggered by the wild beauty of this mountain region, where hamlets clung to the crags and steep valley sides, and the river Drina below seemed to burst out of a wall of rock. Travnik was a village of plum orchards and the scent of fruit was everywhere.

'There was a famous – and staggeringly beautiful – stone bridge over the Drina at Visegrad, built centuries earlier by the Turks using Christian slaves when the Ottoman Empire ruled the area. Muslims, Catholic Christians, Orthodox Christians and some Jews had, for most of the time since then, co-existed harmoniously in the town.

'All that changed with the civil war. Spring 1992. Visegrad was of strategic importance because the bridge took the road from Saravejo to Belgrade over the Drina. There was also a hydroelectric dam nearby that provided electricity to the area and prevented the Drina flooding towns and villages further down the valley.

'Over half the town's twenty thousand or so people were Bosniaks – Bosnian Muslims. A third were Serbians. The rest a mix of ethnicities. When Serbia got its appetite for empire building the JNA – the largely Serbian Yugoslav People's Army – bombarded the Bosniak neighbourhoods and nearby Bosniak villages. Some Bosniaks responded by taking local Serbian bigwigs hostage and taking over the dam. The JNA sent commandos in. They recaptured the dam and freed the hostages.

'The JNA occupied the town for a month or so. When they left they put the local Serbs in charge.'

'Then it started,' Tingley said. 'Local Serbs, police and paramilitaries decided to get rid of the entire Bosniak population. They were the paramilitaries known as the "White Eagles" and "Avengers" – linked to the ultra-nationalist Serbian Radical Party of Vojislav Seselj. They were avenging slights that had happened centuries before.'

'They wanted to kill all twenty thousand?' Gilchrist was pale.

'They probably would have if they could. They attacked all the nearby Bosniak villages and killed whoever they found. Every day they marched Bosniak men, women and children on to the bridge – that beautiful bridge – and killed them, dumping their bodies in the river. They looted and destroyed the homes. They blew up the town's two mosques.

'They systematically raped the women. They imprisoned the rest of the Bosniaks in various detention sites. The most unfortunate were housed in a concentration camp where they were beaten, tortured and forced to work. They were all sexually assaulted, of course.'

'Terrible,' Gilchrist whispered, her jaw tight.

'They herded Bosniaks into a couple of houses then threw grenades through the windows. They burned them alive in other houses. The worst of the atrocities were done by this guy, Radislav. He'd been a barber in Visegrad. He was one of those psychopaths the war let loose. He ran amok. He tortured and raped children of both sexes. Murdered with gleeful ferocity.'

Watts's voice was toneless:

'His men dragged people through the streets tied to the rear bumpers of cars. They ripped out people's kidneys. They took truckloads of people down to the Drina, shot them or knifed them in the guts then pushed them in. For target practice they threw children from the bridge and tried to shoot them before they hit the water.'

'But why the name Vlad?'

'That came after the UN arrived,' Watts said. 'He retreated with his band of men into the mountains, dragging their loot with them.'

A month later, Watts received word that Radislav's band had returned to his village. Watts was ordered to get to Visegrad as soon as possible. Radislav's gang had gone far beyond rape and beatings this time. This one had to be seen to be believed.

Watts and his squadron went down the mountain in four vehicles. It was a blustery day, clouds scudding between the mountain tops. The road was on the whole good, although they passed bombed-out and fire-destroyed houses. At two points they had to skirt deep bomb craters.

They approached the town from the other side of the river, winding down through the hills. The green water roared between the arches of the old bridge. The soldiers' attention was drawn to what looked like a dozen statues in a row on a parapet raised some eight feet above the highest point of the bridge.

As the vehicles dropped down closer to the river they could see that the statues were in crude wooden frames. As they came on to the bridge their progress was halted by a large group of people, looking in horror at the statues, women keening and howling, men tearing at their clothes. A handful of peacekeepers in their bright blue helmets had formed a perimeter in front of the statues. Tingley was standing beside them.

Watts quit his vehicle and led his men through the throng. He could see now that the statues were men hanging in a line from long poles. A corporal stepped away from the perimeter. He was red-faced.

'Bosnian-Serbs came out of the mountains in the night and raided the village. These are the young Muslim men they found here.'

'Why do they look so stiff?' Watts said.

'They've been impaled,' the corporal said. 'Last night.' He gulped. 'Two were still alive this morning.'

Watts looked up at the sky and at the mountains. He looked at Tingley. Tingley shook his head.

'He got the name Vlad the Impaler that day,' Tingley said. 'The lads weren't hot on geography. But Radislav wasn't inspired by Vlad. He was taking revenge for a Christian from his village who had been impaled by the local Muslims five hundred years earlier.'

'Jesus,' Gilchrist said.

'Radislav took off back into the mountains,' Tingley said, 'I tracked him but never caught him.'

'The coastguards have found a blood-soaked boat with a horribly mutilated body on board,' Gilchrist said. 'An Italian industrialist. It seems the boat was boarded in the Adriatic. It was Radislav, wasn't it?'

258

Tingley and Watts exchanged glances.

'Probably,' Tingley said.

Gilchrist shuddered.

'And he's only just started,' Watts said. 'I don't think the police can handle somebody like him.'

Tingley touched his swollen face and grimaced.

'Well, someone has got to take him on.'

Gilchrist looked at the two men.

'Now hang on – don't you two vigilantes go getting any ideas. We don't need you riding to the rescue. This is police business.'

She started to rise.

'I've got to feed this information back, alert some other agencies.'

'There was something else I wanted to talk to you about,' Watts said.

Gilchrist paused.

'It pales in comparison to these horrors but I've been asked to investigate the death of the chair of the West Pier Trust.'

'Great. No offence, Bob, but how are you going to do that?'

'Just ask around.'

'You know I can't help you. I'm a full-time police officer. I can't get involved in private investigations. Plus, I've got enough on my plate if this Radislav is going to kick things off.'

'That wasn't exactly what I had in mind.'

'Then what?'

SIXTEEN

Kate Simpson had joined a scuba club that had been diving in and around Brighton bay looking at wrecks of fishing boats. She loved it, although it needed a clear day to see anything. Phil, the guy who ran the club, was ex-Navy but he now made a good living as a salvage diver. He had a bit of a soft spot for her.

He phoned her one evening when she was practising for a supper she was having at the weekend. Specifically, she was contemplating the mess she'd made of her first attempt to stuff a chicken breast.

'I've been asked to get a crew together to check out the damage the firebombing did under the West Pier. See if there's risk of further collapse. Wondered if you wanted to tag along?'

Kate was a competent diver. She'd got her qualifications at university and had become obsessed with the sport. She'd been rusty when she joined the scuba club but had quickly got the hang of things again. Even so, the storm would have thrown up a lot of shit that would take weeks to settle. Visibility would be poor and if the pier was damaged under the water the dive could be dangerous.

'Am I qualified for that kind of dive?' she said.

'Well, I thought you could stay out of the water until me and a couple of the pro-divers had checked it out, Then you could come and have a look.'

'Will there be anything to see?'

'There's always something. Interested?'

'You're on.'

The dive was on Saturday morning. When Kate got down to the marina she was surprised to see Bob Watts waiting with the others. He grinned when he saw her and gave her a hug.

Their friendship was complicated by the fact that Kate was the daughter of a man he despised. His former friend, William Simpson. Watts was convinced that Simpson, a senior government figure, had been involved in planning the Milldean massacre but he had been unable to prove it. Kate had her own issues with her father.

In addition, Kate and Watts had led the research into the 1934 Brighton Trunk Murders the previous year. She had discovered among old police files an anonymous memoir that, it transpired, had been written by Watts's father, Donald Watts aka Victor Tempest.

'You're full of surprises,' she said. 'I didn't know you were a diver.'

'Nor I you. And, actually, I'm not. I'm just along for the ride. The West Pier Syndicate has tasked me with the job of checking out the damage. I'm the client.' He hesitated for the moment. 'It could be hazardous down there, Kate. Are you sure you—'

'She'll be fine,' said a tall, slender man with

close-cropped hair and startling blue eyes. He leaned over and gave Kate a peck on the cheek, then shook Watts's hand.

'Bob.'

'Phil. I know she's in capable hands.'

'Plus she knows what she's doing.'

'I am standing right here, you know,' Kate said, only half-joking.

Watts coloured.

'I'm sorry, Kate.' He looked around at the half a dozen people gathered round the boat. 'You good to go?'

'Good to go,' Phil said.

The boat was capable of high speeds but Phil kept it steady, heading first out to sea then diagonally into the West Pier. He dropped anchor about fifty yards from the ruined end of the pier. The water was choppy and the boat dipped and rolled.

'We're going to focus on this end today. Kate, you'll come in after we've done the initial exploration.'

The divers had digital video cameras with them. For the next two hours they did fifteen-minute shifts. Visibility was better than expected. Kate went down a couple of times and Watts stayed by the monitors on board ship. He was able to communicate with the divers on an audio link.

Phil's camera was focused on the seabed near to a big rusty stanchion. Watts peered as the monitor homed in on what looked like two iron rods sticking out of the seabed. Particles swirling like a blizzard around the lens.

Phil reached down and dug around their base. More particles obscured the picture. When the lens cleared Watts could see that Phil was holding something at arm's length in front of the camera.

Watts peered, trying to make out what it was. Kate looked over his shoulder. Phil was holding a human skull.

'The Brighton Trunk Murder victim,' Kate said, certainty in her voice. Although there was one story that the victim's head had been sighted over in Black Rock, nobody knew for sure. At the time the lack of a head on the body had prevented the police identifying the victim and hence solving the crime.

Phil came up five minutes later.

'Any other bones?' Watts said.

'I think those two rods are actually shin bones. And I found a foot. I left it all in situ.'

'Is there a wreck or something there?'

Phil shook his head.

'Any idea what age?'

'At this stage, of course not, but probably no more than a hundred years old.'

'What makes you say that?'

Phil glanced at Kate.

'Because there is what appears to be the remains of an old galvanised tin bath down there. That's what the feet and shins are in, encased in what was once concrete.'

'I don't understand,' Kate said. 'Her legs were found at King's Cross.'

'It's what I believe Chicago gangsters used to call a cement corset. During the Prohibition they got rid of business rivals by sticking their feet in quick-drying cement then dumping them in Lake Michigan. You like to hope they killed them first but I'm sure some of them went in alive.'

'Jesus,' Kate said.

'We'd better notify the police,' Watts said. 'You may have just uncovered a crime scene, Phil.'

The next day Bob Watts got a phone call from Karen Hewitt, his successor as chief constable of Southern Police.

'Bob. It's Karen. I wondered if you might like to do a bit of work for us?'

'I'm not a policeman anymore, Karen.'

'We can sort something out.'

'You want me to investigate the Milldean Massacre?'

'I'd be grateful if you'd get that right out of your head. It's done and dusted.'

'Not by me.'

'This force has moved on and so should you.'

'How are you liking my job?'

'Bob.'

'OK. Sorry. What work are you talking about?'

'I believe you were at the crime scene uncovered near Brighton pier yesterday.'

'I'm on the West Pier committee.'

'I know – and you're liaising between the Syndicate, the insurance company and the police about the firebombing.'

'I am.'

'Well, those remains. Whoever it is has been down there a long time. Essentially, anything we

264

do will be as a cold case. I don't have the staff here to examine cold cases—'

'So you wondered if I'd like to take it on. I'd love to.'

'You would?' Hewitt said, surprised.

'Only connect, Karen, only connect.'

The meeting with the grass's partner, Edna the Inebriated Woman, was painful. Her actual name was Dana and she looked like death herself, shivering on the sofa. Tingley, in Watt's experience the most undemonstrative of men, put his arm round her and held her as she sobbed on to his shoulder. She was much taller than Tingley so it looked slightly ridiculous, but Watts was moved nevertheless.

She and Nealson lived in Preston Park in a big Edwardian semi. She'd been slow to come to the door but ushered them in readily enough.

'Will you excuse me?' she said when she'd taken them into a cluttered sitting room.

She was away ten minutes. Watts and Tingley sat side by side on a long sofa and scanned the room. Crumbs on the floor, magazines strewn around, used glasses on every surface.

When she came back into the room her face was a ghastly mess of pancake make-up and red-rimmed eyes. She saw Watts looking round the room.

'Cleaner's year off,' she said. She had a glass in her hand, almost full to the brim with a clear liquid Watts assumed to be vodka.

'As you've probably guessed, I'm an addict,' she said.

'You cope?' Watts said.

'Do I? I don't know. It's a heavy blanket. Anything that requires effort, more especially anything that requires emotion, and this blanket drops on me.'

She took a sip of the drink. Watts knew from observing his wife Molly that alcoholics always started slow.

'Do you know who might have wanted to harm your husband?'

'He wasn't my husband. I'd never marry him. I still have some self-respect.'

She picked at the chair arm with a long crimson fingernail.

'How long were you together?' Tingley said.

'Ten years. He looked after me. He knew I didn't love him. Can't love anybody. But he looked after me. Didn't get much in return. Can't even give a decent blow job these days.'

Watts dropped his eyes.

'How did you meet?' he said.

'Don't remember.' She put her drink down carefully on the coffee table and leaned forward. 'I see most things in a haze. My memory is pretty much shot. Conversations had, arrangements made – forget it. So your next question will be: what good am I? It's a question I ask myself all the time.'

'Dana—'

'I've got a dyke friend who prefaces almost everything she says with "As a lesbian". Fuck's sake, just get on with it. But then I think, I'm the same. As an alcoholic ... so bloody tedious.' She looked at Tingley as if he had said something.

'Am I promiscuous? I've been fucked for a bottle of voddy. Easy for a woman. I just have to let you get on with it.'

'Did Stewart have any enemies?' Watts persisted.

She ignored him.

'Feel sorry for drunk men. They get the horn but they can't perform.' She hacked a laugh. 'Hey – I'm a poet and I don't know it.'

'Enemies?' Watts said.

She finally looked his way, touched a finger to her red mouth.

'Course he had enemies – he was surrounded by enemies – he lived in enemy country. Hostile environment.' She took another sip of her drink, pulled her skirt down. She had good legs.

'You have a child?' Watts said.

'Children. They're with their father. He remarried – proper home for them.' She twisted her mouth oddly. 'I don't see them.'

'Any specific people you'd like to draw our attention to?' Watts said.

She glanced his way.

'Do you know how much I hate waking up in the morning feeling so fucking awful? Every day I decide this day will be *the* day. I'll stop. I'll force a healthy breakfast down – superfoods, you know? But by eleven there's that little thing scratching at me. Then I go: OK, today I'll pace myself. Then someone comes along and says Stewart has been murdered...'

Watts and Tingley watched as she sipped at her drink again. Watts leaned forward.

'Any names you can give us?'

267

Dana looked bemused. Maybe the drink was finally kicking in.

'Of the men I've slept with? Don't remember. I'm not that Tracy Emin, you know. All the same, they are. Slimey.'

Watts looked at Tingley, but Tingley was focused on Dana.

'Not Stewart, though...' Tingley said.

'Why not Stewart? Why else was he with me? Panting for it all the time. He was useless for a woman who's had two kids. Hadn't a clue.' She looked vaguely round the room. 'But he was kind to me.' She sniffed. 'What am I going to do now?'

'Do you have a name?' Watts said.

Again she looked befuddled.

'I know lots of names. How's about John Hathaway?'

Again Tingley and Watts exchanged looks.

'You know John Hathaway?'

'The King of Brighton? Of course I know Johnny. I'm one of his cast-offs. When I was eighteen. He might even have passed me on to Stewart. I can't be certain. My memory is shot – did I say?'

'Stewart worked for lots of criminals, didn't he?' Watts said.

'Accountant to the crooks, that was Stewart.'

'Do you think any of them might have done this? On account of—?'

Watts paused, but Dana looked at him sharply, for the first time.

'On account of Stewart was a snitch? Doubt it – Stewart wasn't a real snitch, you know.'

268

Watts leaned back.

'Meaning?'

Dana looked at him and smirked.

'Meaning that clever bastard knew what Stewart was up to.' She put her hand to the side of her head. 'He was probably pulling his strings.'

'Cuthbert?' Watts said, though he knew the answer.

Cuthbert was a small-time thug in Milldean he and Tingley had clashed with several times.

'Cuthbert?' Dana said witheringly. 'He's a lot of things but clever he isn't. Cunning maybe. I mean Johnny. Johnny Hathaway.'

Watts tried to process this information.

'He fed Stewart selected information to pass on to the police.'

Dana reached for her glass. Missed.

'And the likes of you.'

Tingley leaned forward and handed her glass to her.

'But Stewart was the one who led us to Hathaway,' Watts said, almost to himself. 'Why would Hathaway want that?'

Dana sighed and took a longer drink from her glass, almost emptying it.

'Didn't get you anywhere but involved, did it?' she said, slurring for the first time.

'Involved in what?' said Watts, leaning forward again. Tingley gestured for him to cool his eagerness. He leaned over and took Dana's hand. She looked down at his as if a hand were something alien.

'You know there's a rumpus in town over who

runs it?' she said, looking from his hand to his face.

'You mean between the crime families?'

Tingley released her hand. She smiled at him. A good smile, given she was drunk.

'Perhaps Johnny figured you to be a couple of wild cards.'

'Between the crime families?' Watts repeated Tingley's question.

Dana drained her glass. She looked from one to the other of them.

'Someone is trying to take over. Someone different.'

'Based locally?'

She shook her head.

'I don't think so.'

She jiggled her foot.

'Look, Stewart used to tell me bits and pieces. I never got the whole picture from him. But I used to overhear him on the phone too. He was always cautious. But there'd be bits and pieces.'

She looked at her glass. Tingley took it from her and went into the kitchen. He returned with the glass refilled and set it down on the table in front of her. She looked at him.

'A true gentleman. Stay on after your friend has gone.'

Tingley smiled.

'This person from outside,' he said. 'Any names mentioned?'

She started on the new glass, not sipping now.

'No names that I recall.' She started to put the glass down, then lifted it to her lips again. 'But then I don't recall much. He was the middle-man

270

setting up a meeting with someone here and some foreign people. It had something to do with those police killings over in Milldean.' She looked at Watts. 'That was you, wasn't it? You should know.'

Watts looked at his hands.

'If only I did.'

John Hathaway had a problem with the Palace Pier people. The Boroni family were long gone and for decades it had been a legitimate enterprise. Hathaway had left it at that. He'd moved on from piers when the West Pier closed for good in 1975.

But lately he'd got back in via the West Pier development. And in consequence he'd been getting grief from the new owners of the Palace Pier. Niggly things. Stewart Nealson was supposed to find out who was backing the new owners but he hadn't got anywhere before his terrible demise. Hathaway thought for a moment. Or maybe he had got somewhere.

And then they'd torched the West Pier. Hathaway was in no doubt the new mystery owners of the Palace Pier were behind that. So now it was payback time.

His phone rang. He had his feet propped up on the rail of his boat, looking out over the marina. He reached over.

'Yeah?'

'Is it a go?'

'It's a go. We're gonna fuck 'em during that party on the beach. Do you remember last time DJ Dickhead did his thing? The entire beach was mobbed. People pissing where they stood because they couldn't move. The entire city gridlocked right out on to the Downs, west to Worthing and east to Eastbourne, and nobody getting anywhere near the London Road.'

'So excuse my asking, but how do we get away?'

'By sea, you idiot. Just like those guys who firebombed the West Pier. The thing is, there's no way anyone can stop us.'

'Are we going armed?'

Hathaway didn't even bother to reply.

The boat came in from the east. Hathaway was watching from the window of his room at Blake's Hotel. He could see people streaming past the entrance to the Palace Pier, heading for the sound of the music. The promenade was a solid mass of them.

He could hear the music clearly. On the beach it must have been overwhelming.

He saw the boat slow as the driver eased up on the throttle. It sent out a long wave in its wake as it curved into the far end of the pier.

He saw the line go out to secure the boat to a thick stanchion. Secured, the boat bobbed on the waves. Hathaway adjusted the binoculars and looked at the deck of the pier. It was crowded with people facing towards the west, towards the music.

Hathaway focused on a door at the back of a solid-looking building on the pier. After a few moments it opened and four men in jeans and denim jackets spilled out. All were wearing bala-

272

clavas.

They each carried rucksacks on their backs. Without looking back they walked to the edge of the pier and looked down at the boat. One by one they clambered over the side and down a rusted ladder to the boat.

The first dropped easily into the boat. The second paused as the boat dipped in the swell. One-handed he took his rucksack and dropped it into the boat. The third and fourth lowered themselves in.

The driver reached out and unhooked the rope. The boat roared away from the pier, heading out to sea. It would be in Varengevilles-sur-mer within three hours.

Hathaway smiled and turned back to the girl sitting up in bed. She saw the expression on his face.

'Has it taken effect?'

'Oh yes,' he said, walking towards her.

SEVENTEEN

Watts and Tingley went up to see Hathaway in his mansion on Tongdean Drive.

A black man in a well-cut grey suit answered the door.

'For Mr Hathaway,' Watts said.

The man looked him up and down, nodded. Then he looked at Tingley. Smiled.

'Hello, Tingles.'

Tingley held out his hand.

'David. You're looking trim.'

'You too,' David said, shaking the offered hand.

'You're out of the business in one piece, then,' Tingley said.

David glanced at Watts.

'Bob here is a good friend of mine,' Tingley said.

Watts stuck out his hand.

'Bob Watts.'

David took the offered hand.

'If Tingley vouches for you—'

'I definitely do. He's the ex-chief constable—'

David kept hold of Watts's hand.

'The one who got busted for standing up for his men?'

274

'And women,' Tingley said.

David clapped his other hand over the hand clasp.

'Pleased to meet an officer who knows what his primary function is.'

Watts let go.

Hathaway appeared in the doorway behind David. He saw Tingley, the dapper, slender man he'd met some months earlier and decided he liked. The big, broad-shouldered blond man with the broken nose he recognized from the press as ex-Chief Constable Bob Watts.

'If you're finished with the love-in, Dave, perhaps you'd bring your friends through – where your boss is patiently waiting. Sometime this year would be favourite.'

David turned and grinned.

'Sorry, Mr H. Mr Tingley and Mr Watts.'

'Well, I can see that for myself, can't I?' He looked at Watts. 'I don't know why I bother. Try to ease the unemployment statistics and look what you get.'

'If David is typical of who you're hiring,' Tingley said, looking at Watts, 'then you're hiring the best.'

Hathaway dropped his arm on David's shoulder and winked at Watts.

'David? He's just the trainee. Coming along nicely, though.'

'Thanks, Mr H.,' David said.

'All right, hop off and polish your medals or whatever it is you do for your extravagant salary all day. Come in, gentlemen, do. Mr Tingley – not an unalloyed pleasure to see you again but

275

anyway. And ex-Chief Constable Bob Watts – I know you only by repute – though I did know your father. How is the old rogue?'

Watts was thrown by mention of his father.

'He's fine, thanks – how do you know him?'

'Well, Bob – OK to do first names?' Watts nodded. 'Well, Bob, that's a bit of a convoluted story – but who knows – if we make an afternoon of it there may be time.'

Hathaway took them up to a mezzanine where one whole wall was a window. He pressed a button and the window slid open. He led them on to a deep balcony enclosed in more glass. Another button and the glass retracted. Half a dozen ample wicker armchairs were spread across the balcony.

'Sit, sit. I'm about to have a mojito – my girls make great mojitos – and you're welcome to join me.'

'I don't know what it is but I'll give it a try,' Watts said. Tingley nodded. Hathaway raised three fingers and waved them towards a beautiful olive-skinned young woman hovering by a doorway.

'You obviously don't have kids who hit the cocktail bars,' Hathaway said.

'I probably do,' Watts said.

'You probably have kids or they probably hit the cocktail bars?' Hathaway grinned his perfect white teeth grin. 'Doesn't matter – either way your answer is indicative.'

'How old are your kids?' Watts said.

Hathaway made an odd face.

'I don't have any – but I have a big family.'

276

Hathaway toasted Watts and Tingley.

'Here's to coalitions – may they always fail.'

'You don't like coalitions?' Tingley said.

'Worst of both worlds, then one member takes over.'

'Here's to truth,' Watts said.

Hathaway laughed.

'Yeah. Right.'

When they'd all sipped the cocktails Hathaway looked at Tingley.

'I assume you and David were brothers-in-arms at some stage.'

'More than once,' Tingley said.

'I've always had great admiration for soldiers,' Hathaway said. 'Never had any desire to join up, let me add, and I was the right side of National Service. But, growing up, I was close to an ex-commando who worked for my father. Became something of a mentor.'

Hathaway raised his glass.

'Here's to him.'

Watts and Tingley raised their glasses.

'Does he have a name?' Watts said.

Simultaneously, Tingley asked:

'Is he dead?'

'His name is Sean Reilly, Bob. And he's very much alive, James. Later he worked with me for a few years but eventually retired. To Normandy, actually. His health isn't good but he's still sharp as a pin. I have a house in Varengevilles-sur-mer, a little village outside Dieppe. He lives there. Lovely place. If you're a gardening nut, Gerturde Jekyll did the garden on the side whilst she was landscaping a local chateau. Name means nothing, Bob? Your wife does the gardening, eh? Or you're thinking Jekyll and Hyde. How about Luytens, the architect who refurbished the chateau? No? He created Delhi – or whatever it's called now. Bob, you did go to school, did you?'

Watts smiled.

'Anyway your dad's still kicking? Glad to hear it. He must be a fine old age. I'm afraid, Jimmy, I never had the pleasure of your father, as it were.'

'Nor did I,' Tingley said. Watts gave him a glance.

'Yeah, well, that's fathers for you.'

Hathaway drained his glass.

'The West Pier,' Watts said.

'And?'

'It's been firebombed three times.'

'And you're asking me about this why, exactly?'

Watts leaned forward.

'Come on, Mr Hathaway—'

'John. My name is John. I thought we were doing first names.'

'Nothing happens in this town without your knowledge and say-so. The pier's development syndicate had the money in place to put the pier back in business and you didn't want that because it would impact on your businesses.'

Hathaway looked out over his garden.

'You want a confession?' he said when Watts paused. 'Because otherwise I'm not quite sure what the point of this bombast is.'

'Actually, we want help with something else. At the same time as the pier was being fire-

278

bombed, Laurence Kingston, chair of the West Pier Development Committee, was committing suicide. Pills and booze. Died inhaling his own vomit. Odd coincidence, don't you think?'

'Now you want my advice on synchronicity?'

'Did you know Mr Kingston?'

'I don't associate with many poofs but as it happens I did know him. Not in itself a crime, even when homosexuality was illegal. Can I just say, Bob, that you show shocking research skills in your assumptions about me and the two piers.

'If you knew anything of my history and my family's history, you'd know that the West Pier runs through our lives like the lettering in a stick of rock. I'd no more have it firebombed than I would – well – almost anything. I used to spend my Easter holidays every year giving a small bit of the West Pier a lick of paint to keep the elements away.'

'That was in the sixties, when your father ran Brighton?'

Hathaway kept his eyes on his garden but shook his head.

'The police ran Brighton. First, the town's chief constable, then, when – because of him – the government decided to push town constabularies into countywide police forces, the first county chief constable, Philip Simpson. William's father.'

Hathaway caught the look that passed between his visitors.

'What? You didn't realize I knew William Simpson and his father too? Back in the day, I knew everybody.'

'But you were only a kid,' Tingley said.

'Kind of you to say, but actually I was above the age of consent and I was learning the trade.'

'The trade?'

'My dad's trade.'

'And what trade would that be?' Watts said.

Hathaway sat back in his seat.

'Don't be coy, ex-chief constable. It doesn't become you.' He pointed at Watts's hands. 'I can see the scars on those knuckles. You've got stuck in at some point in your life.'

Watts lifted his hands and examined them for a moment. He let them fall back on to his thighs.

'You still haven't told me how you knew my father,' he said.

Hathaway bared his perfect teeth.

'Oh, that's easily explained. He used to come to our house with his friend, the aforementioned Chief Constable Philip Simpson.'

Watts seemed confused.

'Why?' he said.

'Why? Let's see. My father knew the chief constable, your father knew the chief constable, my father threw a lot of parties. Doesn't sound odd to me – does it sound odd to you, Jimmy? He came to our house many times. Victor Tempest, thriller writer. We read his books, my dad and me. He signed some for us – they'll be around here somewhere. Brighton was small in those days. Still is, really. Not that Larry Olivier ever came to our house from his Regency mansion, but that was more a class thing.'

'So my father knew your father?' Watts said.

'Pretty well. Not from his police days – your

dad was a copper in the thirties with Philip Simpson and Charlie Ridge, wasn't he? Though Charlie would have had a higher rank. Amazing to think he joined the force in 1926.'

'And Ridge and Philip Simpson were both corrupt chief constables?' Watts said.

Hathaway nodded.

'Shocking, isn't it?' He saw Watts's face. 'Oh, I see what you're thinking. Were they corrupt from the start of their careers? And if they were and your father was mates with them...' Hathaway shrugged. 'You'd best ask your dad. I remember there was some brouhaha around the end of 1963 or in 1964 over a lot of files that had gone missing or been destroyed from the 1930s – particularly 1934 when that Brighton Trunk Murder was. Did your dad investigate the Trunk Murders?'

Watts nodded.

'Ooops,' Hathaway said. He reached over and patted Watts's arm.

'I remember when you were born. For that matter, I remember when your friend William Simpson was born. The same year, if memory serves. Now his birth was really something. My mum and dad referred to it as the Immaculate Conception.'

Watts tilted his head.

'Oh, not that Philip Simpson's wife was a virgin.' Hathaway leered. 'Far from it.'

He looked at Watts.

'The good old days, eh?'

Watts was morose. 'I think everything has to do

281

with everything in Brighton. Corruption in the sixties links back to the Trunk Murders in the thirties and forward to now. And Hathaway, from being a peripheral figure, is now taking centre stage.'

'I like him,' Tingley said.

Watts thought for a moment.

'Like him as in you think he's somehow behind the Milldean thing, or like him as in like him.'

'The latter.'

Watts nodded his head slowly.

'Is that going to be a problem?' he said.

'Of course not. But the difference between him and Cuthbert ... this guy has some sense of morality.'

Watts laughed.

'An honest villain – that's all right, then.'

'Dave and I are going to have a drink this evening. Wanna come?'

Watts shrugged. Evenings were when he felt most alone.

'Sure.'

Watts called in on Gilchrist in police headquarters first. It felt strange re-entering the building he used to run. She met him in one of the conference rooms looking out over the beach.

'We've identified the skull,' she said.

Watts looked at Gilchrist surprised.

'So soon. That's bloody impressive.'

She shrugged.

'We had a break. We thought we were going to have to go the familial DNA route, but her father

282

was on a database and there was a missing persons report.'

'From 1934? I thought all that had been destroyed.'

Gilchrist looked puzzled for a moment.

'This isn't the head of the Trunk Murder victim, Bob, though it is a woman. She went missing in 1969. The missing persons wasn't pursued vigorously, if at all, because it was assumed she had gone off to India and joined some ashram, or got caught up with some cult.'

'Any contemporary statements from friends and family? Known associates?'

'Family no help. Father is dead and mother has Alzheimer's. We've got her class list from the university so we're tracking people down through the alumni association. We're checking the electoral roll too, just in case.'

'Who was she?'

'Student at Sussex; hippy by the sounds of it. Name of Elaine Trumpler.'

Watts and Tingley met David in the bar of the Jubilee Hotel in Jubilee Square that evening. The bar was low-lit and the décor was white plastic. David was sitting in a booth in front of a large aquarium. Brightly coloured fish drifted or darted behind him. He was speaking into his mobile phone but cut the connection when he saw them.

'I'll get these,' Watts said to Tingley. 'You've got catching up to do.'

Watts pointed at David's glass and the ex-soldier shook his head. When Watts went over a few moments later and put Tingley's drink in front of him, David laughed.

'Still drinking that fag drink?'

Tingley gestured around them.

'Yeah, keep forgetting what town we're in. Cheers, Tingles, and best of health to you, Bob.'

They drank. Tingley exaggerated smacking his lips after taking a sip of his rum and pep.

'I told the boss I was seeing you,' David said. 'Wanted to play it straight.'

'Whatever way you want to play it – we weren't going to interrogate you, just wanted a bit of an idea of the set-up from your point of view.'

'He said to tell you anything you want to know.'

'You know he's a major crime figure,' Watts said. 'You're putting yourself at risk of jail time getting involved in illegalities.'

'I know policing used to be your business, Bob – what's lawful and what's not – but our government has sent Tingles and me out on many an op where the lines are blurred. In the twilight zone chances are we're helping shore up some regime that has raped an entire country. We must have worked for some of the world's biggest crooks but they're legitimate because they have the power. Terrorists who are now presidents. War criminals with the Nobel Peace Prize tucked in their back pockets. So Mr Hathaway's crimes, whatever they may have been – for I do believe they're all in the past – pale by comparison. What was it the man said? "All great fortunes are based on crimes."'

'Have you been rehearsing that?' Watts said with a smile.

'Bit. How'd it sound?'

'Good,' Tingley said. 'Good enough to convince yourself, right?'

David looked him in the eye.

'I'm working for him, aren't I?'

'What's he like?' Watts said. 'I've only got the police report to go on and, frankly, a lot of that is guesswork.'

'What's he like? A man of his word, I think. A tough bastard – mentally and physically. He's a streetfighter. I've seen him spar with some of the guys and he knows some stuff you don't find in the textbooks.'

'He's an expert in aikido and karate,' Watts said.

'Nah, not that shit. Dirty stuff. The stuff Tingles and me were taught – you too, maybe – you've got the look of a military man.'

'Reckon he learned those from Sean Reilly back when?' Tingley said.

'Obi-Wan Kenobi? Maybe.' He saw their look. 'Hathaway reveres that old commando guy. Talks about him far more than he ever talks about his dad.'

'And you're certain Hathaway's not involved in anything illegal these days.'

'Well, obviously I can't be certain but there's no heroin lab in the basement or brothel in the greenhouse, if that's what you mean. And the kind of meetings I accompany him to are with legit businessmen – as far as any businessman can be legit. I'm sure you wouldn't regard Laurence Kingston as a nefarious character.'

'Laurence Kingston?' Watts said.

'Last meeting I took Mr H. to was over at his place in Hove.'

'When was that?'

'Some time last week – Thursday, I think.'

'You're sure it was him?'

'Mr Kingston's hard to miss, wouldn't you say?'

'You know he committed suicide the other night?'

David looked at Watts.

'I didn't know.'

After a moment, Watts said:

'Is that it? The sum total of your grief?'

'Bob—' Tingley said. David raised his hand.

'Give me a break,' he said, a look of disgust on his face. 'I didn't know Mr Kingston. I don't entirely approve of suicide – though I would argue the toss in certain situations – so I've no reason to feel grief for the man. I've lost a number of friends and too many close friends to violent death. I'll keep my grief for such as those, if you don't mind.'

'I'm sorry,' Watts said. 'That was crass of me.'

'Yes, it was,' David said.

'You know the pier has been firebombed too,' Watts said.

'I heard you thought Mr H. had done it – rather an odd thing for someone to do who planned to invest, I'd say, but I'm just a jarhead not a former top cop. What I do know is that Mr H. was well pissed off when he heard about the firebombing.'

'And you maintain he's legit.'

'Why would he not be? He's made his money – why run the risk of doing crooked things? You know better than me, Bob, how these things go. He owns restaurants, nightclubs, a chain of dry cleaners, office buildings and a couple of boutique hotels. He's a legitimate businessman.'

Watts smiled.

'So why does he need you and the others like you?'

'Everybody needs security. And, unfortunately, in the past Mr H. has mixed with a lot of unsavoury characters who want to drag him back into the mire. He has to protect himself.'

'How many people like you does he employ?'

'A dozen round the house, on shift. I wouldn't like to guess with regard to his businesses, especially as – I forgot to say – he also runs a security firm. Operates all along the south coast.'

There was a pause whilst they all sipped their drinks.

'I assume you've heard about his accountant, Stewart Nealson?' David said.

'We've heard,' Tingley said.

David looked down at his hands.

'It's starting, then.'

EIGHTEEN

Watts met his father in a pub at Kew tube station, a couple of miles from his Barnes home. Donald Watts, aka Victor Tempest, best-selling thriller writer, womaniser, husband, all-round bastard. Through a wall of windows they could see on to the platform where crowds waited for tube trains that took their time arriving.

His father was looking frailer than the last time he'd seen him, some six months earlier, but still darned good for ninety-seven.

'Got a job yet?' Donald Watts said.

'Sort of.'

His father looked at him. One eye was watering. He reached in his pocket for a cotton handkerchief and dabbed his eye. Watts took a sip of his wine. It tasted corked but he took another sip anyway.

'It's about Brighton in the sixties, Dad. Skeletal remains have turned up near the West Pier. I wondered if there was anything you could remember about those times.'

'Giddy times. Paisley shirts. Men wearing silk scarves knotted at the neck. Kipper ties. Or was that the seventies?'

'You were friendly with Philip Simpson, the corrupt chief constable.'

'We'd been in the force together back in the thirties.'

'He destroyed the Trunk Murder files. Don't you think that's odd?'

'Oh, you're back on the Trunk Murder again. How are these remains connected?'

'They're probably not. I went off at a tangent. This is a woman with her face punched in as best we can tell from the skull. I was just intrigued by the destruction of the files.'

'What year?'

'1964.'

Donald Watts nodded.

'Thirty-year rule. Standard thing to do.'

'It seems to have been virtually the first thing he did. An unsolved crime.'

Watts's father shrugged his bony shoulders. He wiped his eye again.

'Did you know Charles Ridge?' Watts said.

'Of course – he was another one. He'd been in ten years or so when I joined. Moved through the ranks. We were part of the same social circle in the fifties, early sixties.'

'And you stayed friends with Philip Simpson. I don't remember meeting him.'

'He died of cancer – 1969, I think. You were but a bairn, as was William.'

'We found the remains of a skeleton in a block of cement. The old Chicago waistcoat – feet in a tub full of concrete.'

'Cement shoes, eh? And you think I did that too?'

'Of course not. We're trying to figure out what was going on in Brighton in the sixties. You

289

knew Dennis Hathaway. Went to his parties. Did you ever meet a young woman called Elaine Trumpler?'

'Never. Dennis Hathaway. Good parties. And he liked my books.'

'You know he was a villain.'

'I was aware of him hoping to take over from Charlie Ridge, the ex-chief constable and his merry men – you knew about that?'

Watts nodded.

'Charlie had been in the force since 1926 – he joined at the time of the General Strike. Then Philip Simpson came along.'

'You knew they were bent?'

'Most of them were bent back then.'

'You?'

'Not particularly. You know my crime.'

'Selling stories to the newspapers.'

Donald Watts shrugged.

'That was about it. A few backhanders but that was part of the system. Charlie refined it. Took over the whole bloody town. Controlled the abortionists, took a percentage from the brothels and the arcades.'

'From when?'

Donald Watts looked at his son. Grinned. He looked vulpine.

'Clever boy.'

There'd been a society abortionist based in Hove who'd been suspected of committing the Brighton Trunk Murder. Watts's father had sent a French girlfriend of his there who may have been the murder victim.

'You mean, was the phony pharaoh, Dr Massiah, one of his?'

'Did Ridge protect him at the time?'

'From the investigation into the Trunk Murder? We'll never know that now, will we?'

'Dammit, Dad, don't do this again. Do you know?'

'I had my suspicions.'

'What about Simpson destroying the Trunk Murder files?'

'I told you that was at his discretion – the thirty-year rule.'

'There were thousands of statements. Numerous people accused.'

'What is it you really want to know?'

'Everything.'

Watts's father took a long pull of his beer and stared out at the departing tube train.

'I think you think I know more than I do know.'

'Telling me anything you do know would be a start.'

Donald Watts scratched at his cheek.

'My memory isn't what it was. Perhaps you'd be best reading the rest of my memoir.'

Although Simpson's father had admitted he had written the fragments of a diary Kate Simpson had found, he had not mentioned the existence of anything further.

'You sod,' his son said.

Gilchrist met Watts on the seafront.

'We have a hit from a classmate of hers who was also her flatmate for a time. Claire Mellon. Want to come with me?'

Watts nodded. She drove him up to Beachy Head. They spoke little in the car. She found that awkward. He didn't seem to notice.

'I've been here before,' Gilchrist said, looking up at the slope of the cliff edge and the house above it. 'Woman who lost her cat.'

'The cat in the burned-out car?' Watts said.

'The very one.'

During their investigation of the Milldean massacre they had traced a car used to dump a body off the Seven Sisters to a burnt out hulk at Ditchling Beacon, all thanks to the remains of a cat that had disappeared from Beachy Head.

The house on the cliff top was a converted lighthouse that had been moved back a couple of hundred yards some years before because of cliff erosion. A slender, upright woman answered the door. Gilchrist remembered how the woman's grace had made her feel lumpen the last time they'd met.

'Hello – we've met before,' Gilchrist said.

'Not something else to tell me about my cat, I hope?'

The woman smiled. She was as elegant and graceful as before as she led them into her pristine living area. Watts looked around.

'Lovely,' he said.

'*Grand Designs* thought so, though Kevin was worried about our budget and our timescale.'

Gilchrist and Watts both looked blank.

'TV programme? Never mind.'

'It's about Elaine Trumpler.'

'Yes, Elaine.' She ushered them to her white sofa. 'A wild child if ever there was one. Would

292

you like green tea or, in the circumstances, some herb?' She saw their expressions. 'Just joking – sorry. What is it you want to know about her?'

'When did you last see her?'

'After your call, I gave this some thought. Sometime in 1969. We lost track of each other when we stopped being flatmates and because she was filming for a long time, and then there was her townie boyfriend, of course. Then she took off for India.'

'Whoa – you're saying a lot there. She was filming?'

'She was in several films being made in Brighton. *Oh! What A Lovely War. On A Clear Day You Can See Forever.*'

Watts and Gilchrist both looked blank.

'There were quite famous films at the time. First one directed by Sir Richard Attenborough, second by Liza Minnelli's father? Filmed on the West Pier and along the seafront? Anyway, she was a speaking extra. She wanted to be an actress – sorry, I think women call themselves actors now as they don't want to be seen as adjuncts.'

'Were you an extra?'

'For a couple of days. I was one of Vanessa Redgrave's suffragettes. But dance was my thing and I was going up to London for dance auditions, so couldn't do more.'

'And this townie boyfriend?'

'She kept him very secret, though I met him a couple of times. Great-looking but kind of straight, you know. I only met him early on but they were together for a couple of years after that. We kind of thought they'd gone off to India together.'

'Even though he was straight?'

'Well, he wasn't exactly Peter Fonda and Dennis Hopper but everybody was going to India. Mia Farrow went out there and she was married to Frank Sinatra around that time. We all talked about going to India and we were mostly well-brought-up middle-class kids.'

'You weren't worried about her?'

'At the time? Hard to remember, but I think all of us were rootless. People disappeared off all the time so it was no big deal.' She tilted her head. 'Should I be worried now? I'm a bit scatty – I realize I didn't actually ask why you wanted to know about her.'

Gilchrist told her about the remains. Claire Mellon put her hand over her mouth.

'How awful. Poor, poor Elaine. How did it happen?'

'That's what we're trying to find out. Did she say any kind of goodbye?'

'Not that I recall, but at the time that was cool, you know? We were accepting of whatever people did. If I'm honest, that's largely because we didn't really understand what was going on, so we adopted this air of coolness.' She shrugged. 'We were just kids – far less mature than the kids these days.'

Mellon offered names of other students who were close to Trumpler. Gilchrist wrote them down.

'And this townie – do you remember his name?'

294

'No. I remember the name of his band, though. The Avalons.'

'Why does that stick in your mind?'

'The King Arthur thing, you know? Except I remember Elaine telling me the bass player used to work in a furniture warehouse and it was the name of its most popular three-piece suite. We laughed about it.'

'And you don't even remember his first name?'

'I'm sorry, I don't. But he's still around Brighton sometimes.'

'What?'

'I've seen him a couple of times in that bar in the marina – the Asian-looking one.'

'The Buddha?'

'I think that's the name. I'm pretty sure it was him. Much older now, of course, but aren't we all?'

'You didn't speak to him?'

'To say what? Elaine and I weren't that close, my life went in a totally different direction, and I'm not in the least interested in him. What's to say? The older you get the more memories you want to forget – don't you think so, ex-Chief Constable?'

Back in the car Watts rubbed his hands.

'The local history archive in the library will have old newspaper cuttings so we can find out who was in The Avalons,' Watts said. 'I'll get down there. I'll dig out what I can find out about the West Pier then too.'

Gilchrist dropped him off beside the Royal Pavilion. As he walked through the gardens into the museum he was thinking about his parents living in Brighton at that time. Watts had been born there in 1968.

He walked through the gallery, skirting a gaggle of schoolchildren rushing from object to object then scribbling in their notebooks. Watts went upstairs and headed into the local history unit.

Gilchrist had scarcely reached her desk when Claire Mellon rang.

'Hello, it's the cat woman.'

'Cat woman?' she said, dropping down into her seat.

'Claire Mellon from Beachy Head?'

'Sorry, yes. How can I help?'

'I remembered after you'd gone that I have something of Elaine's. She left it by mistake at my flat after a heavy night and I hung on to it. Over the years I could never quite bring myself to get rid of it in case she turned up again. I dug it out of the attic then forgot to give it to you. Would you like it?'

'What is it?'

'It's her diary.'

Gilchrist sighed.

'I'll be right back.'

Half an hour later Watts phoned Gilchrist on her mobile as he walked past the statue of Max Miller beside the Pavilion Theatre. He couldn't raise her nor was there a facility for leaving a message. He walked on to the end of the street. He was hungry. Carluccio's was to his left but he was fond of a little bodega next to the Coach and Horses. A Spanish family had opened it a couple of years before to sell produce from their Spanish estates, but they also sold glasses of wine and tapas. It was tiny, with scarcely room for the six small tables they crammed in.

Settled there with a glass of tempranillo and little plates of manchego and chorizo stew, he phoned Gilchrist again. This time she replied.

'You'll never guess what I've got,' he said.

'You go first,' she said.

'You've found something too?'

She arrived twenty minutes later, by which time he'd ordered paella and frittata and more wine. Gilchrist had the diary with her. It was big – A4 size.

'It's full,' Gilchrist said. 'The last entry is dated Easter 1968. Just about to go off on holiday with her guy to Greece. There must be another diary after this.'

'Does she identify the townie?'

'No,' Gilchrist said, licking her fingers, 'but it does refer to going to see the band the night before the last entry.'

'It's OK. I found some press-clippings about the band. There's even a photo.'

'Does it name the band members?'

'It does.'

'And?'

'Does the name John Hathaway mean anything to you?'

'Bloody John Hathaway.'

She gobbled some more frittata.

'This is great. I'm starving.'

'I noticed.'

He pushed the other plate over.

'I've already fed my face.'

'Do you think he killed her?' she said between mouthfuls.

'His dad owned that end of the West Pier,' Watts said.

'Where the remains were found. Looking bad for Johnny boy. But is he known as a killer?'

'He's known as being above the law,' Watts said. 'And every one of his generation got his hands dirty at some time or other. Every one.'

'I remember checking his file before. He's never been down for anything.'

'No. Nor done time. And that's unusual. But he's dirty. We know he's dirty. Maybe this is the leverage you need.'

'I've got enough on my plate without going after a crime kingpin.'

'I'll take Tingley with me,' Hathaway said. 'Boys' night out.'

NINETEEN

Watts went with Tingley to the Buddha, Hathaway's bar at the marina. It was another blisteringly hot day. Hathaway met them in his office on the first floor and took them out on to a private balcony. They sat in the shade of an awning, the glittering sea and the brilliant white boats almost impossibly bright.

'I'd get a headache, looking at this every day,' Tingley said. 'One of those boats yours?'

Hathaway smiled and shot his cuff to check his watch.

'Just setting off back from France, I think. I lent it to a mate. This marina was a long time coming, you know. Twelve years of enquiries. The site kept shifting. There were referenda and parliamentary bills. The first version in 1970 was just a boat harbour. It's been added to ever since. I own four places here altogether. And my boat, of course.'

'John,' Watts said. 'As we're on first name terms, tell me about Elaine.'

'Which Elaine?' Hathaway pushed his sunglasses further up his nose. 'There have been a lot of Elaines.'

'The one we just dug out of the seabed under the West Pier.'

Hathaway mimed applause.

'I admire your sensitivity. That's years of customer care training coming into its own, is it?'

'So – what about her?'

Hathaway's face was impassive.

'I'm no wiser, so let me ask you the same question. Which Elaine?'

Watts turned in his seat to look at Hathaway directly.

'Elaine Trumpler. Believe you knew her. When you were in a pop group. Didn't know you had that in you.'

Hathaway wafted his arm towards the dozen or so guitars on display in a corner of the bar.

'Some detective you are. I can see why your police career was cut short.'

Watts smiled.

'I'm slow but I get there in the end. So, Ms Trumpler?'

'Yeah, I knew her. We had a thing. I was in a band – I had lots of things.'

'When did you last see her?'

'You're joking, of course. I can't remember.'

'Try.'

'Well, she did a bit part in that film on the pier, I know that.'

'Were you still together?'

'No. She was screwing some actor by then. Several actors, I believe. Then I heard she'd gone off to India.'

'You heard?'

'We weren't talking really. Originally she'd wanted me to go with her but I couldn't do it

300

and, in any case, she then got off with these actors.'

He shook his head.

'You OK?'

Hathaway looked like the wind had been kicked out of him.

'Yeah. Funny how old memories catch up with you.'

'So you cared about her?'

'Suppose I must have done.'

'You've never married. Never had kids.'

'This is Brighton, darling. Nothing conventional here.'

'Nevertheless.'

'What, you think my heartbreak at losing that bint wrecked my emotional life forever?' He reached over and began shaking a small bell. 'Where is that Sigmund Freud when you need him?'

A big blond man hurried out.

'It's OK,' Hathaway said. 'Just a fire drill.'

The blond man looked puzzled. Hathaway shooed him away. He looked towards Watts and Tingley.

'So Elaine has turned up under the West Pier, has she? I'm distressed to hear that.'

'You don't know why that would be?'

'My distress? Because I cared about her.'

'Why she should turn up there.'

Hathaway steepled his hands.

'She was filming there. Perhaps you should be talking to the film people – and whichever actor was shagging her.'

'I think you're mixing up your years, John.

She was filming there in 1968 but disappeared in 1969.'

'That right?'

'That's right. Your father had premises at the end of the pier.'

'An arcade and a shooting range, yes.'

Watts grimaced. Hathaway looked towards him.

'Do you think we could assume we're all adults here, Mr Hathaway?'

'John. I thought we agreed on first names.'

'John. You know what we're asking. Was this something to do with your father?'

'Absolutely not.'

'You can see our problem here. Your father was a known gangster. Elaine turns up in a bucket of cement, which tends to exclude the notion she committed suicide or was killed in a crime of passion—'

'My father was not a gangster.'

Watts laughed.

'OK, clearly we're not all adults. Maybe it's because we're talking about your dad and that reduces you to infantilism. Do you want to call your blond bimbo for your potty?'

Hathaway measured Watts with a long look. Watts was up for a fight. Perhaps Hathaway sensed that.

'It's a long time ago, John. Your father is dead. We just want closure for Elaine.'

'Closure? If only life were like that.'

'It can be,' Watts said.

'Really? How's your life since those people were shot in Milldean?'

302

Watts started to speak then stopped.

'Things are going down the pan,' Hathaway said. 'It's back to the old days. There was a moment, just a moment mind, when this city could have been great. It could have been among the great cities of the world. But no, small minds and local greed won out. I'm from a local family but I hate that this city is run by local families. Jesus, we have a leader of the council so thick he has to have somebody write a synopsis of committee reports so that he can understand them.'

'There's a rumour you were behind the firebombing of the West Pier.'

'Really? And there's a rumour you and Sarah Gilchrist are still fucking like rabbits. Care to comment?'

Watts flushed.

'It's not true.'

'There you go, then. Rumours. What can you do with them? As I was saying, things are going down the pan. The Geary plan for the Lord Alfred Centre is gone – and there are a number of villains past and present who are grateful those foundations aren't going to be dug up. Brighton Centre, that fucking seventies eyesore, that, if I was going to firebomb anything, would be top of my list, is now not going to be refurbished. And the West Pier, of course.'

'We're just trying to find out about Elaine.'

Hathaway leaned forward.

'I know you won't believe this but I am a sentimental man. An emotional man. Over the years I've thought a lot about Elaine. I've imagined her safe in some ashram all this time or living in Australia or America, settled with a family.'

He rubbed his face.

'But here she is in the ocean under the West Pier in a block of cement.'

Tingley and Watts glanced at each other, then both focused on Hathaway.

'It's a sea, not an ocean,' Watts said. 'And where her remains were found I'm not sure that even constitutes a sea, it was so near the shore. More like the basement of your dad's place really. But thank you for your time. We can see you're upset. Perhaps we can come back on another occasion to discuss her diary.'

Hathaway raised his head.

'Her diary?'

'Oh yes. Didn't we say? It goes up, presumably, right to the day of her death. She was a good writer. Lyrical. Factual too, though. Very factual.'

'How have you got it?'

'Now that's a funny story. You probably thought you'd cleared her place out after you killed her.'

Hathaway stood.

'I didn't kill her.'

'Really? Didn't take some cold-blooded revenge when she went off with these actors? Didn't see it as a slight on your manhood?'

'I'm not like that.'

'She was living in a flat owned by your father, wasn't she?'

'I don't remember.'

'Yes, you do. Forty Kemp Street. Next door to

304

the house where Mancini killed his mistress in the 1930s, though they renumbered the street to stop the ghouls gawking at the house. The second Brighton Trunk Murder. Famous in its day. He did it and got off. Remarkable. He confessed to a newspaper early in the sixties. You might remember.'

'I do, actually. And my father remembered him doing a music hall show in the late thirties and forties in very poor taste. It was based around killing women – sawing them in half, that kind of thing. Played on the same bill as Max Miller. You're too young to remember Max Miller.'

'I've seen the statue in town.'

'My father's favourite. He was that cut up when Miller died. Could quote his act almost word for word. Did not a bad impression, too. "I was on this narrow ledge. Very narrow. And coming the other way was this beautiful girl. Very beautiful. So beautiful, I tell you, I didn't know whether to block her passage or toss myself off."' Tingley smiled. ' "'Ere, you've got a dirty mind you have, mister." '

'Not a bad impersonator yourself, John,' Watts said.

'You should have heard my Peter Sellers doing Laurence Olivier reciting *A Hard Day's Night*.'

Watts frowned.

'You had to be there. In the sixties, I mean.'

'I thought if you remembered the sixties you weren't really there?' Watts said.

'Exactly my point, Bob, exactly my point. You're asking me these questions but how am I supposed to remember?'

305

'You're not doing too badly,' Tingley said. 'We know where Elaine lived because she was a civic-minded young woman. She registered to vote when she was twenty-one. Her name showed up on the electoral register for the property. We can't find you, though. Not so interested in politics? Or wanting to keep under the radar?'

Hathaway had a far away look on his face.

'I remember the diary. Used to carry it with her everywhere. Always scribbling in it. She had a thing about Anaïs Nin.'

Hathaway looked at their blank faces.

'I had no idea who she was either. Wife of a businessman in Paris, wanted to be a writer. Hung out with Henry Miller – the dirty writer? His lover apparently. Her husband was loaded and she took his money and slept around. Nice. Did the rounds, though, I think. She wrote porn herself – you know, female porn. Arty farty. And she kept this diary. There were volumes of them – must have been millions of words. All about her and what she was up to in Paris. Elaine was doing American studies and I think three of these volumes were part of her reading list. Anyway, Elaine started to keep her own diary in this big book. More like a series of big books, actually. How have you got hold of it?'

'Cat woman came to our rescue,' Watts said with a grin.

Hathaway looked from one to the other.

'I've no idea what that means but I assume the diary is how you ended up with me.'

'Actually, no. It was through the band you were in – the three-piece suite.'

306

Hathaway laughed.

'Fuck you and the horse you rode in on,' he said good-naturedly. 'Who told you about that? It's true. Billy, our bass player, came up with the name. Didn't tell us for years where it came from. We were so pissed off, especially as, by then, that whole Avalon and Grail thing was part of the zeitgeist.'

'The zeitgeist?'

'I know a few big words, Bob. You don't get to where I am without a brain.'

'Seems your band was pretty good.'

'The funny thing is we were pretty good.'

'Why is that funny?'

'Doesn't matter.'

'Come on, John. Share, since we're getting along so well.'

Hathaway pointed back at one of the guitars on the wall.

'That was my very first. A Rosetti. Sounds crap now but at the time ... well, actually, it sounded crap then. Then my dad bought me a Fender Stratocaster.'

He nodded to himself.

'My dad. I didn't know for ages we were only getting gigs because my dad was leaning on publicans and club owners. It saved him giving me money if I was earning it myself, you see. So we thought we were great when actually we were rubbish. But as time went on we did get better. Very much better. Dan could really sing. Charlie the drummer, despite all the jokes about drummers, never screwed up the beat, however drugged-up he was. Billy had a really fluid bass line. Then Tony joined us on rhythm guitar. He could play anything.'

'And you?'

'Me?' Hathaway looked wistful. 'I could carry a tune.'

'So what happened? You seem to have disappeared off the music scene around the same time that Elaine disappeared for good.'

'There's no connection.'

'No?'

Hathaway sat forward in his chair.

'No. The band split up because of – what do they say? – creative differences. Five guys with big egos – it's surprising we stayed together so long.'

'What happened to the others?'

'You don't know?'

Watts shook his head.

'Billy turned out to be a poof and moved to San Francisco to be with others like him.' Hathaway caught Tingley's look. 'I know. If he'd waited in Brighton a few years he could have saved himself the plane fare. Got involved in gay politics with that bloke Harvey Milk. Died in the gay plague.' Hathaway looked at the ceiling. 'Had quite a life journey, our Billy. Always the quiet one.' Hathaway tapped his head. 'But a lot going on in here.'

'The others?'

'Dan stayed in the music business and did pretty well. He had a good voice and he started writing songs. Ended up in the States. Hung out with the Brits – Graham Nash, Terry Reid – that crowd. We knew Graham from when he'd been

308

in The Hollies – we'd played support a couple of times. Good bloke. Got friendly with Graham's old lady, Joni Mitchell, and Stephen Stills, Dave Crosby, Neil Young. Couple of minor hit albums, lot of session work doing backing vocals. Later he used to play footie with Rod Stewart's team.'

'And now?'

'He went into record producing then Al Stewart – no relation to Rod, this was the Year of the Cat guy – advised him to get into the wine business. Al had got some vineyards for himself – so Dan bought himself a winery up in the Napa Valley. Got in at just the right time. Does pretty well. We're still in touch. Sends me a case of a rather special Merlot every Christmas. You can try a glass if you like next time you're over at the house – you seem to be regular visitors.'

'And Tony?'

'He joined us late on so he wasn't really one of the gang. I think he went back to being a butcher.' He spread his hands. 'So there you go.'

'You've missed out Charlie the drummer?'

Hathaway looked over at his guitars.

'Charlie went his own way. We lost touch.'

'Drugs?'

'Yeah, something like that.' Hathaway cleared his throat. 'So, that's all I can tell you about the good old, long-gone days.' He looked at Watts. 'And if you've got Elaine's diary that'll tell you anything else you need to know about me.'

Watts stood up, maintaining eye contact.

'Actually, John,' Watts said. 'I hate to disappoint you but she doesn't mention you at all.'

Hathaway gave an odd smile.

'That so? Well, there you go, then. Told you our affair was something and nothing.'

Outside, Tingley looked at Watts.

'I don't think he was disappointed at all.'

Karen Hewitt met Bob Watts, her predecessor as chief constable, in a restaurant under the arches near the West Pier. It was a regular haunt for her. She liked fusion food. Their table was on a mezzanine, right next to the semi-circular window that looked out on to the shingle beach and the remains of the pier.

Hewitt knew she looked tired, her long blonde hair framing a haggard face. Watts was drawn too but his eyes still flashed an amazing blue. Hewitt chinked her glass of Prosecco against his.

'To results,' she said.

He nodded and put his glass down.

'Have you got anything for me yet?' she said.

'It's only been two days, Karen. But, yes, actually, on the Elaine Trumpler front. John Hathaway or his father are in the frame.'

'Elaine Trumpler?'

'The remains under the West Pier?'

Hewitt put her own glass down.

'Sorry, Bob. It's been a bad week. That man on the Downs. That bloody party on the beach. Laurence Kingston. The West Pier—'

'No news on Kingston or the Pier, I'm afraid. But Trumpler was Hathaway's girlfriend. She lived in one of his dad's flats. If you want to go for Hathaway, maybe this is the way to bring him down. I don't think he did the firebombing.'

310

'How do we prove a forty-year-old crime?'

'Not my area of expertise,' Watts said. 'Have you got anything for me?'

'Nothing on the pier. Fire services think it probably was arson but most of the proof is in the sea. Kingston died of a mixture of pills and alcohol. Choked on his own vomit. There were two glasses in the room where he was found, as if he'd been entertaining somebody.'

'Odd – he should have been entertaining me – but great news—'

'Except that the cleaner put them in the dishwasher. Scene of crime have got some samples for DNA analysis but Kingston was a party animal – had people over all the time.'

'It could be suicide but there's a strong suspicion of fraud. Karen?'

Hewitt was gazing out of the window watching people fooling around on the beach. She looked back at him. He was starting to look jowly. He'd have to watch that.

'The other thing that has been ballsing up my week is the official report about the Milldean massacre.'

Watts sat back, watching her intently.

'You're cleared of any operational misdemeanour but criticized for your actions after the incident.'

Watts shook his head.

'No surprise there. When is it being published?'

Hewitt picked up her glass then put it back.

'It isn't. I wanted to give you a heads-up. The press will be on it tomorrow. You'll be back in

311

the limelight again, I'm afraid.'

Watts clenched his jaw.

'Not published? Karen, that will look like yet another police cover-up.'

Karen reached into her handbag and pulled out a packet of cigarettes. She placed it on the table beside her knife.

'That's as maybe but it was a unanimous decision. Not just me. The Home Office...'

Watts emptied his glass.

'And there I was thinking this was a social occasion.'

Hewitt took a cigarette from her packet and rolled it between her fingers. She looked at the varnish chipped on one nail. Policing and looking good didn't necessarily go together.

'Bob, I can't let the past divert us just at the moment. Something very worrying is happening in Brighton. New criminal rivalries emerging. There's a rumour the Palace Pier got robbed during the Party on the Beach. The heist team got away by sea. The Palace Pier people deny it but there are witnesses talking about masked men breaking into the pier offices.'

'CCTV?'

'Not working on the pier that day. Apparently.'

They shared a look. Ambitious as she had been to get on, Hewitt had nevertheless enjoyed her time as deputy to Watts. They had worked well together. She now understood what a poisoned chalice the chief constable's job was.

'I'd say that's something to do with Hathaway,' Watts said. 'Has Gilchrist passed on to you the intel about Miladin Radislav – Vlad the

Impaler?'

Hewitt put her cigarette back in the packet and sipped her drink.

'She has. We're in touch with the Transnational Crime Unit in London and with Interpol, who are trying to track him down. You think he's after Hathaway?'

'Stewart Nealson was linked to a lot of Brighton crime families but Hathaway is the biggest. It seems likely.'

Hewitt was conscious the waiter was hovering a couple of yards away. She glanced at the menu.

'How's your appetite, Bob?'

Watts made a sour face.

'Dwindling fast.'

They both ordered salads. Hewitt decided against a fag outside and put the packet back in her bag. One small triumph for the day.

'The Balkans is the breeding ground for a vast amount of crime in western Europe,' she said to Watts. 'It started with cigarettes – diverting Duty Not Paid fags destined for the Sahara, or wherever, through Montenegro, then across the straits to Italy for the Italian Mafia. Then narcotics and women. Afghan heroin. Now it's that, plus people smuggling and even organ smuggling – livers and kidneys.'

Watts was nodding.

'I was in the Balkans when it all kicked off. These criminals were supported by their governments and the paramilitaries – hell, they usually *were* the governments and paramilitaries. During the civil war Croatia and Bosnia were banned from buying weapons legally so this was a way

313

to get money to buy them illegally. When I was in Kosovo, the smuggling routes went right across the frontlines. Kosovo was the hub for distributing Turkish heroin.'

Hewitt had forgotten about Watts's military experience.

'I'm behind on all this – though I shouldn't be,' she admitted. 'I'm hearing that these gangs cross racial and ethnic boundaries. Syndicates of Turkish, Serbian, Macedonian and Albanian criminals working together with a common goal. Money. It's like a United Nations of crime.'

Watts nodded again.

'And Radislav is embedded in it.'

Hewitt reached into her handbag.

'We're in deep trouble,' she said. The cigarette packet was back in her hand. 'Have you got any matches?'

TWENTY

A woman was lurking downstairs when Dave let Watts and Tingley in to the big house on Tongdean Drive. She looked at them with cold eyes, then went into the kitchen, closing the door firmly behind her.

'Who's that?' Tingley murmured as Dave led them up to the mezzanine. 'New mistress?'

'Hardly,' Dave said. 'He likes them young. Maybe his mother.'

She looked like a junkie in rehab. Beautiful once, now stringy and lined, in a shapeless dress. Tingley thought he had seen faded trackmarks on her arms.

Hathaway remained seated when the three men walked in.

'You two again – you're like a bad fart. What is it this time?'

'Do you know anything about the Visegrad genocide?' Tingley said.

'I've a feeling I'm about to,' Hathaway said. 'You two want a beer? Afraid I've got standards. I drink it out of a glass. I drink my wine the same way.'

Tingley told much the same story he'd told Gilchrist. Hathaway watched Tingley carefully as he talked.

'The Serbs practiced eliticide, systematically killing the political and economic leadership. Then moved down the hierarchy, killing and raping at will. And the ethnic cleansing worked. These days Visegrad is a Serbian town. There's hardly any Bosniaks living there.

'Terrible,' Hathaway said when Tingley had finished. 'But there were war crime trials for these people.'

'For some people. Eight men were charged with war crimes at The Hague for this and imprisoned. But some ringleaders got away – as we know, the two biggest Serbian war criminals did – Radovan Karadic and General Ratko Mladic. As did a certain Miladin Radislav. He parlayed the plunder he took from his victims into criminal wealth and a criminal empire. Ended up

315

after the war in some fortified mountain eyrie as a white slaver and drug baron.'

'I don't know the name,' Hathaway said.

'Better known by his nickname. Vlad the Impaler.'

Hathaway looked off into the distance.

'Nealson's death, eh? You think Radislav is here.'

'I think,' said Tingley, 'that he came across the oceans bringing plague and pestilence.'

'That's very poetical.'

'I was thinking of Nosferatu. Dracula? Came from Transylvania in a plague ship. Killed all the crew. Captain tied to the wheel?'

'You're making him out to be a nightmare figure. But he's just a gangster. I've known gangsters all my life. He doesn't scare me.'

'He should. He's not just a gangster. He and his men are hardened in war. Trained killers. And he's part of a pan-Balkan crime syndicate, thanks to the war. Which means he has a limitless supply of money and manpower. If they want to take over Brighton, they will. If they want you dead, you're dead.'

Hathaway chewed his lip.

'And you think I'm weaker than them?'

'I think you're twenty years older than them. And you have some sort of moral compass, skewed though it might be.'

'Do you know why they're here?' Hathaway said.

'Specifically? No.'

Hathaway stood and walked over to a desk against the wall. He picked up a small, plastic-covered red book then put it down.

'You know about Mohammed?' he said.

'Which Mohammed are we talking about?'

'*The* Mohammed.'

'Your point is eluding me. He was from the Balkans?'

'He died in 632 and within twenty years his followers had conquered half the Mediterranean. North Africa fell in about two years, then they were all over Spain and Italy and Sardinia. You know how?'

Watts turned to Tingley.

'Seems it's our turn for a history lesson.'

'Alliances. Always alliances. They came in when areas were in trouble and they came to deals with the guys who were losing, then they took over the whole thing. The Spanish conquistadores did the same in South America.'

'You think the Balkan guys have been invited in. By whom?'

'Whoever their friend came to talk to in Milldean?' Hathaway said. 'Maybe the person who is behind the Palace Pier people now?'

'What's the Palace Pier got to do with it?'

'Somebody is making a play for Brighton. That's why they bombed the West Pier.'

Watts sat back in his chair.

'There's a rumour your guys heisted the Palace Pier the other weekend.'

Hathaway turned, a small smile on his face.

'In a way,' Tingley said, 'that doesn't really matter. Nor does why these people came. They came for revenge but now they are here to take over, as they have in France and Italy and

317

Germany. And they will take over.'

'Over my fucking dead body.'

'I believe that's their intention, yes. They intend to kill you. And they will succeed.'

'Bullshit. If you think I'm going to let a bunch of Balkan gangsters take over my town – *my town* – you're fucking mad.'

'Now don't go all Bob Hoskins on us. It's over. Embrace change and get out alive. If you can.'

'Bob Hoskins? The mockney actor? You lost me.'

'It'll come to you.'

'*The Long Good Friday*.' Tingley said. 'Thought he could take on the IRA. Ended up in the back of a car being taken to a very bad end.'

'Saw it. Down in Worthing. Got my car keyed that night. Maybe that was a message.'

Hathaway sighed.

'So, you're saying these guys have come into town and they're intending to take over all crime as we know it.'

'Not just crime. They'll want what you have. Your legit businesses. And they will take over. These guys are killers. They're at a different level. They're war veterans. Mercenaries. They live by the feud, by torture. They are more barbarous than you can imagine.'

Hathaway walked over to his balcony. With his back to them, he said:

'You don't know what I can imagine. To frighten naughty children Romans used to warn them, "Hannibal the barbarian is at the gate."'

'More of your classical education, John?'

'A Kevin Costner film called *The Postman*,

318

actually. Much underrated.'

'Sounds riveting,' Watts said.

'Oh, it was an epic. But you know the history of postal services is a history of adventure and of secrecy.'

'I'll tell them that the next time I'm at the sorting office,' Watts said.

'You should read *The Crying of Lot 49*.'

Watts was growing exasperated at Hathaway always talking in riddles.

'I don't have time to sort that title out, John.'

'I've done a lot of reading over the years.' Hathaway looked at his hands. 'It feeds the soul.'

'I'm sure it does. We need to move on, John.'

Hathaway ignored him.

'You know how many times Britain has been invaded? We think we're this island and that protects us, but that's bullshit. Before 1066 and all that we were invaded by every bugger that took a fancy to us. Brighton got burned down by the French more than once in the Middle Ages.

'Have you heard of the Barbary pirates? Muslims again on the north coast of Africa. In the sixteenth century, they took entire villages into slavery. Cornish and Irish villages left deserted for decades.'

'John. Please—'

'But that was then. No foreign invader has landed on these shores since the nineteenth century and, as far as I'm concerned, no fucker is gonna. Yeah, we'll take their cockle pickers and strawberry pickers, we'll pay their slaves shit but we aren't going to let them get a hold.'

319

'Jesus,' Watts said, jumping to his feet and striding over to Hathaway. 'They've already got a hold. Russians, Triads, Yakuza. They run Britain now. The Serbians have been running crime in the Midlands since the end of World War Two.'

'They don't run Brighton.'

'For the moment, King Canute. For the moment.'

Hathaway pushed his face towards Watts.

'Yeah, well, if that's all you have to say, you can go. I hate negativism. Can't abide it.'

Watts eye-balled him.

'It's realism.'

'Yeah. Do you know how many years I've heard people talk of pessimism and say it's realism? It's not. It's pessimism. That's it. End of story.'

Tingley walked up beside them.

'They're going to kill you, John.'

Hathaway half-turned so that he was facing Watts and Tingley.

'Then I'll be the last king of Brighton. And after me – the dark ages all over again.'

'Oh, they weren't as dark as people think.'

'These will be. But why are you sticking your noses in this? I thought you were trying to find out who killed Elaine Trumpler.'

'And what happened to the West Pier,' Watts said. 'And Laurence Kingston.'

Hathaway stepped back from the two men.

'Kingston? I thought he was a suicide? Probably in a hissy fit. He was that kind of guy.'

'He may have been murdered. The crime scene

320

guys will move it along.'

'Who would have killed him?'

'We were thinking you might have. You had a meeting with him the week before, didn't you?'

Hathaway moved back to his chair.

'He was in a funk. Wanted to back out of a deal we were doing.'

'Good motive for murder.'

'Please. I persuaded him to hold firm.' He looked up at the two men. 'But you two can't be investigating that – that must be an ongoing police investigation.'

'I've been retained by the West Pier Syndicate to look at recent events.'

Hathaway smiled.

'Should I start calling you Marlowe, ex-Chief Constable?'

Tingley had drifted over to the desk. He picked up the little red book.

'What's this? The thoughts of Mao Tse-tung.' He looked inside. 'First printing, 1966. Wow. Bet this is worth something.'

'They printed ninety million so I doubt it.'

'Didn't take you for a Maoist, John.'

'It was a gift,' Hathaway said. 'From Elaine Trumpler. There's an inscription somewhere in the middle of the book. She hid it there so she could check I'd actually read it. Thought you might want it as evidence.'

Tingley closed the book and put it back on the desk.

'You're going to need to give us more than that.'

Hathaway frowned.

'I don't need to give you anything at all.'

In Tingley's car Watts said:

'Can he do it?'

'Not a chance in hell. These guys are unstoppable. The police will have to come to an accommodation with them as they have in London. I saw the same thing in Israel in the nineties. Hundreds of thousands of Russian Jews took Israeli citizenship. They included a lot of criminals so they could get easy access to the West. They brought drugs and prostitution to Israel. They thrive and the Israeli cops turn a blind eye as long as they don't take the violence out of their own communities. If the Israelis can't deal with them we don't stand a chance.'

When the two men had left, the woman who had withdrawn to the kitchen walked in on Hathaway. He was standing by the window, looking out. He had a mojito in his hand, she had a diet cola in hers.

'I'd kill for you,' she said matter-of-factly.

He didn't respond.

'I'd kill for you,' she repeated, touching the side of his face.

Hathaway turned and raised his glass to her.

'You said that. I hope it won't be necessary. But thank you, Barbara, thank you.'

Hathaway made some calls then took his boat over to France later that day. Barbara came with him. She observed him on the crossing. She'd thrived in his home. Relaxed. She knew he was on the lookout for drug use but there was none. She thought he recognized that she was devoted to him.

It was odd for her that she'd slept with both father and son. Odd but not significant, given all the other men she'd slept with in all kinds of combinations. Odder was the fact that she'd forgiven him for abandoning her. All she could think was that in the scale of things he had still treated her better than anyone else. He was the only one who had genuinely cared for her, even if only for a little while.

He'd been astonished when she'd turned up on his doorstep three months earlier. Astonished and cruel. Her sister had died and left her some money, and she'd come back to see the lawyer.

Unusually, Hathaway had actually answered the door himself.

'Hello, young man,' she said cautiously.

It took him a moment to recognize her. She had lost a lot of weight over the years. She recalled the last time he'd seen her, hurrying down the police station corridors after him.

'Barbara, a long time. I thought you were dead.'

'Didn't bother to find out, though, did you?' she said, without bitterness.

He stood aside to let her enter. She stopped in front of him and looked up into his face.

'Still got my looks, though, wouldn't you say?'

She grinned revealing artificially white false teeth.

323

'What the fuck happened to you?' he said. 'You're a fucking mess.'

She reared back then leaned in, hissing:

'You mean before or after your father sold me to a brothel in The Hague? Before or after the heroin they stuffed into me to make me compliant? Before or after stag parties did what they wanted with me? What happened to me? Your father. Then cancer. They took my tits but left me alive.'

He couldn't keep the disgust from his face.

'Christ,' he said sourly.

She saw his look.

'Yeah, that's right. Blame the victim. If it makes you feel better, you were my first trick.'

'What?'

'You think I slept with you for your baby blues?'

He looked down.

'Actually, you didn't care why I slept with you. You only cared that I slept with you.'

'So you blame my father for everything.'

'He made us both what we've become.'

'We make our own destinies.'

'Is that right? So, if you hadn't seen your father beat somebody to death and oversee the murder of your girlfriend you would still have turned out a right bastard would you?'

'That's right. I was a bastard long before those things happened.'

She shrugged.

'I don't really care. I'm just saying.'

She clasped her hands in front of her, veins standing out on arms and neck.

324

'Do you want something from me?' he said. 'Money? A flat? A fuck, for old times' sake.'

'I've had enough fucks to last three lifetimes and then some.'

'Good, because that bit was a joke. I don't fuck senior citizens.'

She stepped away from him.

'Jesus,' he hissed. He put his hand on her shoulder. 'I'm just being honest. I thought women valued honesty.'

'Personally,' she said faintly, 'I think truth is much overrated.'

'Let me give you money.'

'I need money but not from you.'

'What, then?'

'Such a lot of things.' Sadness behind her words. 'Don't you wish we could have another try? Do it better? Different.'

Hathaway gave her a look.

'I don't mean you and me. I mean life. By the time you realize you've only got one shot, it's already too late. You, above all people, know that.'

'It would have turned out the same way for me whatever.'

'You keep saying that.' She picked at a scab on her bare arm. 'I think you're hard on yourself.'

'Do you? Do you? You have no idea what things I've done.'

'I think you were fundamentally changed in those teenage years.'

He patted her arm.

'Nah. I found myself.'

She went and sat down on the sofa. She looked

up at him.

'Does that mean you're happy?'

'Are you? You look fucking dreadful so I can't imagine there's much happiness in your life.'

'Actually, Rilley's been after me.'

'Rilley?'

'Yes. Wants his life back.'

It took him a moment. He laughed. Then:

'Stay here.'

'What?'

'I don't mean in my bed. I already said. But there are lots of rooms in this house. Empty rooms. Choose one. Stay here.'

'And do what? The cleaning?'

'Please. I'll help you get on your feet.' He moved behind her and brushed his index finger across her back. 'Barbara – you were more important to me than I think you realize. It grieves me to see you like this. And I want to help.'

She tilted her head back to look at him. She had difficulty hearing as he said:

'There are few things in my life I remember fondly. It's a short list. You're near the top.'

She looked at the ceiling. Neither of them acknowledged the tears sliding from the corners of her eyes.

TWENTY-ONE

Sean Reilly's retirement home was Hathaway's big house on the outskirts of Varengeville-sur-mer, not far from the church where the artist Georges Braque was buried and the road ended at the cliff edge. Reilly lived there under the vague protection of the family of one of Dennis Hathaway's old smuggling partners, Marcel Magnon, a man who had also known Reilly during the war.

When Hathaway's boat docked at Dieppe they took the waiting car along the coast road. The tide was out and a score or so people were picking mussels from the rock pools.

The house had high walls around it with barbed wire along the top and security cameras set at intervals. Hathaway buzzed the intercom at the outer gate and it swung open. A man with a bulge under his jacket escorted them into the house. Barbara waited whilst Hathaway went ahead.

Hathaway was led down a corridor that smelt of floor wax, toilets and harsh disinfectant. The whole place smelt like a hospital. The smell was more intense in a large drawing room that had been converted into a hospital room.

Sean Reilly was propped up in a bed facing out

through open French windows on to a long, landscaped garden. He looked up from the book he was reading. Smiled a winning smile, his false teeth too big in his skeletal head.

'John.'

'Mr Reilly.'

Reilly smiled again.

'Sean.'

'You're looking well, Sean,' Hathaway said.

'I look like shit – and smell like it mostly, thanks to this bag. Sit me up higher, will you?'

Hathaway leaned over and pressed the button that lifted the top end of the bed. Reilly's head and upper body rose towards him.

'That OK?'

'Grand. So what's happening?'

Hathaway proffered the bottle of single malt.

'I'm sure you're not allowed to but flowers are frowned on by your warders – nurses – I recall and I don't remember you having a sweet tooth.'

'Hope it's Irish.'

Hathaway smiled.

'Of course.'

With difficulty, Reilly raised a hand.

'There are a couple of pretty decent glasses over there.'

Hathaway walked over to the table beside the open windows and poured two hefty measures of the best Irish he'd been able to find.

He handed a glass to Reilly, pulled over a chair and sat beside him.

'How's things?'

Reilly looked beyond Hathaway.

'I've been thinking about the past a lot. Things

328

I did. Things I didn't do.'

'Not regretting things?'

Reilly grimaced.

'No point. Just wondering how my life might have been different. Alternative lives.'

'The road not travelled.'

Reilly smiled, nodded down at the book he'd been reading.

'I'm enjoying stuff that makes me think.'

'Jesus,' Hathaway said. 'I used to have that.'

'It's your copy. I found it lying around. Hope you don't mind.'

'*Zen and the Art of Motorcycle Maintenance*. Bit late to turn hippy, isn't it?'

Reilly smiled.

'Did you know I started a philosophy degree at Trinity before the war? Then the war came and I went over the border and enlisted – don't ask me why, that's a long bloody story. And then, after the war, well, things had moved on for me.'

'So you were going to be the new Bertrand Russell?'

'Or James Joyce. I was all over the place. But then life took another course.' He took a sip of the drink, closed his eye. His cheeks reddened within seconds. 'That's good. Slainte.'

'Slainte.'

'Never understood before why in Westerns cowboys would come into town dehydrated and go to the saloon and down whiskies. Wouldn't a beer have been better?'

'But?'

Reilly grinned again.

'But this whiskey is just the drink for the

thirsty man in the desert.'

Hathaway smiled, nodded down at the book and quoted from memory:

'The truth knocks on the door and you say "Go away, I'm looking for the truth" and so it goes away.'

'Personally, I've always thought truth over-valued.' He passed his glass to Hathaway, his hand shaking. 'Stephen Boyd was the best James Bond.'

Hathaway looked puzzled.

'Who?'

'Who?' Reilly laughed. 'The first one.'

'Wasn't that Sean Connery?'

'Sean Connery? The guy who played Taggart? Runs the bar in *Emmerdale* now?'

Hathaway looked at Reilly's glass.

'That's had a quick effect.'

'I told you – I've been thinking about different ways life might have gone. But not just mine. Michael Caine didn't get the posh part in *Zulu*, so the cockney actor who played Private Hook got all the attention, ended up doing *The Ipcress File* and went on to have Caine's career.'

'What happened to Caine?'

'He did *Steptoe and Son* and now he's a stall-holder in *EastEnders*.'

'And you?'

Reilly took another sip of his whiskey.

'Me? I'm Seamus Heaney. Or Monet.'

'Wouldn't you have missed the action?'

Reilly looked away to one side. Hathaway put both glasses on a table beside Reilly's old display cabinet. He glanced down at Reilly's

330

memorabilia. The guns, the knives, the medals. He recalled the first time he'd seen them, so many years before.

'What's happening with you?' Reilly said eventually.

Hathaway turned.

'There are some very bad men in town.'

Reilly cleared his throat and looked up at the ceiling.

'Tell me something I don't know.'

'I don't mean the usual scum. These people have come from outside.'

'What do they want?'

'They want to kill,' Hathaway said. *'Plus ça* fucking *change.* You get rid of one set of scumbags and another one comes in.'

Hathaway leaned in.

'I've seen enough films about this but I can't believe it's happening to me. I want out but I can't seem to get out.'

'You know that from your dad,' Reilly said, fixing Hathaway with a watery stare.

Hathaway looked down.

'Aye, well.'

'Who's coming after you?'

'Foreigners. Serbians. Mad fuckers. Real hard bastards. The kind who burn your neighbour's house down just because they live next door to you.'

'What do they want?'

'Long term? Everything. Short term? Revenge for the death of one of theirs and his pregnant girlfriend in that Milldean thing.'

'The massacre?'

'Yeah. They think it was targeted at their guy.'

'Was it?'

Hathaway shrugged.

'Not for me to say. But they're here and they're starting up their own mayhem.'

'That man on the Ditchling Beacon?'

Hathaway smiled.

'I see you're keeping up with the Brighton news. Yeah. Stuck a skewer right up him. Came out next to his ear. Left him there to have a slow, painful death. What are things coming to?'

'We've done our share.'

Hathaway looked at his father's old ally and his own mentor.

'True,' he said. 'True.'

'What are you going to do?' Reilly said.

'What do you think I should do? I was so nearly out of it and now I'm being dragged back in.'

'You know you've got to go pre-emptive, John. It's the only way. Nuke the bastards.'

'That brings me right back in.'

'But it's your only way out.'

'I don't know.'

'You can do it, John. I know you can do it. I know what you've done.'

'I know you know,' Hathaway said, then caught something in Reilly's tone. 'We never really talked about that.'

'Your dad was my friend but he'd gone rabid. It was something you had to do. I didn't like that you did it, but I could see why you thought you had to. So I let it go.'

'And worked with me over all those subse-

332

quent years.'

Reilly reached out a thin, purple veined hand and laid it on Hathaway's.

'It's a strange world you and I inhabit. I doubt anyone living outside it would understand. I think you had enough dealing with your guilt. I don't think you've had a happy life, John.'

Hathaway smiled at him.

'Are we supposed to have?'

'Don't let the guilt emasculate you. You can handle these Balkan johnny-come-latelies.'

Hathaway sighed and looked down at Reilly's gnarled hand.

'If I start it, they'll come back with everything. You'll end up in the firing line. I don't know whether I can protect you.' He indicated the passage outside the door. 'I've brought Barbara with me. I'd like her to stay here. I'll leave men too. Good men.'

'Barbara – that will be nice. As for me?' Reilly shrugged his bony shoulders. 'I can protect myself, don't worry about that.' He grimaced. 'The only thing I can't do is change my own bloody shitbag. Can you get Hattie Jacques?'

Hathaway left Barbara with Reilly and had dinner in a private dining room in a quiet restaurant in the backstreets of Dieppe. His hosts were Marcel Magnon, frail and thin-voiced, and his children, Patrice and Jeanne. Hathaway had been doing business with them for years and they greeted him warmly.

Marcel Magnon's first question remained the same whenever they met.

'Any word of your father?'

As always, Hathaway shook his head.

'No word but we don't give up.'

Magnon sighed and his head sank on to his chest.

The four of them shared a large tureen of *La Marmite Dieppoise*, the local fish stew, all dipping their bread in to soak up the liquor. Jeanne fed her father, who sucked on the wet bread as best he could. Conversation was kept general until the cheese course. Then:

'Albanians control all our major ports now,' Patrice said. 'Even Marseilles.'

'Dieppe?'

Patrice shook his head.

'Too small but we pay them a tithe for the quiet life.'

'We know of your problems,' Jeanne said, cutting a small sliver from a hard goat's cheese. 'But I do not know how we can help. Our rough stuff days are in the past.'

'I don't expect anything,' Hathaway said, reaching out to pat her hand. 'Just keep an eye on Sean, if you would, and let him know if bad men are heading his way.'

'That we can gladly do,' Jeanne said, and Patrice nodded vigorously in agreement.

'I'm sending men here,' Hathaway said, 'but let me know if there are developments.'

Jeanne contemplated her sliver of cheese then looked intently at Hathaway.

'And you?'

'Things are in hand.'

'You could get out,' Patrice said. 'You have

made your money.'

Hathaway reached over for the cheese plate. 'It's not my way.'

His phone trembled in his pocket.

'Excuse me. A call I am expecting.'

He took out a pen and small pad and listened to the voice on the phone.

'Spell that, please,' he said. And twice more. 'And Radislav?'

He ended the call without saying goodbye. A few moments later his phone made a series of beeping noises and he scrolled down the photos that had appeared on its LCD screen.

He put the phone on the table and Jeanne looked down at the last photograph.

'I know that face. He has been here.'

The man who had just spoken to Hathaway phoned Jimmy Tingley next. Tingley and he had served together in the SAS before the man had joined the special Transnational Crimes Unit at Scotland Yard. He gave Tingley the same names and suspected British locations of four Balkan gangsters recently arrived in the country.

When he had finished he suggested Tingley and he meet for a drink the next time they coincided in London.

'And, Jimmy, this is just intel for you, right? You're not going to do anything illegal?'

After a moment, Tingley murmured:

'*Moi*?'

TWENTY-TWO

Hathaway's boat drove into the setting sun. Seeing the sun go down always made him think of illustrations in a book he had as a kid of the wounded King Arthur being carried towards the setting sun on a fairy barge.

He made a number of calls on his crossing back to England, waking most of those he called. He gave Dave two instructions. One to deliver a message, the other to collect a parcel.

'Do the first in a public place – don't want any of that shoot the messenger shit happening to you.'

'OK,' Dave said.

'Be careful with the parcel too – take a few of the lads with you. Deliver it to our storage place near Shoreham. Storage room 2020 should do nicely.'

'Will do, Mr H.'

Hathaway was sitting on his boat by the break-water at the outside edge of the marina when the Serbians torched his restaurant. He had his feet up watching the sun rising in a golden glow. Then there was the faint noise of an explosion and a surge of orange flame gushed out of the front of his restaurant and reached out over the water.

'The fuck?' he said, scrambling to his feet. Joggers and dog-walkers scattered along the boardwalk. He thought he could hear screams, then pops as bottles of alcohol exploded.

Dave came up from below.

'Want us to cast off, Mr H., or go in?'

Hathaway waved him away.

He stayed on the boat, watching the black smoke spiral up into the sky, masking the sun. Emergency services arrived. Police milled about whilst firemen went in.

His mobile rang and he realized it had been ringing on and off for a while. The number was blocked.

He put the phone to his ear.

'This is just the beginning,' a deep, lightly accented voice said.

'You're wrong,' Hathaway said. 'This is the end. You and your oppos are toast.'

'Oppos?'

'I warned you. I told you to get out of my fucking country. I told you I was coming for you. Didn't you get the message?'

The man chuckled, surprisingly warmly.

'Think of what happened to your bar as my reply. Do not threaten us, Mr Hathaway. Aside from anything else, it makes you appear foolish. You don't even know who we are.'

'Don't I? Well, you're one of four. I'm guessing you're Drago Kadire? What kind of name is Drago? You sound like a toilet cleaner. The Grand been treating you all right, have they? Hope you've had the afternoon tea. It's known

337

for it.'

There was silence on the other end of the phone.

'That room you're in – it's the one Norman Tebbit and his missus were in when the bomb went off. Refurbished since, of course.'

Hathaway gripped his phone more tightly.

'Now you listen to me, *Drago*. I had nothing to do with the death of your friends in Milldean. Let it go and I'll let you flush back to your hovel in the Balkans.'

'And if I don't?'

'Well, Mr Kadire, when you get that knock on your door it won't be room service.'

Although he'd owned it for years, Hathaway hardly ever went to the storage facility near Shoreham. It was one of his legit businesses but he kept a couple of dozen spaces at the back end of the building for his own use. He had an armoury there, for instance, although he had another, more substantial, in the house in France.

There was a back entrance so his men could come and go unnoticed by the people who stored up their lives in the units at the front. The front was noisy, since everything was metal, including the corridor floors. A walk down those corridors set up a horrible, clanging reverberation.

The back, though, was all rubber. And the storage unit he was headed for had sound-proofing. And an extractor fan.

Hathaway's shoes squeaked just a little as he walked along the corridor to the pool of light spilling from unit 2020. It was empty except for

338

Dave and two other tough-looking men leaning against the wall, looking towards a chair bolted to the floor in the centre of the room. All were armed with handguns.

Stevie Cuthbert, in an England football shirt and khaki cargo pants, was taped to the chair.

'Stevie, my old mucker,' Hathaway said, walking into the room. He clamped his hand around Cuthbert's jaw, tilting his head. 'God, that Jimmy Tingley really did a job on your nose, didn't he? Surprised you can still breathe through it.'

Cuthbert jerked his head away.

'He got his,' he snarled.

Hathaway recalled the faded bruising on Tingley's face the first time he had seen him again.

'Hardly, Stevie.'

He looked down at the man squirming against the ropes tying him to the chair.

'God, this scene takes me back.' He looked over at Dave. 'A word, Dave.'

Outside in the corridor, Hathaway put his head close to Dave and whispered.

'You've got a decision to make, son. So far I've kept you away from the dark side, but if you stay for what's about to happen you will definitely have crossed over. I won't think the worse of you if you want to walk away. But I need to know now.'

Dave scanned his face. He glanced back into the room.

'Those Serbians were tough-looking fuckers,' he said.

'But you delivered my message. Good lad.'

Dave looked at the floor.

'I need an answer. And if it's yes, there'll be no turning back.'

Hathaway waited. Finally, Dave looked up, squared his shoulders and walked back into unit 2020.

'You never knew what happened to your father, did you, Cuthbert?'

Hathaway was standing to Cuthbert's right, Dave behind his left shoulder.

'What do you mean?' Cuthbert said, twisting his head to look at Hathaway. 'We both know he died in a car crash.' He frowned. 'What are you saying, you fucking tosspot?'

Dave cuffed him across the side of his head.

'Watch your language.'

Cuthbert looked up at him.

'You're fucking dead for that, dickhead.'

Dave hit him again. Blood splashed bright red on to the white football shirt. Cuthbert looked back at Hathaway.

'Don't you think a man taped to a chair making threats is utterly ridiculous?' Hathaway said. 'And pathetic?'

'What's this about?'

'Well, originally, it was about you taking the piss as a loan shark and antagonizing the people we all need to be on our side. But something else has come up – to be precise, somebody has burned down my club in the marina. So, this is now about finding out what the hell is going on.'

'How would I know?'

'Oh, you know, compadre. You're in this up to

your bloody stupid cauliflower ears. Now the word I'm hearing is that these are Serbians and other Balkan riff-raff. I know they're already over here doing drugs and girls in London and slave labour out in the country, but this particular lot have something else in mind. And I want to know what.'

'How would I know?'

'You a student of history, Cuthbert?'

'Is that likely?'

'Good point. OK, well most big changes happen because of local bickering when there's a big bloody threat hanging over everyone's heads. And some idiot, looking only at the narrow picture, invites this big bloody threat in to help him. And once they're in, that's the end – they take over the whole country.'

'You've brought me here to give me a history lesson.'

'No, Stevie, I've brought you here to whack you because you're as thick as shit, and that's why I think you might have been the moron who invited these Serbs in. But before I whack you, I just want to know what deal you made with them. And whether you do, in fact, get out of this room somehow by your own volition depends entirely on the quality of your answers. '

'You're fucking bonkers. Two things. You want to whack me, why the fuck should I tell you anything? Second, you whack me, you'll start a war you can't win.'

'I'm already in a war and I want to know why.'

'Cos you're past it. Your day has gone. You can't fight the future. You mention the Serbians.

These guys are in another league.'

'Are you helping them?'

Cuthbert laughed.

'You don't get it. These guys don't need my help. They don't want my help. I don't even figure on their radar. I'm irrelevant to them. They'll kill me, sure, but they don't want me dead in the way they want you dead. You want to talk history? These guys are the fucking Mongol horde. Attila the Hun drank milk compared to these guys. You point a gun at them? They'll point a fucking rocket launcher back at you.'

Hathaway grabbed at Cuthbert's England shirt, getting flesh with it.

'You're wearing an England shirt and spouting this crap.'

He tore the England shirt across the front and tried to rip it from Cuthbert's body but it got stuck in the tape. He left it in tatters, Cuthbert's gut exposed, hanging over his belt. His chest was heavily tattooed.

'What do they want?'

'Payback.'

'For that Milldean thing?'

'Of course.'

'Is that why they want me dead?'

'Of course.'

'But I had nothing to do with that.'

Cuthbert grinned.

'They think you did.'

Hathaway moved in front of Cuthbert.

'And why would they think that?'

Cuthbert attempted to shrug but the tape round him gave him little room for movement.

'You?'

Cuthbert just looked at him.

'Does it matter?' he said. 'Pandora's out of the box.'

Hathaway gave him a contemptuous look.

'Pandora was never in the box.'

Cuthbert looked puzzled.

'Who was in the box, then?'

'How would I know? Jack, probably.'

'So where was Pandora?'

'How the fuck do I know?'

'I mean, what's she got to do with it?'

Hathaway sighed.

'It's her bloody box. Now, I was saying about your father.'

Cuthbert watched him.

'That car accident.'

'What about it?'

'It wasn't an accident.'

Cuthbert narrowed his eyes.

'But, actually, that doesn't matter because your dad wasn't in the car.'

Cuthbert's face reddened.

'His dentures were, for the purposes of identification.'

'Who was it?'

'What the fuck do you care who it was, you muppet?' Dave said, hitting him across the side of the head again.

'Because we fucking buried the pathetic remains in the family grave and now you're telling me we've got some toerag in there with the rest of the Cuthberts?'

'Believe me – whoever he is he'll be a step up

343

from your blood. Your dad was as much a pain in the arse as you. You're like a family of fucking hyenas. My dad was sick of him just like I'm sick of you. I'm surprised I've let you live so long.'

Cuthbert stared into Hathaway's eyes. His own were dead.

'So, anyways, your dad was toast, obviously. It was just a matter of who else. My dad had scruples. I wanted him to do the whole bloody lot of you. Pest control. Fumigate Milldean. But you and your sister and brother were just kids. And he totally underestimated how much your mother was involved in the family business. He thought that if he got rid of your dad that would be the end of it.'

Cuthbert's look burned.

'Anyway, Steve. Finally, you and your scum family are getting what your breed deserved back then. Just so you know. Everyone is going.'

Hathaway was aware that Dave's attention jerked to him when he said that. He continued: 'Your wife. The not-so-little uns – they've already got ASBOs, haven't they? Your brother and his family. Your sister – and she's definitely no loss, scag that she is. You were scum. You are scum. And none of you deserve to smear the future.'

He nodded at Dave. Dave looked uncertain. Hathaway waited. Cuthbert started to turn his head. Dave raised his hand and shot Cuthbert through the temple. Cuthbert's head snapped away then rolled sharply forward, his body tilted in the chair.

344

Dave looked at his handiwork, then down at the floor.

'Wish he'd said more,' he said finally.

Hathaway turned away.

'Nobody ever says enough. Or they say too much.'

TWENTY-THREE

Tingley looked at the drinks Watts brought over to their table in the garden of the old pub beneath the Downs.

'What is that?' Tingley said.

Watts picked up his glass and peered at it.

'This year's black. Or something. Cider. Nice.'

Tingley tutted.

'Cider is either for teenagers sitting on park benches or – well – old winos sitting on park benches. Which are you?'

'Ha. There's not a park bench in sight.'

Tingley's phone rang. He didn't recognize the number. He shrugged at Watts and put the phone to his ear.

'Tingles, it's Dave. Don't say anything, just listen.'

He sounded winded.

'Thought you should know things have kicked off. Hathaway's restaurant at the marina was torched and he sent me to the Grand with a message for three Serbs staying there.'

'Was one called Radislav?' Tingley said.

'I said just listen,' Dave said fiercely. 'Then we snatched Cuthbert. Thought you'd be pleased about that.'

'Where is he?'

Dave was quiet for a moment, though Tingley could hear his ragged breathing.

'I've crossed a line. I don't regret it. Cuthbert was a shit. You know his loan sharking? Once people borrowed from him he had them for life. He charged interest rates that worked out as high as a couple of thousand per cent.' Dave was speaking more quickly. 'He lent this nurse five hundred quid to buy a computer for her daughter. Over seven years he's demanded eighty-eight thousand pounds from her. She had two strokes and a brain haemorrhage from the stress. He was a bastard.'

Tingley saw Watts get up from the table and walk away, fishing his own phone out of his pocket. Watts put it to his ear.

'But Hathaway was talking of doing Cuthbert's entire family. Blaming the Serbs. There's no need for that, so I'm letting you know. The other – well, it's a kind of war.'

Before Tingley could say anything, Dave hung up. He put his phone on the table and watched Watts walk back over.

'That was Dave. It's kicked off. Hathaway's restaurant at the marina was torched. Something has gone on with Balkan gangsters at the Grand and I think Cuthbert might be dead.'

Watts slumped down.

'That was Gilchrist. She can't join us as she's

346

down at the Grand. There are three dead Balkan gangsters there after a gun battle on the fourth floor.'

'Radislav among them?'

'Apparently not. Was Dave one of the shooters?'

'I don't know. But I think he might have killed Cuthbert.'

Tingley told him the rest of Dave's message. Before he'd even finished Watts was phoning Hewitt to get protection to Cuthbert's family as soon as possible.

Watts put his phone back in his pocket and he and Tingley just looked at each other.

Tingley had never known peace. He knew how he appeared – calm and matter of fact. It was a front he maintained by rigid self-control. He couldn't remember the last time he'd felt relaxed, though he also couldn't remember when he could afford to relax.

Gaza, Lebanon, Iran for the Israelis. Iraq, both times. In the nineties, the Balkans, of course, that cesspit. Just back from Afghanistan. And now this. The Balkans on his doorstep.

'Strictly speaking this isn't any of our business,' he said. 'You're examining a cold case and liaising between different people about the West Pier.'

'True. But Stewart Nealson was a friend of yours, wasn't he?'

'Not exactly a friend...'

'And Radislav is the one that got away.'

'Not the only one...'

Watts gave him a long look and Tingley nodded. He brought out a sheaf of papers from his jacket pocket.

'Radislav is somewhere outside Birmingham, lying low with his men. Drago Kadire, an Albanian, and another big name – Miklos Verbalin – were the Brighton forward brigade at the Grand. Verbalin is one of the dead. The other two are presumably foot soldiers.'

'But Kadire got away with some of his men.'

Tingley nodded.

'And Radislav will come running.'

'Who will they go for?'

'Hathaway – who else?'

'Did Dave say where Hathaway is?'

Tingley shook his head.

'Let's find out,' Watts said.

Hathaway answered on the first ring.

'It's Bob Watts.'

'How nice to hear from you, ex-Chief Constable, though your timing could be better.'

'Got a lot on your plate, have you?'

'The cross all entrepreneurs must bear.'

'Sorry to hear about your restaurant.'

'Yes, that was uncalled for. A malicious act.'

'So was whacking three of the Grand's paying guests.'

'Well, they've paid now, that's for sure.'

'You know that isn't going to end it?'

'I think it might.'

'Vlad is still out there.'

Hathaway said nothing.

'What have you done to Cuthbert?'

Again silence.

'His family are in protective custody by now.'

Hathaway sighed.

'Oh dear. Dave did seem to take that very hard, though I did warn him that once he came in, he was in all the way.'

'You're not going to hurt him?' Watts said. Tingley raised a questioning eyebrow.

'No, no. Just reassign him.'

'We need to talk to you.'

'I get that a lot. OK. Come down to the marina. I'm on my boat. I might have something for you.'

Sarah Gilchrist and Reg Williamson got there first. They'd already been to the house on Tongdean Drive to try to question Hathaway about the torching of his bar and the deaths at the Grand.

They stood on the boardwalk now looking at the charred remains of The Buddha. Williamson had his jacket over his shoulder, his belly straining at his crumpled shirt. He looked out over the harbour, shading his eyes with his hand.

'He's on one of those boats.'

They walked along a narrow wooden walkway past boats of every shape and size. There was a large double-decker cruiser at the far end with a gaggle of tough-looking men standing before it. Subtle. As they got nearer, a broad-shouldered black guy stepped towards them.

'Can I help you?'

Williamson produced his warrant card.

'Looking for Mr Hathaway.'

The man shrugged.

'Can't help you.'

349

Williamson smiled thinly.

'Won't wash, mate. Either we go on or he comes off.'

'It's all right, Dave.'

Williamson and Gilchrist looked up at the sound of the voice. The tall, good-looking man standing on the rear deck gave a startlingly Simon Cowell-like grin and waved them aboard.

The two policemen were still there when Watts and Tingley arrived. Dave had come on board to alert Hathaway of their approach when they were a couple of hundred yards away.

'Thanks, Dave. You make yourself scarce.'

Watts smiled at the sight of Gilchrist and Williamson when he and Tingley came on to the rear deck. Hathaway excused himself from the two policemen and came over, hand extended. He looked fit and lithe in navy linen trousers and a white silk shirt. He also looked remarkably relaxed considering what had been going on.

'Gentlemen, good to see you. I've just been accused of several murders by proxy. I think you know DS Gilchrist, Bob – rather well, in fact. But have you met acting DI Williamson?'

'We're disturbing you,' Tingley said to Williamson.

'Mr Hathaway was being unhelpful,' Williamson replied, shaking his hand. 'But he assures me he has something to tell us all.'

Gilchrist nodded at Watts and Tingley.

'Well, isn't this jolly,' Hathaway said. 'Drinks all round? Oh, I know our coppers are on duty but this is a boat so pretend you're in international waters.'

They all had beers.

'You were about to confess,' Gilchrist said. 'The Serbians in the Grand?'

'You're a one, DS Gilchrist. No, I have a bit of a roundabout story to tell. It starts with Elaine Trumpler.'

'That's a cold case,' Gilchrist said.

'But the police would be arresting the murderer.'

'If he's still alive,' Watts said. 'Are you saying it was you, not your father?'

'Not so fast,' Hathaway said, putting his hand up.

'Your father was not known for turning the other cheek,' Watts said. 'Your father was known for violence. Competitors disappearing without trace.'

'I can't comment on his business methods.'

'Really? Even though you inherited them. Where's Cuthbert?'

Hathaway looked down at his hands on his knees, tilted his head and looked at the four people facing him.

'And here was I thinking we were getting on so well.'

He spread his hands.

'My father was a psychopath – I think you call them sociopaths these days. And for years I worried that it was a genetic thing, that I was the same. But I'm not. I know that. My fear that I carried the gene is the reason I never had children.' He looked out over the marina. 'One of the reasons.'

'Who do you think topped your father?' Ting-

351

ley said.

'Who said he was topped?' Hathaway said, menace in his voice.

'He disappeared. Your mum died of grief.' Tingley saw Hathaway's look. 'That's what I heard anyway.'

Hathaway jabbed his finger at Tingley.

'You've got a cheek, Jimmy, saying such things to my face. But I'll answer your question. I don't know who topped my father and after all this time I don't care. All that bollocks about revenge is a dish best eaten cold is just that – bollocks. No dish meant to be served hot tastes anything like as good cold.'

'Thanks for the gastronomic tip,' Gilchrist said.

Hathaway turned to her.

'Let me tell you my dad's philosophy. Courtesy of some Persian wise man. "The moving finger writes and having writ moves on. Nor all your piety nor wit shall lure it back to cancel half a line, nor all your tears wash out a word of it."'

The four of them looked at him. He shook his head.

'Nobody has any culture any more.' He pointed at Watts. 'Your father would know it. *The Rubaiyat of Omar Khayyam*, written in the eleventh century, as translated by Edward Fitzgerald in the nineteenth century. Very big for most of the twentieth century. Words to live by.'

'No good crying over spilt milk, you mean?' Watts said.

Hathaway gave him a curious look.

'I made a decision to live in the present and the

352

future. Decided not to get bogged down in revenge. Wasteful emotion. What's done is done. Move on. Carpe diem. All that.'

'You've seized a few days since then,' Watts said.

'That I have, ex-Chief Constable. Though, actually, you're mistranslating. Everybody does. Horace was actually using the word "carpe" in the sense of "enjoy, make use of" – it actually means "pick, pluck or gather". And it was the start of a sentence that went on "quam minimum credula postero" – "enjoy the day and put little trust in the future". The ode is all about tomorrow being unknowable so focus on now – and drink your wine.'

'The wonders of a classical education,' Gilchrist said, almost admiringly.

'You're a constant surprise, John,' Watts said.

Hathaway shook his head.

'Just good at Latin at school. '

'"Eat and drink, for tomorrow we die",' Williamson said. '"Gather ye rosebuds whilst ye may."'

Hathaway laughed.

'Or as old Omar would say: "Here with a little bread beneath the bough, a flask of wine, a book of verse –"' he looked at Gilchrist – '"and thee".'

Gilchrist smiled, despite herself.

'That's all very well but who killed Elaine Trumpler?' Watts said.

'Anyone here know of a guy called Keith Jeffery?' Hathaway said. 'Apropos the Swinging Sixties.'

'Another hoodlum?'

353

'He's the guy who either murdered or ordered the murder of Jimi Hendrix.'

'Whoa,' Williamson said. 'Nobody killed Jimi Hendrix except Jimi Hendrix. He drowned in his own vomit after a drug-drink overdose.'

He sensed Gilchrist staring at him.

'It's a pub quiz question.'

'Rather like Laurence Kingston, you mean?' Hathaway said.

Gilchrist laughed.

'Hang on – Elaine Trumpler, Jimi Hendrix and Laurence Kingston? This Keith Jeffery killed them all?'

Hathaway sipped his beer.

'Jeffery was Hendrix's manager. Insured him for two million dollars. He was worth more to him dead than alive. '

'Hendrix was a megastar,' Williamson said. 'He would have made far more than two million.'

'After his death he was a megastar. And Keith wasn't exactly au fait with the music business. He didn't really get Hendrix. In 1967, Jeffery put Hendrix on as support for The Monkees – the first boy band, I guess.

'But he'd put a lot of money into building Electric Ladyland studios in New York. He owed the Inland Revenue a fortune. He'd had to pay off various ex-managers. He was spending money without getting much return. Then Hendrix said he wanted to change managers.'

'So Jeffery killed him?' Tingley said.

Hathaway nodded.

'Took the two million dollars insurance,

354

bought a house in Woodstock, took control of the studios in New York, made a packet out of Hendrix's heritage. You know these guys can definitely be worth more dead than alive.'

'He ordered it or he did it?' Tingley said.

Hathaway spread his hands.

'One or the other. He claimed to be in his nightclub in Majorca at the time. Claimed he didn't know about it until the police turned up a few days later. But he was a Geordie wideboy who didn't mind getting his hands dirty.

'He started with a little night club that wasn't doing too well on the outskirts of Geordie-land. It conveniently burned down. Then he had a coffee bar in the centre also not doing too well. That burned down. With the insurance money from both he opened up a dance place. The house band he booked and then managed was The Animals.'

'I've heard of them,' Gilchrist said.

'Yeah. Well spare me your rendition of "House of the Rising Sun". Jeffery was their manager. They had a string of hits. They weren't The Beatles or Gerry and the Pacemakers and they weren't as pretty, but that Eric Burdon had a voice on him.'

'Is there a point to this pop history lesson?' Williamson said.

'The Animals split up in 1966. Creative differences. After all those hits they scarcely had a pot to piss in. Jeffery had persuaded them to put their money in an offshore account he set up in the Bahamas. Called it Yameta. Eric Burdon called it the Bermuda Triangle because all their money disappeared in it.'

Williamson put his empty glass down hard on the table in front of him.

'I repeat – what is your point?'

'The acting DI needs another drink,' Hathaway called over his shoulder. 'My point is that the pop scene in the sixties was like the wild bloody west. You may have heard about hoodlums muscling in on Tin Pan Alley in the fifties but, Christ, the sixties. Forget no law west of the Pecos – there was no law at all. There were all these managers getting rich off these pig-ignorant rock stars who were too busy getting high – and laid – to worry about their money.'

He put his hand up to placate Williamson.

'OK, someone broke into Hendrix's place, forced booze and sleeping pills down his throat. Autopsy showed a lot of wine in his lungs but little absorbed into his bloodstream, which means he hadn't been on a drinking binge, as suggested.'

'You knew Keith Jeffery?' Watts said.

'I knew him. I knew all the gangsters back then, but of course I was a generation behind.'

'Did you manage anyone?'

'You betcha.'

'Did you rip them off?'

Hathaway laughed.

'Of course. These guys were morons. Morons are fair game.' He clasped his hands. 'But they did OK too. I wasn't a total louse.'

'Is that going to be on your tombstone?' Gilchrist said.

'Not for a long time yet,' Hathaway said,

baring his white teeth at her.

'Are you going to get to the point?' Tingley said.

'Two people have been fingered for killing Hendrix. One is Jeffery, who has his alibi. The other is a man he went into business with. A couple of years later, Jeffery died in a private plane crash and this man took over his empire. If you want to get into conspiracy theory, when Hendrix died he'd been with a German druggie who'd nipped out for cigarettes. In the mid-nineties she started mouthing off about how Hendrix was murdered. Then she killed herself in 1996. Supposedly.' Hathaway turned to Williamson, who was pouring his second beer into his glass. 'Have they checked Kingston's lungs?'

Gilchrist laughed again.

'Whoa. You really are saying the guy who killed Hendrix also killed his manager and his ex-girlfriend and, *then*, fifteen years later, Laurence Kingston of the West Pier Syndicate. Any chance he did JFK and the Pope too?'

She looked at Watts and Tingley for support. Both were looking intently at Hathaway. Hathaway picked up an envelope from the table beside his chair. He stretched his arm out to Tingley.

'Read it aloud, Jimmy,' Hathaway said.

'It isn't dated,' Tingley said. 'It says: "Hello Johnny. Time's up." I can't read the signature. Charlie somebody?'

'Charlie Laker,' Hathaway said.

Watts had a flash of a newspaper cutting he'd found in the local history unit. He shook his head in disbelief.

'Charlie Laker. Drummer with The Avalons pop group.'

Hathaway should have killed Charlie in 1970. He intended to. He had the gun to his head. He was going to shoot him in the face, like Charlie had shot Elaine. Charlie was pretty calm, in the circumstances.

Then Reilly was standing beside him.

'John,' he said quietly.

Hathaway had lowered the gun.

'We're even,' he said to Charlie.

Charlie had buggered off to America. He thrived in the music business, first under Jeffery then on his own. Bought a house in Hollywood next to Cary Grant. Surfed the seventies, found a way to profit from punk and the US New Wave. Then sometime in the eighties he disappeared off the radar.

But here was the thing. The other reason Hathaway had let him live.

'He and your sister are back together,' Reilly told him that evening in Spain. 'She loves him.'

'So now you're saying your drummer Charlie killed all those people *and* Elaine Trumpler and Laurence Kingston?' Gilchrist was almost harrumphing in her disbelief.

'He had form in the music business here in Brighton. Rough tactics against rival managers. He went off to the States, did well for himself.'

'And he killed Elaine Trumpler?' Watts said.

'I watched him do it,' Hathaway said quietly. 'Shot her in the face.'

358

'Why?'

'My dad ordered it and at the time I was too weak to stop it.'

'But why did he order it?'

'She'd seen something she shouldn't have.'

Gilchrist thought for a moment.

'Are there other remains down there?'

Hathaway shook his head.

'Maybe one. The rest he took out to sea.'

The others exchanged glances. Hathaway stood and looked up at the sky.

'I think Charlie is behind all this, this shit that is raining down on the city. He bears me a bad grudge.'

'Aside from you threatening to blow his head off?'

'He killed my girlfriend.'

'So something else?'

'Something only one other person knew about. My sister. I'm guessing she told him.'

'She told him how?'

'She was his wife.'

They all paused at that.

'And you think he's behind the Balkan gangsters?' Tingley eventually said.

Hathaway nodded.

'I think he owns the Palace Pier.'

'So he's after revenge – revenge that's so cold it's frozen?'

Hathaway nodded again. His bravado seemed to have deserted him. Williamson stirred.

'If Charlie is back in Brighton – why now?'

'My sister died,' Hathaway said. 'I heard from a cousin. She and Charlie were married for forty years. They couldn't have kids. She'd had an abortion. She blamed me for that, I don't really know why. A stand-in for my father, I suppose. I never saw her in all that time. I'm guessing he never did anything before because of her. Plus he was inside for a while. In San Quentin. That would have slowed him down.'

Williamson sniffed.

'So you're saying that Charlie Laker is making a major move to take over the town and to do that he has brought in Balkan gangsters, taken over the West Pier and killed Laurence Kingston?'

'At least all that.'

Williamson stood and Gilchrist followed suit.

'Don't suppose you've any idea where we might find him?'

Hathaway grimaced.

'Don't you think I've been looking? But he shouldn't be hard to recognize. He got into bad trouble in San Quentin with the Hispanics. A turf war thing. They almost killed him. He spent three months in the infirmary. He got better but he still carries the wounds.'

'What kind of wounds?' Tingley said.

'Well, for one thing, his face was pretty badly sliced up.'

Watts let out an exasperated sigh, remembering the scarred man in the Grand the night Laurence Kingston had died.

Charlie Laker knew how to bear a grudge. He'd never knowingly forgiven any slight, however minor. Anything major? Well...

360

He stood beside the windmills high on the South Downs above Clayton watching the black Merc pull up. The wind tugged at his jacket, flattened his trousers against his legs.

Radislav, the Serbian torturer, and Drago Kadire, the Albanian sniper, got out of the back. Charlie watched them as they walked towards him. Radislav, slight, grey-faced, kept his head down. Kadire, always alert, looked around.

Charlie touched the rough scar on his top lip.

'I want you to take a pop at him,' Charlie said to Kadire before they had quite reached him.

Kadire looked up at the long white arms on the nearest windmill.

'I want him,' Radislav said. 'My way.'

'I think that's overambitious,' Charlie said. 'I'm grateful for what you did, but I want to finish this.' He turned to Kadire. 'You could do it from up here?'

'The distance is no problem,' Kadire said. 'I once shot a general from a mile away. But there are obstacles. His house is hidden. The boat too.'

'Then get closer.'

Radislav was walking in circles.

'And me? I've been here for two weeks for nothing?'

Charlie watched him bare his teeth. He chuckled.

'I'm sure we can find someone for you. Do you kill coppers?'

TWENTY-FOUR

Hathaway took the old acoustic guitar out on to the balcony and sat on the front edge of a wicker chair. He picked at the strings, running the damaged fingers of his left hand up and down the frets. Long ago he'd burned his fingers. The scars remained, though he always tried to keep them hidden. But some chord shapes he'd never been able to do because the scars made his fingers too stiff.

All those years ago, Dawn had tried to deal with the burns with butter from the kitchen and snow from the garden. Before her love for him turned to hate.

He couldn't say he missed Dawn. When she'd gone off with Charlie, she'd cut herself off from him. Whether because he'd killed their father, he didn't know.

The lights in the garden threw up random shapes and deep shadows in the undergrowth. The pool was opalescent green beneath its glass roof.

There was movement in the trees to his left. A miniscule alteration to the depth of shadow. It might have been nothing. He continued to play, head bent over his guitar. He knew better than to try and sing. He was thinking about John Martyn the night he'd chased his manager down the centre aisle and whopped Dan in the chops. Then of the last time he'd seen Martyn, bloated, missing a leg, performing in the Dome concert hall.

Martyn's fingers had seemed too thick to separate the guitar strings, his voice had been nothing more than a growl. One of Hathaway's men running the get-out had told him that Martyn's stump was bleeding at the end of the evening.

Hathaway hadn't gone backstage to say hello. Some things are best left to lie.

Hathaway liked his balcony. The bulletproof, matt glass canopy did not reflect light, although brightly polished, so it was difficult to see that it was there. The sniper didn't know.

When the first bullet pocked the glass above Hathaway's head, he carried on playing. There were two more rapid attempts. Hathaway could see the sniper was good by the way the pock marks were grouped so closely together.

He put down his guitar and went back into his house to wait for the sniper to be brought to him. He assumed it would be the Albanian, Drago Kadire. He walked to the bar, nodding at Jimmy Tingley as he passed him.

'Rum and pep?'

Kadire proffered a photograph from his pocket. It was the bridge at Drina.

'You know this bridge?'

'I know this bridge,' Tingley said.

'Do you know that the Turks built it. They

buried twins in it to placate the spirit of the river Drina. Stoja and Ostoja. The mason couldn't bring himself to kill the twins so he left a loophole through which their mother might feed them. The bridge took seven years to build. She lived on the riverbank each day and sold herself to the builders to get the food to feed them. But in seven years they grew. Their quarters became too small for them. As they crouched there, moaning, the mason did what he should have done years before. He sealed them up.

'Their mother still had milk in her breasts for all those years. She had suckled them all that time. Over the centuries the mother's milk still flowed from the bridge – a white stream from between the stones that was scraped off and sold to mothers without milk. Wild doves nest in the loophole now.'

Kadire looked down at his hands.

'I was born in this village.'

'You were a barber like your friend Radislav?'

'He's no friend of mine,' Kadire spat out. 'I am Albanian. He is Serbian. I tolerate him.'

'So you had a better job?'

Kadire laughed.

'No education. I was bright enough but my father lost his job – taken by Mussulmen, of course. I had to go to work young.'

'How many times has that bridge been fought over? How much blood has been spilt over it? Spilt on it.'

'I am no historian.' Kadire leaned forward and pointed at the picture.

'I was born in that house there – that one,

364

below the bridge on the right. The one with the moss growing on the roof. You see it?'

Tingley looked closer.

'I see it.'

Kadire dropped the photograph on the table.

'My mother was raped on that rock there. Beside the bridge, stretched out on that rock, held down by two men whilst the third raped her. And then they swapped. When they had finished with her they cut her throat and threw her in the river.'

'I'm sorry,' Tingley said, and he was. 'During the Civil War?'

'Before. Long before.'

'They were Muslims?'

Kadire didn't answer.

'I'm sorry.'

'The men who did it were sorrier. I was watching from that small window up there – the one with the bars upon it? I saw them clearly. And I followed them. I was stealthy even as my eyes burned.'

'Were they Bosniaks?'

'I learned patience. I took them all some years later. I made them suffer. And their families. Rape. Slow roasting.'

Tingley looked down.

'Revenge in the Balkans.'

'Revenge.' He dropped the photograph on the table in front of him. 'It is a beautiful bridge, is it not?'

'Drago, if you don't talk to me you'll have to talk to Hathaway. He's not a gentle man. Where is Radislav and where is Charlie Laker?'

'I am a soldier. A sniper.'

'Where are they, Drago? We have to stop this.'

Kadire spat on Hathaway's oriental rug and closed his eyes. Hathaway touched Tingley on the shoulder.

'My turn now.'

The men crowded into Reilly's room. Four, five, six of them. Reilly opened his eyes and waved the one hand he had above his sheets.

'Bit mob-heavy aren't you?' he croaked. 'No wonder your country was always getting pissed on if it takes six of you to deal with one old man.'

'You are the man who is going to be pissed on,' the nearest man said, stepping towards the bed. 'Then much worse. And you can blame Mr John Hathaway.'

'He's going to have your mates,' Reilly said. 'If he hasn't already.'

'And we're going to have you.'

'You Serbians. You know, I'm a great reader. Always have been. I've read a lot of your greatest writer. Ivo Andric. You've probably never even heard of him, have you?'

None of the Serbians responded.

'Typical lowlife scum. Read him and you might learn to take proper pride in your country.' Reilly tucked his hand back under his blankets. 'In fact, come a little closer all of you and I'll quote his words.'

'We're coming closer, old man,' the first man said, yanking Reilly's blankets off him.

They all looked first at his wizened, naked

366

body and the tubes coming out of him. Then they saw the curled piece of metal in his right hand. The pin of the World War Two grenade that he proffered in his left.

Tingley looked at Kadire sprawled on the plastic sheets on the garage floor and thought how pathetic he looked, one ear hanging off, his nose mashed to one side of his face, blood pumping out of him.

'This is not the way to get information,' he said.

'We'll see,' Hathaway said.

Then his phone rang.

'Yes. Patrice.' His shoulders slumped. 'Did you warn him? And Barbara? Thank you, Patrice. I'm on my way.'

Hathaway dropped his phone into his pocket. He turned to Tingley.

'Sean Reilly is dead, but he took six of them with him. I'm going to France.' He gestured at Kadire. 'Do it your way – but do it.'

Miladin Radislav killed coppers. He killed any-thing and anybody if the mood was upon him. He watched the copper jogging along the sea-front. He itched to kill her.

Gilchrist was feeling both overwhelmed and out of her depth. So many deaths; so much violence. She'd worked out ferociously at the gym but now enjoyed the sight of the sea, calm after the fury of the storm some days before.

She dropped down to the lower promenade

beside the beach and ran towards the West Pier. She loved running, loved getting the breath and the legs in rhythm. Sometimes felt she could run forever. She'd applied for the London Marathon but hadn't yet heard back about her application.

She looked out at the tangled remains of the West Pier as she approached it. A group of teen-age girls were gathered at the water's edge. She watched them as she ran. She could vaguely hear their shouts. They were throwing stones into the sea.

After another hundred yards Gilchrist realized from the angle of their arms that they were throwing them at something.

When she also realized that some were using the cameras on their mobile phones she lost the rhythm of her breath. She had guessed what they were doing. Stumbling and gasping, she headed across the beach towards them.

'Hey,' she yelled, her voice breaking as her breath went again. She stumbled as she crunched through the pebbles. She called again.

Only when she was within fifty yards of the girls did they turn at what were by now her screeches. And only then did she recognize that she was running into a bad situation. She didn't know what they were up to, but she did know there were about ten feral teenage girls now interested in her. Each one with a stone in her hand.

Gilchrist was big and strong but she knew about pack animals. She slowed to get her breath and her footing. The girls, hyped up, were actually snarling. Gilchrist was thinking that a

Sussex University academic she'd briefly dated would have made a meal out of this apparent proof that pubescent girls are so overwhelmed by hormones they can become wild animals.

Personally, Gilchrist believed they were just horrible girls, though she was also thinking about vampire films as she slowed to a walk.

She was about twenty yards away before she saw the huddled form lying on the pebble beach below them.

'Police,' she called. 'What are you doing?'

The girls gave her that same feral look.

'Police, right,' said a blonde with a lot of metal in her face. 'Fuck off, bitch, or we'll tear your tits off.'

Sarah, breathing deeply, walked steadily towards them. The girls watched her approach, intense looks on their faces. The body lying on the beach didn't move.

The girls looked to be about fourteen or fifteen, some younger. One of them pointed her phone and photographed Gilchrist.

'Who is that lying on the beach? They need help.'

'You really a copper?' a mixed-race girl with her red hair in dreadlocks said, her chin thrust out.

Gilchrist wondered about knives. Her training told her to withdraw and call for backup, but she didn't want to leave whoever was lying on the shore to the mercy of these savages. She made a decision.

'Get on your way now,' she said, trying to keep the tremor from her voice.

'What – you not going to arrest us?' metal-face sneered. 'Why have you stopped? Don't want to lose your tits?'

'Just go on your way. All of you.'

'Nah,' the red-haired girl said. 'Come on down and we'll help you with your inquiries.'

The other girls laughed but Gilchrist had never heard a chillier sound.

'Go along now or you'll be in serious trouble.'

'Ain't we already?' metal-face said. 'We've really messed her up, you know.'

Gilchrist took a deep breath. Fuck, fuck, fuck. She didn't have a phone with her, didn't have her warrant card. Could she bluff this out? She had to try to help the girl lying so still. She needed to get to a phone to do that. The nearest phones were just ahead of her, snapping her picture.

She put her hand in her tracksuit trouser pocket. Gripped the oblong piece of plastic there. Her dirty little secret.

She walked slowly towards the metal-faced girl. She was expecting that at any moment they would throw their stones at her. At this distance she wasn't sure how accurate they would be.

'You're making such a fucking serious mistake, bitch,' the girl said.

'You've already made yours,' Gilchrist said, stopping two feet from the girl, towering over her. As she stopped, the other girls started to move round her.

The red-haired girl looked beyond her. A man's voice came from behind. Accented.

'You sluts – we have a present for you unless you go away.'

She heard crunching footsteps, more than one.

The teenage girls stared resistance, then, as one, started to run off down the beach.

Hathaway turned. Four men were approaching her in a loose line. The grey-faced one slightly ahead of the others smiled, but there was no warmth in it.

'Thank you,' she said.

'No problem, policewoman Gilchrist,' he said.

Gilchrist stepped back, her feet sinking into the shingle. This wasn't right. She risked a look at the unconscious girl beside her. There was blood everywhere. A bruised and bloodied face. Water was swirling nearer to her as the tide rose. Gilchrist looked down the beach at the gang of girls scrambling across the pebbles. The men were just a few yards away.

Gilchrist used to carry Mace. Illegally imported from the US, illegally carried. Now she had something better. Certainly better than the officially sanctioned Taser she used to carry when on duty.

The Taser was fine in its way. You could use it from fifteen feet away. You fired its two darts on the end of their fifteen feet wires and pumped 50,000 volts into your antagonist. Screwed up their neuromuscular system – for the next fifteen minutes the person on the receiving end was useless.

But it was a one-shot weapon and came under firearm regulations, so she was no longer allowed to use one after being stripped of her firearm privileges.

Her dirty little secret didn't have wires. The

XR5000 Nova Stun Gun was powered by a nine-volt cadmium rechargeable battery – the kind used in transistor radios. It produced, through two brass studs, a sawtooth 47,000 volts in around one and a half seconds at up to twenty cycles per second. Didn't burn, bruise or damage tissue. Just incapacitated somebody within three seconds.

Four men. She wasn't sure it could recharge in time for four men. She swept it from her pocket and pointed it at the leering, grey-faced man. At least she'd get him.

Tingley phoned Watts.

'I've crossed the line too.'

'I didn't know you had a line.'

Tingley was silent.

'Sorry, that came out wrong.'

'I know where they are.'

'And Charlie Laker?'

'Him next.'

'I'll come with you.'

Tingley looked out of the flat's window at the Ravenscourt Park below. A Polish neighbourhood since the Second World War. Now the hidey-hole for Serbian gangsters.

Kadire had talked.

'I'm already here.'

Tingley had meant it when he said the Balkan gang couldn't be stopped. But maybe they could be stopped from coming to Brighton.

He watched a car draw up. A big man got out of the front passenger side and scanned the street. The back doors opened and the other men got out on either side. Both were lean, wiry. One of the men scanned the street whilst the other moved to the door of the apartment block and was lost from view. The car drove away.

Tingley moved away from the window and went to stand beside the door. He heard the ping of the lift down the corridor, then nothing until the key in the lock. He hefted the Sig Sauer Hathaway had given him.

The two bodyguards came in first. They scanned the room but weren't really expecting anybody to be here – Tingley had made sure he'd replaced the couple of security indicators on the door. They had no reason to suspect anyone was in the room.

They didn't look behind the door. When the man they were escorting was halfway in the room, Tingley slammed the door into him. He shot the two bodyguards, the first in the back and the back of the head, the second, as he turned, in the chest and the side of the head. Perfect double taps.

The bullets made 'phtt' sounds because of the silencer. Tingley swung back the door and kicked the man trying to get up from the floor in the side of the head. He grabbed his feet and dragged him into the room, swung him over and dropped on to his back, swiping the door closed with his left hand. He grabbed the man's head and pulled back.

'I want names or I'll break your back as well as your nose,' he said, bearing down with his knees. 'All the way back to the slum you came from.'

'Go fuck yourself,' the man said between gritted teeth.

Tingley grabbed his hair.

'All the way back.'

TWENTY-FIVE

'You did well, Sarah.'

Karen Hewitt dropped her hand on Gilchrist's shoulder and left it there for a moment. Gilchrist stared at the ground between her trainers. She wanted to vomit.

'How's the girl?' she said, gulping down air.

'The girl?' Hewitt said. 'Oh – she'll be fine.'

Gilchrist was being debriefed in one of the station's ground-floor interview rooms. There was hot coffee on the table in the centre of the room, but even in her state she knew better than to drink it. The coffee in this place spawned as many jokes as microbes, if the jokes were to be believed.

She smiled at the thought. Tried to smile. She was flashing back to the beach. And still trying to figure out how she had missed the man she now knew was Radislav with her electric charge.

He had moved so quickly, knocking her arm to one side as he bowled into her. The charge had gone into the man to his right as she fell.

She had scrambled away from Radislav, twisting his arm to get his hand off her throat. She

374

still clutched the volt gun as the other two stopped in their tracks, watching their friend writhe and judder on the shingle beach.

She looked down at the grey-faced man, who was scrambling to his feet with difficulty, his attempt to propel himself up with his left arm failing because his hand was sinking into the shingle.

She stood at bay, her arm extended with the volt gun pointing at each man in turn. From the corner of her eye she saw uniformed police making a slow progress towards them. Radislav saw them too. With an almost pantomime snarl he set off down the beach towards the West Pier, followed by the other two men.

Gilchrist's legs were shaking by the time the uniforms arrived. Her volt gun was back in her pocket. Radislav and his two cohorts were too far away to chase. She abruptly sat down.

Charlie Laker had followed Hathaway to France or was already there. This much Watts surmised. He met Tingley on the Old Steine and drove them down to Newhaven.

'I'm not quite sure why we're doing this,' he said. 'How far are we willing to go in support of a gangster?'

'It's relative, isn't it?' Tingley said as they waited in the line of cars to board the ferry.

'Are you willing to kill?' Watts said. 'Did you kill Kadire?'

'I called the police to take care of him,' he said.

'And from now on?'

'We'll see what happens.'

They took the overnight ferry. The only time either had crossed to Dieppe before had been on a hovercraft that had done the journey in a bouncy two hours. This was a ferry brought up from Sicily.

The crew and stewards were Italian. They spoke little English or, indeed, French. It was a four-hour journey that turned into six because the captain, more used to the calmer waters of the Med, deemed the sea too rough to get into port without the help of tugs.

It took an hour for the tugs to arrive, another hour for them to haul the boat in backwards to its dock.

Tingley and Watts were only partly aware of this. They'd bought a bottle of duty-free brandy when the boat first left Newhaven. They'd laid on the narrow beds in the narrow cabin and sipped the brandy until around midnight. Conversation had been muted.

Both had dozed off, fully clothed, lying on their backs, lulled by the sea. They woke at four and went upstairs, expecting the boat to be docking. They waited aft by a big window, watching the lights of Dieppe as the tugs manoeuvred them into port.

They went down to the car deck, huge trucks dwarfing them on every side. Off the boat they drove around town looking for somewhere to get coffee and croissants.

The sky was drab, shedding reluctant light on sodden streets. They parked outside a neon-lit worker's café on the other side of the harbour and sat peering out of the rain-streaked windows at the deserted promenade.

'You a fan of Jean-Pierre Melville?' Tingley said.

Watts looked blank.

'French film-maker influenced by Yank gangster movies. Did one that starts with a bank robbery on a seafront just like this – rain sweeping across it.'

'I'm not much of a movie-goer,' Watts said.

The coffee was good, served in bowls. The croissants less so. The little pats of butter were straight from the freezer. Tingley put a shot of brandy in his coffee. Watts shook his head.

After twenty minutes Tingley looked at his watch.

'Time to go.'

The road out to Varengeville wound along the coast, rising and falling. They passed the remains of World War Two gun emplacements. Tingley drove slowly, occasionally checking the rear-view mirror for anyone following.

On the ferry they had scoped out the other passengers. Mostly men, mostly rough-looking. Poor, blue-collar, lorry drivers and low-paid workers. None of them looked particularly like Balkan gangsters but how would they know? Besides, the grey-faced Miladin Radislav kept to his cabin for the entire journey.

They dropped down into a village right on the sea. People in hooded anoraks or raincoats were walking dogs on the shingle beach, the undertow of the water dragging at the pebbles, sucking it out to sea.

The road rose and curved away from the

beach, up and inland. Varengeville was little more than a single street with a few shops along it. A boulangerie was open.

Tingley watched the road until Watts returned with some kind of quiche and two more coffees in Styrofoam cups.

'We go through town and turn right on to a semi-paved road to get to the church. There's a big car park.'

Tingley waved away the coffee and tart.

'I'll have it when we're there.'

The unpaved road was narrow and went past a number of large houses protected by high walls. The church was on a promontory looking out over the sea. Tingley parked at the back of the car park off in a corner. They ate and drank their coffee in silence.

'You know I'm going to follow the trail back,' Tingley said.

'Why?'

'Because I hate this tidal wave of sewage washing over us all. It's my duty to try to stop it.'

'Your duty?'

Tingley shrugged.

'Besides – what the hell else have I got to do?'

Watts looked over at the church.

'Live?' he said. 'You know I can't go with you.'

Tingley reached out and squeezed his arm.

'You've got a family to win back,' he said. He pushed open his car door. 'Let's take a look around.'

There was a headland beyond the church,

378

reached by a path that dipped down into a little shingle cove then climbed up a sleep incline. They slithered in the rain. When they reached the top they could see the back of John Hathaway's house.

Charlie Laker sat in the thirteenth-century church of St Valery, contemplating the gaudy, abstract stained-glass window done by Georges Braque in 1954. He'd seen the artist's tomb in the graveyard earlier, topped by a mosaic of a white dove.

'The Tree of Jesse,' Patrice Magnon said, following Charlie's look.

'Could have fooled me,' Charlie said. He patted Patrice on the back. 'Thanks for coming in with us.'

Patrice smiled thinly. Glanced at the grey-faced man sitting alert in the corner.

'Did I have a choice?'

After some discussion, Watts and Tingley went in by the front door. Watts had declared he was too old to be scaling walls. They buzzed at the gate and walked through a cobbled courtyard to where Dave was waiting for them in an open door. There was the scent of honeysuckle around them. Clematis hung from the front of the house.

Dave had an uncertain smile on his face and a gun in his hand.

'What the fuck are you up to, Tingles?'

'Unfinished business with Radislav.'

'And you?' Dave said to Watts.

'Making a stand.'

Dave frowned.

'This is ... unexpected.'

Tingley walked right up to Dave.

'Are you going to let us in?'

'More bloody coppers,' Hathaway said when Dave led them into a long, gloomy drawing room. He was sitting in a wing-backed chair, a pistol on the table beside it. 'I've only just got rid of the French *flics*.'

'Ex-copper,' Watts said. 'Are they going to protect you?'

'Hardly. They don't know anything. Neighbours heard an explosion. I fobbed them off. Do you know what happened?'

'I'm not psychic,' Watts said.

'Lippy, aren't you?' A woman's head appeared from behind the wing of another chair. Hathaway gestured at her.

'This is Barbara. Very loyal. First love of my life. It's just his way, Barbara. Barbara was close to Sean Reilly back in the day. She's in mourning. Barbara, this is ex-Chief Constable Bob Watts and Mr Tingley.'

'Reilly's dead?' Tingley said. He'd been looking forward to meeting the old soldier.

'They came in through the garden. I have a dozen men here but these scum waltzed in through the French windows to Sean's room. He had a surprise for them.'

Hathaway looked down.

'Sean took care of them. Well, most of them. My men, once they got their arses in gear, took care of the rest.'

'Radislav?'

Hathaway shook his head.

'Is Charlie Laker over here?' Watts asked.

'Don't know. I expect so – every other bugger is. So much for my weekend retreat. Why the hell are you two boy scouts here? Gone soft on me or something?'

'Must have,' Watts said. 'Where's Cuthbert?'

Hathaway glanced at Dave, standing by the door.

'Thought you knew. He was long past his sell-by date. But the rozzers don't need to keep a guard on his family. I was just winding him up. I would never harm them. I'm evil but I'm not a monster.'

'Subtle difference,' Watts said.

'Life is all in the subtle differences,' Hathaway said.

Barbara stood.

'I need a fag.'

As she passed Watts, she said:

'I met your dad once.'

'I hear that a lot,' he said.

'He made a pass at me.'

'That too.'

She left the room. Hathaway was looking at Watts, sizing him up.

'Your dad, yes. Somewhere in this house is something that might interest you.'

'I'm sure there are lots of things,' Watts said.

'The bulk of the police files for the Brighton Trunk Murders.'

'They were destroyed,' Watts said.

Hathaway shook his head.

'Nah. Philip Simpson desperately wanted them destroyed for some reason but my dad got hold of them, gave them to Sean for safe keeping.'

'Why would I be interested?'

'Family history?'

Watts glanced at Tingley.

'I'd be more interested in what you meant when you said William Simpson's birth was the Immaculate Conception.'

Hathaway stood.

'Is this the time?'

He saw the look on Watts's face.

'Well, I guess we have nothing else to do until the barbarians reach the gate.' He made a wry face. 'I just meant that his pretty young wife confided in my mother, who told me and my sister, that they never had sex. Had separate bedrooms, in fact.'

There was movement in the corridor outside the drawing room. Dave turned then looked back, an odd expression on his face. A bunch of men crowded past him into the room. They were led by a man with scars on his face.

'Mr H.,' Dave said. 'Charles Laker to see you.'

'What happened to the man on the beach?' Karen Hewitt asked Gilchrist. 'The uniforms said he looked as if he'd been tasered.'

Gilchrist held Hewitt's look.

'Beats me. There was a lot of confusion. Maybe he got in the way of one of the others. What is he saying?'

'Nothing,' Hewitt said.

382

'And Kadire?'

'Kadire's out on bail.'

'What?'

Hewitt threw up her hands.

'Tell me about it. Hathaway has disappeared, so has Tingley, so we just have an uncorroborated claim that he tried to shoot Hathaway. Smart lawyer and a lot of cash behind him, he's out the door.'

'Where is he?'

'Disappeared.'

'And Radislav?'

'We don't know where he is either. So it goes on. Do you know where Bob Watts is?'

Gilchrist shook her head.

'That's three strikes,' Hewitt said.

'Am I out?'

Watts was unconscious on the floor, a vicious blow to the back of his head with the butt of a machine pistol doing the damage. Tingley was inelegantly bound to the wingback chair. Dave stood over him.

'Sorry about this, Tingles.'

'You switched horses?'

'Strictly speaking, no. I was Mr Laker's man from the start.'

'So all that hand-wringing about crossing the line?'

'Well, Cuthbert was Laker's man so I didn't think he'd want his family wiped out. Had to think of some reason to phone you.'

'Why are you doing this?'

'Why?' Dave was almost jeering. 'I'm a soldier

of fortune. A mercenary. I go where the money is.'

Barbara came in shooting. The recoil of the sawn-off almost knocked her off her feet but she kept her balance. The blast was a terrible violation of the room. Dave fell against the fireplace and lay, still and broken, arms flung out. The Serbian by the window was writhing on the floor, blood spreading from his right hip down his trousers and up his shirt.

A shattered hip, Tingley judged. He tried to stand, taking the chair with him. Barbara looked at him and the chair hanging down behind him. She looked at Watts, slumped on the floor.

'Where's my John?' she said.

'They took him,' Tingley said, turning sideways on to her. 'Could you? I can't reach.'

'What good are you going to be to me?' she said. 'Scrawny guy like you.'

'I'm better than I look.'

'Then why are you tied to a chair?'

'Misjudgement. But I won't make another one.'

Barbara took a knife from her jacket pocket. Tingley laughed.

'You come prepared.'

She sawed at the rope.

'You have no idea.'

She cut him free and pointed at Watts.

'I'll take care of him,' Tingley said. He looked over at the man with the shattered hip. 'What about him?'

Barbara was already striding out of the room. 'Fuck him.'

Tingley gathered up Watts. Though his friend outweighed him by a couple of stone, he hoisted him up and brought him out of the room.

'You are deceptive,' Barbara said as they went down the corridor.

They got into Tingley's car, Watts laid out on the back seat.

'What now?'

'We find Hathaway.'

It took until dusk. They'd driven to Dieppe, haunted the ferry point, driven out into the country. They found him on the cliff-top beyond the church, silhouetted against the sinking sun in the west. He was hanging in a crude frame, a black silhouette outlined in orange flame from the sun beyond him. Naked. Impaled.

Barbara gave an animal moan and dropped to her knees. Watts, who'd come round in the car hours before and immediately vomited, looked at Tingley.

'He's still alive,' he whispered.

Tingley and Watts moved closer. Hathaway was keening.

'John?' Watts looked up at him.

'We should kill him,' Tingley said. 'Put him out of his misery.'

'How?' Watts said.

'Barbara has a knife.'

Hathaway's eyes were rolling. He worked his mouth.

'Where...?' he gasped. A gout of blood streaming from his mouth made his next words indistinguishable. He gave a terrible cough. He raised

385

his head. He gargled part of a word.

'Aval...'

'Jesus,' Tingley said. 'Where's the lady of the lake when you need her?'

TWENTY-SIX

'You OK?' Tingley said.

Watts was looking out of the window watching the kids they passed on the streets. They went past the King Alfred centre and Tingley kept to thirty mph until the speed camera was out of view. There were brightly painted beach huts on their left, a series of blocks of flats on the right. They passed the one that Philippa Franks lived in. One of the shooters at the Milldean massacre. Watts glanced up to see if she was sitting on her balcony. He was sure there was more information to be got from her about the massacre in which she'd participated but now wasn't the time.

'What kind of shit eco-friendly car is this?' Watts said. 'I could walk more quickly.'

'I'll take that as a "No",' Tingley said. 'And, as a point of information, it's the traffic, not my shit eco-friendly car that is inhibiting our speed.'

'What a fucking mess,' Watts said. 'Charlie Laker, Radislav, Kadire – all disappeared.'

'Do you fancy Laker for Laurence Kingston's death?'

'As Hathaway guessed, there was hardly any booze in the bloodstream and a lot in the lungs.'

They were silent for a moment.

'Sarah had a lucky getaway.'

'I know it,' Watts said.

'Maybe the Balkan guys were here earlier than we thought,' Tingley said.

'Meaning?'

'Maybe they were involved with killing your policemen who did the Milldean thing.'

Watts roared. Tingley nodded. Watts, coughing, laughed.

'Sorry, Jimmy.'

'Listen to the lion,' Tingley said.

'We still don't really have the links in the chain.'

'What chain?' Tingley said.

'Only connect, Jimmy, only connect.'

'Yeah, the prose and the passion. I know the quote, Bob. I've read a book or two. But that's got nothing to do with our situation.'

'You read Forster? I didn't know that.'

'I said I knew the quote. I didn't say I'd read that particular book.' Tingley grinned. 'Now a couple of tanks in the front garden at Howards End, that might have piqued my interest'

Watts smiled reluctantly.

'The point I'm trying to make,' he said, 'is that everything connects somehow. There's a thread linking the Trunk Murder – groan if you want to but listen – the stuff that went down in the sixties and the Milldean Massacre and hence these Serbians.'

'And what is that thread, O Master Weaver?'

387

Watts sat back and threw up his hands.

'I wish I knew.'

'But it's none of this that's bothering you, is it?'

Watts shook his head.

'Go and see your father.'

'Didn't know you were one for family history, Dad,' Watts said as he sat down opposite his father in the cafeteria of the National Archives.

'Just checking on a couple of things.' His father gestured vaguely. 'Remarkable place this. The amount of stuff they have available. Even if I were fifty years younger and going at it every day, I wouldn't be able to scratch the surface in my lifetime.'

'Have you always kept diaries, Dad?'

'Who said I ever kept one?'

Watts sighed.

'Come on, Dad, coyness doesn't suit you. You're a call-a-spade-a-spade man. You mentioned there was more of your diary. Are you going to let me see it?'

'What do you know about the Great Train Robbery?' his father said.

Watts eyed him carefully.

'Two, mebbe three, were never caught,' his father said. 'Never caught, never identified.'

'None of the others gave them up?'

Donald Watts shook his head.

'For all their memoirs and all that Ronnie Biggs posturing, none of them ever really said how it happened or who did what. And the Bucks police didn't have a clue.'

Watts sipped his coffee and watched his father.

'These people who were never caught?'

His father looked at him again.

'You know there was a strong Brighton connection? Half the gang had been robbing trains on the Brighton to London line. Penny ante stuff at first but then they figured out a way to stop the trains by fiddling with the signals. Same method they used in the Great Train Robbery.'

'These people who got away with it – they were from Brighton?'

'One was a train driver they took along whose nerve went on the actual job. A couple of the gang wanted to kill him to stop him talking, but in the end they paid him off.'

'And the other two?'

Donald Watts leaned forward. His tongue darted out to lick at his dry lips.

'One is certain. The other more speculative.'

'I like certainties.'

His father smiled. His teeth were yellow. He looked very old, and he gave off a rancid smell.

'I recall going to a house-warming party with my friend Philip Simpson. Lively do. Very lively. Our host had been living in some squalor on what we would now term a sink estate, but here he was in a better part of town with a big garden and a lot of influential people paying court to him.'

'And you concluded?'

'I concluded that family fortunes can change very quickly.'

'A little showy, wasn't it?'

'Oh, he'd waited. This was a couple of years

down the line.'

'And the name of this gentleman?'

Watts' father rubbed his cheek.

'I think you know.'

'Dennis Hathaway?'

Donald Watts inclined his head and looked down at his liver-spotted hands.

Watts thought for a moment.

'And the speculative one?'

His father shrugged.

'My friend Philip Simpson was never what you'd call a straight arrow.'

'The chief constable of Brighton was one of the Great Train Robbers?' Watts sat back and laughed. 'I don't believe it.'

Donald Watts picked up his drink then put it down again.

'I'm not saying he was actually on the track with a pickaxe handle in his hands. I'm just saying that he was implicated.'

'Implicated how?'

'Look, Philip Simpson ran crime in Brighton. Do you remember staying at their house in Spain? Did you never wonder how somebody on his salary could afford a bloody castle?'

'OK, so you're saying he was implicated in the robbery. That he got a share of the dosh. And everybody kept schtum about it.'

'That's what I'm saying.'

'So what did he do for the money?'

'Kept Dennis Hathaway out of the frame.'

'And that's it? How about all the others who were caught? He didn't do a very good job with them, did he?'

'Two of them were broken out of prison, three others were on the run for years. Who do you think bankrolled all that?'

'What about the files he tried to destroy? Did they contain the identity of the Trunk Murderer?'

'Don't be gormless. It were nothing to do with that. It were his deal with Dr M.'

'Dr M?'

'Massiah,' Watts said. 'The society abortionist. Philip were the one who egged that idiot policeman from Hove to go and try to get him. He knew he'd muck it up. But he couldn't afford to let anything come out about him.'

'Because he protected him?'

'And some.'

Watts looked around the café.

'Dad, I've got to ask—'

'Do you?'

'Yes.'

'Then ask away.'

Donald Watts put his coffee cup down.

'This isn't easy,' Watts said. His father just stared. 'You made a career of chasing women. You were a bastard to my mother. We all knew. She never let on. She never once commented on it whilst we were growing up, but I'm sure it helped kill her.'

Donald Watts continued to stare at his son.

'Did you have an affair with Philip Simpson's wife?'

His father sat back.

'Nice lass.'

'Someone told me that when she had William

Simpson it was the Immaculate Conception,'
Watts said. 'Is William Simpson related to me?'

His father sat back.

'I don't quite understand you, son.'

Watts looked at his father.

'Simpson takes after his mother and I take
after you, so the fact we don't look alike doesn't
mean anything.'

His father absently watched another group of
people arrive.

'We never talked about it.'

'That's it? Why are you so cold, Dad – and
don't give me that Graham Greene sliver of ice
in the heart thing.'

'Why are you so wet? Do you have any backbone?'

'Don't be fatuous, Dad. It doesn't become you.
I've proved I've got backbone.'

'But you haven't proved you're not an idiot.
An idiot who doesn't see what's in front of his
face and who gets too exercised over unimpor-
tant things.'

Watts reached over and grasped his father's
scrawny hand.

'Dad, you've got to stop being the tough guy.
You haven't the strength for it and it comes over
as bombast.'

'Bombast. Nice word. You should be writing,
not me. Philip assumed the boy was his. His
mother never said he wasn't. William had no
reason to think otherwise. Why don't you leave
it at that?'

Watts looked round as people began to fill up
the tables around them. Why indeed? He looked

at his father's clasped hands and down at his own. He laughed grimly.

'Because I can think of only one thing worse than not being able to nail William Simpson for what he's done. And that is to discover that, because my father was fucking his best friend's wife, William Simpson is my half-brother.'

Jimmy Tingley crossed the Kings Road near the Palace Pier and went to join Barbara at the railings overlooking the beach. Below him were the tables of a bar, chairs stacked on them.

It was a still night, the water calm, the moon high. The Palace Pier lights had been extinguished but there were others flickering on the horizon. Fishing boats, passing ships.

Tingley watched the lights. He was tired. Tired of killing. But what to do in a world of wicked men?

'I was scared of him at first,' Barbara said, still facing out to sea. 'John. Then I fell in love with him. Then his father sent me away...'

'John didn't stand up for you?'

'No?'

'Nor when you had cancer?'

She shook her head.

'Then why?'

'Go back to him? I didn't have anywhere else to go. My sister dead, my husband long gone, my life a nightmare. He was the best I had. And he took me in.'

Tingley turned and tried to see beyond the lights. He imagined himself standing at the Ditchling Beacon, looking down on the town.

393

Looking at himself, standing here tonight. He turned back to look out to sea.

'I'm going after them, you know.'

'Why?'

The men he had killed had been wicked men. He hadn't hesitated.

'I've got something of the trail back to the Balkans. I'll set out on it in the next few days. Kill everybody I can find. Including Radislav and Kadire.'

'Why?'

'That's what I do best. All I do well.'

'It won't stop it. You know that.'

'But there'll be a lull. Until the next flood forward.'

'Nature abhors a vacuum,' she said. She reached out and put her hand on his. 'I inherit, you know. He left me everything. If you need money.'

'What was Hathaway's guilty secret?' Tingley said. 'What had he done to Charlie Laker that would make him take such revenge on him after so many years. It had to be more than the abortion thing.'

'It went way back,' Barbara murmured, then the bullet shattered the back of her skull and exited through her left eye socket, taking eye, brain matter and shards of bone with it.

EPILOGUE

November 2nd, 1959. It was cold in the den. Roy Laker pulled his duffel coat hood over his head and curled his fingers in his mittens. He shuffled on the makeshift orange box seat. His brother, Charlie, and Charlie's mate, Kevin, had gone down to the café to get warm but Roy wanted to stay in the den. After all, he was on guard.

He peered out through the boards and crates and tree branches piled against each other. The den was right in the centre of the stack of wood and he'd had to crawl on his hands and knees to get in. The bonfire was big but would be lot bigger by Guy Fawkes night.

'Penny for the Guy,' Roy muttered as he saw an indistinct figure approach the bonfire. His heart jumped. Rival gangs tried to set fire to each other's bonfires before November 5th. Roy couldn't see properly but followed the figure flitting around the stacked wood. He heard the splash of liquid and smelt paraffin.

The flame shot up the side of the bonfire. Roy heard the sharp crackle as tree branches caught. He scuttled backwards for the tunnel. His feet slipped on the torn pieces of lino that had been laid across the mud floor. He turned awkwardly, seeing flames shoot up on every side, and stuck his head into the tunnel. It was blocked with a large crate and a railway sleeper.

Gulping down panic, he pushed against the crate, for the first time feeling the heat of the blaze. He coughed as smoke swirled round him. He vaguely heard singing. 'Remember, remember the fifth of November. The Gunpowder Plot...'

He could vaguely see someone peering in at him. With a whoosh the entire bonfire took flame.

Young John Hathaway walked away without a backward glance.

To be continued in *God's Lonely Man*

AUTHOR'S NOTE

Let's get the covering my back stuff out of the way first. The Palace Pier and the West Pier and their owners in this work of fiction are fictional creations, bearing no relationship whatsoever to any piers or owners that might exist or have existed in the real Brighton. Similarly, criminal input into sixties' Brighton building works is entirely in my imagination.

Charles Ridge, disgraced chief constable, did exist and was acquitted on charges of corruption. He sued the then police authorities for unfair dismissal and won the case and his pension rights. Philip Simpson, who succeeds him in this work of fiction, is my invention and bears absolutely no relationship to anyone who might have been chief constable in Brighton or Sussex in subsequent years.

Dr Say Massiah was both a society abortionist and a suspect in the Brighton Trunk Murder case.

Milan Radislav is a figment of my imagination.

Sadly, so too was the Visegrad Massacre during the Balkans conflict. For knowledge of Balkan gangsters I am indebted to Misha Glenny's *McMafia, Seriously Organised Crime* (Vintage,

2009). For knowledge of how to impale somebody, I turned to Ivo Andric's Nobel Prize-win-
ning *The Bridge Over The Drina* (1945).

For stories of the pop scene in the sixties from
the point of view of a support band, I am indebted to my brother, Michael, whose group did
support Little Richard, Duane Eddy, The Who
and many others. I am grateful to him and to
vocalist Dave Parkinson and to other members
of The Avalons for allowing me to borrow their
name (and trash it).

Peter Guttridge, 2010.